THE GOVERNME
THE GRAY WOMAN...

And they are determined to use her unique skillset against terrorists and make her an offer she can't refuse.

When Homeland Security is alerted to threats against a retired army sniper made real with a bounty on his head, they offer the impossible task of keeping him safe to Julia Pelletier. Accepting her role as an agent of the government, she travels to Jackson, Wyoming, and learns the enormous scope of what's been assigned to her—cover a vast area with his extended family and friends possibly included with him under the gun. To shadow a man once known for his stealthy ability to infiltrate and terminate opposing leaders will tax her ability to remain invisible. Kill teams arriving from the Middle East hope to collect on the death of Early Hollister.

But to earn the huge payday, supporters of ISIS must battle their way past the gray woman.

What Readers Are Saying About Sanctioned Hitwoman

"Jeffrey A Pitts' descriptive writing has you so involved in the storyline and characters that you find yourself on the edge of your seat wanting more. I had to put the book down so I wouldn't read it all in one day. I wanted to savor it to make the book last longer."-- *K.L. Wright, Educator*

"Backed by the U.S. government, J takes on an international threat against a military hero. The anticipation of her going full out guns blazing kept me frantic for the next page. I couldn't stop till it was over."--*David Heye BA in English from WSU*

"Jeffrey A. Pitts has done it, once again! He has a tremendous talent for creating characters and making them believable. I felt I was right there with Jules in Wyoming. Her friends and family become your friends and family. I became lost in *Sanctioned Hitwoman* and could not stop reading until I finished the whole book. The ending does not disappoint, and I feel leaves it open for more to come in this great series. I have purchased this series for gifts, and they can't wait for more. Keep up the AWESOME work."—*Tracy Stowell, Human Resource and Safety Manager*

"Jeffrey A Pitts has shown how true love between two people will go the extra mile for each other even when the death of one of them could be the end. Jeff takes you on a journey into Jackson Hole and other small towns in Wyoming, A real heart thumper!"—*Dennis Schlenker, Mossyrock WA*

Excerpt

Rather than worry about her partner, I drew my gun and focused on my target. Not comfortable with a fifty-foot moving headshot, I prayed Father Timothy followed through while I strode quickly, the suppressed Ruger held against my leg. She pulled, then jerked at the door when it didn't open. Twenty feet, fifteen, I closed the distance. My gun raised only to hear a staccato blast I ignored to my right. The woman turned in surprise at the noise to face my muzzle. One shot to the center of her forehead, and she collapsed at my feet. While she spasmed on the concrete, I administered another four to her temple before I turned to find the reason for the explosion and neutralize any partner...

SANCTIONED HITWOMAN

Jeffrey A. Pitts

Moonshine Cove Publishing, LLC
Abbeville, South Carolina U.S.A.
First Moonshine Cove Edition Jul 2021

ISBN: 9781952439131

Library of Congress LCCN: 2021912885

© Copyright 2021 by Jeffrey A. Pitts

This book is a work of fiction. Names, characters, places and incidents are products of the author's imagination or are used fictitiously. Any resemblance to actual events, locales or persons, living or dead, is entirely coincidental.

All rights reserved. No part of this book may be reproduced in whole or in part without written permission from the publisher except by reviewers who may quote brief excerpts in connection with a review in a newspaper, magazine or electronic publication; nor may any part of this book be reproduced, stored in a retrieval system or transmitted in any form or by any means electronic, mechanical, photocopying, recording or any other means, without written permission from the publisher.

Cover photo by Teresa Fox illustration and design by Stacia Stojanoff, Edited by Chase Nottiongham

www.espialdesign.com; www.espialdesign.blogspot.com
www.chaseediting.com

Acknowledgment

I must always express gratitude to my wife Jodi for her unwavering support for my passion of writing. Many thanks to Frank Petrino and Chase Nottingham for their insight and knowledge of Catholicism. Also, Darrell Tevis for his answers to my many questions surrounding law enforcement, and my son-in-law Dave for his continued support and valuable comments.

About the Author

Jeffrey A Pitts grew up on farms in Oregon and Washington, and spent most of his time in whatever backcountry he could reach on horseback or afoot. Now, this dedicated storyteller's characters walk in the same tracks. Seldom does he utilize a wilderness setting he hasn't hiked, camped, fished, or hunted. Jeff loads, tests, and maintains important ballistic data of his own ammunition, because the harvest of wild game is a way of life to him, not a hobby.

After graduating from high school, Jeff worked as a carpenter, log home builder, logger, and heavy equipment operator. Fascinated by the roughest wilderness areas the US has to offer, he's spent much of his life exploring the wildest country possible, sometimes living off the land as he traveled. From the Goat Rocks Wilderness of Washington state, the Bob Marshall of Montana, to the Frank Church River of No Return Wilderness of Idaho, he's hiked thousands of miles on and off trails.

After the loss of a special German shorthair pointer, he filled the void with wirehair pointers and adds dogs into much of his writings.

An avid powerlifter, Jeff enjoys the big loads of squatting, benching, and deadlifting. He is married to Jodi, his childhood sweetheart, they have two children, Tyrel and Terin, son-in-law Dave and three grandchildren, Noah, Hayden, and Kody.

A lifelong reader, he began writing stories when they could no longer be contained in his head and spilled over onto paper and computer screens.

Jeff derives pleasure from a slow rural life, enjoying friends and family, crafting his stories, growing a garden, and living off the grid in the Pacific Northwest with wife, a German wirehair, and a flock of chickens

www.jeffreyapitts.com

Sanctioned Hitwoman

Chapter I

Leaving both bodies where they lay, I switched magazines and slid the handgun behind my belt, then retraced steps through the tall sage and found the lookout squatting at the driveway entrance, a rifle I recognized as a full-automatic Kalashnikov 400 in 7.62mm rested across his thighs. With no way to reduce the remaining forty yards to him, I flipped the selector of my own carbine from SAFE to FIRE and stood high enough to clear the thick vegetation. Fixated on the home they intended to invade some two-hundred yards away, he never looked in my direction. I put my Aimpoint dot an inch above the junction where his jaw hinged to the temporal bones of the skull. A spray of particles hung in the air for a moment after he collapsed.

Pulling my phone as I closed the distance, I made a call. A baritone answered. "KC."

"Ariel. Three down. One at the driveway entrance and another on the porch. The last is at the end of the house. Need cleanup ASAP."

"Copy." The cell went back into my pocket. A quick glance showed no reason for finishers in the lookout since most of what should be inside his skull was no longer there.

I was almost to my Suburban when I heard the first heavy whap of rotators in the distance. I stowed gear and prepared to leave. Detaching my carbine from the sling, it got propped against the seat within reach alongside my work pistol. Three helicopters appeared and slowed, then dropped from sight over the hill above. I started my truck and turned around. Three down, four to go.

I am extremely good at what I do. As an elementary school teacher, I receive student appreciation and respect, while staff and administration seem to like and value me. Hard work earned a third-grade position and my own classroom. Yet I'm asked to give it up for what? To keep an honorably discharged soldier safe in the heart of the United States? What of my husband, Dawson...and Jake, my best friend and four-legged hunting companion? Where do they fit into my life? I want babies—soon—or we may never have any. Nearing my mid-thirties, I can hear my biological clock tick louder each day.

If there's anything I'm better suited to than reaching young minds and preparing them for the next grade level, it's hunting and killing miscreants who don't value the lives of others. Believe me when I admit to being fully aware of the incongruity and irony of my statement. I am responsible for extinguishing the lives of psychopaths who don't appreciate the sanctity of creation. How dramatic if a bit grandiose. This wasn't a job I chose for myself—it was forced down my throat. Oh, I took to the task willingly enough after the murders of my family. Finding myself the executioner after my client was deemed guilty was a role I came to relish. I'm a damned good teacher and wife but an even better assassin. Time to put everything I learned and experienced to good use.

High peaks surrounding Jackson, Wyoming, were capped with a dusting of snow. I braked gently for a young mother pushing a stroller into a crosswalk ahead. The windows of my Suburban were down, letting in fresh air warmed by a sunny afternoon. The woman waved and smiled her thanks as I waited. I passed the Come Horn Inn where a rented room awaited to drive to the south end of town to a popular watering hole. Only forty-eight hours after landing in the quaint village, I was already learning the best places to eat. An open spot on the street was big enough for my lumbering vehicle, and I swooped in to park.

A board and bat exterior promised a rustic dining experience I'd already enjoyed. I put my windows up before stepping out and locking my rig. Cash and cell phone zipped inside my hand purse, its strap encircled my left wrist. My trusty Glock 17 resided in a shoulder holster beneath a light jacket with two magazines opposite providing balance. For the first time since losing my parents so many years ago, I didn't have to hide in plain sight—although few would remember a short, skinny blonde with no redeeming features, neither old nor young. Even my hair was put up in a bun with letter openers pinned Geisha-style. With their razor-sharp tips, the five-inch shafts were my last line of defense.

A life-sized grizzly reared on his hind legs greeted visitors when they first stepped inside. Antlers and horns adorned every wall to their high eaves. I recognized most because of my husband. An avid outdoorsman, Dawson hunted or was familiar with most species I could see. Moose, sheep, mountain goats, elk, and deer—even buffalo looked down at patrons. Full mounts of cougar, wolf, and martin watched from lofty shelves.

I stood at the sign asking to wait to be seated. A woman my age or older came to greet me. "Just one?" I nodded. "Follow me, please."

Her choice of tables didn't leave me feeling safe. I didn't want to sit in the open where others could pass behind, leaving me vulnerable. "I'm sorry...would you mind if I sat over there?" I pointed to a table for two against the wall.

She didn't seem to care. "Certainly." I took the menu she offered, glancing at her nametag. Angie. It fit her. "We'll give you a few minutes to look at our choices. Russell will be your server." I'd noticed a tall man leaner than my Dawson behind the bar and tallied sixteen diners at seven tables: five were men, eight women, and three young children. Few cast more than a cursory glance in my direction—exactly how I wished to be barely noticed and never remembered.

A *table d'hôte* lunch listed a half-sandwich, a bowl of corn chowder, and drink at a reasonable price for a tourist town. Removing my phone from its tight pocket in the little purse, I texted Dawson. *Everything okay at home?*

"Have you decided?" I looked up to a tall man Angie mentioned as my server.

"I have. The lunch special, please."

"Chicken, beef, or turkey?"

"Beef."

"For your drink?"

"Coffee. May I have a carafe?"

His stern and aloof countenance dissolved into a smile. "Ah, another lover of java."

I couldn't help but grin back. "Only reason I don't mainline it is I'd miss out on its flavor." Russell chuckled until out of earshot.

Jackson felt empty. Plenty of residents and pedestrians, but not like I expected a tourist town to be. Of course, early October came after the summer rush and before hunting and skiing seasons. I did note pickups with pointers and flushers, so bird hunting was underway in Wyoming as in Idaho. A few trucks sported fishing poles protruding from beds. With the town lying on upper banks of the Snake River, rods and boats weren't out of place.

Without much of an appetite, the meal was almost more than I could eat. The place emptied without more customers before I finished. My phone knocked after I paid my bill on the way out. I waited to check until closing the door to my Suburban. The interior smelled fresh. With less than ten thousand miles and a year old, it looked and handled as if brand new. *No problems on the home front. Situation on your end manageable?*

I hated to lie and loathed those who told them. *Still on the road. Will contact you when I arrive.* The untrue text proved difficult to send. After staring and wishing not to, I capitulated to need.

His answer was immediate. *Jake and I love and miss you.*

His missive tore my heart out. I lie, and he extends affection. *Love you, too. Hug my boy for me.* Christ, what have I become? Certainly nothing I recognized nor embraced. How can I deliver such a falsehood to the man I love more than life itself? Another part of me answered. Easy. I want him safe and alive.

With a couple hours until dark, I drove south to Hoback. As Early Hollister's guardian angel, I needed to familiarize myself with where his family and close friends lived. From a report provided, both Angie and Russell were important to Early Hollister. Too many peripheral friends and family members made my task an impossibility. From Jackson to south of Hoback and east to Dubois, I wasn't sure a dozen angels could provide safety the army demanded for their former sergeant.

Locating Early's parents proved easy enough. I stopped to watch their ancient log home with my Swarovski binoculars. An old barn in good shape could be seen beyond. A Ford pickup was parked nearby. I wondered if the couple owned more vehicles but could spot no garage from my angle.

I drove past Russell Endicott's driveway without a way to view their home. I'd scrutinized it carefully from Google Earth, leading me to believe he and his wife Ionella lived in a travel trailer. I parked across the highway where the Snake River flowed below it. A lone angler fished its bank. Watching through my field glasses, I could only see the back of a woman with jet black hair. She hooked one, but the line broke as she attempted to net it. I guessed the loss made her angry, because she whipped the water with the tip of her pole. I could only sigh after turning to drive north. Too large an area for one shadow to cover.

* * *

Dawson and I spoke or texted a minimum of twice daily. The days after scouting Hoback south found me in Dubois, a town significantly smaller than Salmon. Somewhere nearby were four of Hollister's closest friends. Jack and Marta Boyd were the parents of Emerson and Anna Boyd and grandparents of Lola and little Jack. I found their family tree a bit odd until realizing the elder Jack was Emerson's father and Marta the mother of Anna. As single parents, they hit it off and later married. More information made me wonder why I'd been involved. Mrs. Boyd was worth more money than I could imagine, and I'm fairly well off. She possessed the funds to hire a platoon. I couldn't wait to see the McMansion where she resided with her husband.

I stopped at a steakhouse, hoping for a late morning burger. A rough old cob of a cowboy waited my table. "Bill" according to his nametag. Judging by his voice, he'd spent quality time getting downright comfortable with whiskey. He didn't ask—simply turning over a cup and filling it with coffee before offering a menu held under one arm. "Got a BLT and fries for my lunch special."

Crap. I'd been looking forward to a burger but loved his daily choice. I smiled at the guy, wondering how he'd ended up waiting tables. Didn't see any obvious physical limitations—although that meant little. I held a hand up. "Your special sounds great. A little on the crisp side for my fries if you could." He grunted and left for the kitchen. As the only customer, I wondered if he cooked, too.

My phone vibrated with the ringer turned off. Cursing the tight handbag, I tugged it free to check the number before answering. "Ariel Woodman speaking." Archangel Ariel is known as the Lioness of God. I thought her name fit my present job. Woodman meant huntress in Old English. Both apropos.

"KC. I should have heard from you before now. What's the holdup?"

I learned super-secret agent Kevin's last name was Carter, and he went by his initials. "Sightseeing takes time," I answered coolly. "Quite a distance between points of interest. I'm in Dubois as we speak."

"Have you put eyes on Hollister?"

"Huh uh, but I might know where to find him." He and his family were in the apple orchard business south of Jackson. Early was also partners with the younger Boyd, owning more trees outside of Dubois, and it was easy to figure one spot or the other would be a good place to start.

"Get to him. Intel suggests our infiltrators have gone dark. No word since they entered the country approximately seventy-two hours ago."

A bell over the door rang when a group of customers entered, and Bill appeared from the kitchen with my meal shortly thereafter. "Will do. Gotta go." I didn't wait for an answer before ending the call.

A couple of the newcomers were loud and boisterous. Six in all, they pulled two tables together. Four seated themselves on one side with two on the other due to the great size of one man. Even wearing a heavy jacket, I could see his dense muscularity. Blond hair matched his short, thick beard.

The sandwich tasted better than I expected as did the fries, crisp the way I preferred. I ate slowly with the plan of taking what I couldn't finish with me. No telling how long my drive would take through the mountains to Moran and south to Jackson. The task Kevin asked of me seemed impossible. Checking any texts, I saw one from Dawson. Somehow, I missed its arrival hours before. *I'm leaving Jake with Mom to ride into the backcountry with Scotty and Robin. Falconberry, I think but not sure. Should be back in a week or ten days. Take care. I love you with every beat of my heart, Jules.*

My Lord. Eyes welling immediately, I could only dab at my cheeks with a napkin and wipe my nose. What was I thinking? It wasn't as if we needed the money. I'd not shared the news of our recent windfall with Dawson. My former employer—The Company—lost seventeen of their voting members to my guns, plus another six sent to assassinate me. After being laughed at, my price was increased to two-hundred thousand each. With the muzzle of my Ruger pressed against his chin, the member who agreed to my demand was happy to pay. Four point six million was deposited into my account before I slid my work gun behind my belt. As far as I was concerned, Dawson and I possessed more money than we knew what to do with. If I'd known about the eight men and two women my husband took on, I'd have charged them an extra two million. I still might.

I texted back, hopeful he would read it before out of cell tower range. *Sorry I didn't make contact sooner. Have fun with our friends and take care. I love you, Dawson. More than you could ever know. Hope to see you soon.*

My ears perked up at the banter coming from my lunch compatriots over menus. "We'll have pruning finished in a week or less, Em," one said. "You'll only miss the first couple days of season."

"We depend on venison. Ain't no way the two little bucks Anna and I tagged will be enough. Never mind Lola, little Jack eats enough for three. Tell him, Dad."

Speak of the devil, and he falls into my lap. Not much of a surprise with Wyoming's population around a half-million, meeting someone

I'm looking for in another town isn't rare. I kept any observation to a minimum while they conversed. The oldest of the group nodded. "He's right. Can't hardly feed the kids enough when they stay at our place. Must be going through a growth spurt."

Sounded as though the men were working in their orchards. No way could they be vigilant. Tough to prune, drag, and burn while watchful of others planning your death. Bill returned with his paper and the stub of a pencil for their orders but stopped to fill my cup first. I sipped the scalding java as cover to scan the men.

The giant addressed as "Em" and calling his elder "Dad" could only be Emerson Boyd. Then the younger man of normal size was by default none other than Early Hollister, the target. Any doubt disappeared when his searching sniper stare swept to me and paused. I nearly startled. No way could he know who I was or my mission. Yet his short-lived attention burned its way through me. I met it as coolly as I could before glancing at my phone in a pretext to avoid his concern. "Tell you what." Peripheral monitoring assured me Hollister no longer found me a point of interest. "I've got a couple herds spotted on Burnt Ridge above my place. You strike out, I'll guide you in and help pack home game if we get lucky."

I dawdled over my meal and drank enough coffee to strain even my large bladder. Most of their conversation revolved around deer season ending and elk beginning. It caused me to wonder about Dawson and whether he planned to hunt wapiti with his friend and local guide. Once it became apparent I would focus on a job other than teaching, my husband rarely went anywhere without me. With our freezer devoid of venison, he chose to tag a respectable whitetail buck along our driveway with his revolver. I hoped he did well in the backcountry with Scotty. The idea of thick elk chops made my mouth water.

Not wanting to miss a word of conversation, I breathed a sigh of relief when the crew of tree-trimmers trooped out. I raced for the bathroom after leaving more than enough for my bill and tip. They were piling into a four-door green F350 and matching canopy when I closed the steakhouse door behind.

Nightfall caught me watching Hollister and Boyd with my spotting scope from a window mount. Nearly three miles away, I hoped they didn't notice my blue Suburban parked above. I kept an eye for anyone else performing recon. Rather than follow my quarry, I saw them disappear on a long driveway leading to a log home. I sighed when they vanished into pines kissed by dying light. Their night would be far more comfortable than mine. With a small amount of shifting, I made a place for my air mattress and sleeping bag in back. I'd asked to have rear seating removed for the circumstance I faced. Settling inside my warm bag, I braced myself for a long vigil.

* * *

Rather than give myself away, I filled a cheap Styrofoam container to bursting with bread, condiments, cold cuts, and cheese. It would be nice to gain weight on a job rather than return home emaciated. Gallon jugs of water and a 12-volt coffee maker kept me fueled. A hole dug in the soil beside my rig allowed me to relieve myself and sprinkle dirt after each time.

Expectation of the kill team infiltration was through Jackson. I wasn't so sure. If they wished to murder Early Hollister and no others, my prediction was hostiles moving north from Rock Springs. If my guess proved correct, they could storm his home—or more likely reconnoiter—then catch him coming and going.

Returning to the Come Horn Inn after I no longer needed to check out orchards, I wished to shower before scouting Jackson. With a nice rear parking area, my vehicle wouldn't draw attention. It took me three trips to move my guns and gear inside. The upscale room offered laundry service, and I took full advantage. After a long time under invigorating spray and quick nap, evening streets beckoned.

Strolling quietly, I smiled and nodded in a friendly fashion to anyone. A family of four stopped at one of the town's antler arches caught my attention. "Excuse me." The man offered me his phone. "Could you take a picture for us, please?" I snapped a half-dozen, and they barely got their phone back and offered thanks before rushing after their pair of toddlers running loose.

A bench along the sidewalk provided a restful place from which to observe tourists and residents, hunters and anglers, shopkeepers and laborers. It was my father's favorite pastime before his untimely end. I'd sit beside him, while he pointed out the majority of genuine people at work and play—and show me an occasional pretender. I watched for those giveaways in passersby's now, aware of the irony that I'd left my real deal of a husband at home while trying to find fakes here hundreds of miles away, unable to turn my back on doing what I do best.

* * *

KC proved no help over the next couple days, nor did my targets accommodate by raising their heads. Even though I expected them to be dark haired with long, heavy beards, I knew my quarry the moment they stopped for gas in Pinedale. My tank was full while I waited to peel a banana and an orange. Two rentals, both white Nissan Rogues, stopped at nearby pumps. The first with three men and the second carrying four. All seven stepped out to stretch as if the first time in hours. I wouldn't recognize their language even if the low tones they used carried better.

Two were as light haired as Emerson Boyd, yet not as much as me. The rest were swarthy, and all were clean shaven, showing chins not kissed by the sun in years. I'm not sure if the oldest was more than thirty, and the youngest was a skinny boyish teen. Their apparent leader passed out cash to the fair skinned pair. He was battled hardened and ready for more. After tanks were filled, the pair sent inside returned with arms laden with gas station food. I lowered the passenger window to better hear any conversation, but the only term I understood were repeats of *kaffir*, Arabic for "infidel." If the two blond men understood, they must agree, because they didn't seem to take offense.

Already a few minutes after noon, I wondered how and from where they arrived. I'd been up early, eating a light breakfast of fruit on my way to the Hollister home. I hoped to study the surrounding area to find a suitable location from which to observe the house. Meeting Early and his family at the restaurant gave me time to reconnoiter better than I might have. A short hillside to the east consisting of a couple acres heavily timbered with thick underbrush would work. Silver sage surrounding their log structure would allow me to make my way closer if needed.

I moved my Suburban aside for other cars and pretended to be absorbed in texting. Instead, I poured a coffee while keeping a sharp eye on whom I hoped was my prey. The aroma of java from the Upchuck made my mouth water.

The bastards separated after poring over a map. The leader—his name sounded like Aahil—gestured east toward the center of town before pointing northwest. The blond pair split up with one in either vehicle. When four of the men turned toward town, I followed Aahil at a distance. Straight roads through farm country made the job of keeping them in sight easy. My heart thumped hard as they turned north from the main highway, driving toward the Green River and Hollister's log home. Each mile made me surer I located the first team.

A fishing pole and license made for a handy blind. To haul it out and cast a lure might keep me alive. I waited until the Nissan disappeared from sight before following. If they turned west to leave the river, the trio were fair game as far as I was concerned. Whether or not the Hollister family already returned home worried me. It wouldn't be hard for three armed men to catch Early unaware. Nor would it be difficult to develop an ambush by hurting family members or friends, drawing him into a one-way trap.

I'm not sure if they missed their turn or purposely stayed straight. Rather than cut up the steep hill where their target lived, the Rogue traveled as if they planned a backcountry excursion to Union Gap or beyond. Stopping at the Y leading to Hollisters', I watched them head up the mountainside leading north to Dubois. I wasn't sure of my next move. Following wasn't an option, and I didn't dare leave the log home unprotected. Without traffic on the dusty dirt road, I stepped out with my binoculars. The door made for a good brace as I located the Rogue parked high on a switchback. As I suspected, the trio were performing their own reconnaissance.

My outside temperature gauge on the Suburban read thirty-five degrees. Combined with a stiff breeze, it seemed to blow through me. I tossed my jacket and shoulder holster for my Glock aside, opting for a much larger and thicker coat. Before donning, I unfastened the one-point sling from Al's carbine and slid it over my shoulder. Should my opportunity arise, I needed only to clip it to the rifle swivel. Buttoning my coat would serve to hide or make it difficult to see. Sliding the Austrian-made semi-auto beneath the seat, I opened the case my work gun was kept in.

I preferred twenty-round magazines for my Sig Sauer MPX 9mm Carbine given to me by a friend. They made for a more compact long gun under my coat. Two extra mags for both the carbine and Ruger MK-IV semi-auto .22 rimfire got dropped into my pocket. As a believer in making sure my target was dead, I went overkill when it came to extra rounds.

The river below was beautiful, showcasing the gorgeous Wind River Mountain Range beyond. A swift current promised big trout. I thought of Dawson when it came to fishing. While he rarely went, it seemed he always came home with his wicker basket full of trout or a big salmon tossed into the sink. My heart hurt to realize I'd not thought of him after my hunt began. I suddenly wanted to go home. Instead, I made a call.

* * *

The Rogue disappeared on the ridge where I first watched it stop. Above me was the hillside sloping down to the back of the Hollister place. Attaching the Sig Sauer to the sling, I left it to hang along my side after setting the ambidextrous switch to SAFE, and chambering a round. My trusty work gun got the same treatment and then slid inside the waistband of my jeans. I left the rod and a small box of fishing gear on the hood of my vehicle before jogging up the graveled road leading to the driveway of the log home. I hoped no one felt free to liberate it before my targets got a chance to see my cover prop.

The graveled route proved steeper than I imaged. Short of breath before I reached the top, the crunch of gravel supplied a burst of fear and adrenaline. I left the rough thoroughfare and raced through sage almost as tall as me. Cutting and dodging, I dashed in the direction of the house. A log-sided garage loomed between me and my goal as the white Rogue turned onto the driveway.

A parked Jeep hinted someone could be home, but unless the brown F250 I met earlier in the morning was garaged, the house was empty. Dressed in black jeans with a charcoal-gray coat, I remained motionless while the men inside the car idling at the driveway entrance came to a decision. An incoming text vibrated against my thigh. Drawing back behind thicker vegetation, I checked it. *EH - ETA fifteen.* Damn! The Hollisters were driving in my direction and closer than I hoped.

I peeked after hearing more tires on gravel. One man stayed behind—I suppose to act as a lookout—while two others drove to the garage and parked. *Stall,* I typed back.

Aahil and the blond stepped out, stopping to check their surroundings before strolling toward the massive front porch. Neither carried a rifle, but I didn't miss the handgun behind the belt of the nearest before he closed his jacket. I hoped like hell they weren't friends of the family, because I'd made the decision to kill all three. I swallowed a tremor of excitement and justified fear. Careful of the pair of eyes left behind, I eased behind the garage the moment the two men turned their backs. Rather than ready a gun, I waited to learn their plan.

Hardly exposing the side of my head, I monitored both men cross to the porch to knock on the door less than fifty feet away. A dog barked inside, making me wonder if I made a dreadful error. Didn't I recognize Shaye Hollister on the passenger side? Raising Al's suppressed Sig carbine to my shoulder, I switched the selector to FIRE and rested the pad of my index finger on the trigger. A second vibration in my pocket went unanswered.

My chance came when Aahil peered in the front window and gestured. The blond man left the porch to circle around back. Lowering the short rifle to hang again, I drew the quieter Ruger MK IV and released the safety. The garage was a buffer between me and the lookout on the road. Walking slowly and carefully with the gun hidden within the folds of my coat, I halted at the end of the porch. My lips pulled back when the leader stood at less than twenty feet. With a gun in his fist and peering inside, my hand steadied as I raised the suppressed .22.

He never knew what hit him. A clacking of the bolt ejecting the empty into a custom catcher was the only sound until his body collapsed. I aimed for the top of his ear and softer bone than his forehead. Rather than have the decency to die quickly, he made a loud groaning sound. With his crown facing me, I put another bullet into the top of his head.

I stepped onto the first stair at a hint of movement to my right. Blondie either finished his recon or heard his commanding officer die. He drew up startled to face the muzzle of my handgun. The sight was the last for him, with the first going into his right eye. The moment he stilled, four more went into his temple. I wished to administer extra *coups de grâce* to the first but didn't have time.

Three down, four to go.

Chapter II

The second white Rogue hadn't moved since I returned to Pinedale. I'd stopped at a drive-in for a chocolate milkshake, a thick turkey sandwich, and to fill my thermos. The car was parked in front of a rundown motel on the eastern outskirts of town. Street lights came on as the sun descended. So focused on my targets, I didn't realize my drink was empty until the hollow sucking sounds from the straw. With only half my supper gone, I forced myself to nibble the rest until finished.

More than once, a curtain got pulled back and a face peered out. It didn't seem to be the same person each time. I guessed three men and a pimply teenager attempting to grow a beard became more nervous by the minute. A lack of contact with their comrades likely worried them. I couldn't allow the quartet to escape. What if they were to scatter until another opportunity arose? No, they were cornered whether they knew it or not. They would die by my hand rather than disappear into America's heartland.

A police cruiser slowed for its driver to look me over before continuing. My coat hid both guns lying next to me. I nudged my binoculars under cover, too. Truthfully, I was checking my phone for any texts, and the officer saw, I guess putting her mind at ease. Two final bites, and my sandwich was gone. I hoped the meal got a chance to settle before I left to finish my hunt.

I found a country music station to fill the silence. I waited where few cars passed, less as darkness fell. Too many broken marriages and pickup trucks were sung about for my taste, making me search for something different. Boston, Air Supply, and Fleetwood Mac almost made me smile with their 'seventies rock and roll. Embroiled in cleaning up after federal government inadequacies, I suppose my attempt to grin was feral and ugly.

The light in their room went out. Checking my wristwatch, I saw the time neared one a.m. Whatever I decided needed to happen quickly. Rather than let opportunity come to me as it would, I decided to face the matter head-on. Not long after I started driving back in high school, my dad gave me the gift of a safety hammer to break a car window. Although I'd not needed to use it, I still kept it in my large purse. I started the Suburban and idled past the motel some quarter mile to a restaurant closed for years and parked in the lot. My keys were left in the ignition, and the doors unlocked. Woe to any thieves attempting to steal it. A knit hat with eyeholes covered my face and thin doeskin gloves my hands. The hammer went into a rear pocket when I left my heavy coat behind. Damn the temperature. What I planned couldn't be hampered or hindered by a bulky body.

The Rogue was still parked outside their room. Other accommodations some five doors down were taken by two men driving a work truck. It looked to me as if they stumbled into their quarters—both were either tired or inebriated. I hoped for the latter. My plan of action relied on stealth and speed.

Shattering the driver's window with the hammer caused the car alarm to sound. Not hesitating, I sprinted the few yards to stand outside their door on the poorly-lit porch. Wearing jeans, a dark knit sweater, and my head and face covered, flattened against the outside wall might give me the edge I needed. Exclamations sounded from within, and a light switched on. As I hoped, a face looked out from behind the curtain, and moments later, the alarm stopped. My grip tightened on my work gun as I waited for one from inside to check on their vehicle.

The door opened as a man stepped out to assess before committing. Another stood within to guard the entrance. I shot the latter in the inside corner of his eye before turning the muzzle on the former standing perhaps six feet away. He probably didn't know the first man died when the bullet entered the back of his skull. I stepped across the threshold to face a scared kid standing in his underwear and gripping a handgun, and the second blond still lying in bed. My eye stayed fixed on the front sight—two shots and the remaining fighters were finished. A second magazine was required to add my signature. It was something I couldn't leave unsettled in the past. If I'm paid to kill—the term was difficult for me to admit—I wanted my target to stay dead.

The voice answering my call as I hurried to my vehicle was alert, considering the hour. "KC. Tell me good things, Ariel."

"Send your cleanup team to the Dusty Sunset Motel on the east side of Pinedale. Remaining four targets have been neutralized." Rather than stay on the line, I ended the call and lengthened my strides. The Suburban was moving seconds after I closed the door.

* * *

The clock read after eight when I woke. Working late and wound tight took its toll. Slipping my work gun from under the pillow, I took it with me into the bathroom. I trusted no one but Dawson. My eyes welled with thoughts of my husband. He deserved better than I treated him. Nevertheless, I would love him with every fiber of my being until the day I died—preferably of old age at his side. My man was devoted to his woman, yet I left him behind with barely a second thought. It wasn't about the money. Nor was it about stopping the scourge of narcotics any longer. Sanctioned by—and with the full weight of the federal government at my back—the muzzle of my gun turned to enemies of the state. I shivered and smiled while still sitting on the commode holding my suppressed Ruger. Who knew I would continue plying my trade for the good of the Homeland?

A shower came before cleaning my guns. A quick glance out my window treated me to a winter wonderland. Flakes drifted down on my early morning return trip to Jackson. With temperatures hovering in the low twenties, I figured it would stick around. Not more than two or three inches blanketed streets. Washing and drying my hair left me feeling like returning to bed. Cleanliness combined with the memory of a soft mattress almost drew me back. Instead, I dressed before scrubbing my Ruger handgun, SIG Sauer carbine, and suppressors. No corners could be cut when taking care of the tools keeping me alive.

Seated for a late breakfast in the Upchuck Restaurant and Lounge, I'd barely ordered steak and eggs and checked my phone when a presence loomed. "May I sit?" I glanced up to KC—I guess he was my boss. It seemed he needed to run anything we discussed past his commanding officer. Behind him was the short burly soldier who once pushed my face and then Dawson's into the dirt when we were intercepted. Although I glared while trying to catch the bastard's eye, he didn't glance in my direction. My payback then for treating my husband roughly while Dawson tried to protect me was a broken nose. I wasn't sure I'd finished with him.

Impeccably dressed as usual with not a hair out of place, KC smiled when I offered a chair and gestured. "Be my guest." His second sat at a neighboring table.

No other patrons were within thirty feet, but he kept his voice low. "Nice work. You've impressed me, although I expected the professionalism exhibited. Housework was exemplary, where the job inside city limits was spectacular." KC glanced over my head an instant before our waitress reappeared with her coffee pot in hand.

The beautiful woman offered both men a menu. Her dusky features framed by thick black hair cut Cleopatra-style were stunning. "Would you like time before you order?" she asked my tablemate. Her nametag read *Nellie*. Both KC and I knew exactly who she was. Married to Russell Endicott, the woman about my age was one of those on my list to shadow. Either her clothes didn't fit or the woman was pregnant.

KC and his second shook their heads. "Just coffee, please," my boss said. "We've already eaten."

I waited until she left before replying. "You're saying cleanup went okay, and the homeowners didn't arrive before you?"

He tested his hot drink. "We contacted state and county for assistance. State Patrol offered a roadblock, and our team accepted." KC noticed my raised eyebrow. "We often work with local law enforcement. A slight stain remained on the decking. Otherwise, no one would guess."

"Downtown?" Where Hollister's home was very rural and secluded, the motel was inside city limits.

"The owners were promised a room renovation after we secured it. New carpet, paint, and mattresses. All they know is law enforcement got reports of a murder-suicide."

"What now? Am I free to return home and go back to work?" I'd been doing my best to catch the eye of KCs gopher and finally succeeded. I was staring intently when he threw me a glance. He needed to know not all was forgiven. Judging by the way his eyes widened and blood drained from his features, he got the message. I wasn't going to kill him, but when circumstance offered, I was going to ruin his day. Mess with me, and you may survive—but don't touch my man. By his reaction, I guessed he took part in both cleanups. Good. Perhaps he learned a valuable lesson.

Again, KC paused before answering. Nellie brought my breakfast and to top our coffee cups. I checked immediately to make sure the kitchen didn't overcook the meat. Kevin offered a gagging sound. "Jesus, did they even warm it?" Already crimson soaked into my hash browns, where I used some to create a dam.

I speared a bloody chunk and chewed slowly. "Perfect," I assured our server.

KC waited until she was out of earshot to respond. "To answer your question, I'd prefer you stayed in the general area a little longer. Keep surveilling."

"You suggested seven. All are accounted for. Is intel offering insight into more arriving? Infiltration you weren't expecting?" I was surprised to be so hungry, and my table manners were less than ladylike.

"We're standing by for chatter...when they learn their target survived, and there's no response from their comrades."

I pointed my fork at KC after stabbing a centerpiece of the steak. He stared with open revulsion while I spoke. "Maybe the new guys know of the 'sow and reap' scripture and scattered to the winds after tasting real US freedom."

He shook his head. "Doesn't work with this group. Many have already sampled western fruit and know what we offer. We've identified five of the deceased. Two grew up in Norway and one in Portugal. It's obvious we fight ideology."

I feared the answer before asking my question. "How old was the kid?"

"Old enough to know better." His response was delivered in a belligerent tone I didn't appreciate.

My voice dropped to a monotone whisper. "I asked a question I expect to be answered."

He swallowed and wet his lips. "We have video of the kid involved in torture and murder. Don't let it bother you."

I leaned forward tightening my grip on the steak knife. "Last chance." I didn't break eye contact nor blink. Boy Friday shifted in his seat, and I held up a single finger as warning. Stay where you are or risk your wellbeing.

"Fourteen or fifteen. We believe he's fifteen," KC said.

I mulled the number while spreading blackberry jelly on my toast and cramming half into my mouth, wondering what hell would be like. Men, women, and now a child fell to my gun. Did God grant mercy to those who killed murderers? Were my sins less grievous than those I exterminated? Perhaps a stop at one of Salmon's churches could offer insight, although the genie was out of the bottle. "Three days. I'm giving you another seventy-two hours of service before I go home. If no one appears locally, and you don't get news of imminent infiltration, I want a few weeks of teaching before Thanksgiving." My hackles still standing, I tried to stare KC down. He wasn't having any part of it and looked toward the kitchen. "My students depend on me."

"More than your kids depend on you, Ms. Woodman. Those you shadow along with a grateful nation give thanks for the expertise you offer." He stood suddenly as did boy Friday. "Stay in contact. We'll provide long term parking for the Suburban and air service for your return home." He tossed thirty dollars to the table. "Allow me to pay for our coffee and your meal."

* * *

Our place looked incredible when I asked my driver to stop so I could admire the new house. Dawson's F250 sat parked next to the garage as always. We could probably squeeze it into the old building if need be, but he protested having not enough room. I unlocked the door and looked inside to check on my Jeep. After my ride left me behind, I needed only to ferry a suitcase with clothes inside, along with my work guns. For so many years, I considered only the Ruger MK IV my go-to firearm. Now, the suppressed Sig Sauer carbine fell into the same comfortable category, far more than my AR15 in 5.56mm.

Dawson strolled and Jake raced outside when I put a foot on the bottom step. My pup took one look and bolted to me. "Jakie!" I dropped the duffle and braced myself for his exuberance. He smelled like my best boy when I hugged him. The German shorthair wasn't ready for me to stop when I did, but I needed my man. It didn't surprise me when Dawson stayed where he was and watched rather than help carry my things. He relented enough to meet me at the top of our porch steps.

I set my belongings down and fell into his open arms. Jake tried to force his muzzle between Dawson and me. To be honest, I'm sure there wasn't room for a single sheet of paper. My body automatically molded against his. Tears I wasn't prepared for made my nose run. As always, I needed his flannel shirt to rub it against. "We missed you, girl." My legs weakened and almost gave way to feel as much as hear his rumbling bass.

I choked trying to answer. "M-me, t-too...I mean, I-I missed you, too." My arms couldn't have coiled tighter around his waist. The ever-present Colt Anaconda on his belt dug into my ribs. Over a foot taller than me, my crown barely reached his collar. With him lanky and me just plain skinny, I figured our kids would have to graze all day to grow. My mom was very thin, too, while Dad was always fit and muscular from his job as a forester. Perhaps our children would take after him.

We went inside where I left my bags on the kitchen floor. Jake sat nearby to watch. The absolute silence I longed for permeated my soul—if indeed I still possessed one. A box of tissues sat on the counter, and I used a couple to blow my nose and dry wet cheeks. Dawson leaned next to the toaster to take my measure. "You look good," he said. "A bit ragged but healthy. No bullet holes I can see. Reckon Nurse Ratched can set her stethoscope aside for the time being."

It's hard to tell when Dawson is joking. His dry humor occasionally caused friction between us—usually when I thought he was kidding and found he wasn't or other times the opposite. I sat at the big oak table we bought for our new place, after the last one was hit by an RPG, exploding and burning it down. The attack almost killed my husband and Jake. Those days were behind us as The Company no longer existed. Dawson and his friend Scotty rebuilt it as a story and a half, rather than the single floor it used to be. Finished with a knotty pine interior along with board-and-batten exterior, our new place was far more spacious and inviting. I sat at the table and smiled after a heavy sigh. "It's so nice to be home." Already I could feel muscles relaxing.

"When's the last time you ate?" Dawson asked. "I was about to put a peanut butter and jelly sandwich together."

I'd noticed the strawberry preserves his mom, Melissa, put up for us on the counter. "About six this morning. I wouldn't mind a half while you've got the makings out. Is the java fresh?" About a half-pot remained in the coffee maker, and the light was on.

As it turned out, he'd warmed it from hours before. Not willing to drink a form of black lye, I opted for a new batch—just a few cups. Jake sat next to my chair where I could stroke his head and muzzle while I nibbled and sipped. Dawson didn't press me nor offer any news. We were simply comfortable together. After we finished, I followed him into the living room. Rather than the couch, he opted for his recliner and held his arms out. The chair easily handled our combined weight as he made us comfortable. I knew he knew it was coming, and he knew I was waiting. Only the comfort and relaxation of home could suffice.

The warmth and safety of my husband's arms lulled. Unfortunately, I didn't rouse when the first spasm struck, and I vomited, throwing up into Dawson's lap. Convulsing before getting to my feet, I could only cling to my mate as he hurried me into the bathroom. Holding onto the toilet and praying to the porcelain gods, I understood why we sat in the chair instead of on the couch. We were closer to the bathroom. The door closed quietly after he made sure I was situated best to empty my stomach. The built-in stereo got turned on only moments before my bowels emptied while I still purged. I would have laughed at his attempt to give me privacy if not in so much discomfort. Little wonder there was no bottom to the depths of my love for him.

Dawson came in to throw his clothes and mine into the washer while I showered. A cup of chicken noodle soup and a glass of milk awaited me after dressing. "How're you feeling?" he asked.

"Better," I answered truthfully. I'd never grown used to the toll I paid for taking life. A quick sample of the meal made me grateful Melissa put up a dozen quarts of the wonderous soup after we butchered. I learned a delightful lesson from my husband and his mother. Food wasn't to be wasted. Especially chicken carcasses for stock and soup. Gardens were carefully preserved, along with farm raised animals and wild game. My longtime goal was self-sufficiency, and Dawson helped teach me.

"May I ask why you're back and for how long?"

I hadn't bothered to alert my husband before leaving Jackson. Swallowing a mouthful of hot soup, I washed it down with ice-cold milk. None of that two-percent crap. We bought ours from a neighbor with a freshened cow. She produced too much for the old widower, but he loved doing what he'd done all his life. Raise a couple cows and milk them. Whole milk was the only way to go as far as I was concerned. Plus, Melissa gave me an old churn to make butter from the cream standing on top. I'd never eat margarine again. "I'm back because the job is done."

He seemed surprised. "Done? You're out?"

I stirred the hot soup while considering my answer and finally shrugged. "Out? Probably not. I intercepted the group KC hired me to stop, but others are on the way. I'll be contacted when they hear more."

Dawson surprised me when he opened the refrigerator door, and I could see two cases of beer. One was already opened, and he retrieved a can before sitting across the table—nearly draining it in a single drought. I watched in consternation. My husband wasn't much of a beer drinker and never before noon. Rarely before three. He set it on the table before running a sleeve across his mouth. "Is this our future?" he asked. "Never knowin' what tomorrow will bring?"

His question wasn't one for which I could provide an adequate response. Not even my boss knew the answer. Dawson drained and pushed the empty can aside. The soup tasted good, and I finished it and the milk, making my stomach feel much better. I answered truthfully. "I hope not. In the short term, yes. Got to put an end to this group. We can't have enemies of Americans sending men to kill our citizens." Christ, I sounded like KC's trusty sidekick.

His gaze was cool as he regarded me across the table. "You made contact with the kill team?" I nodded my answer. "How many?"

"Seven...the suspected number. I hung around a few extra days to make sure we weren't wrong."

"Seven," he repeated.

I found myself biting a piece of skin on my bottom lip, waiting for Dawson's response. Love is a funny thing. While I demanded respect from my students, and J took action without thinking twice, as Julia I needed my husband's approval in the worst way. Don't get me wrong. He didn't validate, but his respect for the person I was meant everything. Not Mrs. Pelletier, nor J. Me, Julia. I shrugged and offered a quick dip of my head. "Uh huh. It went pretty smoothly after I made contact."

Dawson scraped his chair back and stood. "Goddamn it, Julia..." He came around the table fast enough to scare me. Pulling me to my feet and swinging me into his arms, I didn't have to look where we were going. He closed our bedroom door with the heel of his boot and tossed me on the bed. Both of us were in a mad dash to disrobe the fastest. I beat him by a pair of underwear because of his laced boots.

I woke later to open one eye and peer at the wall clock. Almost four. We'd made love twice—his desire made clear by how my body ached. So much larger and heavier than me, Dawson was always tender and careful. Not so this time. I sighed happily. He couldn't have made it clearer I was his woman. His arm rested across my side holding me to him. I took his hand from where it lay on the mattress and raised it to my lips. "I love you, Julia. More than I can explain." His soft voice rumbled with his mouth close to my ear.

I twisted in his arms to face him. "How did I get so lucky as to find you? You're my everything. I couldn't stop thinking about you while I was gone." A single tear escaped to soak into my pillow. My sight cloudy, I could no longer stop more from coming. As he'd done so many times before, Dawson pulled me to him and held me while I cried.

He waited until I finished, his neck and chest wet from weeping. "Reckon we were both blessed, little hawk." Goose bumps raised across my body. Was I no longer his dove? "Never thought finding love was for me in this life. Then you came."

"You loved Nancy." I couldn't help myself. Dawson never spoke about his ex.

His deep chuckle reverberated through his chest and into my ear. "She was nothing more than a young man's infatuation. Now that I know love, what I felt for her was a candle compared to the sun. To a supernova."

I smiled against his chest. "Hyperbole will get you everywhere."

The earnestness in his voice came across loud and clear. "I meant every word," he responded seriously.

A whine outside the door stopped our conversation. "We'd better get some clothes on," I suggested.

An arm of iron stopped me from rolling away. "Leaving so soon, Mrs. Pelletier?" Dawson purred into my ear. "I think we have a few minutes for unfinished business."

* * *

Bess Mueller, the school vice-principal and Dawson's aunt, sounded glad to hear from me. Arriving home on a Thursday and calling her the next day, she was open to me returning to work the following Monday. I got a chance to spend some time with my chickens—it seemed Dawson did a good job taking care of my bantams. After assuring me they still gave eggs, I found seven from twelve hens. Seemed he wasn't kidding when I opened the refrigerator to see five dozen stored inside.

I followed my two boys on a bird hunt, although I didn't tote a shotgun. We lost my Browning and Dawson's Ruger in the explosion and house fire. Dawson replaced his Red Label after a call to his friend Scotty Rich. Thus far, a substitution for my Citori hadn't been located. If need be, I was prepared to purchase new. One pheasant fell to my hunting partners, enough for a Sunday meal. Jake pointed well and held it until Dawson flushed the bird from a tuft of grass. For a fleeting moment, I thought he wasn't going to squeeze the trigger until the fowl fell from a cloud of feathers. His quick boyish grin made my heart leap to feel his joy. Dawson wasn't slow—he was deliberate.

I spent late morning and afternoon baking bread. Dawson kept my sourdough starter fed during my absence, leaving me with plenty to use. The first pair of loaves were eaten while still warm. We were equally guilty—I love fresh bread hot from the oven almost as much as my husband. The second pair went into plastic sacks while I mixed more dough for rolls.

The driveway alarm Dawson installed during my absence while I destroyed The Company tolled. Not an unpleasant sound, just a tone letting us know someone not only drove through the first but the second remote laser as well. We were going to have company. I opened the second drawer under the silverware and withdrew my spare Ruger MK IV. A cursory look assured me the magazine was loaded, and I worked the action to put one directly into the chamber. Rather than engage the safety, I merely covered it with a dishtowel and left it on the countertop.

Dawson looked through the kitchen door window. Up so high, I could see little but sky and usually watched from the big one. "Scotty and Robin," he drawled. "Crisis averted." At least he winked. So soon after a hunt—although relaxing at home—my nerves were tightly strung. Dawson glanced in my direction again before opening the door to see me taking deep breaths and trying to slow my pounding heart. "You okay, Jules?" He threw the bolt and hurried to me, ignoring the footfalls on the porch.

I grasped the sleeves of his shirt and rested my forehead against his chest. Four or five breaths later, I drew back and nodded. "Goddamn it, Pelletier..." Scotty shouted. "...the damned door is locked."

"I'm good," I assured him. "Let them in."

Dawson seemed deaf to his friend about to tear a new opening into the kitchen. "Are you sure?" he asked staring a hole through my head. I nodded, if only to stop the racket.

Robin saw me first. "Julia!" It seemed like everyone around Salmon was a giant compared to me, and Scotty's girlfriend was no different. Her hug pulled me against a breast far larger than mine put together and multiplied by five or more. She held me at arm's length after a brief time. "You look good. A little pale...but healthy. We missed you the last few times we've stopped."

Scotty seemed friendly enough. "Julia." He nodded and didn't bother to shake my hand. He would have hugged me if I demanded one. According to Dawson, his friend still struggled with what I was—more than even Robin whom I nearly killed. He lifted his nose and smelled. "Something tells me we got here at the right time."

I wanted to show Scotty my appreciation for helping a friend. "Thanks for taking Dawson elk hunting." I looked back and forth between the two men. "Did you get one?"

Scotty's brow furrowed as if not understanding my gratitude as he looked at my husband. "He went el—"

"Snow missed and stayed north of us, Jules," Dawson spoke over his friend. "Didn't see a hair. We'll have to make-do with the whitetail I tagged along the driveway."

An awkward silence caught me by surprise. Even Robin seemed mystified. No matter, I needed to be a better host. "We planned to have tacos tonight. Can I interest you in staying for dinner?"

Our guests committed to stay the moment Scotty saw Dawson's beer in the fridge, much to Jake's delight. Our pointer—I no longer thought of him as only mine—loved the attention Robin always showered. We went into the living room to catch up and enjoy the warm stove, while my sourdough buns rose. I figured a half-hour, and they could go in the oven.

Scotty regaled us with stories of deer hunters he already guided. One man was so obese the guide feared for his horse's back. Unable to walk far alone, he surprised everyone and killed the biggest mule deer buck of the season thus far. While everyone else but Robin was out of camp, the man literally shot it from his chair while sitting next to the fire. Scotty could only shake his head and chuckle while telling the story. Worse, the rest of the party were skunked, although having hunted hard.

I loved Robin's enjoyment of working deep in the backcountry with her boyfriend. Like Dawson and me, they fit each other perfectly. She wasn't afraid to jump in and help where she could and told of guiding a hunter herself. Left in camp feeling poorly, he lamented spending so much money while sick in his sleeping bag. Robin cajoled him into going out and went along to show the way. Scotty howled his enjoyment while telling of returning to find them both bloody and trying to skin a small buck. The man figured it was his only chance and took it. One of their group returned home with an unfilled tag, while the sick hunter took meat back.

During his antics of storytelling, Scotty spilled his beer on an end table. I was already up to check my bread, but he beat me into the kitchen for a dish towel. Before I could help, he'd already swept the one covering my suppressed Ruger. He froze, unable to tear his gaze away. "Go sit," I implored. "I'll clean the mess."

"Julia..." Scotty dragged my name out and didn't move. "...are you working again?"

My tone was sharper than I planned. "I said I've got this, Scotty."

"What's going on? Jules?" I turned to see Dawson and Robin standing at the edge of the kitchen.

Scotty frowned. "I thought The Company disbanded. Why...?" He pointed at what I considered my kitchen or backup gun.

Dawson came to my defense. "Jules was cleaning while she cooked. Found it in a drawer while you were banging on the door. She didn't know who was here and left it covered. Don't make this into something bigger than it is, dumbass." As one of the pet names for his friend, I figured Dawson used it to set Scotty at ease.

Robin helped to diffuse her boyfriend's worry. Soon we were laughing and cooking as a group, then stretching a pound of ground venison with plenty of vegetables. Before I knew it, the boys were in the living room telling stories—I called them lies—and drinking more beer. Robin and I could only shake our heads while we cleaned the kitchen, knowing headaches the following morning would be severe. Yet it was nice to be home, to enjoy my newly constructed house and host close friends. Already I dreaded getting the call to go east.

Chapter III

I love my classroom and don't get tired of saying it. The kids missed me, and my substitute teacher followed the lesson plans I left. With few exceptions, my students did well in my absence. Although class started at 8:05 and teachers were required to be available by 7:30, I arrived at my room before 6:00. My job was to be prepared.

"Hi, Mrs. Pelletier." Amy Jo Gossen was the first to make an appearance. Her mother waited tables and dropped her daughter off early as to not be late for work. I knew they struggled financially by the worn albeit clean clothes the nine-year-old wore. Her mom drove a beat-up Buick that likely used too much gas.

The little girl didn't have anywhere to go but my room. "Good morning, Amy Jo. Did you work hard during my absence?" I pretended to check my grade book.

"Yes, ma'am. I didn't like Mr. Garrison. He was always cross."

Voices in the hall and slamming doors meant children arriving for breakfast provided in the cafeteria. Amy Jo stood uncomfortably close, and I heard her stomach gurgle. "Did I hear your tummy tiger growl?" My little visitor blushed. "Why don't you hurry and eat breakfast before class?"

"Okay. Maybe I can get seconds. Momma didn't have anything for my lunch."

"You need to eat later, too. It's difficult to learn when you're hungry." I pretended to consider. "Mrs. Mueller said the cafeteria has extra food left each day. It makes her sad to throw it away. Would you like me to see if we could get you set up to eat some of it instead of letting it go to waste? You would make Mrs. Mueller very happy."

"A-are you sure?" It broke my heart to know she was famished. Children should never go without a meal.

I nodded and held out a hand. "You bet I am. Why don't I go, too, and we'll set up lunch for you?"

Later Dawson's aunt caught me by surprise as I passed her office on my way to the teacher's lounge for my noon meal. "May I have a word with you, Mrs. Pelletier?"

Bess was one of my favorites at school—not to mention an in-law. A no-nonsense administrator, she was tough but wore her heart on her shirtsleeve. Many were the times we cried together. I offered my brightest smile. "Sure."

She waited until we sat. "First, I'd like to welcome you back. Your kids missed you. Apparently, your substitute wasn't their favorite." I set my lunch aside and noted her gaze travel over my body. She knew and personally approved of me carrying a firearm, even if she wasn't sure where or how. No other teachers or administrators were aware as far as I knew.

I chuckled. "My class mentioned something similar."

She sniffed before I noticed welling tears. "I want to thank you for buying Amy Jo's lunch. Mrs. Hill stopped to tell me you filled the girl's account for the year." Mrs. Hill was the woman my students called the lunch lady. "Is she correct?"

"Her stomach growled this morning, and she was worried about breakfast not lasting through the day." I took a tissue from a box on her table to dab at my cheeks and nose. "Her mom works hard...I know she does. But a single mother with three kids, two of whom go to daycare...it must be difficult. Free school breakfasts must be godsend to young parents like her."

Bess nodded. "I remember Noel as she went through school. I find it difficult to grasp she's not only a mother of three but already divorced. None of us could figure out what she saw in Wayne. Little bastard never seemed trustworthy. Glad he's in prison instead of still knocking her around and knocking her up."

I was struck by an epiphany. "Bess, how many more are there in the district like Amy Jo? Those whose circumstances are difficult at home and may go hungry?"

She made a face. "More than you'd think."

With my own stomach growling and two freshly baked buns filled with sausage patties and cheese in my brown paper bag, I stood to leave. "Will you be here this afternoon after school lets out?" She nodded. Bess rarely left before six. "Maybe I'll see you then."

* * *

"You what?" Dawson sounded incredulous on the phone. "Are you serious?"

"As a heart attack, my husband. Please?"

"I'll be there. Ain't no skin off my nose." I almost laughed. Beneath the gruff tone was a gentle and considerate man. He didn't mind at all.

My kids were gone at 4:00, and teachers stayed until 4:30. Dawson appeared at my door at 4:35. "Mah hero," I praised and offered my lips as recompense. Judging by his soft smile and rumble, it was enough.

He walked with me to Bess's office. Her secretary was already gone, and I knocked on the door. "Come in." She smiled the moment she saw Dawson and came around her desk. "I don't see you often enough, nephew." She gave him a peck on his cheek. "What brings you to school? I seem to remember you swearing you'd never set foot in these halls again."

"You know me, Auntie. Jules tells me to jump, and I ask how high." She made herself comfortable behind her desk when Dawson and I sat.

"What can I do for you? Need us to keep Jake again? The kids certainly love him."

Dawson sat back and made a zipping motion across his lips and gestured to me. This was my idea. He handed me a paper bag folded tightly against contents secured with strapping tape. I stood enough to lean forward and set it on her desk. "Mrs. Mueller...Bess...I'd like to make a donation. I want it kept anonymous, but I'd like to request it go toward school lunches. Kids shouldn't be required to learn while they're hungry."

Bess looked from me to Dawson, who shrugged and nodded. She pointed to the package. "May I?" She produced a letter opener at my nod. It wasn't anything like the pair I sometimes wore in my hair for self-defense. She worked at it long enough Dawson finally offered his jackknife, a "weapon" not allowed on school grounds these days. Bess sent him a disgusted look, but accepted the razor-sharp blade. Slicing through and opening the sack, she peered inside and gasped. Within moments she formed two stacks of cash. "H-how much is here?"

"I asked Dawson to bring twenty-five. Is it enough?"

"Twenty-five thousand dollars?" She sat back slack jawed and stared.

"Will it pay for children kindergarten through twelve with low income families meeting the threshold for reduced meals?" I asked anxiously. "We can bring more if you need it."

"No, I mean, yes. No, we don't need more. Yes, this is plenty. I'll personally make sure it goes to the neediest students and isn't wasted."

"Are you positive?"

"Cash, Julia? Did Dawson stop at the bank and get a loan? This is over half your yearly salary."

Dawson finally opened his mouth. "Never mind, Auntie. Our only stipulation is anonymity. Do we have your promise?"

"Of course. Does Melissa know?"

"This's Jules' money and her decision," Dawson said. "Mom's got nothing to do with it."

We left Mrs. Mueller's office with her firm promise no one would know. While I had great feelings inside, I believe Dawson felt equally as good. Other than what I gave Scotty after almost single-handedly ruining his guiding business, money I earned while working for The Company could finally do good.

* * *

A notification from my money manager caused me to check my savings account. True to his word, KC made sure I got paid for services rendered. Unlike The Company who typically settled within minutes or even seconds of signing a customer, the federal government was hamstrung by rules and red tape. Each of the seven meeting their end at Hollister's home and in Pinedale paid $25,000. Somehow, the money didn't seem as tainted as what I earned from The Company, perhaps because it was sanctioned by the United States government. $175,000 would look good when added to my growing portfolio.

The backdoor opened, and I peeked over our second-floor railing to Jake squirting past Dawson on his way to his water dish. "Got skunked," my husband said. Empty hands held out meant no grouse. His shotgun went into the corner before holding cold fingers over a toasty stove. "Whatcha doing up there?"

I love sitting and working at our beautiful desk. Although open to below, the office seems quiet and private. All my schoolwork got hauled upstairs. "Got an alert from my savings account. KC made a deposit for us." I thought it important to make Dawson a part of the money. It was his as much as mine.

He glanced up to where I leaned on the handrail. "Already? The government doesn't normally work so quickly." He didn't ask the amount, and so much less than what I'd grown accustomed to working for The Company, I fretted over whether to tell him.

"I get the feeling these folks are a little different. Tough to respond to an emergency without a sizeable budget." Time to change the subject. "How was Jake?"

Dawson hung his hunting vest behind the stove along with his coat. Daytime temperatures were hovering in the low twenties. We'd probably get snow before long. "Good. He held point on a native, but there wasn't a shot." For some reason, my husband called ruffed grouse natives. He searched for his cellphone in a side pocket and set it on the charging station. "Got a text from Scotty. He and Robin wondered if we'd be interested in meeting at The Jumping Salmon for dinner. They packed their clients out, and it'll be a few days before going back with the next bunch."

Less than a week before school let out for Thanksgiving, it would be our first time together at a restaurant in months. "Sure. What time?"

"Five. Reckon it's because he heard a new band will be playin'. Sounds as if he plans to wear Robin's shoes off. Prime rib is the special tonight, and he knows how much I enjoy it."

We got there a few minutes before the preplanned time. Scotty and Robin were thirty minutes early, which was unusually prompt. She once told me how funny she found her boyfriend when he prepared to go out. He spent an hour choosing his outfit and combing his hair. Like me, Robin could change her blouse or trousers, run a brush through her tresses, and be ready to leave. Dawson was even quicker—he didn't mind wearing rundown work boots, dusty jeans, or sweat-stained shirts.

Pretty sure I spotted Scotty's grin before anything else. As much as he lived for the backcountry, the man loved social life. As his girlfriend warned, he wore his go-to-town Stetson, new red and black checkered shirt, clean Wranglers, and polished cowboy boots. Robin chose a simple blouse and long skirt—a much different look from my jeans, undershirt, and blouse to make carrying my .38 more comfortable.

Scotty noticed my lemonade and Dawson's coffee we carried. "Jesus Christ," he shouted over the music. "Looks like an old prim and proper married couple. You folks park your walkers in back?" he hooted. I noticed he pulled a chair out for Robin and seated her. She tried to shush him, but her boyfriend wasn't having any of it. "I'll buy the first round."

I shook my head. "None for me. I see a few of my students' parents here tonight." Besides, as far as I was concerned, until KC told me the job was over, no alcohol would pass my lips. I was on the job until it got finished. Quiet as he normally was when we went out, Dawson nodded.

Allison Edwards brought menus to our table. We didn't need them, and each ordered a different sized prime rib. Scotty asked for a Moscow mule using a spicy ginger beer, Robin a Coors, but Dawson went with a high proofed whiskey. Although I may have frowned, it wasn't my place to say anything. I didn't want him to feel henpecked. If my husband drank whiskey neat, it meant he was in a reflective mood, one that could turn dangerous. Lord knew I gave him enough reason to imbibe.

I turned to Robin. "How's hunting season this year? I'd ask Scotty, but he'd tell me about antler size."

She made a face and lifted a shoulder. "Good as could be expected. Down about fifty percent from two years ago. We're going to have to tighten our belts to feed the horses through spring."

Their lack of work could be directly attributed to me. After I killed four hunters in his camp—there to murder me—most of his deer and elk seasons were lost to investigations. Other paying customers were left without a hunt they'd planned and most salted money away to pay for over years. Poor reviews on his website didn't help. Scotty would've been ruined if I didn't step in and provide working capital. I figured my fault—my cash. I put a hand on the back of her forearm. "I'm really sorry."

"We'll bounce back," she assured as Allison returned with their drinks.

"Got pictures of two dandy bucks and a bull on my website taken this season," Scotty crowed. "They're getting a lot of internet hits. Bet next year will be a good one after hunters see their quality."

Dawson drank three whiskeys before asking me to dance. His mediocre skills didn't matter. What did were his arms clasped tightly. He chose a slow one and held me closer than normal. Almost as if—I peered up into a countenance filled with desperation. It was as if he feared our time together was almost over. I squeezed him tighter, only to cause his arms to do the same. I could barely breathe when the song ended. Catching him looking, I pulled his face lower for a kiss. "I love you, Dawson. Please don't worry...I'll always be here." His return gaze was unfathomable. Seeing our meals waited, I led him by the hand through the crowd to our table. A fourth tumbler awaited his return, and he downed it in two swallows.

I couldn't help but compare my meal to the ones I ate at the Upchuck in Jackson. Both were very good, but I was forced to give my nod to the Wyoming establishment. Scotty kept Dawson entertained with hunting stories, while Robin and I buckled down to eat. I wasn't half finished before Robin dropped her fork and turned to me. "We're getting married," she said.

Although I wondered if a long-term commitment was in the cards, her announcement caught me—Dawson, too—by surprise. I could only stare for a moment until her words made sense. "Oh..." I put a hand over my mouth in shock. "I'm so happy for you...for both of you. When? Do you have a date?" My dinner was forgotten.

Dawson finally smiled. "You ol' dog!" He slapped Scotty on the back. I caught our friend watching Robin and me hug with a grin. Seeing his pleasure at sharing the news made me feel good.

"Next summer," Robin said. "We'll tie the knot and spend our honeymoon in the backcountry cleaning trail." I guess she caught my look of surprise, although it made sense. "It's my dream. Oh, to sit on a warm beach would be nice, but we can't afford it, and this is what I want."

"Dawson?" I glanced at my husband and wondered if he could read my mind. Seemed four whiskeys aided any innate ability, and he nodded with a smile. I turned in my chair to face Robin. "We'd like to offer you our gift now. You can't use it yet, but we'd like to send you to Belize for your honeymoon."

"No!" Scotty and Robin exclaimed simultaneously. "Absolutely not," Robin said. "I've known friends who spent time in Central America, and it can be expensive...outrageously expensive. I want only one thing from you—"

"It won't cost us anything. Dawson has interest in a villa outside of Belize City. Melissa wintered there last year and plans to again in a few weeks. You could spend as long as you want...a month or the whole summer." To have a way of showing how much we cared for our friends was exciting.

Scotty turned to Dawson. "What? You own a place down there? How?"

Dawson shrugged lazily. "I never think about it. Jules and I are part owners with my business partner." It made me feel good to have him include me. I didn't want to overstep unseen boundaries.

"What about airfare? Scotty inquired, excited but biting his lip nervously. "Can an underpaid guide and his penniless sidekick afford it?"

"Didn't you get one helluva windfall?" Dawson asked. "You didn't piss it away yet, did you?" All of us knew he meant the money I gave Scotty.

"Blame me," Robin said. "We replaced two tents and bought an extra, along with the Ford. Scotty got tired of borrowing his Dad's truck to pull the horse trailer. We invested the rest into high yield bonds. It's growing slowly, and we don't plan to touch it unless we expand the business."

I did my best to murder Dawson with my stare. The money was Scotty's the instant he accepted my gift. "Pay no attention to my insufferable husband," I said, still not able to make eye contact with Dawson. "It was yours the moment I offered." Scotty's hurt look improved at my asseveration.

Robin took my hands in hers. "Julia, will you be my matron of honor?"

Her excited question left me shocked. Although we'd become good friends, I struggled to believe she would choose me. "I-I'm at a loss for words. Isn't there someone else...an old friend or family member you'd rather have?"

Her hopeful look didn't change and she shook her head. "No, there's no one more important to us than you and Dawson. She shifted forward in her seat. "Will you?"

"Of course, I will!" I leaned forward to embrace the much larger woman.

I barely heard Scotty over the music. "I need a best man, bud. Interested?" Dawson nodded and offered his hand. Grasping it and drawing my taller and leaner husband in close for a bro-hug, Scotty turned his head where I could see to grin and wink.

***

With Dawson's Aunt Bess and family sick with the flu, Melissa agreed to Thanksgiving at our new home. Scotty and Robin attended, making the day even more special with their planned nuptials the focus. Melissa learned of Dawson's friend's good news within moments of arriving at our place in her son's truck. Melissa didn't drive and relied mostly on Dawson. Our guests left early with Melissa in tow. I flopped onto the bed in exhaustion about my normal bedtime. "A successful dinner, don't you agree?"

"Yep. Mom loved our turkey. Her praise is nothing short of miraculous."

"How long since she celebrated anywhere but home where she did the cooking?"

Dawson's chuckle was a deep rumble. "At Grandma and Grandpa's house before she married Dad."

I turned to my side and faced him. "You're joking? She's always held the celebrations at her place?"

"Except for last year."

We'd forced Melissa south for the winter while I tried to keep Dawson and me alive. We survived two hit-teams hired to kill me, then later Dawson. A duo got sent to Belize to murder Melissa, but friends of my husband intercepted, killed them, and disposed of their bodies. We'd been too busy keeping our chins above the dirt line to consider holidays. "Wow..."

"Forgot to mention Mandy gave birth to a bouncing baby girl. Mark contacted me while you were working for the government."

"What?" I slapped his shoulder. "You neglected to tell me until now?" Mark and Mandy were in Dawson's army unit. They helped save my life more than once. Only the death of Mandy's mom in a traffic accident stopped their efforts to continue helping Dawson and me. She was pregnant the last time we met.

"Sorry, it slipped my mind," Dawson said. "She was born in June."

"They didn't bother to let us know for five months?"

"I think they attempted to contact me, but that's when I was working on the house and didn't return their call." He left out being angry with me for not calling or texting while I hunted and killed those who led The Company.

Seemed to me as if many things were slipping my husband's mind. Since I got approached to work for KC and his governmental employers, he wasn't the same. "Honey, what aren't you telling me?"

A sigh told me I wasn't wrong. He turned his head toward me from where he stared at the ceiling. "I'm about to turn forty. You're thirty-four. If we're going to have a family, it's a subject we need to discuss."

"We have, Dawson. I thought we agreed to start after I got situated in my job."

"Your job." He sounded angry.

"I'll go off birth control when this schoolyear finishes. We can while away the summer in the Middle Fork of the Salmon like we planned and work at starting our family there." I grinned to ease the tension. "Spend time fishing and hiking but mostly in our sleeping bag." I waggled my brows lasciviously.

"What of your other place of employment? When's it finished? How can we even consider the next phase of our life with it open-ended?"

I made my decision in an instant. "It's over the moment I'm done with this assignment. I'll tell KC I quit once this man and his family I shadow are safe." I smiled and traced an index finger across his lips. "We need to start soon if we're going to have a half-dozen."

His next question was no different than my own and apropos. "Can you stop working? Can you say no?"

Indeed. Could I?

* * *

"Mrs. Pelletier?" I turned to see Bess Mueller standing in my open doorway. "May I see you for a moment?"

"Class, I'd like you to open your books to page one-nineteen and study chapter ten while I step outside." When I stopped in the hall, more than Mrs. Mueller awaited. Rather than as a civilian, KC stood at attention in his dress blues. I glanced at Bess before turning attention to my other boss. "Yes?"

"We have transportation waiting." he said. "We need to leave immediately."

"I've got my Jeep in the parking lot. Besides, I have students to teach."

Bess touched my shoulder. "There's a substitute coming. I'll take your class until he gets here. Will we need another longtime sub like before?" Her question was directed to KC. He nodded.

A day into December and I was expected to leave my class, my town, my home, and my husband. Begin making plans for a family, and duty rears its ugly head. "Let me get my things."

Transportation was a ride to the airport where our helicopter awaited. Kevin explained on the way. "No chatter until this morning when the airwaves went wild. We believe a single ISIS infiltrator is already in Wyoming...possibly in place. We've been monitoring airports and as much as possible along our borders." Our car drove onto the runway to the waiting 'copter—rotors spinning and ready to liftoff. KC helped me in and buckled my straps. He nodded to the pilot when his own belt and shoulder harness were secured. Although I'd ridden in Al's Bell 407, the smaller corporate supercharged version was far more powerful. It seemed only seconds before I saw my home below. With instructions from me, the pilot set down behind the buildings near our shooting range. I wasn't surprised to see Dawson seated on the back porch with his AR10 resting across the railing.

"Jules?" He met Kevin and me at the top step, and though letting me pass, Dawson stopped my boss with an upraised palm. He followed me into our bedroom with Jake close behind. KC stayed outside in the cold as directed. "What's goin' on?"

"My boss got word ISIS has got a man very close to their target. Sounds as if it's a race to see who gets there first." I threw clothes into my duffle after changing into black jeans, long underwear top, heavy long-sleeved blouse, hiking boots, and my warmest coat. A few clothes awaited me in the Suburban, though not nearly enough.

"I guess I'll see you when you get home," he said bitterly. "If you come back."

Stopping my packing, I went to where he sat on our bed. "Honey, each time I leave we're one step closer to starting a family." I kissed his cheek when he turned his head. "I'm no happier than you about this, Dawson. I want it finished before school ends, and our new life begins."

I packed the same guns as before. My work gun, SIG carbine, and Dad's Glock—along with three magazines for each. After giving it a little thought while I zipped the soft cases, I tossed in another box of 9-millimeter and CCI .22 Long Rifle standard velocity lead. Didn't really matter I brought the extra. If sixty rifle rounds weren't enough, I was dead. Same with fifty-one rounds from three Glock mags. When it came down to brass tacks, I'd likely use the Ruger MK IV handgun and five rounds.

Once again Dawson refused to kiss me goodbye. KC offered his hand to my husband who ignored it, and for a moment I thought he might punch my boss. I'm absolutely certain the thought crossed his mind. If Kevin realized how angry Dawson was, he wouldn't have waited at the backdoor. I kissed and hugged Jake, telling him to be good and mind his master. Then I ran for the 'copter with the duffle strap over my shoulder. Although my boss offered, I wasn't willing to let him carry the tools of my trade.

The same room awaited me when I checked into the Come Horn Inn. A setting sun gave me just enough light to check on my Suburban and see if it would start. It fired immediately, and I noticed the fuel gauge at half. A foot of snow lay on the ground and my vehicle. I used a long brush and ice scraper to clean the windshield enough to navigate. A drive to the nearest station to fuel and wipe the rig of snow would leave me ready for morning. I could only hope I wasn't too late.

An aged Ford Taurus stopped across the pump from me. With my head on a swivel and hoping for the same blind luck as with the first group, I smiled when an old man stepped out. I guessed him at least eighty if I was a day. Wearing a heavy fur-lined coat, he fumbled with the hood a couple times before it covered his bald pate. I smiled again when he forgot his wallet inside the car after slapping every pocket in his search. He reached back into his rig while I watched. Laboriously pushing himself upright, a foot slipped in snow frozen into compact ice. He fell hard before I could react.

I ran to where he lay. The wind obviously knocked from his lungs, the ancient fellow rolled to his side gasping for air. "Are you okay?" I knelt to put a hand on his shoulder.

"I-I..." he gasped. "...can...hardly catch my breath."

I kept my hand where it was to keep him from standing. A woman watched from across the station but didn't offer help. I'm sure she thought I got the situation under control. "Are any bones broken? Can you stand?" He needed help to sit. "Should I call an ambulance?"

"I suffer from a simple bruised ego, young woman. I can do only half of what I could five years ago, which was fifty percent of what I could do the decade before. Getting old sucks."

The struggle to stand him upright wasn't difficult. Probably not more than three inches taller than me, he likely didn't weigh twenty pounds more. My grip compressed his coat sleeve enough I could feel a thin arm. If Dawson thought me skinny, I wondered how he would view this tiny man. The codger favored a hip, shuffling slower than before. The pumps required either a credit card or pay with cash inside. He drew out a twenty and cast a long look at the hundred feet or more to the cashier. "I'll do it," I offered. He didn't hesitate to trust and handed me the bill. A glance showed me his pump number was eight, and I hurried inside to pay. I returned to find him fumbling with his gas cap. "Let me help." He stepped away until I got the nozzle situated. With my Suburban filled, I replaced the nozzle and capped the tank. Rather than leave the old fellow alone, I waited until his twenty dollars turned into gasoline.

"I can't thank you enough, young lady." He looked up after I helped him into his car. "Do you live around here?"

My lie came easily. "I'm staying in the area for the next few weeks while I visit family and friends."

"Here for Christmas, eh?"

I shook my head. "Not if I'm lucky. I'd rather spend the holidays with my husband at home."

"I wish you the best, and coffee is on me if we meet again."

He stopped at the highway before entering far too slowly. A speeding pickup braked hard, and for a moment I wondered if it might slide out of control and hurt someone. Old folks, I snorted to myself. Going to get someone killed if they weren't more careful.

I got up early with visions of leaving long before daylight. An available continental breakfast was my first stop. I took enough hotcakes, floppy bacon, sausage, and buns to fill me—and more for a small lunch. Without others awake to partake, I drained the pot of coffee into my thermos.

My first stop was at the home of Early Hollister's parents. Only a few miles out of my way, I parked on a hill to watch the house and surrounding area as best I could in lowlight conditions with my binoculars. The expensive Swarovski glass drew in all available luminescence. A herd of feeding mule deer were visible, although well before sunrise. Not sure how long to wait, I stayed thirty minutes after rays appeared over the horizon. Then I pointed my rig east toward Pinedale and the Green River.

My second stop was Early Hollister's log home. I knew the area intimately and drove past to stop about where the white Rogue did my first time in the area. Another vehicle—I hoped a local—made tire tracks sometime after snow stopped falling. My aggressive tires didn't slip in what I estimated fifteen inches, but my location wasn't quite high enough to see over the timbered hillside behind the house. I backtracked and made the bold move of driving up the hill and past the intersection of their driveway where I killed the third ISIS fighter. The graveled road led past a ranch I'd seen on a map with its own airstrip. On such a dismal day, I wasn't surprised to see lights on in the Hollister home as I idled past at some three hundred yards.

Nothing suspicious caught my attention. A car, truck, footprints along the road, I could find nothing to alert me. Yet knowing a single member lurked nearby—or soon would—made hair on the back of my neck raise.

My phone alerted me to a text while I pondered my next move. *I'm sorry about my reaction yesterday. Forgive me? I love you, little hawk.*

My heart lurched. No matter how others saw my husband, I knew him as a remarkably passionate man. Although outwardly quiet, he loved intensely. Slow to anger and rarely showing it, I couldn't imagine a more dangerous human. He could frighten me with a look even when I worked as J. If he knew I was in danger, he would find a way to raze entire cities and flatten mountains to see me safe. *Of course. There is nothing to forgive, but I understand. I love you, too, Dawson.*

Is everything okay?

Yes, I'm out now. Lots of binocular work.

I'll leave you alone. We can talk tonight. I' see you.

His texting was horrible with occasional mistakes he blamed on "fat finger," swearing the tiny keys on his phone weren't made for his rough digits. I laughed at him missing the two letters after the apostrophe on "I'll." Unless in a terrible hurry, I always reread what I typed before sending. Auto-correct could cause massive blunders. Dawson and I worked through more than one technological miscommunication threatening our marriage.

Once again, my job felt impossible. Too many opportunities existed to reach Hollister without my knowledge. While I'd gotten lucky before, what if the assassin planned to hunt at night? Or take hostages of friends or family members? What of a rocket attack such as the one used against my home and husband? Too many possibilities existed to reach the man I shadowed before I could target an unknown nemesis. I poured my insulated travel mug full of coffee before idling back toward the Hollister driveway. Somehow, I needed to get closer. Setting up camp inside the small stand of timber behind his home was impossible at minus ten degrees Fahrenheit.

Stopping when I reached Green River, I parked to step outside. A hard wind buffeted my truck and me when I wandered away. The extreme temperature acted as a blowtorch to my face. It got cold at my place, but never with the gusts I experienced, making me retreat inside. If a different plan existed to save Early Hollister's life, I needed to find it fast.

Chapter IV

How do I search for a single person I've never met, don't know what he or she looks like, or how my target may arrive? He—I assumed it was a man—may have already taken hostages. Perhaps he planned to lie low until the cold weather broke. Endless alternatives made my head spin before I was struck by an epiphany. I should have quit after the first seven. Dawson and I could be snuggling on the couch with Jake. Governmental resources were unending—someone else could have easily and more efficiently taken my place

The day got wasted, along with a significant portion of my truck's thirty-nine-gallon fuel tank. Spending so much time in four-wheel-drive, I noted thirteen miles per gallon until I sat and let it idle for heat. Then the thirsty V8 caused it to drop below seven.

After another three days straining my eyes through binoculars, mental exhaustion due to lack of sleep drove me to the breaking point. I even bent my rule of never imbibing on the job late in the evening at the Upchuck. My head hurt as I cradled it in a palm while sitting in a darkened corner. Few patrons were in the joint on a Thursday night at eight.

A voice caught my attention enough to raise my head. An old man in a fashionably long coat of black wool stood near my table apparently awaiting a response. "Excuse me?"

"I asked if you've saved more age-challenged men who fell on their butts lately?"

"Oh." The tiny man from the gas station wasn't going to leave without my answer. Weariness crushed any pleasure from our second meeting. "No, I certainly haven't." I'd barely touched my cosmopolitan and tasted it again.

"Drowning your sorrows?" Although hard to see in the dim light, I thought he winked.

His comment caused the corners of my mouth to lift into a smile that didn't stand a chance of reaching my eyes. My waitress—Angie—watched from a distance, waiting to see what the talkative old man planned. I hoped my burger and baked potato would soon be served. I was famished. "No sorrows here, sir. Just a long day."

"You look exhausted. May I sit?" He didn't wait for my answer and drew a chair out, removing and draping his coat neatly over another chairback. The moment he sat, Angie walked toward us with a drink and stopped at my table.

"Your Glenlivet, Father Timothy." I didn't see his Roman collar until he lifted his chin and twisted to express gratitude.

"Thank you, Angie. May God reward your kindness."

"Anything to eat for you, Father? Your usual?"

"Please." He turned to me after Angie left.

I blurted the obvious. "You're a priest."

His smile warmed me as though a ray of sunshine. "Guilty. Although without a flock any longer...in the Roman Catholic church, once a priest always a priest. I help out where needed around our parish."

Although initially wishing to be alone, the old dominee intrigued me. "Have you always lived in Jackson?"

He chuckled. "No, this was my last assignment before retirement. I stayed after my replacement requested help. Most of my life was spent in the northeast before landing in Wyoming." He tasted his drink, then downed a significant portion of the expensive whiskey.

"I've never traveled east of Chicago." Even then my sightseeing was limited to the meatpackers union workplace. I remembered The Company's shock when I walked into the president's office and immediately put a bullet into his brain and that of the vice president. Another two of the upper hierarchy—one a woman—died by my hand before I blended with and escaped among terrified employees.

I noted his interest after focusing on him again. "Hordes of humanity wherever you go. I like the isolation of my adopted state best."

Angie brought my meal and a baked potato for the cleric. Where I ordered mine with basic sour cream and butter, his was a meal. Toppings were not only pieces of bacon but also thick chunks of ham and turkey and covered in chives.

I found him to be an interesting soul as we chatted over our food about the places he'd been and his congregations. I thought it sounded as if he'd have to be a hundred to fit his stories into one life. "If you don't mind me asking, how old are you, Father?"

His sly grin made me smile. "Don't you know it's impolite to ask oldsters their ages? We're as private as any woman with hers."

"I'm thirty-four."

His shrill bark of laughter caught even Angie's attention across the floor. "Fair enough. I turned eighty-eight last month. Since you know mine, what's your name?"

"Ariel. Ariel Woodman."

"Ah, the patron saint of animals and the environment, once called the lioness of God. Are you?"

His question confused me. "Am I what?"

"A lioness of God." I was far more than a female great cat, capable of giving the grim reaper a run for his money. More would soon have their lives snatched away at the muzzle of my gun. I figured it likely God cringed when He took note of my life. Men, women, and now a child got struck down by my hand. Chances were I'd never bask in His glory. I sniffed and wiped an errant tear. He gave me a start when he repeated a word I'd been thinking: "Child?"

"I-I'm just a lost woman. One who's made a lot of poor choices."

He gestured at my simple wedding band. "I see you're married. Happily?"

"Oh, yes. I love my husband. He's my life and makes it worth living."

"I see the truth in your eyes and hear it in your voice. Is he nearby?"

I shook my head. "Huh uh. He's at home.

"If I may ask...where do you live?"

"West of here." My suspicions rose during what felt more like an interrogation.

"You aren't a trusting woman, are you, Ariel?"

"Few in my life have given me a reason to trust, Father." I ducked my head to power through my meal. He watched for a moment before duplicating my efforts. Knowing I needed to put on more weight if Dawson and I were to have babies, I planned to eat until I could stand no more. I finished and caught Angie's eye with a raised finger. She brought a ticket and waited while I checked her work and dug in my handbag for cash. "I'd like to pay for both of our meals, please."

She smiled and shook her head. "Father Timothy's money is no good here."

"Be that as it may, I'd like to pay for his meal and drink, please." She left with sixty-five dollars for a sixty-four-dollar bill. I tossed another twenty on the table and rose to leave.

"My door is open to all who wish to step through it, Ariel. Are you saved?"

I hesitated at his question while leaning forward to push my chair in. My answer stopped when I noticed his gaze. Looking down, I saw my open jacket draped to expose the grip of my Glock. A hitch of my shoulder and tug of the garment hid it again. "Do I believe in God? Yes. Am I saved? Only He can answer your question. I've asked him into my heart, and I pray daily. Is that enough?" My tone was clipped, although I tried to keep my growing angst from showing.

He shrugged. "Walk in His light, Ariel Woodman. Remember, my door is always open. I'm not a perfect man by any means. However, I'm willing to be your guide and help you with any questions. Is there a chance I'll see you here again?"

"Perhaps, Father," I answered before turning to leave. "Good night." I was tired and a long hunt lay ahead.

* * *

With Christmas eighteen days away, I was no closer to locating my quarry. My solace lay in the knowledge Hollister and his family still lived. If anyone watched and waited, he or she did so under my nose.

My eyes continued to sink deeper into their orbital sockets each morning I critiqued myself in the mirror. While I seemed to gain weight from little physical activity but driving and glassing, growing stress over the unknown took its toll on my body.

Happy shoppers lined the streets each afternoon and evening, and even I spent time attempting to locate something Dawson would appreciate and enjoy. It was difficult to buy for a man who owned all he wanted and asked for little more. I sat at a window seat in the Upchuck to observe every passerby. My eyes burned and lids drooped until I leaned my head where the wooden backrest and plank wall came together. A brief moment to rest, and I'd continue my vigil.

Even the bell over the door didn't rouse me. "Aren't there better places to sleep, Archangel?"

I forced my lids open at the voice enough to recognize the elderly priest. "It's been a long day, Father." I rubbed my eyes and yawned.

"May I sit?" he asked.

"Be my guest."

Although Russell Endicott worked the bar, where we sat was his section, too. A long walk from where he spent most of his efforts—two tables didn't take much time and the other sat empty. I could mentally check him and his wife Ionella from my worry list while she waited the busier section. Apparently, the ancient clergyman was a beloved fixture in the premises by how quickly our waiter arrived. An amber liquid filled the tumbler. "What can I get you, Father?"

The priest tasted the whiskey and smiled. "You're a good man, Russ. No matter what others say." He winked at me and chuckled. "Yet I've never understood how you coerced such a beautiful woman into marriage. She must have fractured a leg and gave up running."

I enjoyed the tall young man's chuckle. "You aren't far from wrong. Wear 'em down is my motto."

Even I joined in their laughter. Timothy asked for another potato, and Russell left with his order after filling my water glass. I sat with my half-eaten cobb salad pushed aside. "Seems like a nice guy." I said. We watched as Ionella intercepted him with an order and a smile and a touch to his forearm.

"Salt of the earth. His wife, too. Their story is a painful one."

"Oh?" I knew little of him other than as a friend to Early Hollister.

"It's no secret he landed in our town while evading his wife. The woman tracked him across the country like a bloodhound and located him here. I'm not at liberty to discuss the backstory, but I believe we can hold God directly responsible for their reuniting. Ionella refused to live without him."

"Mm...true love." Once sure I'd never find it, I was a big believer in the concept. I could understand Ionella. Dawson was my one and only. If he left me behind, I could do no less than Russell's wife.

"I believe so." I tore my eyes away from the couple to find my table partner studying me. "Is Mr. Woodman *your* true love?"

"Absolutely. He's my other half. My soulmate."

"Yet here you are in Jackson and not with him."

"I wish I was home but I'm working."

He studied me over his glass. "What is it you do?"

What, indeed. I fell back on an old story. "I make contact with potential clientele for a large entity to express our interest in what they offer. If my diligence pays off, I contact my employer for cleanup."

"By cleanup you mean..." His question tailed off.

"Nail the lid closed on our negotiation. I don't get into the minutia when my part is finished. My job is simply making contact so they are aware of our strengths and what we can do with them. Beyond that is above my paygrade." I hoped they tossed the bodies into a landfill.

Russell appeared at our table with the priest's meal. I picked at mine again while they spoke. Like Salmon, it seemed everyone in town knew everyone else. I tuned out their chatter and turned my attention outside. Throngs of shoppers passed while I had no way of knowing for whom I searched. "Ariel?" Timothy waited expectantly.

"Sorry, got thinking about work and zoned out. Did you say something?"

"I asked what your husband does for a living."

"He farms." I racked my brain to remember what crops were raised on part of his and Melissa's bottomland by another rancher. "Alfalfa and oats." My return gaze was steady, but everything about me was a lie—an affront to God.

"Are you often apart?"

I didn't care for his line of questioning and changed the subject. "How does a sinner go to heaven, Father? What if their transgressions are unpardonable?"

It seemed I gave him the opening he wanted. The priest pushed back into his chair to regard me carefully. "Nothing is unpardonable, child. Forgiveness is given when it's asked for."

To restrain from unburdening myself was difficult. If anyone could answer my questions, he sat across the table. I leaned forward. "Terrible sins." I whispered, showing my teeth. "The kind told to keep young children manageable at night." I wanted to avoid the inevitable Hitler clichés, but wasn't entirely successful. "Man's inhumanity to man."

A lively gaze met mine. "God forgives all. His only son gave His life for us."

I broke eye contact by closing mine. "Will He absolve monsters performing abhorrent deeds?"

"Ariel...Mrs. Woodman...may I ask a favor of you?" I cracked my lids to see. "Is it possible you might take a day away from work and see me in my living quarters?"

I shook my head. "As much as I'd like to, I can't. My job directly affects too many lives."

His gentle smile almost got me until he spoke. "A few hours spent unburdening yourself shouldn't be life and death, young woman."

I stood suddenly and tossed a couple twenties to the table. Russell could divvy it how he wanted. "You'd think so, wouldn't you?" I swung my heavy coat around my shoulders to stave temperatures hovering in single digits. "Not everything is as it seems."

* * *

Other than meeting a woman coming from the direction of the ranch past Hollister's log home and driving toward Pinedale, I met no one to catch undue attention. Already, I was familiar with most vehicles within twenty miles of their property. More hours were wasted scouting his parents place—even two days in Dubois brought me no closer to my quarry. My temper grew short as days dragged. With a week and a half to Christmas, I wanted to spend it with Dawson. Our conversations were sometimes lengthy during evening hours. Otherwise, they were kept to short text messages. I needed to hear his rich bass to keep an even keel.

KC began to feel my wrath. His calls for information angered me. "I'll make contact when there's something to report," I finally shouted over the Suburban Bluetooth. "I can't be everywhere at once. Give me some men...three, at least. We can cover Dubois, Hoback, and Jackson, while I shadow Hollister in Pinedale."

"My guys and gals are military, Ariel. They'd stick out like sore thumbs. Anyone but the blind would ID them and redirect their plans elsewhere."

"Then send me some goddamned killers," I shrieked, hurting my own ears inside the cab. "Find a couple more like me."

For a moment, dead air made me fear he ended our call. "There is no one like you," he said quietly. "It's why we made contact and offered you the contract instead of someone else."

"There's plenty more. The Company employed hundreds."

"Many of which you terminated...others were killed by your husband. For now, you're our best hope. Besides, you understand small towns better than most. I cannot move military assets into the area without garnering attention."

We were getting nowhere fast, so I changed the subject. "Any fresh chatter?"

"Negative. Most operations we're following are taking place overseas. Al Qaeda is branching into areas once held by ISIS, who seem to be on a killing spree in North Africa. They've also struck again in western Europe. So far, Hollister appears to be the only American targeted."

A glow to the north meant I was closing on Jackson. "What in the world did the guy do to rack up so much animosity?"

"Few have clearance for this kind of information."

"You want his ass saved, but you're not going to level with me?"

"Can't. I'd lose my rank and possibly draw a court-marshal."

"Fine. Don't call again until you have information." He didn't get a chance to respond before I ended our conversation.

Instead of stopping at the Come Horn Inn for a shower before eating, I continued north. Struck by a whim, I turned onto West Pearl Avenue, then South Jackson Street. There I passed Our Lady of The Mountains Catholic Church, and wondered if Father Timothy were home. Didn't matter I told myself. I wasn't going to spill my guts to the clergyman. I believed in and prayed to God daily. What else did He expect of me? I chose a small café for dinner, only to learn a reservation was needed. Instead, I found a nearby grill to avoid the Upchuck and any chance of bumping into the priest.

Parking and waiting for a pickup to pass, my heart almost stopped. Although long after nightfall, street lights and businesses cast enough illumination. The driver didn't look in my direction, but I could see his dark complexion and a thick braid reminding me of Dawson. Not recognizing the truck and waiting to cross the street, I'd stayed partially hidden. If I'd stepped out, the driver certainly would have noticed and glanced my way. I waited until finding a seat before checking my phone. Nothing. Instead of a text, I rang his number. He answered on the fifth ring. "Hello?"

He sounded as if woken from a nap. "I'm sorry. Did I get you up?"

I heard a yawn. "Fell asleep on the couch. What's up? Any closer?"

"Nothing," I grumped. "At this rate, the guy I shadow is going to find himself dead before I can do anything about it."

"Wish there was something I could say or do."

"There isn't. Honey, we may miss Christmas together." I squeezed my lids closed to hinder tears. "I want to be there with you and Jake.

Scotty, Robin, and Melissa, too." A young woman came to my table with a menu. "Hold on for moment, will you?" I set my phone aside.

"Would you like something to drink?" she asked.

"Water with lemon. What's your soup today?"

"Split pea."

I thumbed quickly through their choices and decided. "A bowl of your soup, breadsticks, and a garden salad, please." I waited until she left my table before speaking to Dawson again. "I love you...I miss you."

"I love you, too."

"Did you put up a tree?"

"Nope. Jake didn't seem to find it important enough to mention. Got one for Mom, though."

Almost in tears when we finished talking, I drank a full glass of water before sending Dawson a text. *I love you.* I couldn't say it enough. Thinking of him too often made my chest feel tight. A return missive came as fast as his slow fingers could type.

I'll always love you.

My meal filled me, although I don't remember how it tasted, nor driving to my room. Instead, I found myself crying in the shower, unaware of how I got there. Tired, exhausted, and unsure of myself or my next move, I made a decision. Father Timothy would have a guest in the morning.

* * *

I don't know if the doors were locked, but a sign listed church hours as 8:30 a.m. to midnight. Only 6:30 when I got there, a voice startled me as I turned to leave. "May I help you?" A woman came around the corner with a set of keys.

"I was hoping to find Father Timothy."

She sounded surprised. "Oh. He's an early riser and should be up by now." I thanked her when she pointed the way to the rectory.

A large brass doorknocker called my name. I couldn't help but grin and pound hard three times. "Just a moment," a voice called. There were sounds of shuffling before the door opened, and I was met with a broad smile. "Archangel Ariel! How nice it is to see you."

"May I come in?"

He stepped aside with a gallant flourish. "Certainly."

His place was small. One room for the kitchen, dining, and living area with two more I guessed were the bath and bedroom. Other than a desk covered in papers, a computer, and knickknacks, his furnishings appeared sparse. It held the musty odor of old folks. A well-used recliner faced a small television with a couch to the side. I pointed after removing my coat. "Do you mind?"

"Make yourself comfortable. I was about to have tea. Would you like a cup?" I hate tea. Stuff gives me a blistering headache. He must have noticed me make an inadvertent face. "I've got cocoa if you'd rather. Sorry about no coffee. Stuff gives me terrible indigestion."

"Cocoa is fine. Thank you."

We didn't speak while he fixed our drinks. Without an end table nearby, he brought out an old metal TV tray from the previous century for my cup. I almost offered to hold his while he sat. For a moment I wondered if the ancient priest might fall. We sipped in silence before he set his aside. "I didn't expect to see you. How may I help?" he asked.

I'd thought of little else in regard to my life ending since killing the boy in Pinedale. Young man might be a more apt description. A deep breath released slowly helped me to relax. "How do I get my sins absolved?"

"Some Protestants believe by asking Christ into your heart."

"I've done that."

I guessed his nod meant he knew. "You worry it's not enough?"

"I know little about organized religion, Father. My parents didn't attend church, and although we were raised with a strong belief in God, I..." I thought for a moment. "...I don't know what I don't know."

He chuckled. "None of us do. However, I can tell you what I am sure of. God forgives all. You merely have to ask." His words were powerful, yet I wasn't sure they were enough. My eyes misted, and a tear escaped before I could stop it. I brushed it away while he absorbed my silent battle. I leaked quiet squeaks while trying to seal my lips, knowing he watched. "Are you the monster?" he asked quietly.

Emotion tore through me at his question. "Y-yes…" I couldn't help sobbing, and for a moment couldn't catch my breath while considering the sanctity of where I sat. Nowhere on earth could I be closer to God than seated beside His mouthpiece.

"No sin but denying our Lord can't be forgiven, child. If you continue to pray, you haven't turned away from Him. You could confess if you were Catholic," he said with a twinkle in his eyes.

A box of tissues sat on a shelf across the room. I wobbled over and retrieved them. Dabbing at my nose proved futile, and I finally honked it clear of snot. I blotted my eyes and cheeks while regaining enough control to speak. "I don't have time to go through catechism. There're more pressing issues, such as life and death. I shouldn't even be here."

"We face the same choices. All of mankind must make important decisions. Are you well? Do you fight a life ending or altering disease?"

I stared for a moment, surprised at where his suspicions took him. "I'm as healthy as a horse."

Timothy cocked his head. "I'm afraid I don't understand. Young people such as yourself are often confused…usually after the death of someone close. Sometimes a breakup with a spouse or partner. Yet you purport to be happily married with a strong belief in God. What drives you to fear the hereafter?"

I needed to gather my thoughts. "May I use your bathroom?"

"Certainly." He pointed to a door.

The room was very small, featuring a toilet, porcelain sink, and cozy shower with space for little more. Towels and sundries were on shelves above the commode. I took my time washing and drying my hands before rejoining. "I mean no disrespect, but are you afraid to die, Father?" I asked without warning.

His chuckle surprised me. "No, I'm not. Am I ready? I certainly don't think so. My life is obviously nearing its end, but there are so many things I need to finish." He winked. "Not the least of which is helping you, Ariel."

"How? You can't. No one can."

"To find and provide the answers you search for, thereby assuaging your fears."

"How do I confess? Will my sins be forgiven?"

"You must be baptized as a Catholic. Our tradition calls for completing catechism first."

I shook my head. "I don't have time.

"I could aid you...help you get done faster." He chuckled before asking, "I certainly hope you don't expect to stand at the Pearly Gates anytime soon." His jest fell flat. While I hoped to live to a ripe old age, my parents were murdered in their early fifties. Dad was adopted and never knew his family, Mom's parents perished in a car accident in their sixties. But her grandparents both lived almost to a hundred. Genetics might see me through to an advanced age if a bullet didn't take me—which might happen before I returned to my room. "Ariel?"

"Anything can happen. Especially when we least expect it." Except I did anticipate a sudden and violent end. "I don't live here and need to return home when my task is completed."

"They don't have Catholic churches..." He gestured vaguely as I once did. "...to the west?"

His question and the way he delivered it lifted my somber mood. I chuckled. "Probably, but they would be missing the most important thing." He lifted a brow. "No Father Timothy."

He joined my laughter. "True...we have complete agreement on your point." The priest sipped his tea and appeared to consider, while I finished my cocoa gone cold. He seemed no closer to an answer, so I stood and gathered my coat. He leaned forward, and standing looked like it hurt. "I need to pray on our path forward. May we meet again? Perhaps tomorrow?"

I'd already wasted valuable time, although my target certainly didn't need light to do dirty work. I simply prayed subzero temperatures at night would stop any attempts. "I'm busy between five each morning to after seven every night. Doesn't leave much time for meeting."

"At the Upchuck, then? Say tomorrow evening around seven or seven-thirty?"

"No promises, Father, but I'll do my best to be there. Say..." I stopped at the door after zipping my coat. "...why in the world is a restaurant as good as the Upchuck named after someone vomiting?"

His watery eyes crinkled when he smiled. "You haven't met Bonnie and Jake?"

I shrugged, having met many but introduced to few. "I don't know. Probably not. Who're they?"

"They own the place and used their name. Bonnie and Jake Chukkas, and it was opened uptown. The Upchuck." He laughed hard enough to snort.

I was still shaking my head—although grinning—when I started the Suburban and drove south toward Hoback.

Chapter V

Fresh snow overnight let me know the Endicott's south of Hoback hadn't left for work. Perhaps they got the day off or the afternoon shift, because new white powder on their driveway lay undisturbed. My Chevy indicated the outside temperature at minus seven. Working my way north with the plan of reaching Pinedale before it bounced toward lunch, I stopped at a place where I could use binoculars to watch around the elder Hollister ranch. A tractor with a round bale of hay left the large barn below their house, and closed in on a half-dozen cows. I racked my brain trying to remember what kind were black, and remembered as I looked for the information on my phone. Angus. They're a popular breed.

A truck stopping along the highway about a mile from where I sat caught my attention. It looked to be within a few hundred yards of the Hollister driveway. With the window up to warm chilled hands, I lowered it again and attached my spotting scope mount. Glare kept me from viewing through the windshield. Ready to put my Suburban in gear and move closer, I relaxed when it pulled onto the highway to travel in my direction. Stowing my binoculars and scope on the seat, I tracked its progress visually. Adopting my oft-used pretense of stopping to text, I braced my forearms on the steering wheel while holding my phone in plain view.

The driver appeared to be the same one I passed on the way to the ranch beyond Early's place. A woman about my age or younger—she seemed prepared for cold temperatures, wearing a coat and a scarf over her head. She passed—never glancing in my direction.

Snow lay deep above the Green River and Early Hollister's log home. Not sure my rig could make the hill, a glint from something shiny drew my eye. Binoculars and then my long-range scope allowed me to observe a truck passing near where I sometimes parked to see across the valley to the log home. With my first option gone and no tracks leaving the road they lived on, I retreated to Pinedale for a meal and fuel.

After topping off my Suburban, I found a clean café on Main Street with a widow seat. Spending my morning with Father Timothy and missing breakfast left me famished. I finished downing a thick greasy burger and all the onion rings it came with, when a truck parked on the street. Near as I could tell, it was driven by the woman who passed me. She got out to disappear into a hardware store. Not one to believe in coincidences, I'd already paid the bill and sat in my rig when she returned with a bag. Both our vehicles pointed east. I waited until she was almost out of sight before following.

I noted about where she turned. Slowing and taking my time, I got there as she exited her truck at the Sundance Motel. I marked the door she entered before passing the lot and continuing around the block. A good spot at the grocery allowed me to view the area.

An hour without any movement passed before I checked closer. Although using my binoculars sparingly, I threw caution to the wind and set up my spotting scope. Dialing it in to bring the truck and room door close, I finally realized what gnawed in the back of my mind. The license plate was Minnesota instead of Wyoming. I'd watched it pass Early's house, his parents', and even disappear south toward the Endicotts. I wondered if she worked alone or did the leg work for someone else.

I left my position after dark with enough time to find a place to stay. Rather than drive to Jackson and return to Pinedale early, a room at the Best Western saved time and energy. The grocery provided dinner—deep fried chicken and potato chunks. A couple breasts were more than I could eat, especially after delving heavily into their produce aisle. My craving for vegetables grew almost insatiable.

My belly bulged and was still complaining when I could stand to wait no longer. Although almost 9:00, I needed to hear Dawson's voice. "Hello, beautiful." His bass rumble filled my senses.

"I needed to hear your voice, handsome. Talk to me. Just talk."

I love his chuckle, caressing me like a warm breeze. "Oh, hell. Let me think. Got the oil changed in the Ford today. I planned to do it, but the damned engineers built 'em where the filter is near impossible to get at. Took it into the dealership and got the twenty-point checkup, the interior vacuumed, and a wash-job. Looks pretty damned good."

"Don't stop."

"Bought Mom a turkey and delivered it today. Turns out I was too late. She'd already got one a few weeks ago. One of her friends took her shopping. Robin texted to say they picked up a ham. They plan to spend Christmas Eve at home, then come over on Christmas Day. Everyone including Aunt Bess is askin' about you."

I lay on the bed with the covers turned down and wearing a heavy nightgown. My Glock was next to the alarm clock, but my work gun was only inches from my right hand. "Ohh...tell me more. What'd you eat for dinner?" His voice lulled me so much I was afraid of falling asleep while he talked.

"Oh...ahem...two whiskeys."

"Dawson—"

"I was tired...didn't feel like cooking'"

"A peanut butter and jelly sandwich would've been better."

He ignored my comment. "Scotty's been doin' pretty good on geese. This storm has 'em socked in around here. Said every hunter limited and plans to return next year." His announcement relaxed me more knowing his friend's business was on its way to recovery. "The big news is Al's having the engine in his flying contraption replaced." Dawson didn't care to ride in his business partner's helicopter.

"Mm..."

"Cost him more than the initial price of the 'copter..."

I woke to pee at a hair before 2:00 a.m.—long after Dawson put me to sleep. Chilled from lying on top of the covers, I snuggled in and used the pillow to help me burrow. With a small opening in front of my mouth for oxygen, warmth drifted me back into the sandman's arms.

I waited in the same grocery lot long before daylight. The truck still sat parked where I'd last seen it. Hoping I was on the right track spending time observing the woman and anyone else with her, I dialed KC. "Tell me you've got news," he said without fanfare.

"Not certain. Could there be a second?"

I got a few moments of silence. "You believe two have infiltrated?"

"Don't know for sure." I brought my boss up to date on what I found and suspected.

"Sounds plausible. Are you planning to move into termination phase soon?"

"What? Of course not. She might not have anything to do with this." I swallowed hard. "I've never murdered an innocent and don't plan to now." I wasn't going to admit to him I came close more than once while working for The Company.

"Are you familiar with the term *collateral damage*?"

"You're suggesting I kill her?"

I heard a sigh. "No, I'm not proposing anything of the sort. However, I need you to keep in mind there may be instances where you're not one hundred percent certain. We need you able to pull the trigger."

Breath escaped in a hiss. "Never worry I can't do it." I whispered into the receiver. "Be ready to go on standby when I call again." I refused to kill if not absolutely sure of guilt.

KC didn't call back after I ended our conversation.

Keeping tabs on the room and truck proved long and fruitless. The woman—tall and lean in need of a heavier coat—left on foot to the grocery where I waited. Parked to the side in case of this exact situation, she never came closer than fifty yards. Though my heart screamed to follow, my brain cautioned me to wait. Fourteen minutes and thirty seconds later, she passed me again with a small bag.

Temperatures rose to almost twenty during the day. My quarry didn't appear again. After nightfall, it dropped a degree below zero. I started my rig a few minutes after 6:00 p.m., less than an hour before the earliest time I agreed to meet Father Timothy at the Upchuck. Snow fell only lightly during the day, making me hope the road was clear.

A ninety-minute drive in good weather took me only ninety-five. No parking spaces were available close by, making me jog to the restaurant after stopping a block away. On a Thursday night, the place was less than half-filled. Angie saw me enter and pointed to a table in the back. I waved and went to find my date. "You made it," Timothy said. "I started to believe you stood me up." His smile belied any worry.

"I'm sorry—" I started to say while hanging my outer coat on the back of my chair, when Angie appeared from behind.

"Can I get you anything to drink?" she asked. The whiskey in front of the old priest was almost finished.

"Water with lemon, please." I looked at my table mate. "Have you ordered supper?" I turned back to Angie when he nodded. "I'd like your chicken oriental salad."

"Half or whole?"

"Whole...and a couple warmed buns if you could?"

My dominee companion waited until Angie left before asking, "A busy day of keeping your nose to the grindstone?"

I rubbed my eyes and nodded. "I'll be right back." I needed to pee in the worst way and splash water on my face. Feeling fresher and more awake when I finished, I found he hadn't moved when I returned. "Have you discovered a way to solve my dilemma?" I asked. He didn't move or say anything, simply studied my face. I met his gaze while carefully unsnapping the light jacket worn beneath my heavy coat. It worked well to conceal my Glock.

The priest finally nodded. "I have. Although seldom prescribed by today's church, I've employed it many times in the past."

I learned forward over my chair. "I'm all ears."

"I'm planning to baptize you."

"Baptize me...I don't understand. Don't I need to go through catechism beforehand?"

He shook his head. "Not always or in every case. In some circumstances having to do with not much time before admission of sins, baptism may come before instruction. If you agree, I can take your confession afterward."

I could only stare for a minute while containing my growing enthusiasm. "Tonight? Could we do it after supper?" I tried to curtail my excitement but failed.

He grinned. "Why not tomorrow? We could use the baptismal and do it properly. There's a winter carnival in town, too. We'll have the church to ourselves."

I sighed and sat. "Tomorrow may be too late."

He didn't probe my statement and waited when Angie appeared with our meals and my water. "I wish you were more forthcoming in relation to your job. It would certainly make mine easier," he said.

"I've already explained."

He frowned—I think to himself. "You've told me little except you fear your life may end abruptly." He didn't miss my lackadaisical shrug. "However, it's one of the legitimate reasons we might delay instructions for joining the church."

After eating what little chicken remained from my dinner the night before—forgotten and left to freeze overnight in the Suburban—I ignored his statement and tore into my salad. He looked on for a minute before following suit. I finished long before him. Catching Angie's eye, I ordered an apple pie alamode. Although it took time to heat, I still finished at the same time as Timothy. "Are you ready?" I asked. The time on my watch indicated a few minutes after eight.

After paying our bill, I followed him to the rectory and accompanied the dominee inside. Not having the slightest idea of what was to come, I waited while he disappeared into a backroom. If I harbored any reservations as to whether he was a real priest, they were quashed when he reappeared. Dressed in a beautiful white robe, he carried a large bowl. I watched as he filled the metal tub from the tap and blessed it with a prayer. He turned while situating the holy water on a table and said, "Although not required, a person being baptized into our church is expected to dress in white to symbolize purity of faith and the cleansing power of baptism. It also symbolizes the white garments Jesus wore when he was placed in the tomb after his death on Good Friday. If you would be so kind, a robe awaits you in my room."

The way I figured, his house—his rules. A robe could go over my jeans and blouse but not my jacket. I hesitated, then realized I was going to bare myself before him and God soon enough. I opened my outer garment and set it aside. My belt was next, going through my jean loops and one hanging from my holster to keep it snug, the other side holding my spare magazines. These I rolled in my jacket to cover. Father Timothy's watery eyes merely looked from my weapon to me but opened wider when I removed the shoulder-length dark brown wig. I set it aside and brushed my natural blonde hair with nervous fingers. He squinted and cocked his head—a smart man capable of drawing lines between the dots.

The baptismal rites went quickly. He didn't press me, but dawdling through the ceremony didn't fit my circumstances. Offered prayers struck me with the power of God—I took none of it for granted. He made the sign of a cross, poured water over my head three times as he prayed, and finished by saying, "I baptize you in the name of the Father, and of the Son, and of the Holy Spirit."

I accepted the towel he offered. "Is that all?" I wondered aloud.

He chuckled while moving the bowl onto a counter. "You wanted the quick version. I can't think of a faster way."

"Now what?"

Timothy glanced at the clock. "You'll confess your sins. We can do it here...or inside the confessional. You may prefer the anonymity of the church for your first time."

"You'll be the one to take my confession, won't you?" I wasn't ready for a nameless and faceless person hearing things no one should.

"I will unless you're more comfortable with Father Charles."

"You," I said. "We'll do it here if you don't mind."

After we moved two chairs from the table to face each other, he showed me how to make the sign of the cross, and I repeated his movements. "Bless me, Father, for I have sinned. This is my first confession."

My tongue stopped working and felt tied. For some reason I couldn't make a sound. Father Timothy recognized my stage fright and smiled gently. "Simply tell me of your sins, child, starting with those you feel are the largest and most important, then work down in magnitude to the smallest. I understand you won't remember every sin you've committed. Unburden yourself to me before God, Ariel."

A deep breath shook badly as I let it out. A tear trickled, followed by another before I got hold of myself. I was a damned killer—not a crybaby—except I was talking to God through His mouthpiece. "First, my name isn't Ariel Woodman. It's Julia Marie Pelletier. I live in Salmon, Idaho, with my husband Dawson. Ariel is a pseudonym I use with my employers."

He nodded when I didn't know how to continue. "What is the sin of which you most wish to unburden yourself, Julia? Stay as general as you'd like...or as in-depth as you wish."

I swallowed hard and looked down before meeting his gaze. "I have killed a hundred and six men and women, and now one child in his teens..."

The priest allowed me to confess with few interruptions. Though it wasn't required, I broke down working for The Company and the reason I took the job. Then why I killed those sent after me in self-defense, and of later going on offense against the hierarchy. Finally, I spoke of my contract with the government, although I didn't mention department or branch.

He was obviously shaken. It was abundantly clear he'd never taken confession from a contract killer. I wanted him to understand my defining moment came when I terminated the young ISIS warrior. While the boy wasn't an innocent by any standard, he was considered a child in our society. I needed Father Timothy to understand the importance of my work in Wyoming without giving it away.

I couldn't remember lesser sins by the time I stopped. He waited for a moment and asked if there were any others I wished to confess. I shook my head. "I'm sure there are...I just can't think of them now."

"Very well. Now, I'd like you to make an act of contrition."

Since I didn't understand, he helped me to say the prayer. After I finished, the priest offered absolution: "I absolve you of your sins in the name of the Father, and of the Son, and of the Holy Spirit." I swear to God a weight lifted from my shoulders. Perhaps it was only in my mind, but I don't care. Eternal damnation no longer frightened me. He stood slowly and painfully, and I with him. "I expect much more from you, Julia...such as attend church when you can and return so I can help where I may."

I nodded. "Is it okay if I repay you monetarily in some small way?"

"If you wish. It isn't required, however."

The old priest observed silently while I replaced my wig, then the holster around my shoulders, which I fastened to my belt. Snapping my jacket, I withdrew my wallet from a pocket. More government-provided cash was stored in the duffle inside my room, and I counted what I carried. "Thirty-one hundred, Father." I handed it to him. "I'd like you to keep it. Will the church accept a check?"

* * *

Four hours of sleep was all that was afforded me after retiring to my room. The alarm on my cellphone woke me at 4:15, and I prepared for the ninety-minute journey to Pinedale and Early Hollister's home. Grumpy and grouching at myself, I started the trek southeast.

My supposed target remained at the motel. A dusting of snow from overnight still covered the windshield and hood. She definitely hadn't started it. Finding a different parking spot, I settled in to wait for the grocery to open—or my quarry to move—all while hoping to be right and the man I shadowed still lived.

The store opened at 7:00, but I needed to bide time until 8:00 for the deli. A rumbling stomach tied into my lack of sleep and general crabbiness. A thermos of their strongest coffee along with a dish of potato salad and two breakfast burritos would hold me until lunch. I almost felt like my old self after eating the entire haul and drinking most of the coffee. With no movement inside the door and window I surveilled, I dashed to the store again and refilled my thermos. A Danish called my name, and I finished it before leaving the grocery.

I wasn't to the Suburban when my quarry stepped outside, followed by a male. Unlike the previous seven, he wore a long beard. The female kept her head covered by the scarf. Tamping down a burst of satisfaction over my gut feeling, I started my rig and buckled the seatbelt. It took them almost ten minutes before they were ready to leave with the woman driving. I hung back, barely able to see them over a mile ahead.

They led me to the cutoff turning north to Hollister's home. When the duo took the road and pulled to the side, there was no alternative for me but to continue west and wait on a long private drive. Two or three long minutes passed before an epiphany. I got a response after the first ring. "Tell me good things, Archangel," KC demanded.

I caught him up to date before explaining. "I need eyes in the sky ASAP. If I drive back, and they're still parked, I'm likely busted. Hate like hell to find the attack has started while I wait."

"We can be there in forty-five."

"Not fast enough."

"I suggest you redirect east. If they're still waiting, continue driving. I'll give you an update on the vehicle after we're in theater."

Sounded as plausible as any idea I'd discarded. As luck would have it, the truck was still parked where I left it. Rather than look in their direction, I passed with my cell held as if I searched for directions. Backtracking a couple miles until I found a likely spot, I stopped where it was only wide enough for a single car to park.

I could barely hear KC when he called. The thunder of a turbo engine drowned his voice. "Target still parked, but we're picking up movement around the Hollister residence."

"Movement of doing chores or preparing to leave?"

"Prepar..." I couldn't make out the rest.

Damn. If I was right, the couple would smoke the whole family when they came into view. Any weapon could be purchased if enough money were offered. I'd witnessed the results of a black-market RPG on my home. The pickup or Jeep Hollister's drove stood no chance. They were walking—driving—into a trap.

"KC?" I wasn't sure if we were still in contact.

"I'm here." I could hear him far better than before. "Hollister is moving in the direction of your quarry."

Damn. The 9mm SIG lay on the seat next to me. I worked the action to load a round and put it on safety before switching on the electronic sight and removing the scope caps. The fight was getting real, and my heartrate increased. Rather than fear, all I could feel was excitement at the culmination of my hunt. The time neared to cap them, and I prayed they weren't innocents with the unfortunate luck of finding themselves in the wrong place at the wrong time.

A snowplow almost hit me when I started to enter the highway. I stood on the brakes with both feet and breathed a sigh of relief when it missed, blaring its horn as it passed. Tunnel vision while focused on the job at hand blocked out a thirty-ton truck. I followed at a safe distance after sand and bits of gravel bounced from my windshield.

Apparently, God watches over the uncorrupted and unwitting—such as the Hollisters. With the rifle on my lap, I planned to lower my window, stop next to my targets and open fire, killing them before they recognized me as a threat. Instead, the plow switched on its turn signal to let me know it was going where my quarry waited. I slowed and held back until I could better see. My phone rang. "Another truck with snow-clearing equipment is leading Hollister's movement south."

I wasn't given a chance to open fire. Both trucks met at the intersection where the drivers could compare notes. If the pair I thought of as my targets planned to catch Early there, they didn't get an opportunity because of blind luck. Before I knew it, Hollister swung wide around the meeting, inadvertently using the trucks to shield him and his family. With the plow drivers showing no signs of moving, I continued east toward the Hoback-Jackson cutoff, monitoring the family following me. I drove the speed limit on 189 until the Ford caught me, and I slowed enough so Early passed on a short straight section. A glance in my mirror reassured me the pickup filled with those I hoped were members of ISIS lagged far behind but tagged steadily along.

The young family was still in sight when we entered the southern outskirts of Jackson. They'd surprised me by not turning south on 26 to Hoback until I remembered the winter festival running Friday through Sunday. Vendors were lining the street to offer a change from the multitude of fine dining establishments. Kids were on their Christmas break and families would soon inundate the town—the perfect place to target Hollister and disappear into a crowd. I slowed when Early turned to use rear parking at the Upchuck. The two following me quickly swung onto the preceding street. Seemed to me the dance was starting.

I found a place on Main to park. Fearing the Hollister's safety in the rear lot, I stuffed my work gun inside my waistband after chambering a round and sliding a spare magazine into my back pocket. Keys, phone, and wallet went into my coat as I jogged down an alley and around the building. The man I'd identified as Early Hollister already helped his family from their truck. His wife was short, muscular, and very pretty with wavy brunette hair. Two kids, a boy of at least five and a little girl perhaps three, rounded out their household. One look at their excited faces made me more determined to not fail in my mission.

Getting to the back entrance before them, my head was on a swivel watching for an attack. Holding the door open and stepping aside, I motioned for them to pass. "Go on in. I'm in no hurry," I said.

"Thank you," Hollister replied, his wife adding her own with a friendly nod and smile. The exuberant quartet went in, and I waited a moment to search for a target. If either would have appeared, I'd've gone straight to termination and contacted KC. As it turned out, there was still time to prove their innocence by disappearing with Hollister's life intact.

Crowd noise after I entered made me groan. Stopping to get my bearings, I retrieved my phone from a pocket and sent a text. *Shadowing in the Upchuck restaurant. Quarry is somewhere near. Standby for cleanup.* Damn, I felt like a secret agent rather than a hunter.

KC's response was immediate. *In place waiting on your timeline.*

I leaned my hip against a stool at the bar. Russell Endicott and his wife were pushing three long tables together where the Hollister family waited. Damn, it looked as if they expected more. I felt a nonthreatening presence at my shoulder. "Can I get you something to drink?" Angie stood across from me.

My answer was short and clipped. "Coffee."

She filled a cup and slid it across the top to me. "If you're looking for Father Timothy, he's sitting along the wall." I ignored her and didn't bother to look—I'd already spotted him. Of thirty-six tables, thirty-one were occupied, and none of those left open offered a good vantage. I gritted my teeth to realize the priest sat in the best one for my purposes.

Dismissing Angie from my mind, I wove between seated patrons. The priest sat facing the door some fifty feet away, with only an alcove and two tables behind him. I didn't recognize the couples at either one. Hollister's arrangement was almost in the center to my right—his back to us, and beyond lay the bar, kitchen, and rear entrance.

The old man slurped clam chowder and drowned a bun in the bowl. He looked up when I stopped. A smile lit his face when he recognized me, quickly fading. "Ariel. How are you?"

I didn't stop surveilling both entrances. "I need your seat."

"Excuse me?"

"Leave your meal and go home. Now, Father." I kept my voice low enough nearby tables couldn't overhear.

"I'm sorry, I—"

"Move. I need your spot."

The dominee complied but didn't leave. Rather, he pushed his meal across and slowly changed chairs. Twenty-four hours prior, I would've cringed at the pain it caused him. I moved to his spot and sat abruptly, setting my coffee in front of me. The front door opened to put me further on edge, but an older couple hurried to the Hollisters. I twisted my chair until the back was against the wall, allowing me to view the floor without craning my neck. I recognized the male from lunch in Dubois. The man was Emerson Boyd's father and possible target for the enemy. Although I shouldn't've placed his female partner, she looked vaguely familiar. "Are you going to explain what this's about?" my tablemate asked. I ignored his question—sipping coffee and watching. More people entered and left when they observed the crowd. Others made their way to the center group. One I recognized without doubt—Emerson Boyd. Big enough to produce his own gravitational field, he entered with two children and a blonde woman who resembled his father's wife. I figured the girl at eight or nine, the boy no more than five. "Nice folks." I glanced at Timothy, who hitched his chin toward the gathering I shadowed. "The Hollister family has lived in this neck of the woods for generations." I guess he didn't mind I wasn't engaging with him. "They aren't Catholic, but I've known them since I moved here two decades ago."

I watched Ionella coming to our table. Her husband Russell worked the bar and the Hollister's group. "Would you like a menu?" she asked.

"No."

"Coffee?"

"Yes." I didn't need more—the stuff was boiling in my stomach. She reached across me when I didn't slide my cup closer.

"Father? More tea or bread?"

"No, thank you, Ionella," he said. "I think we're fine for a while." He turned his attention to me after she left. "You're working."

"Go..." I stretched the words. "...home."

"The Lord *is* my shepherd; I shall not want," he prayed. "He maketh me to lie down in green pastures: he leadeth me beside the still waters. He restoreth my soul: he leadeth me in the paths of righteousness for his name's sake. Yea, though I walk through the valley of the shadow of death, I will fear no evil: for thou *art* with me; thy rod and thy staff they comfort me—"

"Father, not now."

"Thou preparest a table before me in the presence of mine enemies: thou anointest my head with oil; my cup runneth over. Surely goodness and mercy shall follow me all the days of my life: and I will dwell in the house of the Lord forever." His eyes widened when I turned my gaze on him. "I do not fear, Ariel. Neither you nor death."

A low hiss escaped me. "We're one in the same, priest. You just can't see my scythe."

I could only wait for what might come, although in the back of my mind I envied the obvious joy of the nearby group. It seemed as if a family reunion went on while we watched. Unfortunately, it was my job to ignore others' happiness or pain to focus on what I did best. Timothy finished his meal before pushing back to make himself comfortable. Didn't seem he was leaving anytime soon.

"I remember very well when the Boyds moved into the area. While they live in Dubois, they spend much time here visiting friends." Russell was stopped from leaving the table by the older blonde woman's hand on his arm. Her eyes were full of mischief as she spoke and got a laugh from him before glancing toward his wife, Ionella, and appearing embarrassed. The bell of the opening door snapped my attention away, causing my hand to inch closer to the Ruger inside my waistband. Two women stepped forward to give their names to Angie and wait to be seated. I glanced back to the happy tables only to find the elder female staring. Our eyes met, and we held our gaze until she leaned toward her husband. Only a whisper before he lifted an icy glare. The priest continued his story. "There was a big shootout in the mountains east of here. Somebody messed with the wrong people, and the Boyds did all the killing. Did away with more at their house during a home invasion a few years later."

I sensed a warning in his tale and looked away from where I watched to pin him with a frown. "Are you trying to tell me something, Father?" My voice was kept low and monotone.

He used his chin to point. "The Hollister boy spent quality time in the military. Army sniper, I believe. He and his future wife were attacked in the Wind River Mountains by three scoundrels. Way we heard it, he went out of his way to only kill one and spare the others."

I offered my most bored look. "Your point?"

Father Timothy finally smiled when he leaned forward to whisper. "Three out of the four most dangerous men I can imagine are seated over there." He nodded to Russell returning with drinks. "The man at the bar would be the fourth."

"Endicott?" The notion seemed ludicrous. Tall, athletic, with a short thick beard and a ready smile, I couldn't imagine anyone appearing less dangerous, except perhaps Scotty. The priest nodded.

I noted the blonde woman spent too much time looking in my direction. Thankful to notice her phone lifting to aim in my direction, I learned an elbow on the table and used my hand to shield my face. The other dug into my jacket for a jamming device KC remanded to my custody. With five short antennas to do its dirty work, a collective groan went up across the bar and grill the moment it was activated and the televisions went to black. The woman seemed surprised as she stared at her phone before lowering it and looking up in confusion. While I didn't smile, a smirk was impossible to stop until motion at the front doors caught my attention.

My target wearing her head covering stood outside staring into the restaurant.

Chapter VI

The female would have appeared far less conspicuous if she passed or entered the restaurant. Instead, with the sun high and shining brightly, a hand on either side of her face to see through the reflection gave her away. I waited—sure she intended to come in—until fearing she may well be a diversion. Timothy noted my alarm and twisted in his chair to look. "Are you prepared to die today, Father?" I asked when he turned back. The young woman stepped away from the window to glance in either direction. Although I'd been closer in the past, she appeared heavier than I first thought. Certain it was her, I thought perhaps it was the way she wore her coat.

"I'm ready when my Lord God calls me home."

My quarry cast one last look inside before disappearing. "You may meet him soon, but first I need your help. Go to the rear entrance," I whispered. "Lock it, block it, do whatever you can to stop anyone from entering or exiting. Fight them if you have to, because you battle for everyone's lives." I stood and pointed to my coat. "Take care of it for me if you can." Temperatures were rising to the freezing level, and I didn't need anything to hinder movement. I hurried to the front, cognizant of the blonde woman's following gaze.

The shawled female was nowhere to be seen when I ventured out to run down the steps. I worked my way through less pedestrians than I expected, stopping at the next street corner. I glanced to my left and saw my target vanish behind the Upchuck. Even though sustained speed isn't my forte, I am initially quick. A burst of adrenaline added speed to my feet. She was almost to the rear entrance when I came around the corner. Rather than try to enter through the door I prayed was barred, she faced away with her hands high, opening and closing each one three times.

I couldn't be in two places at once. Rather than worry about her partner, I drew my gun and focused on my target. Not comfortable with a fifty-foot moving headshot, I prayed Father Timothy followed through while I strode quickly, the suppressed Ruger held against my leg. She pulled, then jerked at the door when it didn't open. Twenty feet, fifteen, I closed the distance. My gun raised only to hear a staccato blast I ignored to my right. The woman turned in surprise at the noise to face my muzzle. One shot to the center of her forehead, and she collapsed at my feet. While she spasmed on the concrete, I administered another four to her temple before I turned to find the reason for the explosion and neutralize any partner. I ejected the partially filled magazine and exchanged it for one fully loaded—sliding the former into my jeans pocket.

Their truck was barely visible in the back of the lot against a line of trees. Using a parked moving van to hide my progress, I sprinted to get into position. Edging around the rear, I aimed the barrel of my Ruger at the open pickup window only to find I was too late. The male was unrecognizable after a bullet exited the center of his face. Gore still dripped from the windshield and dash, a sure indication as to the direction of the shot. Someone got to him before I could. Ducking and moving away, I searched for anyone nearby. I switched off the jammer after giving up looking and tapped a number on my cell. The answer was immediate. "KC."

"Cleanup behind the Upchuck restaurant. Female at the rear entrance, a male in a parked gray Dodge pickup."

"Copy that. On our way."

I'm not sure from where they came, but I'd barely returned to the female's body when two large Mercedes vans cornered so fast that I feared they would tip over. An SUV version of the German high-end vehicle followed. They strategically blocked views from side streets. I let cleaners led by KC approach my kill. My boss used a toe to turn her body when the coat she wore pushed up. We could only stare. "Back!" KC shouted. "Everyone back." His arms swung with urgency.

I retreated in horror. My quarry wore a vest filled with wired sticks of dynamite. Her hand signals suddenly made sense. Opening and closing them thrice may have been an indication of time—likely thirty seconds. If I guessed right, we were a half minute from a human bomb going off inside the packed restaurant even if I terminated her on the eatery floor. Most patrons would have been killed—any survivors badly wounded. Early Hollister—along with family and friends—would have perished.

The sound of scuffling inside the door caught my attention. Somehow, the rear entrance to the restaurant opened, and a female stepped out. I could see Father Timothy behind the older woman who watched me—the priest proving too elderly and weak to stop the female mature enough to be my mother. He glanced at the dead woman before the clergyman jerked the door closed, locking her outside. "Arrest her," came the stern demand from KC.

I raised my Ruger to arm's length—the muzzle trained on her forehead. "On your knees, cross your ankles, and hands behind your head," I ordered and got a curious glare in reaction to my command. However, she complied and laced her fingers together.

Two agents cuffed and moved her away from where the body lay wired to explode. I could hear them reciting Miranda rights. "The male?" KC asked.

I pointed. "Over there. I can't thank you enough for neutralizing him." I could think of no other explanation for his death and rationalized my target's hand gestures as we walked. "Good chance he would've triggered the bomb the moment he realized why I was here."

My boss appeared flummoxed. "Us? We didn't do it."

Confusion reigned as we viewed the male body. A phone lay on the floorboards—one I wondered if he planned to use for detonation. Surrounding agents who knew a hell of a lot more about it than me took careful possession of the cell. "I don't get it," I said. "Someone killed him as I closed on his accomplice. If not one of you, then who?"

KC shook his head. "We'll figure it out." Rather than scrub the scene and leave quickly, they erected a tent over the dead female and secured the perimeter. Without X-ray vision, no one could see what went on. "We need you out of here. There's a car parked a block north on Main Street. Get whatever you need from your vehicle. The driver will see you to your room and then the airport. My boss drew his heels together and raised his hand in a snappy salute. "Ariel Woodman, we thank you for your service to our country."

* * *

I couldn't leave—not yet. My imposing driver waited with the door open the moment I crossed the street from the Suburban, my SIG wrapped in a blanket under my arm. "The Come Horn Inn, please," I informed Jeremy. My job performance had been nothing less than spectacular while pedestrians milled about on Main as if nothing happened. My shots were almost soundless, and the explosion from the single round killing the accomplice could be explained away as a backfire. When I left the rear of the Upchuck, it was walled-off and unavailable to civilians. I'd gotten away with a big one without anyone the wiser.

Jeremy toted my bag filled with clothing and personal items from my room to his car. I carried my guns and work paraphernalia. Some of my gear was only to be touched by me. He glanced in the rearview mirror. "If you're ready, Ms. Woodman, your flight is fueled and standing by on the tarmac."

I considered his question before deciding I wasn't. "No, I'm not. Can you take me to Our Lady of The Mountains, please?"

"Excuse me?"

"The Catholic church."

With a plan in mind, I'd dawdled in my room to make sure everything got packed and nothing was forgotten, until ninety minutes passed since I left the Upchuck. As we turned in, the car I hoped to see was in the private parking area where I instructed Jeremy to wait. It made me uncomfortable when the driver opened my door, but he stayed near our vehicle rather than follow. I knocked and listened for slow footsteps inside. A familiar face peered out when it opened. "Mrs. Pelletier." The priest looked over my shoulder. "Make sure your thug stays out," he said before stepping aside. "I've already dealt with him today. Apparently, I didn't see what I saw, according to him."

I stayed where I was. Father Timothy didn't appear angry—worse, he seemed disgusted. "What if he's Catholic and wants to confess?" I asked.

He seemed startled and peeked over my shoulder again before a slow grin crept across his features. "Is he?"

I shrugged, my smile meant to match his. "Want me to ask?"

Finally, the priest laughed. "Please, come in, Julia." He closed the door behind. "I'm sorry all I have to offer you is a headache." My confused reaction earned a chuckle. "You said before how tea makes your head hurt."

"A glass of cold water would be nice." He shuffled to the small kitchen while I absorbed his little place—again noting the smell. I remembered my great grandparents' home with the same musty odor. Like theirs before, the place needed a good scrubbing and airing.

Timothy took his customary spot after giving me a filled glass. "I owe you an apology." he said.

My brow lifted. "For what?"

"I misunderstood."

"Doesn't matter." I lifted a shoulder—my mood souring.

"It does to me. Although hearing your confession, I still feared you were here for people I love. By the way..." He pointed. "...I have your coat.

It hung from a rack inside the front door. I tipped my head. "Thank you." The warm fur-lined garment was far more expensive than any I'd owned, and I hoped to wear it for years to come. "No, I'm not here for anyone you know. We'll cross paths again, I'm sure. However, neither you nor anyone living in the area has reason to be concerned." I considered for a moment before realizing my declaration wasn't factually correct. "That wasn't exactly right. As long as I'm successful, no one you know is in danger."

No doubt he mulled my change by the way his eyes narrowed. "I'm glad to hear your news," he said, then grimaced. "Especially after seeing a body loaded with so much dynamite."

I glared. "Not for your eyes, priest."

He ignored my reaction. "Oddest thing. A dead woman during a celebration without so much as a peep. It's like no one in town noticed a killing. How does something so unchristian happen?" I continued to stare daggers, but he didn't look away. The man possessed a self-confidence I couldn't match.

Although I'd stopped a plot of mass carnage, it could never be made public. No one but me, KC and his team, and now this priest would ever know. The woman arrested couldn't pass it on from inside a cell. I slipped from the couch to my knees. "Father, will you take my confession?"

* * *

Damned if my Jeep wasn't still parked in its normal place at school. It surprised me to find Dawson hadn't bothered to move it home, so I was glad I swung past first. A foot of snow covered the hood, windshield, and top. Ken, one of the guys working at Salmon Air agreed to drive me home after I couldn't contact my husband. He waited until my rig started and helped me brush the snow away. I appreciate him and the guys he works with. Always helpful when I need them most.

A goose of the throttle to make it rock, and the old Wagoneer broke free of its frozen mooring with a throaty roar. Felt good to drive my favorite vehicle. I preferred it over anything new. The fuel gauge sat at a hair below half, so I pulled into the Shell station. I couldn't wait to get home to see Dawson and Jake, but I hurried into our grocery to pick up a few things—mostly fruits and vegetables.

Instead of the homecoming I hoped for, our house sat cold and empty. Following three trips to pack my gear from the garage to the front porch, not even Jake met me when I opened the door.

A fire was the most pressing issue after I hauled and deposited my things into the living room. In the teens outside, the interior felt positively frigid with the electric heat set at fifty-five. Cold permeated from the walls and floor, telling me Dawson hadn't been home in a few days. This was more than the fire going out after leaving early in the morning. It didn't take me long before a cheery blaze roared in the new wood cookstove Dawson bought. I waited a few minutes before loading it with larger chunks and closing the draft.

Rather than an impersonal and quick shower, I ran water into our clawfoot tub. I waited as it filled before climbing in with a steaming cup of coffee set within reach. Sliding deep into the warm water, I waited until my body acclimated to it before adding more. The room filled with steam, providing the illusion of a sauna. I relaxed with only my chin above the waterline and sighed my pleasure. It was twenty minutes before I emptied the insulated cup, while I struggled to stay awake. Watching twilight give way to darkness through the high window nearly put me to sleep.

As it turned out, except for temporary relaxation and rejuvenation, my bath got wasted. Rather than dress, I found my robe and belted it over a long nightgown. With the inside temperature finally comfortable, I settled into Dawson's recliner with a pocketbook started while in Jackson. A retired fighter was about to rescue a damsel in distress from bad guys. I needed to see how he accomplished the task. While I enjoyed the novel, nobody needed to save this girl. Should a man wish to hurt me, I'd put a bullet in his head as a courtesy simply to save him from my husband.

I barely got a chance to start the next chapter where the hero is giving the girl a ride to safety when the first spasm struck. Tossing the book aside, I rushed to the bathroom with my focus on reaching the toilet. On my knees and holding tightly to chilly porcelain, everything in my stomach sought to be the first expelled. Convulsing, choking, and bobbing about, I gripped the throne with all my might. I wasn't able to stop my diarrhea, adding tears of shame to my physical difficulties. My robe and gown were tossed into the washer after I finished purging and shaking, and I cleaned the mess on the floor before dragging my skinny butt into the shower.

I didn't bother trying Dawson again until after finishing supper. Cream of chicken soup got warmed on the woodstove, but I couldn't find any bread. My husband loved it, so I was surprised not to find even a partial loaf. My stomach was queasy at best, and I wasn't able to finish my pottage.

I made myself comfortable in Dawson's chair again, wearing his robe over a clean nightgown to make the call. He answered on the second ring. "Hey, gorgeous." Jesus, it wasn't his compliment making my heart sing—it was the richness of tone.

"Ohh...say it again," I moaned.

Even—or especially—his return chuckle made me go weak in the knees. "When are you expecting to be home, Mrs. Pelletier? Anytime soon?"

"I'm sitting in your chair wearing your favorite robe, my belly already filled with soup."

His gentle laughter—so deep and rich—made me want to tear off my clothes. "Favorite robe?" he questioned. "I've got more than one now?"

"Okay, my favorite robe." Its fleece was thicker and far plusher than mine. "Where are you?"

"Al's place in Missoula," he answered. "He asked if I could give him a hand for a couple days. Should be home early tomorrow."

"What kind of work?" While Dawson's business partner was an IT genius, my husband was lucky to locate a computer's *on* button.

"Mechanical. Made some changes to his 'copter's turbo engine. Should boost horsepower and cut fuel consumption."

I couldn't imagine what my man might do on a helicopter, but didn't put anything past his resourcefulness. Even so, his ability to do almost anything made me want him even more. "Wish you were here. I need some quality time with my favorite guy. Speaking of which, where's Jake?"

I realized my *faux pas* at Dawson's immediate belly laugh. "So, Jake's your number one now?" he barely finished before more guffaws.

Although home alone, my face burned with embarrassment. "You know what I meant, mister," trying to scold and switch blame.

He didn't take the bait, and I didn't need to see him to know of the broad grin he wore. "I heard you loud and clear, woman."

Dawson stayed on the phone until I no longer felt the overwhelming need for his voice—at least control my want—promising to return home soon. Since I planned an early bedtime, he offered to pick Jake up from Melissa's on his way. I considered dressing and driving to my mother-in-law's house for my boy. Exhaustion won in the end, and I retired for what I hoped would be a twelve-hour night.

***

I was almost right. Crawling into the sack at 6:30 and not remembering my head hitting the pillow, I awoke at 5:30, giving me eleven. After stumbling into the bathroom with a stack of clean clothes, it was time to face the day. The house seemed too quiet while I waited for my boys to arrive. I turned the radio on for noise and any local news on my favorite rock station. A Beach Boys song got me to dance my way to the computer. I possess a good sense of rhythm and moderate grace, but my moves are best performed bereft of prying eyes.

A quick glance at my savings account surprised me. I dialed KC immediately. "Good morning, Ms. Woodman. I trust you enjoyed a night spent at home?"

I dispensed with idle chitchat. "Why the big deposit? I was responsible for one, you paid for three."

His tone was matter of fact. "You earned it. Consider it hazard pay beyond what you normally face."

"I don't understand. Seventy-five grand for one because she was wired to blow?"

"No. A hundred percent bump for her, and standard pay for the other."

"He wasn't mine," I argued. "Why pay me?"

"We...I...considered denial. However, someone tapped him, or there was an accident we aren't yet privy to. No matter. He's deceased, and you were hired to make him dead. If we need to quibble over who performed the task, we're analyzing data and hoping to understand better what happened."

"All right. I guess I can live with your pay scale. Got news for me?" I tried to keep any eagerness from my tone, but my heart skipped with the question. A single night of sleep at home was enough to rejuvenate needed enthusiasm. Another spent with Dawson would prepare me for what may come.

His chuckle made it evident he saw through my unconcerned tone. "We're picking up chatter with none of it aimed at our man. Assets believe our enemy continues to wait for confirmation."

Hair on the back of my neck stood at his shared intelligence. "You don't think…I mean…did we miss something? Are more in place I failed to identify?" God, I hoped not. Tomorrow was Christmas Eve. Not only did I need to be with family over the holidays, I hated the idea of what even an unsuccessful attack would do to the Hollister family.

Our call went silent long enough I lifted the cell from my cheek to see if we were disconnected. I pressed it against my ear when I heard his voice from afar. "…don't think so," he was saying. "We'll contact our ears on the ground to see if anything's changed."

"Who was the woman?" I asked. "The one we arrested who was seated with the Hollister party at the Upchuck?"

KC groaned. "You don't want to know."

"The hell I don't. She made me while I acted as his shadow. I don't know how or even why, but she knew something was wrong."

"Marta Stephanopoulos, née Boyd. She's married to her second husband, Jack, father of Emerson. You couldn't miss the son. He's the size of a small mountain, and he and his wife are close to the Hollister clan. We've got a hell of a dossier on the father and son."

I remembered the giant. He reeked of raw physical strength. "Stephanopoulos. Why does the name sound familiar?"

"She once owned a shipping company based in New York. Although no longer affiliated with the firm, she's got more money than God. Rarely spends any outside of charitable foundations. Oddly enough, she and her husband live in a damned cave above Dubois."

"Huh?" His revelation didn't make sense.

"You heard right. They live in a goofy eclectic home set into a mountainside and rarely leave the area. She hasn't returned to New York City since being taken hostage and tortured a few years ago. Tough woman."

"Are you still holding her?"

"Oh, good Lord, no. We didn't have a chance to get her out of Jackson before the wrath of God deluged us. Seems your Father Timothy confided to someone he saw her taken into custody. At least we only contended with lawyers and not her husband. I know you were warned, but let me emphasize it again. Do not, I repeat, do not cross Jack or his son Emerson. Early Hollister will simply kill you. The other two will tear you limb from limb."

Christ, was there anything KC didn't know, including my growing relationship with the priest? I hoped like hell my boss wasn't listening to my confessions, too, although he stood not to be as horrified as was Father Timothy. "Does she know who I am?"

"Not that I'm aware. We'll do everything in our power to protect your name, Ariel. However, not even the government is infallible. Don't underestimate the power of money and the drive of Marta Boyd. Nothing is impossible if you know the right people. She continues to wield clout in financial markets of numerous governments around the world. A simple frown could cause a stock to plummet. Do not misjudge her tenacity and influence."

My rumbling stomach stopped our conversation. KC promised to make contact if he learned anything. Not yet eight a.m., I prepared to break my fast with a plate of fresh pineapple, a sliced apple, blueberries, and strawberries. Switching my focus from money to news, I searched for anything to make me nervous over returning home. English news sites from Bagdad, Cairo, Istanbul, and even Dubai were studied in great detail. Aware the scourge known as ISIS spread to countries in North Africa, along with the Philippines and Indonesia, I didn't neglect readily accessible information from other parts of the world. Aside from a suicide bomber killed trying to enter Israel, nothing stood out. Perhaps a lull was an indication of a storm to come?

My chickens were out of feed and water and were both ravenous and thirsty. Even the snow outside their coop was beaten down in their efforts to find food. Dawson surprised me. He always took great care of my small flock. I hadn't yet replaced my bunnies after losing them the prior winter. A couple handfuls of scratch made my babies happy, as did fresh water and layer crumbles. Somehow, twelve hens gave four eggs since the last time my husband checked. I noted a light snow falling as I barred the chicken house door.

The first indication my boys were home was my dog racing around the house and finding me outside the coop. "Jakie!" I set the wicker basket used to gather eggs aside before he bowled me over. He missed me as much as I did him. He squirmed and jumped while in my arms, standing almost as tall as me. I don't care to have my face licked and avoided his tongue at all costs.

"Thought I might find you out here." My husband's rumble was music to my ears. Jake took his cue to leave us and check his markers. "Welcome back, lady."

My chickens forgotten, I fell into his arms and snuggled inside his open coat, pressing my ear against his flannel shirt. The beat of his heart was strong and steady. "I needed this," I whispered. "I need you."

His arms made me feel small and vulnerable but protected. As long as my Dawson held me, he was my shield from all things frightening and dangerous. I felt him nuzzle my crown. "You smell nice," he whispered.

The reverberation inside his chest was food for my soul. "You, too," I murmured. It was true. I loved the odor of my husband. It wasn't offensive—he smelled like a man, not a perfumed dude. Dawson didn't even use aftershave the occasional times he trimmed his beard and shaved his neck. I almost forgot my egg basket. After I retrieved it, we walked hand-in-hand to the back door. "How were the roads this morning?" I asked.

"Not bad. Snowplows are doin' a good job of keepin' Lost Trail Pass open. Puttin' it down pretty hard up there," he drawled standing aside to let me enter. Jake caught us instead and blew past to go in first.

Dawson stopped automatically for an armload of firewood stacked on the porch.

He left the load next to the stove. I followed him into the kitchen. "Have you eaten breakfast?" My question wasn't dumb. He sometimes got busy and didn't think about it.

Dawson stopped at the front door. "Yeah, Al puts together a good spread. Be right back...gotta get my stuff from the truck."

I waited on the couch with Jake. At first he mauled me, then lay belly up to get it scratched. His master returning and slamming the door earned the opening of a single eye. Focused as I was on reconnecting with my boy, Dawson surprised me when I glanced up. "A Christmas tree! You got one!" It wasn't big—not as tall as me, but I didn't need something huge.

He grinned. "Place south of Hamilton were givin' their last few away. The guy and his daughter were so nice I gave 'em twenty bucks anyway."

Not one to dawdle so close to the holiday, I quickly located our small box of ornaments and lights. It didn't take us long to get it in the stand and decorated. I stood back to gaze critically, looking for any bare spots after running out of mostly homemade ornaments. I moved an angel too far back to the front. "There. Looks pretty good, doesn't it?" As far as I was concerned, the little amount hanging was enough. I liked a simple tree trimmed with baubles made by my hand.

Dawson draped an arm over my shoulders. "It's perfect." Pressure applied by his strong limb turned me, and I saw what he planned. Very high on my priority list, I skipped away and beat him to our bedroom, closing out Jake before he could follow.

I woke alone. Our bedroom was cool with the door still closed, and cocooned inside our blankets contributed to my long nap. Smiling and rolling to my back, I stretched and remembered our lovemaking. As much as I missed and desired my husband, it seemed he wanted me as strongly. I rose and dressed again. I needed to spend more time with my man and make sure our bond remained strong.

Chapter VII

Christmas Eve at Melissa's was kept lowkey except for her festive dress with a snowman print and spectacular decorations adorning the tree Dawson cut for his mom. A light supper of homemade chili and cinnamon rolls would suffice until our anticipated feast on Christmas Day. "I haven't seen much of you, Julia," Melissa remarked after our bowls were filled, and all three of us got a bun. "Bess mentioned you took time away from your classroom."

"We talked about this, Mother." Dawson's disapproval was in his tone.

I put a hand on his thigh. We'd discussed the cover story KC provided to my school district. "My friend and his family are doing better," I said.

"Is he someone you knew through your previous line of work?"

While Melissa knew I dealt with bad people, she didn't know exactly what my job description was. Tough to explain to a mother-in-law my job was terminating bad men...and women. "In a way. The friend of a friend. We were introduced and found we shared a common background." Early Hollister was an army man—I simply killed those my employers deemed detrimental to a thriving society.

"I'm sure your students will appreciate having you back after Christmas break," she said.

Her comment made me smile. I loved my classroom and kids. Dawson sometimes made mention the time I spent at school. My day began long before class commenced, didn't end with the final bell, and I enjoyed every second. It seemed odd, but during school hours, I never thought about my second calling. Yet when I was on the hunt for a chosen target, I thought about school—and Dawson—constantly.

We opened presents after finishing our meal. Although the custom was strange to me, I didn't say anything. Dawson always talked about each opening a gift Christmas Eve, then saving the rest for the next day. My family was the opposite. We unwrapped all but the big one from Santa the night before. I got two nice dresses reaching my calves from Melissa with the promise she'd take them in if needed. Clothes tended to hang unless I shop in the children's sections.

Dawson gave me three expensive outfits. Each came with a jacket to cover my shoulder holster. Getting five new sets of clothing for school made me happy. I'd worn the same things for almost two years. My coworkers were familiar with anything I dressed in—especially after I was certified to carry a gun on school grounds.

I got Jake a bag of his favorite treats and offered him one. He seemed happy enough playing with wadded wrapping paper—pawing, mauling, and tearing it into shreds. Dawson was harder to buy for, but I knew I found the right thing in Jackson. I got him a gift certificate to a custom bootmaker who accepted few new clients. A call to him from Father Timothy made all the difference. They were costly, and Dawson was required to make a trip to have his feet and calves measured for a perfect fit.

Melissa burst into tears after she opened the small box I passed her. Dawson admitted he didn't know what to buy his mother when I texted and agreed to let me choose. Her gnarled fingers shook when she struggled to dislodge the string of pearls from its display. The elder Mrs. Pelletier didn't bother to look at her son. "Julia, you shouldn't have. They're too much."

I wiped my own cheeks from her reaction. "You let me decide what's too much." I took them from her trembling hands and fastened the necklace around her neck. "They look beautiful, Melissa."

Dawson was ready to go home long before me. To see my mother-in-law constantly finger and admire the string of gemstones in the mirror was heartwarming, but my husband prodded me to leave. "Can't thank you enough for the boots, Jules," he said while unlacing his worn pair at our bedside. "Might give Al a call to see if he could give me a lift. Flyin' contraption of his could get me there and back in a day." One thing about Dawson—probably from his stint in the army—he didn't care to fly in a helicopter.

"Don't forget it would cost twice as much in fuel," I said while pulling a nightgown over my head. "I hoped we might make the drive during spring break when I've got a week off work." Jake turned three times at the foot of our bed before collapsing into a ball.

I made sure my .38 Diamondback lay within reach a last time before switching off the lamp on my side. As usual, Dawson slid into bed wearing his birthday suit. With our room cool, he pulled the covers to his neck and rolled to face me. "Sure," he said. "I got no problem waiting. If you wanna tag along and explore a new town, sounds like fun to me."

His response nearly blew my secret when I almost protested how well I knew the city of Jackson. As far as he was aware, I might be shadowing Early Hollister in Maryland or Florida. Instead, I swallowed my retort and gave him a kiss before he twisted to shut his lamp off and throw our room into darkness.

* * *

Dawson was fixing breakfast when I woke at my normal time. I padded into the kitchen wearing my bathrobe and pink kitten slippers after a visit to the bathroom. Deer steak, scrambled eggs, and toast awaited. My husband handed me a filled coffee cup and kissed the tip of my nose. "Good morning, beautiful."

"Up awfully early, aren't you?" Knowing I enjoyed time alone, he usually rose a few minutes later than I did.

"Got a busy day ahead of us. How many pieces of venison do you want?"

"Three." He slid my plate across the table with the small steaks, too many eggs, and one piece of toast. "What time are we supposed to be at your mom's?"

He was constant motion until he sat across from me with his own plate and coffee and shoveled a forkful of steak and eggs into his mouth before checking his wristwatch. "Forty-five minutes."

I stopped with a bite halfway to my mouth. "What?" I waited for the punchline.

"We're meeting her at six-thirty." He motioned to my plate. "Get a move on."

Whatever game my husband was playing, he kept his cards close to his vest, answering very few of my questions. When I got out of the shower and dressed, the kitchen was clean with the dishwasher running. Dawson waited impatiently while I dried my hair. "Okay," I said walking into the living room, "What do I need to take?"

He shook his head and pointed to the travel bag next to his foot. "Got everything we need right here."

"My gun." I turned to the bedroom. No way was I leaving the house without one.

"Got it," Dawson said.

I stopped. He rarely if ever touched my firearms. "Which?"

"Your Glock. Now, c'mon."

We took his truck with Jake in the backseat. I noted fifteen degrees outside our kitchen window before going through the door. Too cold for this skinny girl who planned to sit next to my fire and travel to Melissa's later.

I guess he texted her, because Dawson's bundled mom sat outside with a bag next to her foot when we drove in. "Wait here," he said.

Something didn't add up. He helped Melissa down her porch steps while carrying her suitcase, then into the backseat behind me. "Move over, Jake," she huffed making herself comfortable. Her things went into the bed. "Good morning, Julia."

I twisted in my seat as Dawson let more of our warm air out and cold in. "Morning. Is anyone planning to tell me what the heck is going on?"

Dawson chuckled. "Patience, my little sparrow hawk."

We stopped again, and he didn't allow me out. Instead, he led Jake onto Scotty and Robin's porch where they both laughed and waved to me. Dawson looked at his phone and hurried back to the truck, leaving our pointer in the capable hands of our friends.

99

"Doggone it," I said. "Won't anyone spill the beans?"

Part of the puzzle was solved when he turned into the airport. Only thing I could see was a Leer. "Everyone out," Dawson said after he parked.

He helped his mom with her luggage and led us to the jet with its engines whining. I clutched our small carryon bag, wondering what he was getting us into. Flight attendants who might double for Ryan Reynolds and Scarlett Johansson waited on either side of the door after we climbed the steps. "Good morning, Mr. Pelletier," the pretty young woman greeted. "It's nice to see you again. These must be your wife and your mother?"

Again? My hackles rose while my eyes narrowed. As far as I was concerned, Dawson was the catch of a lifetime. If a girl appreciated a rugged man, mine was far more desirable than mere eye candy. He introduced us. "My wife, Julia...and this's my mom, Melissa. Jules, Mom, this is Annette and...?" He gestured to the male counterpart.

The man stepped forward with a hand outstretched. "Michael. Nice to meet all of you."

I waited until we were in the air and leveled at thirty thousand feet before turning to Dawson. "Who is this Annette, and how do you know her?" I demanded with an edge to my whisper. We were seated in front with Melissa behind us.

Dawson's gaze was cool. "We wouldn't have met if I wasn't left alone in Laredo." He reclined his seat and tipped his Stetson to cover his eyes. Damned man was snoring in less than a minute.

The blame lay squarely on my shoulders. I'd left him behind in Texas—sure he was going to get one or both of us dead. I was there to systematically hunt down and kill the hierarchy of The Company I once worked for—not worry about my husband and his friends. He got left behind after I sent him off on a wild goose chase. Apparently, he wasn't over it yet.

Neither Dawson nor my mother-in-law was willing to relieve my curiosity. I finally gave in and found our seats were equally as comfortable when used as a bed.

Our landing was soft enough I didn't wake. Only when the engines throttled down and the brakes were applied did my eyes open. Dawson was talking to our Reynolds lookalike, and Melissa sat next to me. My husband grinned and winked when we rolled to a stop. My heart skipped a beat and I half stood against the seatbelt when I glanced outside and recognized tropical flora. Were we back in the Bahamas where I was once nearly killed? "Jules?" Dawson was at my side in a blink.

"Why?" I clutched at his arm and murmured, "Why bring me here?"

He cocked his head. "I don't understand. Where do you think we are?"

"Freeport?"

He recoiled. "Absolutely not. How could you think I'd do something so cruel?"

I pointed out the window. "Palm and coconut trees." The door opened and the steps lowered behind me. Much of what I could see reminded me of the worst time in my life. Thrown from a twenty-second story balcony after fulfilling a contract, I survived for weeks along the shoreline with a broken arm and both eyes swollen almost closed. For a moment I thought I'd be sick.

A familiar voice boomed from outside on the tarmac. "You in there, Double-D?"

Dawson didn't break eye contact nor release me. "Be right there, Donny," he called. My lids widened at the name. "We're in Belize City, Jules. This's your Christmas present. Ten days at our villa."

Lurching guts quieted at his revelation, but my legs gave out, and I fell onto my seat again. "Oh, God, I'm so sorry." It took everything I could muster not to weep. I pointed at the window again. "I panicked."

Melissa was ignorant to the reason for my anxiety and patted my arm. "Don't worry. It's hot and humid, but you'll grow to love it here, Julia."

Our attendant carried our bags outside where Donny demanded them. Annette helped Melissa down the steps and delivered her to

Jose—he and Donny having served in the army with my husband. It dawned on me when I followed with Dawson's arm around my shoulders that I hadn't seen either man since Laredo. While I rampaged across the US, both men flew to Belize to protect my mother-in-law. According to Dawson, they saved her life and both were considered blood brothers to my husband. Ignorant of what happened, Melissa enjoyed the time of her life.

We followed Jose to a van. Donny already stowed our luggage and waited with a wide grin. "Julia," he called and waved a hand high over his head to get my attention. As if I couldn't see a man who made my husband seem small. Well over six feet, Dawson weighed almost two-hundred—yet Donny dwarfed him. His prosthetic leg disappeared under loose island shorts.

I lifted a shy hand, although Donny—Ox to his friends—and I already bonded. The man was larger in stature than even the high-profile hit I'd made in the Bahamas. "Hi, Ox." Jose stepped back from where he helped Melissa into second row seating. "Nice to see you again, Jose."

Suave with the ladies, he didn't hesitate to take my hand. "Señora," Jose said. "You are a beautiful sight for sore eyes." He lifted it and kissed the back of my fingers.

"Easy, bucko," Dawson said. "Little hawk's got razor-sharp talons," his murmur low enough his mother couldn't hear.

Of Mexican lineage, Jose's white teeth gleamed within his olive visage, made darker by a year in Central America. "Yes, I know, Captain Pelletier." He added flourish to his Spanish accent and winked at me.

Jose drove. I sat between Dawson and Melissa, apprehensive about our vehicle by how it groaned when Ox sat on the passenger side. Rather than use air-conditioning and cool the hot interior, our windows were lowered and caused us to raise our voices. "Glad you could make it, Julia," Ox shouted over a shoulder. "You're going to love it here."

Our self-appointed driver took corners like a man on a mission. I feared for the wellbeing of locals and tourists alike as we snaked through town—breathing easy only after we passed into the country. "Sorry we didn't catch a hopper from Belize City," Dawson said.

"No problem, Cap." Jose made eye contact in the mirror with my husband long enough I worried over oncoming traffic. "Been a while since we've gotten out to see the sights."

Our journey lasted about ninety minutes before we turned off the road at an imposing gate. It spanned between two massive pillars. I wondered if Jose was lost until Ox aimed a remote and pressed a button. The barrier swung inward, and after we entered, I turned to see it close behind. The van stopped next to a Jeep. "Home, sweet home," Ox announced.

I followed Dawson out his side while Ox helped Messila. "Oh, Lord," I whispered and gazed at the place. Where I imagined the villa as a small bungalow on the beach couldn't have been more wrong. Beautifully manicured grounds surrounded by a massive stone fence featured an astounding house thrice the size of where Dawson and I lived. Even the garage was large with three wide bays and an apartment overhead.

Jose unlocked and opened the door, standing aside for us to enter. "You're gonna love it, Julia," Dawson said as we walked through the foyer into an imposing great room. A cathedral ceiling rose twenty feet over our heads. Ocean surf was visible through a wall of windows.

"You've got four bedrooms and three baths," Ox said. "The master has a walk-in closet, too."

"You and Dawson take it," Melissa said. "I'll sleep in one of the others."

"A big closet, and I came without even a suitcase of clothes?" I turned to my husband. "Why didn't you let me bring any?"

"Part of your present. Buy all you want while we're here, but remember our limited storage at home."

My wide-eyed reaction got a good laugh from the others. "Oh, you poor man," I said. "You don't understand what you've done." His eyebrows raised at my grin. I turned to Ox and Jose. "Are we putting you guys out? Where you do normally stay?"

Jose stabbed a thumb over his shoulder. "Apartment above the garage has two bedrooms. We sleep there."

Our kitchen was huge. A long island with room to seat a half-dozen, two stoves, fancy stainless refrigerator rather than the basic version I used at home, it appeared ready for a professional chef with more counterspace than I could imagine. I loved what I could see of a magnificent table in the dining room.

"If no one minds, I'm going to lie down," Melissa said. "I could stand an hour of sleep."

Jose and Donny left us with the promise of a late supper. Already the sun lowered to a red ball on the western horizon. Dawson guided with a strong arm. "Let me show you our room."

I was sure I'd died and gone to heaven when we entered. The south wall was a huge glass slider framed between two enormous picture windows. I opened it to step outside onto a stone patio. The roar of the sea filled my senses. Mesmerized, I stared until two arms wrapped around me and I twisted to face Dawson. "My God," I whispered, "Why haven't we come sooner?"

My husband stared steadily without a change of expression. "We've been busy," he said. "You've been gone as much or more than you've been home."

I broke eye contact and sighed against his chest. "I know. It shouldn't be long before this job is finished. Then Thanksgiving, Christmas, and spring breaks here?" I pushed back enough to see his reaction. "Summers in Idaho's backcountry?" His response wasn't needed. I sensed profound sadness when he released me. He sat on a nearby chair to stare into Caribbean waters.

"This place is partly ours, Jules," he finally said. "We've owned it together since gettin' married. Allen considered sellin' because no one came here until Mom."

I took the other seat. "It's one of the reasons we're here, isn't it?" I asked. "To show me what I've been missing?"

He nodded. "Part of it. The other is because you needed time away from the real world. Believe me...there's not many better ways to decompress."

I knew Dawson wasn't happy with me taking KC's offer. Away from our home, Idaho, and filling government contracts, I felt his helplessness. He didn't react when I took his hand in mine. "I'm sorry, so very sorry, my love."

"Your love isn't something I question, Jules." I noticed his emphasis on *your*. He considered me and my alter ego J as separate entities.

I wasn't ready nor willing to discuss my extracurricular work. "I'm going to need bathing suits. If you want to take me shopping tomorrow, are you interested in going inside first and checking my measurements?" A looming clash was diverted by the lascivious waggling of my eyebrows. No different than any other man throughout time, Dawson's attention could be diverted by sex. I stood to pull him upright, then dragged him into our bedroom, closing the curtains and locking our doors.

* * *

I rested on our bed, while Dawson showered. I typically took mine before work, but he swore he didn't want to sleep wearing the day's dirt. A light knock sounded. "Dawson? Julia?"

I opened the door. "He's in the shower, Melissa."

"It's late, but tell him supper's ready."

"Okay, thanks. We'll be there when he gets out."

Jose and Ox had every reason to be proud. They barbequed a large fish of some kind, along with vegetables and pineapple slices. I could see how two bachelors would be ready to eat so quickly. We sat at an enormous picnic table between the house and garage.

Ox tore the fish open to where we could reach the meat. It was a simple and yet flavorful meal. He was the first to break into the sounds of five hungry stomachs being satisfied. "Got any particular plans while you're here, Cap'n?"

"Decompression for Jules," he said flatly around a mouthful of hot fish.

Jose set his fork aside and eyed me carefully. "Are you working again, señora?"

Melissa didn't give me a chance. "She's teaching elementary fulltime for the Salmon school district," she informed our hosts.

Dawson reached for another scoop of steaming flesh. "Yeah, she's workin'."

Ox felt the tension and turned his attention to me. "Melissa knows all the good shops. Buy yourself a suit, and we'll show you the best places to swim. Pretty damned good one in the lagoon below the house."

Although I enjoy fish—especially the freshly caught barbequed version—I filled up mostly on vegetables. What I learned was a red snapper guessed to be ten pounds was reduced to the head and a plate of bones. Cleanup was a breeze, made better when Melissa and I didn't lift a finger.

Donny was right. Dawson's mom knew the best places to shop. She dragged me through streets she knew well. I didn't forget she spent almost four months in Belize and took delight in bartering with the locals. We returned to the villa with bags of clothes and lighter wallets. I didn't need to know what the men talked about when I entered the living room and three sets of eyes swiveled to me.

Dawson leaped to his feet. "Here, let me help," he said and relieved me of half my booty.

"Julia," Melissa called on her way to her bedroom. "I'll meet you in back after we've changed." We planned to sunbathe and perhaps swim below the villa.

The boys kept a small cabin cruiser tied at our private dock. Melissa and I didn't get an hour of lying in the sun before we heard footsteps, and Dawson sat next to me. "Sun's pretty intense. Might want to be careful on your first day."

I'd slathered on plenty of sunblock and turned many times to absorb all the rays I could. Propping my chin on a palm, I craned my neck to see him. "We were about to take a dip and then come in. Interested in getting wet?"

He chuckled. "Not wearing jeans and boots I'm not."

My turn to laugh. "No excuses tomorrow. I bought three pairs of swim trunks just for you."

Our southern vacation was everything I dreamed of and more. While Melissa stayed home or haunted nearby boutiques, I went out in the boat crabbing, fishing, and swimming. We ate fish, lobster, and crabs, notwithstanding enormous chunks of beef Ox procured from a local butcher. No longer concerned I might be pressed into service as an assassin while so far away, I gave in and imbibed more than once. Our mornings were busy with boating and angling, while afternoons and evenings were filled with great food, friends, and laughter. Once, Dawson was forced to carry me to our bed, though I don't remember it. Stress and worry dissipated more each day.

I'd finished a long swim and was soaking in rays when I heard the distinct step belonging to Ox. After losing his leg in Iraq, he got around on a prosthetic. Although facedown, I lifted enough to greet him. "How are you, Donny?"

"Livin' the dream, Julia."

I rolled to where I could see him in one of the outdoor chairs lining our section of beach. "Really? You're doing all right?"

He sighed—we both knew what I asked. He'd lost his wife and daughter to a drunk driver in Baton Rouge. "I ain't gonna lie...it's always going to hurt." He gestured around us. "Being here works two ways. I'm away from all I know which helps me forget. But sometimes I think about how I'd like to share this—" He stopped, sniffed, and knuckled a tear away. Dawson warned me how emotional the big man was, and I'd seen it firsthand more than once.

"Do you plan to stay here permanently?"

"Maybe. I've dated a couple of the local gals. Nice folks around here...far more laid back compared to the US."

"Anything serious?"

"No, not yet. At least, I don't think so. Met a widow woman who seems nice."

"I'm glad, and I'm sure Dawson is, too."

Donny cleared his throat. "Speaking of the Cap'n, he tells us you're on the payroll again. Doesn't seem too happy about it."

I looked anywhere but at Donny. "No, he's not."

"He didn't tell us much, but it sounds like you didn't have much of an option."

"Not really. Not if I wanted to be able to live with myself." Yet I thought of the excitement of the hunt, combined with the two smiling faces of Hollister's children. Nothing compared to searching for and taking down the animals who would destroy their happiness. I bared my teeth and shivered and found Donny staring.

"You're a scary woman, ma'am."

I shook my head. "I'm just Julia, Ox." Movement caught my eye. I twisted to see Dawson, a margarita in one hand and a tequila sunrise in the other. He held the former where I could reach it. "You read my mind, honey," I said. Anything to avoid Donny and our conversation.

Jose announced our lunch as barbequed lobster and loaves of locally baked bread. Dawson kept an arm behind me to keep us moving up the hill to the villa and our meal. Even a little alcohol affected me. With huge tails and claws, it took the sweet meat of only one crustacean to fill me. My husband made up for my small appetite, eating a half-dozen while we got the opportunity.

I learned Dawson swam well. While I was powerful for my size, my husband could swim laps around me. His lean body combined with long arms and legs made it impossible for me to keep up. A half-mile from our dock across the lagoon to breakers marking open sea, we swam the distance and back almost every day. Huge powerful strokes by Dawson allowed him to easily outdistance. Instead of leaving me behind, he dawdled and pushed me hard, making me stronger each time we went out.

We waded from the water on our last day, panting and grinning at the hard sprint we'd finished. I almost caught him until he realized I closed in. A burst of speed to make Michael Phelps proud allowed him to win by at least four lengths. I collapsed in the chair next to him in laughter and exhaustion. "I miss this. Swimming is something I'd love to do every day." Gesturing toward the water I added, "Imagine this each morning after we got up."

Dawson didn't skip a beat. "I'll move here tomorrow if you wanted."

My head spun around. "Seriously? Leave Idaho and live in the tropics instead? You could give up hunting, your friends, and all you know for this?"

"I'd give up everything for you, little hawk. Whatever I have to do to keep you safe."

I smiled, sad in knowing it was all a pipedream. "I've got a classroom to manage with budding minds ready to soak in knowledge like a sponge."

"You could get a job here teaching English."

"What would you do? What would happen to your place?"

He shrugged. "Mom could handle the ranch. Besides, most of it's rented out to other farmers. What would I do?" He pointed to the cabin cruiser owned by Donny and Jose. "Buy a boat and fish."

I found it difficult to wrap my mind around my mountain man's willingness to give up his life and move away from all he knew. "No fall, winter, or spring. Think you could handle endless summer?"

"Like I said, Jules, I'd do anything and go anywhere to keep you safe. I want to grow old with you. Bounce our babies on my knee…and then grandkids later."

"We can do that in Idaho."

"Not if you're dead."

Footsteps stopped our conversation. Jose and Donny passed us with bait boxes. Rods and gear stayed on their boat. "Ready for a little fishing, Cap'n?" Donny said. "Need a couple snappers or jacks for supper. Got enough bait for our crab traps, too."

Our discussion pushed aside, Dawson pulled his shirt on and gave me a kiss before hustling to the boat. His deep laugh floated to me as Jose powered the cruiser to a plane. I retreated to our villa for a shower and nap. Our stay was coming to an end. Time to reenter the world after letting weakened batteries recharge.

Chapter VIII

I arrived at school early after Christmas break with sounds of the Caribbean resonating within my memories. Temperatures dipping near zero were uncomfortable after enjoying mid-eighties for nearly two weeks. We stayed two extra days after our ride home didn't arrive when promised. Allen Fryxell was right when he assured us his Russian friend would ferry us back to Idaho the moment his jet was free.

Even Bess Mueller wasn't in her office when I arrived. Having finished her shift, our night custodian smiled and waved as she passed my room on her way home. I like Rosalee—she does a good job of cleaning and vacuuming my room after I leave and never complains. No matter how hard I try, my little scholars inevitably leave messes wherever they roam.

"You certainly looked refreshed." I jerked in surprise at the voice from where I planned my daily lessons. Bess stood just inside my door. I glanced at the clock and saw I'd been busy for over an hour.

I couldn't wait to share. "Oh, Bess, you've got to come with us the next time we fly to Belize! Our place is so much nicer than I dreamed...within only yards of the Caribbean. Lots of room for everyone. In fact, you don't have to wait for us. You're welcome to take Andy and the kids the moment you have a few extra days."

She smiled and squeezed her long frame into a desk meant for a third-grade child. "I'd love to," she said. "But my job dictates I stay close to home. You'd be surprised at the silly emergencies I deal with daily."

I remembered Jose and Donny's parting words. *Don't let life and your job beat you down, Julia. Come back and recharge whenever you need.* "Can't let a job come between you and living, boss. Work to live, not live to work."

Bess sighed. "Melissa's been telling me the same thing. Problem is this school has become my life."

"Fresh crab, clams, and lobster each day," I teased. "Imagine a barbequed lobster tail for breakfast each morning." While I didn't have it but once, Dawson ate two and sometimes three, along with eggs and toast. Said he'd never enjoyed such fresh seafood—why not gorge until content?

"You're making my mouth water," she admitted. "I'll talk to Andy and see if we can find a way." The tall woman uncoiled herself from the desk to close and lock my door. "Do you mind if have a private conversation about your class?"

My heart jumped. Although she was Dawson's aunt, Bess was also my immediate superior. She would be well within her rights to not renew my contract within the first two years. "Sure. Aren't they doing well enough on their tests?"

She waved a careless hand. "Oh, yes. Scores are up in not only your grade level, but throughout the primary and middle school."

I frowned. "Okay—"

"I'm concerned with your absences. As a first-year teacher, you shouldn't be missing so much time. You've been gone more days than you've been at work."

Her scolding wasn't unexpected. Dawson explained his aunt was a pacifist and leery of the military. She refused to speak with him the first few times he returned home on leave after joining the army. "I'm sorry. It's all been so unexpected." I wasn't sure what to say.

"I don't understand why you sometimes have to leave midday. What is so important the federal government needs a schoolteacher to handle?"

I shook my head. "I'm sorry, Bess. You're asking a question so secret not even Dawson knows."

"Where do you go? Who do you work for? What is your job? Why isn't your classroom most important?"

Her questions were unanswerable. "I can't tell you anything except how much I love working here...how I enjoy my coworkers and class."

She was clearly frustrated. "We've been instructed to expect your occasional disappearance. When you're gone, however, we're not only short a teacher but a substitute also."

I knew Bess was right. I subbed before getting my own room. KC's demands threw the primary into disarray each time I left. "If it helps, I've been led to believe my...my services won't be needed much longer." It all depended on how many of the enemy were able to infiltrate our borders. I hoped they would give up, or Homeland Security would nab them before they could get past my guard. So far there'd been no skill involved. I'd gotten lucky.

A rattling knob and the knock on the window of my door saved me from further grilling. A student peered into my room. Bess stood. "I hope so," she said. "You're a valuable member of our team. We'd hate to lose you."

There it was. As plainly as she could, Bess was warning me my teaching future in Salmon was at risk.

* * *

I poured myself into work and appearing at extracurricular activities. It wouldn't hurt to have my boss and community members noticing my attendance. Dawson didn't grumble over the time I put in at school after I passed his aunt's warning to him. KC stayed in regular contact—I think mostly to keep me on my toes. No further chatter concerning Early Hollister was intercepted, except the enemy considered those who infiltrated dead or captured.

Dawson and I—at my urging—took in junior high and high school basketball games. I knew the names of a few of the older kids—both boys and girls—because I subbed a little in the upper grades. Although not sports oriented while in school, my husband enjoyed both home and away games. We went so far as to travel to Idaho Falls, American Falls, Leadore, and even to Darby, Montana, to follow our team. Melissa kept Jake while we were away, staying overnight rather than make the long trek home in late evenings.

Thomas Howell avoided me. While I taught primary and he middle school, our paths occasionally crossed. No doubt he was still embarrassed over the way my husband manhandled and later tried to kill him. Better for Thomas to steer clear of me rather than face Dawson's wrath again. I always smiled and spoke each time we were thrust together to make it clear our workplace was a Dawson-free zone.

I returned home late from work in early March to a table already set and Dawson checking a pork roast in the wood cookstove oven. Baked potatoes were tucked around it with a pan of dry-cooked vegetables on the bottom rack. I got a peck on my lips as I passed on the way to change out of my school clothes. The holstered Glock got tossed aside while Jake watched me change into pajama bottoms and a torn but clean sleeveless sweatshirt.

Supper was on the table when I returned to the kitchen with my dog in tow. "Scotty and Robin invited us to their place tomorrow," Dawson said. He cut the roast into thick chunks with a kitchen knife he kept sharp enough to shave with. "Told 'em we'd come unless you planned stuff I didn't know about."

"Sure!" Other than ballgames, we hadn't been anywhere on a Friday night for weeks. "Can we take anything?"

"Nope. I asked, but Robin said no."

"Do anything interesting today?" Dawson normally found tasks to attend to, such as mending fence, helping his mom, or simply hiking with Jake. I didn't begrudge his choice of working from home rather than toil at a job from eight until four. He swore he stayed busier than when he labored for other businesses.

"Got in a little shooting," he said. "Stretched out my .308 and burned through a couple boxes of .44s. Got the empties in the tumbler...I'll load them tomorrow."

My husband is a fearsome shooter. Respect given out by others who witnessed his prowess with a firearm was well-earned. He did things I couldn't imagine—such as hit tiny targets at ranges so far away his ability seemed magical. While I demanded my ammunition be factory bought, Dawson handloaded and inspected each round he fired.

The pork fell apart rather than need a knife to cut. "How far?"

"Two, four, six hundred, then eight. From fifty to two hundred with my .44."

He didn't appear disgusted. It looked to have been a good shooting day. "Do well?"

"Fair to middlin'," he said while trying and failing to hide a smile. Must have been better than "fair."

"Groups at two hundred?" I questioned before testing the roasted veggies.

"Best went seven sixteenths."

Christ, he was out of my league at what he considered close range. Four inches would be good for me—meaning each round drove into center mass. "Eight hundred?"

He grimaced, although not looking disappointed. "A hair over seven inches."

Dawson wasn't satisfied with shooting I couldn't approach on my best day. Quick and sure handed up close and personal, my abilities with a rifle shrank beyond two-fifty. I preferred a handgun within twenty feet or less. My husband wasn't shy to point out our differing strengths. His lay in the ability to kill anything he could see. Mine was a propensity to look my target in the eye and not hesitate to pull the trigger.

I didn't go anywhere unarmed, and to our friends' place for supper was no different. Dawson always wore his .44—he looked naked without it—while I carried my little Colt covered by my blouse.

Scotty opened the door at Dawson's knock. "Hey, guys." He stood back to let us in. "Robin's in the kitchen." Ignoring Dawson's revolver—probably invisible after so many years—he gave me a quick scan before his eyes stopped at the bulge on my right hip.

I found Robin bent in front of the stove and waited quietly until she finished. Her red locks were twisted into a bun on the back of her head, and she let out a quiet yelp after noticing me. "Julia," she said. "You almost gave me a heart attack."

She got my brightest grin and fake apology. "Sorry." It felt good anytime I wasn't noticed until too late.

Robin held her arms wide and made me feel like a child during our hug. "How've you been? We haven't seen you since your return from Belize."

"Good. Doing my best to get my class ready to move up to fourth grade next year." I sniffed the air. "Whatcha cooking?"

"I hope you like lasagna. We've got tossed salad, and I'm putting garlic bread in now."

I sat at the table to watch her slice and butter the loaf of French bread. "I love it. Dawson does, too."

"Good. I made plenty."

"Making progress on your wedding plans?" I wasn't sure of her colors or intentions for my dress.

"We're staying pretty low key. Scotty's talked to a minister who's agreed to tie our knot. It'll be in the backyard under the walnut trees. Reception to follow."

"You're going to love Belize, Robin. I'm so happy you've accepted our gift. Two weeks won't seem long enough."

We'd offered our villa as our wedding gift to them. Since it belonged to Allen Fryxell and Dawson long before I married him, I insisted on bearing the added expense of their flights.

Our meal was as relaxed and entertaining as any I could remember. Scotty reverted to the fun loving and lackadaisical man I knew before our ill-fated backcountry hunt, where I defended myself and the rest of the camp from four men hired to kill me. Although Robin nearly met the same fate by my hand, she handled the resulting carnage better than her boyfriend.

"I've got a check for you, Julia," Scotty said. "Ain't much...we only cleared a hair over forty grand this last season. You get a few pennies over two thousand."

I waved it off. "Roll it back into your business. Use it to pay for extra advertising."

Refusing their money was the least I could do. It was my fault Scotty's business suffered. Years of hard work was disrupted by my hand, and I still felt bad. My hefty loan was more of a gift to assuage a guilty conscience. Our friends faced a daunting task to rebuilt lost clientele.

"Not our agreement. How am I going to repay you if it takes longer than I'll be alive?"

"By not worrying about it, my friend. Perhaps someday I'll have need of your payment but not now. Use it as a nest egg to fall back on." I shrugged and gave him my best smile.

"Take her advice, honey," Robin said. "We can save it against a rainy day."

We were in the living room laughing at stories Scotty told of the previous season's hunters when my cellphone vibrated. *Lock and load*, the missive from KC read. *Two simultaneous incursions, but we stopped one at the northern border. Chatter indicates we missed the other from the south.*

How soon? I texted back.

If it's too late and you're tired, we'll send an aircraft.

My heart sank. Not because I wasn't ready to work. Instead, I feared Dawson's reaction. *I'm exhausted. ETA?*

Ninety minutes. Your home?

Yes. Please land west of the house. "Dawson?" I spoke his name before looking up. "We've got to go. Now."

His loud curse was filled with both rage and hatred. "God damn it, J..." he dragged the invective out.

"Sorry." I stood, only to have him tower over me with his fists balled. For a moment I thought he set his feet to punch me, before I realized his anger was directed toward KC and the branch of government he worked for.

Robin leaped forward to force herself between us. I guess she thought my husband planned to attack me. "Dawson, don't," she said.

I glanced at Scotty to find him the only one without a reaction. He watched as if uninterested. "He's not going to hit me, Robin. Thank you for supper, but I've got to get home."

She pulled back and turned to her boyfriend. "Scotty?"

His countenance didn't change. "She's working again. J is," he amended.

Robin turned to me. "Julia?"

I stared at Dawson who still glared. "We've got to go."

We didn't speak during the ride back to our place. With time short, I beat him out of the truck and inside. My suitcase was open on the bed when Dawson stalked in and flopped onto the chair kept on his side. "Keep this shit up, and one of these times you won't be coming home."

I ferried clothing from my bureau and closet to my luggage. Not sure how long I'd be gone meant enough for a week of changes before I needed to employ hotel services. Cold winter temperatures were moderating to a wetter and milder spring. My heavy coat could be left behind, but I included a long jacket with down insulation and a hood. "The quicker I finish this job, the sooner I'm back forever."

"Bullshit. With you...J..." He used my pseudonym deliberately for a second time. "...there's never gonna be an end. Always another job on the horizon." He turned his head and spat—literally hawked a goober onto the hardwood floor. "Seems the gray man was right about you. You're not only bloodthirsty, you love this shit."

"Dawson..." My tone took on a steely quality in only the way it could when I gave in to J. "...don't make this harder than it has to be. I didn't apply for this job...it came to me."

"You couldn't wait to accept their offer. Nor will you next time or the time after." Rather than continue our argument and watch me pack, he stood and left the room. I heard the front door slam, then seconds later the truck start. My husband was angry, and our marriage was in trouble.

***

The blades to our helicopter spun to a stop while I sat motionless. I could only ponder what I feared might be a lonely future if my extracurricular activities weren't curtailed. Dawson was angry with me only because he feared each time I left would be our last together. He didn't worry needlessly—I stalked and killed some of the most ferocious and unforgiving fighters the world offered. One misstep, and my life would end. The pilot and KC waited quietly, while his boy Friday fidgeted and finally broke the silence. "Aren't you about..."

I turned my head slightly to pin him with a stare. "I'm going to need to kill you one of these days."

KC put his elbow into the ribs of the soldier. "Keep your mouth shut."

I could see the lights of Jackson and contemplated the next few days or weeks. Preferably not months. Dawson, Jake, my classroom, and Bess filled my thoughts. The first two would be lost without my return, while the latter might take my position away even if I did survive to go back. My chickens entered into my thought process, along with plans to purchase more rabbits.

I'm not sure how much time passed while I considered my future. "Your vehicle is waiting, Mrs. Pelletier," KC said softly.

My sigh was loud in the quiet cabin. "I'm not sure my husband will." My gaze flicked to him. "You're destroying my marriage."

"I'm very..."

I needn't suffer his platitudes and stopped him. "Keep it to yourself and don't pretend to give a shit." My harsh invective was enough to freeze soil thawing from a cold winter.

"Yes, ma'am."

Instead of the Suburban I'd grown accustomed to, an all-black Toyota Tundra matching my mood awaited me. The same color inside as out, I turned to KC. "Black? Really?"

He shrugged and opened the rear door to stow my luggage inside, while I placed my work guns on the passenger side and tucked my blonde locks under the same wig as before. The new car odor assailed my senses when I leaned in. "Thought you might enjoy some up-to-date wheels. We assume you wore your welcome out with the last rig. This one's wearing less than twenty miles." He handed me a fob and a hotel keycard. "The Come Horn Inn as before...different room. A bit of an upgrade. Enjoy."

He wasn't kidding. I enjoyed the truck's state-of-the-art interior, but my new digs were too much. Two bedrooms and bathrooms with a sunken living area and full bar. Televisions were in each room including the baths. Fifty dollars greased the palm of the late-night *concierge* when he offered to carry my bags. I collapsed in exhaustion onto my chosen bed only moments after the door closed behind the helpful man.

* * *

Arctic air blew from high peaks of the Wind River Mountains while I surveyed the big log home above the Green River. Perhaps three miles away, it was easily visible from my higher vantage. I parked in a foot of rotten snow with my Swarovski spotting scope mounted on the lowered window. Gusts of wind would occasionally rock my pickup, making it impossible to see. Set at thirty-power—the highest I could go and still view clearly—a doe bedded below the house was easily identified.

I drove to my higher viewpoint long before daylight. Stopping first to fill my tank with gas and my thermos with coffee, I left the station with a package of jerky, too. It was meat I savored to break my fast by letting it soak in my saliva and then swallow the sweet juice before the smoky beef. My bladder got my attention after finishing most of the hot drink. Confident no one could see, I squatted between my door and the truck to do my business. A small wad of toilet paper got left under a large rock next to the road's edge. Although I wore my coat, it wasn't enough to keep me from shivering before I got back inside. I even started the engine to warm the interior when my hands wouldn't stop shaking.

An incoming text stopped me from fine-tuning the eyepiece again. A strong gust twisted the scope on its window mount while I waited for the engine to blow hot air. It came from Dawson. *I'm sorry for my reaction yesterday, little hawk. I need to apologize and let you know how much I love you. I'm counting the hours and minutes before we're together again.*

I set the phone aside to wipe wet cheeks. My husband expressed his regret when it should have been me. Movement below caught my attention after I blotted my eyes with a tissue. A truck flew up the gravel road and would eventually pass from where I watched. Unscrewing the window mount, I set the scope aside to avoid any curious passersby. It and my work gun got covered by a hotel towel I brought for just such an instance. My—I always thought of it as Allen's—Sig Sauer was more difficult to hide.

A 'seventies standard cab Ford passed me and fishtailed as it navigated the switchback past where I parked, throwing a rooster tail of snow high in the air. The body was jacked to the max by an impressive lift kit where it sat above the chassis. In four-wheel-drive with a throaty exhaust, three boys—young men actually—were hooting their fun as they went by with their windows down. My heavily-tinted glass didn't allow them to see a woman inside—parked alone in the mountains. Far more worried over blowing my cover rather than the natural fear of males as a solo female, I carefully navigated my way south to Pinedale. Nothing I saw around the Hollister home led me to believe an attack was imminent.

Stopping at the same café from where months before I'd watched the female suicide bomber pass, a late breakfast consisted of a waffle and small bowl of fruit. It reminded me to stop at a grocery before I returned to my room. A pineapple, strawberries, and bananas would go far in keeping my desire for fresh fruit satisfied. I needed to keep my focus and finish this job if I hoped to retain my other employment and a hurt husband. I took the time to respond to his earlier missive and explain how much I loved him. He didn't answer, but Dawson was notorious for leaving his phone behind or letting the battery go dead.

* * *

A week of surveillance from Jackson to Pinedale and around the Wind River Range to Dubois brought me no closer to a solution. A drive around the apple orchard owned by Hollister and Boyd left me with nothing to show for my efforts. Remembering what KC told me about Marta Boyd, I hoped to kill two birds with one stone. Perhaps I could find a place to view the younger Boyd's home, and also the eclectic residence shared by his father and mother-in-law.

I searched Google Earth with my phone to get a better look at both places. While Emerson's home was easy to see, his dad's house was invisible to satellites. A pickup sitting on a small bench surrounded by a modest orchard, wind turbine, and solar panels were the only giveaways.

It took longer than I expected to locate the elder Boyd's driveway. When I did, the ground was far steeper than I envisioned. I passed it and continued around a switchback where I parked and stepped from my truck. Snow reaching above my boots made me glad I wore waterproof footwear.

I worked my way around the hillside in hopes of glimpsing both residences. Far below, I could make out the steel roofed log structure of Emerson. Closer was the orchard, photovoltaic system, and a yard surrounded by a fence. Yet any residence was invisible. It wasn't until I worked farther around before locating what I searched for.

Two huge windows seemed to be eyes of the slope looking to the northeast. I finally understood what KC explained. The dwelling was literally set into the hillside. Hunkered beneath a tall pine, I wished I brought the spotting scope to see better. A large door appeared capable of withstanding anything but a direct airstrike.

My mind was set at ease while I hiked back to my Tundra. Hollister's enemies would find hurting him by attacking his friends in their homes almost impossible. Time for me to get back to Jackson.

* * *

After returning to my room at the Come Horn Inn, I slept late the following morning. Not settling in until almost three a.m. meant my eyes were gritty when my phone woke me. It was a text from KC. *Any news?*

I tossed my cell aside and rolled over in an attempt to fall asleep. No such luck. My mind kicked into gear. Dawson, Jake, my job—worries crashed over me as if storm-generated ocean breakers. Sighing, I turned to my back and stared at the ceiling. Nothing was more important than my homelife—not even this poor man I contracted to watch over.

Sighing again, I ignored the message and threw the covers aside. Time for a shower and something to eat. My habits hadn't been healthy since I arrived, and my weight would drop quickly if I didn't change my ways.

Makeup covered dark bags under my eyes and added color to my cheeks. I used a stencil kit to darken my brows and lashes to match my wig. Mascara completed the look. No one would dream I was a blonde under the dark brown hairpiece. Dressed in double-front Carhartt jeans and long-sleeved flannel shirt, I wouldn't seem anymore out of place in the quaint village than in Salmon.

I'd avoided the Upchuck and other regular establishments since returning. Not sure if anyone would recognize me from before, I found other less healthy places to eat—choosing convenience food instead. After parking on the street, I adjusted the Glock in its harness beneath my jacket and took a deep breath.

A bustling restaurant filled with patrons offered anonymity. Russell Endicott seated me at the very table from which I'd departed to deal with the female bomber. He left me with a menu and coffee after promising to return with water.

I was hunkered over my phone and coffee looking at pictures of Dawson and Jake when I felt a presence and heard a familiar voice. "We meet again, Ariel Woodman."

I couldn't hide the pleasure in my tone. "Father Timothy!"

He gestured. "May I sit?"

"Of course." I put my cell aside. "How've you been?"

The old priest sat slowly, making me wince with his stiffness. "Winters aren't as easy on me as they once were."

"You haven't fallen again, have you?" I asked.

I earned his chuckle. "No, I've learned to avoid ice at all costs." He pointed. "I interrupted you looking at pictures."

"Uh huh. My two best boys." I scrolled through and found a nice one of Dawson sitting on the porch with Jake at his side. Then another of my husband with a heavy pack. We'd been carrying out a big buck he'd shot while hunting in the backcountry. I'd been hurt, and we were on our way to the hospital.

Father Timothy scrutinized the photos. "I see what you meant before. Your husband appears quite the rugged outdoorsman."

My heart swelled with pride. Few knew the depths of what the priest articulated, and only I was privy to Dawson's softer side. "You can't imagine, Father."

Russell appeared at our table with water and a warmup for my coffee. "Ready to order?"

"Two soft boiled eggs and a bowl of oatmeal," the priest said. "Milk and honey, too, please."

His meal sounded good, and unlike what I usually ate. "I'd like the same with a side of bacon and a sliced tomato."

I wasn't thinking when our waiter left, and burned my mouth with the fresh coffee. It caused me to jerk and put the cup down. The dominee was waiting when I glanced up. "Are you here working in Jackson again, Ms. Woodman?"

Chapter IX

I stared back, taking Father Timothy's measure. Years of dealing with parishioners gave him the patience to wait me out. Trying to frame a glib answer made me angrier when I couldn't. Instead, I looked away and mulled what I did before looking at him again. His eyes widened, and he pushed rearward in his chair to cock his head. He had no right to pose the question, and my glare left no doubt of my displeasure. My lips were pressed into a flat line while I considered leaving, but I tasted my coffee again to find it cooled enough, and ignored my tablemate after a text arrived.

Any news, Little Hawk?

No, I typed back. *Flailing and wondering what the hell I'm doing here.*

His return came quicker than I thought he could hunt and peck. *Then come home. Me and Jake need you.*

His missive clawed at my heart. *I'm sorry. I can't. You cannot imagine how badly I want to be there.*

Our messaging ended when Russell returned with our meal. I remembered Dad enjoyed oats when I was little, but I never liked them. Perhaps my taste buds changed in the past thirty years. Watching Father Timothy, I copied how he poured first milk into his bowl, followed by a generous dob of honey. We peeled our eggs while the grain softened.

As it turned out, what I liked switched over three decades. Even the soft-boiled eggs were a delightful alternative from sunny-side up. Bacon served at the restaurant was exactly what I enjoyed, thick and crisp.

I relaxed spine and shoulders against the curved upright to let my meal settle and finish my coffee. The priest took his time and seemed to savor each bite. I waited until Russell cleared our table and left before nodding. "I'm on the clock," I said.

His brows raised. "Should I be worried?"

I nodded. "Uh huh. Terrified."

"Oh?"

"Not for yourself. It's because this time I might fail." I hated to say the words aloud, but they were true. The law of averages would eventually catch up, and this time I might face—if I could locate them first—too many.

"We all have daunting challenges at some point in our lives, Ariel. Keep your faith in God. I'll ask the Almighty for His help, and He will not forsake you."

I pushed my chair away and stood. "I appreciate it, Father. I hope you wield mighty prayers. I'm going to need all the help I can get."

His eyes searched for what he knew I carried, but this time my coat didn't open far enough. "My door is always open, Ms. Woodman. You need only stop, and I'll be there for you."

"Thank you. I'll accept your offer...I need to confess."

"You haven't been to church as promised?"

He was right. I'd struck the bargain with him. I leaned forward on the back of my chair. "Huh uh. Not yet."

I expected him to chastise me, but he didn't. Instead, he smiled and inclined his head. "I have no doubt you won't let me down, Ariel. Stop by when you have time. There's something I'd like to speak with you about." He glanced around before continuing. "This isn't the place."

"Something important?"

Father Timothy smiled and added a little shrug. "Probably, but it isn't life or death. When you get a chance."

* * *

Stakeouts are boring. While patience is my *forte*, I prefer to prowl and hunt rather than wait for my target to come to me. Two days above Early Hollister's home, followed by two more watching his parents' place netted me zero. I retreated to Pinedale to scout and scrutinize each hotel, grocery, and anywhere my quarry could park undetected.

Campgrounds hosted few so early in the season, but I drove through each one on the map to check them out. Hungry and at my wits end, I parked on main street to feed a shrinking body and where I could examine every passing vehicle.

A text arrived from KC before I got out. *Anything to report?*

Boredom. Absolute tooth grinding, claw-my-eyes-out frustration.

Prepare yourself. The infiltration contingent has gone dark. They must be on US soil and may be nearby.

My pulse went up as did my body temperature. Finally. *Their numbers, names, description...is there anything for me to go on?*

Negative. I'm en route to Mountain Home AFB as we speak. ETA six hours.

Excitement and anticipation increased to the point of almost panting. Live or die, this was what I existed for and was born to do. *No hurry...hell, take your time. Drive a VW bug and enjoy the scenery,* I answered sarcastically.

We're traveling at Mach .9. Are you concerned enough we should go supersonic?

Crap. Six hours away and going a shade under the speed of sound? From where in the world was KC returning, and what aircraft was he flying in? *I apologize. Everything is under control on my end. Enjoy your flight.*

Skeleton crew of my attachment is on standby. Contact me and I'll relay if you need anything.

10-4.

Not quite noon, I skipped a meal and drove to the Hollister home. Rather than travel to the mountain range above to watch from miles away, I passed their driveway in the direction of a large cattle ranch. Stopping where I could see best, I uncovered my carbine and Ruger MK IV .22/45. Screwing a suppressor onto the threads of each, I pressed a loaded magazine into both guns and left the chambers empty.

Movement in my rearview mirror caught my attention. My pulse quickened before settling into a slow cadence. Instead of passing where I was parked, a three-quarter ton beat-up Chevrolet pickup stopped next to me. Chambering a round and laying the .22 on my lap, I lowered my tinted window to see two men. "Can I help you?"

"No, ma'am," the driver answered. He appeared to be around fifty with the passenger perhaps half his age. "Better question is can I help you?"

Time to think fast on my feet—something I'm not particularly good at. "I don't believe so. Got a few days off work and thought I'd explore." I pointed at the snow-covered Wind River Mountain Range. It appeared close enough to touch. "I'm new to the area and wanted to get pictures for my parents." Holding my phone to where they could see it, I fiddled with the screen and acted like I took another photo. "Is it okay for me to spend an afternoon or two exploring?"

"Sure," he said gruffly. "Just don't cut any fences or leave gates open, you hear?"

I reengaged the safety on my pistol. "No problem," I said.

A thought occurred to me after my visitors left, and I sent a text to KC. *Need night vision. Leave it in my motel room if I'm not there.*

No response didn't surprise me. He'd answer me when he could. On a whim, I sent another, this one to Dawson. *I love and think about you each moment of every day.*

A second lack of reply irritated me more than it should. Giving him a couple minutes with no answer, I drove toward Pinedale—afraid of not being everywhere at once. With the play about to be cast, I wanted a major role.

I got back to my Jackson hotel room to find KC sent someone in his stead. I haven't the slightest clue who or how they got in. A box waited on my couch reading: PSV-15-HS Military Goggles. A handful of batteries were included. After reading the expected life was only sixteen hours, I understood the spares. Somewhat experienced using a similar unit, I adjusted the harness for comfort and inserted the battery. Didn't want to be caught needing it and have the unit unopened.

In bed at ten—my alarm went off at three. Five hours isn't enough sleep for this girl. I needed at least eight and preferably nine hours for best results. However, I drove southeast mindful of pushing the speed limit too far. As before, I stopped in a sage flat past the Hollister residence. Switching off my lights, I donned the night vision goggles, and laden with my trio of firearms, hiked up a slight incline—stopping when I was high enough to see the surrounding terrain.

Other than a coyote hunting and catching mice, nothing moved except what a cold breeze could blow. Staying in position as long as I could stand, I was eventually forced to retreat to the comparative warmth of my Tundra to await daybreak.

Sunrise brought with it yawns and a wish for my thermos filled with hot coffee. I'd missed supper the night before and now breakfast. Only thing in my truck was an unopened flat of water bottles and three empty beer cans I'd picked up—an epiphany I put into good use after a metallic tap on my driver-side window startled me. Busy rubbing eyes bleary with fatigue, I'd allowed myself to be caught unaware.

A gun barrel thumped the glass again. Lowering it enough to make eye contact with the prowler, I found myself face-to-face with Early Hollister gripping a single-action revolver with a huge hole for a muzzle and his thumb on the hammer. "Um...uh...jess?" I said.

His tone was even and could be considered mild. "Can you tell me why you're parked here?"

I closed my lids and rubbed my face, mindful of leaving the hair of my wig hanging to partially conceal my features. "Closed the...the bar down. Figured I...hic...couldn't make it back to Jackson and took a side road. Ta-da...hic...here I am." Somehow, I conjured a burp as I reached down and lifted a beer can from the floor. I shook it and snorted, tossing it over my shoulder into the backseat. "Gotten...have...uh...you got a beer handy?"

With my work gun and SIG carbine covered by the fluffy Come Horn Inn towel, Hollister didn't worry me when he peered inside. I made a show of checking my other cans, only to toss them aside. Early watched unsure before holstering. "You're in no shape to drive, ma'am. Might want to consider a couple hours of sleep before going anywhere."

"Yeah, prolubly light...err...hic...right." I rubbed my face again before reclining the seat and raising the window with the engine running. Throwing an arm over my face, I blocked out the rising sun and my visitor.

Knuckled rapped. I lowered the window enough to hear. "Might want to shut your engine off, ma'am. Otherwise, you could die from carbon monoxide."

"Shoo...shoo told, uh...shoo cold. Juss...juss ressin' mine eyes."

"Can't let you do this, lady. I'm not letting someone die on my watch. My house is just over the rise. I can drive you there if you'd like. My wife and I have an extra room and bed for you to sleep it off."

I waved a hand. "Nah, I'm good here."

"Ma'am, it isn't open for debate. I insist. At least follow and try not to run over me. Stop in front of the garage and don't hit it. My wife and kids are home, too," he added. Hollister slapped my door and strode toward his driveway.

My truck got left where he told me to park with the doors locked and windows up. I didn't want anyone snooping. Early beat me to the house before I shut off the engine and returned with his wife in tow. I did my best to stumble and catch myself when getting out. For a moment, I couldn't remember her name and went through a quick list, knowing it was different, and started with a shh sound. Cheyenne, Sharon, Shane, it came to me—Shaye. One of her arms went around my shoulders to help guide. Short as I am, she was no taller, although far more muscular.

Appearing large from outside, the place felt enormous within. A vaulted ceiling was impressive by itself as were the massive logs making up the walls. Shaye stayed silent while she guided me downstairs into a basement. Anyone else, and I would have panicked to be in a confined area with no chance of escape. She led me inside a doorway to a spare room with a four-poster bed. Her voice was soft. "The kids won't be up for a couple hours. I'll do my best to keep them quiet when they are. Feel free to nap as long as you need. We'll be upstairs when you wake." She gave me a sharp look. "You aren't going to throw up, are you?"

I shook my head. "No, I never vomit."

She stared hard to make me understand. "Okay, but if you feel sick, there's a sink and toilet in the next room."

Left alone after the door closed and footsteps disappeared upstairs, I checked for messages on my cell. With only a single bar showing, any texts would be slow in sending or receiving. I was working on less than four hours of sleep and removed my jacket to strip off my shoulder holster and Glock. Rolling them into the loose garment, I set my cell alarm and made myself comfortable enough to sleep.

Soft chimes on my phone woke me at eight-thirty. Light footsteps above were audible if I listened carefully. It seemed my hosts were doing their best to help a needy drunken woman. I used their bathroom and washed my face afterward, wondering if becoming known to the man I shadowed was for the best. Only time would tell. Shrugging into my holster and jacket, I followed the staircase to the main floor.

The aroma of breakfast assailed my senses when I opened the door. It led directly into a corner of the kitchen from where I could see my hosts at the table and caught the tail end of a discussion about a trip to a grocery in Pinedale. With Shaye's back to me, Early was first to notice my entrance. "Good morning again."

I did my best to act embarrassed and stayed by the door. "Hi. You must think I'm awful."

When Shaye turned, I faced two wide grins. They both chuckled at my *faux* shame. "Nope. Been there, done that," Early said.

"We were sitting for breakfast. There's more than enough if you'd care to join," Shaye said. "Biscuits and gravy with scrambled eggs and toast." I saw an extra place already set.

Hunger overpowered my good sense, but where else could Early's guardian angel get closer than at his kitchen table? It made me uneasy to know my work guns were stowed in my truck rather than close at hand. I wasn't without firepower, yet a force could be amassing outside while we ate. Early must have felt I couldn't make a decision and offered again. "Please. There's plenty."

A low woof sounded as I pulled the chair out, and a Brittany came from the living room to inspect me. I held a hand out for her to smell. "Enough, Amy. Go back to bed while we eat," Shaye said. The little dog looked at Early who pointed before she retreated to her own place.

"What a beautiful girl," I said.

"Thanks...we love her. Would you like me to take your coat?" Shaye asked.

"I'm all right. A little coldblooded...seems I can never get warm." No way did I want my handgun exposed.

Shaye dished their boy and little girl first—while they eyed me warily—before filling her plate and joining Early and me. "What brings you out this way?" she asked.

"I spent a little too much time in the Red Rooster bar last night. Returning to Jackson, I realized I'd partaken too many. I thought I turned off onto a wide spot...but somehow found myself where your husband woke me."

Early's brows raised. "The Red Rooster? Bad things can happen there. I hope you weren't alone."

I shook my head and grinned. "Nope. Just me and a dozen guys for company. Each one thought he was the second coming of Don Juan...a few with the obvious pale circle on their left hand where a ring was removed."

My hosts glanced at each other. "You seem familiar," Shaye said. "Have we met before?"

Looking over my coffee cup, I cocked my head. "I don't see how. I only recently moved to Jackson from Astoria, Oregon."

She pointed to the plain band on my ring finger. "I see you're married."

"Uh huh. My husband is still in Oregon while I interview at the school."

"Oh," Shaye said. "You're a teacher?"

"Preferably primary, although I'm certified K through eight."

"What's your husband do?" Early asked.

Christ, I needed to keep my lies simple to not get caught in a web of deceit. I made a crappy fibber. "He's retired." For the first time since we'd been married, I wanted to name him as a bodyguard.

I ate seconds along with drinking three cups of coffee. The warm room combined with my full belly, hot beverage, and still wearing a jacket was causing sweat to trickle down my spine. With breakfast finished and the kids making a beeline for their toys, Shaye stacked dishes and moved them to the counter. "Can I help?" I offered.

"Thanks, but this won't take but a minute."

Early studied me while Shaye and I spoke. Not with a creepy stare but taking my measure. I could do little but ignore his attention while hoping any blonde strays were secure beneath my wig. Pushing my chair back, I stood. "I hate to sleep, eat, and run, but I need to get back to my room. Before I leave, I'd like to get your names. You took me in without knowing mine." I held my hand out. "Ariel Woodman."

Early shook it with a firm grip—then Shaye. "Early Hollister and my wife, Shaye. Kids are Tryn and Anna."

"Trying?" I asked. It seemed as odd as his father's moniker.

They both grinned before Early answered. "Nope, Tryn. T-r-y-n. I'm always Early, so we figured he should always be Tryn."

Their names made me chuckle, but I needed to leave. "Can't thank you enough for keeping an eye on a foolish woman." I winked and offered a sly grin. "Should you ever meet my husband, let's keep my little *faux pas* between us, okay?"

My time spent with the Hollisters was enjoyable. I liked them far more than anticipated and wished they lived closer to Salmon, but as long as I was fantasizing, a better request of the assassin's fairy godmother was that they never laid eyes on me. Now, the entire mission was compromised because of my inexcusable blunder. While the assignment was far different from how I worked for The Company, the lives of people who opened their home to me were on the line should I fail.

Cool temperatures on the way to the truck chilled my sweaty body. I hurried, remembering my hosts were planning to drive to Pinedale, and

I wanted to make sure the coast was reasonably clear. I stopped at the end of their driveway and used my binoculars to sweep the area. No rigs or movement that I could see. Nice thing about Wyoming's open country was the ease to spot anything out of place.

When I couldn't find a reason to delay longer, I made the drive into Pinedale—parking where my truck wasn't readily visible, but I could watch the highway. While I sat with my head on a swivel, I called my boss. He answered immediately. "KC."

"Ariel. Need new wheels ASAP."

"You've been compromised?"

I answered with one of Dawson's favorites. "Bigger'n shit. I spent the morning with Hollister and his family after he caught me casing the place."

He muttered a crude obscenity. "Okay...okay. You'll find a different vehicle at your hotel this afternoon. Park the Toyota and leave the keys in the ignition. We'll take care of it. Any other news?"

"Huh uh. I'm in Pinedale after overhearing plans to run errands. If our infiltrators are nearby, I've yet to ID them. Need you to remain on standby."

He chuckled. "We're ready to move. Call it in if you find too many to handle."

"Affirmative." I kind of liked the term. It made me feel like an actual agent.

The Hollisters were in no hurry. They passed where I waited nearly two hours after I parked. They did almost everything as a family—whether visiting or running errands. I liked it, hoping someday Dawson and I could do the same on a more regular basis.

They parked at a grocery off West Pine Street and split up—Shaye carrying Anna on a hip and Early hand-in-hand with Tryn. When the boys hurried across the highway away from the market, I left my truck wearing a hoody with my work gun inside my waistband and an extra magazine in my left rear jeans pocket. My gut told me to shadow Shaye, but I couldn't make up my mind. Pressing the switch on my electronic jammer, I crossed the road at a trot after a Toyota Sequoia parked along the street as Early disappeared into a store. I slowed when his wife entered the grocery.

I was almost too late. Two men departed the Toyota to jog across the highway past me and disappear inside the food store. I stopped at the front after they entered, trying to catch sight of them through the windows. I didn't have long to wait before they came out with Shaye and her little girl between them. None of the quartet noticed me where I was barely visible between commercial ice coolers against the front. Instead of crossing the parking lot and street, the pair leading Shaye and her youngest made an abrupt turn to vanish along the building. I saw the glint of a handgun pressed into her ribs before sprinting along the other side of the store. Behind was a wooded lot I feared could become an execution site.

One man—tall and rangy—bound Shaye's hands behind her back, while Anna held her mom's leg and whimpered. A piece of cloth was stuffed inside the young mother's mouth. I got only a moment to wonder what the duo planned for the girl before the shorter bearded one located a large rock. I looked on in horror as he approached her, lifting the boulder high overhead. Shaye's muffled shrieks increased in their intensity while she kicked and fought for her baby's life.

He didn't get close enough to be a threat to the child before a forty grain .22 drilled through his forehead. I didn't wait for results of my aim before turning my sights to the one holding a semi-auto handgun. His look of surprise when his companion collapsed disappeared when my second shot entered the tall man's temple. With her back to me and two down and dead—I stepped where Shaye couldn't see me if she turned, and I hurried around the neighboring building. If more waited in the Toyota, I planned to terminate them in the open on Main Street. To hell with secrecy. Animals so vicious as to murder a child with a huge rock didn't deserve to draw breath.

Stopping where I could see the van, I closely observed it while speed dialing. KC didn't get a chance to answer. "Two down in the wooded area behind the grocery at the west end of Pine," I said, my tone terse. "I suspect more across the street from me." Shouts not unexpected caught my attention. Good. Shaye found help. "Need cleanup ASAP...perhaps extraction."

The driver's window of the Sequoia lowered, allowing me a glimpse inside. More than one waited behind tinted windows—how many I couldn't guess. "Hold your position if you can, Ariel," KC said. We're close and moving your way."

Early Hollister and his son stepped from the hardware store he'd entered minutes before. A quick glance at the Toyota made it clear I wasn't the only one to identify him. The engine started, and the SUV gunned from the curb. "Now...I need you now," I said and dropped my cell into a side pocket without ending the call.

Their wheels were turned toward me as the vehicle lurched forward. Rather than wait as ordered, I brazenly strode several feet into the street before I fired. A risky headshot administered to the driver caused the Toyota to lunge forward, barely miss me, and slam into a parked car. He slumped over the wheel, dead or disabled. The rear doors burst outward. Seven rounds remained in my handgun, and I faced at least four or five. I opened fire as men stumbled forth—never a care if they were armed or not.

Speed and a silent attack worked in my favor. Two bailing on my side were dead the moment their feet hit the pavement. I put a bullet into another one through the gaping rear before two more took cover. Out of my element in the open and not knowing my next move, I squatted and exchanged magazines. So far with the exception of colliding vehicles, our one-sided battle was silent while I pressed onward with my suppressed Ruger. Cars were stopped on the street, unsure of what had been witnessed.

A hard lesson I'd learned was always attack. Holding back offers too many advantages to the enemy. Lying on my side and peering beneath the vehicle, I could see what had to be the rump and low back of a man sitting on the asphalt, along with the shoes and ankles of another. Taking careful aim, I put three quick rounds into the sitter's spine and a fourth and fifth into the heel of the other. He stood to hobble across the highway and covered less than ten feet before I shot him in the back of his head. I guessed the last man would be badly wounded and unable to stand, yet who knew how well-armed?

Planning to circle the Sequoia and terminate the final terrorist, I was stopped by a shout. "Stand down, Agent. That's an order." Spinning mid step, I found myself facing KC and his boy Friday double-timing it to my side. Although I still wore my hood, my boss threw his coat over my head and upper back.

I tried to pull away. "One could still be able just past the Toyota."

Each man positioned himself on either arm to hustle me out of the hot zone, and I got a good look at what KC brought to the fight. Six agents armed with short carbines sprinted past us to take care of the mess I left behind. "It's over...for now. We'll handle public relations and cleanup." I could hear sirens nearing in the distance. My future was left in the hands of KC.

* * *

Breaking news on the television in my hotel room was fascinating. I found most interesting to be no mention of Early or Shaye Hollister. While a spokesman for KC explained and apologized for conducting a snap Homeland Security drill unannounced, she ignored shouted questions about a shadowy figure key to the situation. No one could agree on anything, including whether the person was a boy or small woman.

My phone rang while I watched the looped broadcast for the sixth time and cleaned my gun and suppressor. "Woodman," I said.

"Find the keys to your new wheels?" KC asked.

"I did. Thanks." My ride from Pinedale to Jackson made sure I understood the new metallic deepwood green Suburban parked in back was mine. A check showed less than a hundred miles on the rig. I could get used to the new car odor but loved my Wagoneer too much to change. "How bad was the fallout?"

"Is."

"Excuse me?"

"The fallout continues. It's ongoing."

"Should I return home? I hate to think I compromised the mission if my face got splashed on the boob tube."

"Negative. I suggest remaining where you are for the short term. We were issued a court order and seized all recordings from nearby businesses with cameras. If you activated your jammer, very few should show us anything. Can you tell me if anyone got a good look at you?"

"Not that I'm aware of. It was cold and drizzling. I wore my hood."

"Mrs. Hollister didn't recognize you?"

"Her back was to me." I went on to explain how I killed the pair before their little girl could be slaughtered.

"Don't blame you," KC said after absorbing the horrid tale. "Anyone with a heart would have done the same. You should know the Hollister family spent a couple hours at the Pinedale Medical Clinic and are giving a statement at the police station as we speak."

"How're they faring?"

"As well as can be expected. The kids are exhausted, and Shaye is still frightened, which makes Early angry. Tread carefully, Ariel. Get too close, and he's likely to shoot first and ask questions later."

"How long before I'm released to return home?"

"You can leave anytime you'd like. I only made a suggestion. You're not a prisoner," he said in a sharp tone.

"Another seven are terminated. You advised they may come in teams of that number.

"Technically, six dead and one still in surgery. I'm told the damage to his spine is irreparable. We hope to learn more about upcoming attacks or if any are planned."

"I'll give you a couple days, then. After that, I'm going home."

"We'll be in contact."

It didn't matter if he was or not. The moment I felt comfortable leaving the area, I planned to be on the road.

Chapter X

Four days were spent lazing about my room eating catered meals. The more I stayed out of the public eye, the safer I felt. Besides, I'd fasted too often while trying to be everywhere at once. My body appreciated regular feedings as much as my palate enjoyed them. Returning home to Dawson as a skeleton wouldn't endear my job to him more. Ninety-six hours passed before showing my face on the streets of Jackson—forty-eight after the news cycle changed.

Entering the Upchuck didn't earn me more than casual notice other than from Father Timothy. Relieved, I ignored the sign to wait to be seated and made my way in his direction past diners who continued to pay me no mind, but Russell Endicott stopped polishing the bar, saw where I headed, and almost beat me to my Catholic friend's extra chair with a cup and carafe.

The priest was nearly finished with his bowl of oatmeal when I looked up at our tall server. "Can I get two waffles with a side of bacon, please?"

"Sure," he said. "Anything else for you, Father?"

"More hot water and another teabag if you please, Russell." He waited until we were alone before leaning back and addressing me. "Saw you in Pinedale on TV a few days ago."

"What?" I almost shouted, and my heart rate skyrocketed. Why didn't KC warn me? How? When? There were no news crews I was aware of.

It took me a couple seconds to realize I'd been set up. "Your reaction tells me everything I wanted to know." He seemed pleased with his subterfuge. "My guess is you got the job finished and you're ready to return home."

"You're an asshole, old man," I said under my breath but loud enough for him to hear.

"It wasn't a training exercise, was it?"

I ignored his question. "You mentioned a need to talk to me. What's it about?"

"A couple visitors stopped to chat."

"Oh?"

"Marta Boyd and her husband."

My stomach jolted with the fear my cover may be blown if the woman whose face once graced financial publications tied me to the priest. "Are either of them Catholic?"

"She didn't say."

"Dare I ask what she inquired about?"

"You."

Mind whirling, I wolfed my breakfast after it arrived and drank coffee fast enough to scorch my mouth. I tossed a couple twenties on our table and stood. "Let's go."

Timothy had thought ahead. A small ceramic coffee pot, beans, and an electric grinder were on the short counter next to his kitchen range. "May I take your jacket?" he asked.

I handed it over. He knew who and what I was and wouldn't be startled by my handgun and spare magazines hanging on either side of my ribcage. He made himself comfortable after hooking it on a peg, while I got the pot ready and left it on the burner. I didn't mince words the moment we sat. "What did she want?"

"To know everything there was about a petite dark-haired woman whom she feared constituted a threat toward her family."

"How did she link us?"

"She recalled we sat together during their family celebration at the Upchuck. Remember, Mrs. Boyd wrestled me from the rear entry where she got arrested. I saw you point a gun at her before I barred the door again."

"I don't suppose you can lie," I muttered.

"Didn't need to," he said. "Besides, I'm too old not to tell the truth."

"Priest..." My tone held cold warning. "...what've you done?"

He stared in return. "Fascinating," the old man whispered.

"Does she know who I am?"

He snorted but didn't blink. "Of course not. My meetings with you have been held in confidence. I'm bound not to divulge. Marta Boyd is only sure you came to the church, but for all she knows, it was about secular matters." His eyes twinkled. "If there was a lie, it was by omission, which priests must often do to protect the sanctity of confession."

"Why is she interested in me? Did she say?"

"You caught her attention. She followed me and found you standing over a dead woman laden with enough explosives to flatten the restaurant. A gun was leveled at her before getting arrested. From those things, she fears you may represent a threat to her family."

"Crap." I needed to contact KC and apprise him of the woman.

"Are you?"

"Am I what?"

"A danger to her family."

I snorted my disgust. "No, quite the opposite." The coffeepot threatening to boil over made me scamper into the kitchen and turn the burner down to get a slow perk.

"Then you know who he is, don't you?"

Planning and plotting my next move—mostly to return home and escape the Boyd woman—his question caught me unprepared. "Excuse me?"

"My gut has been honed by almost sixty-five years of interaction with my flocks. Once I get a feel of my parishioner, it's simple to read them. You've been made aware of young Hollister's history," he said with confidence.

I studied him carefully before retrieving my coat. The priest should know nothing of Early's time served overseas. I'd finally been made aware of a disturbing amount of details. KC realized I needed to understand why ISIS wished to destroy a man and his family inside US borders. Going to an inner pocket, I withdrew the electronic jammer KC provided. Timothy watched curiously as I activated it. If his television were on, the picture would have gone blank. My cell was useless, but so would be the case with anyone else's. "Tread carefully, Father."

He nodded toward the device I stowed in my breast pocket. "If it's what I think, Mrs. Boyd suspected you disabled all electronics on the day she saw you."

I ignored his all too real statement. "What did she *want?*"

"Your name and where you live. Why you were in town and how long I've known you."

"How did you answer?"

His watery eyes twinkled. "I couldn't. We've met to save your soul in the case of unexpected death. I could not confirm we met or disclose our discussions than deny my Lord and Savior. Both are equally important."

The coffee was good. Freshly ground beans made for a robust flavor. I poured a cup and strolled to his front window to gaze outside. A sunny day if a bit windier than I liked. "I'm nobody," I muttered.

"You're everything to God, Julia. To Dawson, too. All lives have the same value, whether a pauper, prime minister, president, or king."

My Suburban and the parish Crown Victoria were parked against two curbs in a long row. A sidewalk meandered past the rectory and our vehicles. I sipped my drink and watched with interest as a muscular man disappeared from sight in the direction of the church. I'd yet to meet Timothy's replacement.

The priest stayed silent while I stared out the window and considered my options. Returning to my seat, I asked, "Should I be concerned about Mrs. Boyd? Is she merely curious or something more?"

"I know her only through hearsay. This was the first time we've spoken. From what I understand, when the woman focuses on a problem, she doesn't relent until it's resolved."

"Damn," I said before remembering where I was. "Oh, sorry, Father."

He waved a hand. "Damnation and its prevention are what I deal with daily. Bless you, my child, for not adding the Lord's name in vain."

I spent the day with my friend. The more we talked, the easier our conversation flowed. We discussed my backstory and how I came to be who I am, but I couldn't stop telling him about Dawson. The priest was an easy man to become comfortable with simply because our meetings were private—kept between me, him, and God. The teacher within him was effortless to discern as he answered my questions about faith, grace, and the hereafter. When the hour grew late, I slipped to my knees and asked for absolution. "Forgive me, Father, for I have sinned. Since we last met, I've taken the lives of six men and wounded another—"

* * *

After a long talk with KC, I stayed in my room and got meals delivered. My boss was equally troubled by news about Marta Boyd. The less she knew about ADS—American Defense Shield—and KC's activities, the better. While I'm with them, we are a clandestine group operating as a subdivision of the Department of Homeland Security, an operation few if any within the halls of congress knew. I was merely a pawn in the struggle to stop America's enemies from attacking within our borders.

I needed to hear Dawson's voice. Three calls went to voicemail before he returned one. "Everything okay, beautiful?" he asked.

I closed my eyes and sighed at his deep tone. "It's better after hearing your voice," I said.

"Will I see you soon?"

"It shouldn't be more than a few days as long as nothing comes unglued, unscrewed, or ripped at the seams."

He chuckled at one of Scotty's favorite idioms. "Good. Me'n Jake miss you."

"How is our boy?"

"Lonely. We've been taking long hikes, trying to stay below snow level."

The mountains shot straight up not far behind our house. "I hope you're burning up enough of his excess energy." Hard to keep the wistfulness I felt from my tone.

"You okay, Little Hawk?"

"No—" I trailed off, not sure what to say.

His voice sharpened. "Are you hurt?"

A horn blast was clear on his side of our connection. "Huh uh. Did I hear a car or truck? Do we have company?"

He hesitated. "I-I'm in town getting feed for Jake. If you're okay physically, what's wrong?"

"I'm homesick." I couldn't control my tears and lost keeping them to myself when I sniffed. "I need you, Dawson." Bedsheets where I sprawled were used to blot my eyes.

"Then come to me. Leave right now. You know where I am."

"Another day...perhaps two. It's almost over, honey," I whispered. "I can't stand it. When KC gives this operation the all-clear, I'm finished."

"Any idea of how long?"

"How long for what?"

"Until Carter's sure the job's done."

He refused to call my boss by Kevin or KC, going by his last name or asshole. "Soon. At least, I hope it isn't long."

"We'll be waiting, Jules. Let me know what day you plan to return, and me and Jake'll be ready."

"The moment I'm sure," I promised and rolled to my back to drink in his steady rumble.

We spoke of home and the future until my eyes would no longer stay open. I barely got a chance to say goodbye and how much I loved him before nodding off.

* * *

KC's call came while I packed my things. Ready to return home to a normal life, his message ruined my mood and foreseeable future. "Overseas assets have issued a warning. Western incursions made by ISIS haven't been for naught. They've assassinated eight targets in Europe and one in Canada. We understand they're emboldened by their successes and plan to increase attacks worldwide."

"Do you believe Hollister is still a priority?"

"Likely. They've spent an unusual amount of blood and treasure to ensure his demise."

"Why have countries overseas been so unsuccessful in stopping them?"

"You need to understand the difference between Europe and Canada versus the US, Ariel."

"I'm listening."

He cleared his throat. "Our team has been given a mandate to operate by a separate set of rules when it comes to how we treat terrorists actively trying to assassinate US citizens on our soil. Europe and our northern neighbor monitors, arrests, and tries them. Often, they're deported or simply released until a court date, giving them more opportunities. Hiring you and those with similar skills are keeping our people safe."

"You've hired others like me?"

"Yes, no...well...none with the same skillset you bring to the table."

"How many?" My services might not be needed if enough who could perform the same task were deployed.

"You pose a question beyond my paygrade."

"Five? A dozen? A hundred? More?"

"Ms. Woodman, I simply don't know. Most are still training. I'm aware of only a handful fielded thus far."

A bad feeling was beginning to grow. "How many others besides myself are you responsible for?"

"Just you. If it makes you feel safer, I lead four squads making up a platoon at my disposal."

I knew nothing of the military except the little Dawson shared. "How many is in a platoon?"

"Forty. Each one is dedicated to our mission, which is to make your job go as smoothly as possible. I command both air and ground assets. A simple phone call can bring an F22 Raptor, helicopters, or even armored vehicles into theater."

"Then you have the resources available to cordon off western Wyoming and do the job you expect me to handle. You ask too much. I'm tired and want to go home."

"Would you like me to fly your husband to Jackson? You could enjoy a few days of R&R before the next push."

"God, no!" Knowing my man, he would put himself between me and what he considered harm's way. I could think of no better plan to get Dawson killed than if he knew where I worked. "I want to go home."

"We need *you*, Julia. Rather, we continue to require the services of the gray woman. She can do the job without raising suspicion...an impossibility for my other people."

"I'm going to lose my real job. One I've worked hard for."

KC's tone changed. "No," he said with conviction. "You won't. Schools have to be funded. If there's an issue, I have no problem leaning on your school board."

"Doesn't mean they'll want me back."

"Give me a few extra days, Julia. If nothing concrete has come down the pipe, return to Salmon."

I sighed and agreed before tossing my phone on the bed and unpacking a bulging suitcase and knapsack. In forty-eight to ninety-six hours, I would be free to see my honey again.

* * *

With nothing to fill my time—television bored me with little but bad news and poorly thought-out sitcoms—I drove south to a speck of a town called Freedom. The name sounded great for a western burg where rugged individualism continued to reign. There, I toured a plant building handmade revolvers. Freedom Arms produces guns from .22 LR up to powerful hand cannons I couldn't imagine firing made for hunting big game. Staff was knowledgeable, friendly, and helpful when I put in an order for one of their high-grade revolvers in .44 magnum for Dawson. Best three grand and change I spent as far as I was concerned. We'd missed our planned mini-vacation during spring break to have him fitted for custom made boots. Perhaps my unexpected gift would sooth any ruffled feathers.

I left Freedom with enough time to reach Rock Springs before supper. A familiar vehicle fell in behind me but far enough back I didn't notice until slowing for a speed zone. The flat green paint of a Kia SUV caught my eye because it wasn't a shade I'd have chosen. It'd followed me south before passing when I turned west at the revolver factory. Somewhere, it fell in to trail me again without me noticing. It could be coincidental—we both traveled the same direction—but I wasn't willing to chance my life to concurrence. When the speed limit increased, I floored the accelerator. Racing south at almost a hundred miles per hour, I left the trailing car far behind.

Rock Springs appeared when I could no longer ignore my stomach. I got directions on my phone to a Mexican restaurant. It was busy with a ten-minute wait to be seated. Without anything else to do, I stayed until it was my turn. The food was good and plentiful, and I ate until my stomach could bear no more. I thought seriously about a tequila sunrise but forewent one of Dawson's favorite drinks. Working on a job where firearms are used, I couldn't risk compromised senses.

Two nights and three days were spent in the southwest portion of Wyoming. Dawson worried and texted me regularly each day. It seemed his missives increased while I prowled far from Jackson. They were sometimes difficult to answer, because I spent so much time on the road. The miles I drove didn't matter. It wasn't my Suburban, nor was the gas I purchased with a government credit card. My meals and room tabs were also unlimited.

The green Kia materialized on my second day in Rock Springs while I waited for breakfast. Seated in a window booth at a mom and pop café where my rig was visible to me, I sat forward and stared out as the car idled past. The driver's head was turned from me as he—no doubt it was a man—deliberately checked out my ride.

My server brought a plate of sliced fruit, scrambled eggs, and toast as I retrieved my cell from a pocket. "Can I get you anything else?" the pretty woman asked.

I gave her my best smile. "I don't think so. Thank you."

My boss answered on the second ring. "KC."

"Woodman. Have you got eyes on me?"

"Excuse me?"

"Someone's dogging my every move. Is he one of yours?"

"Absolutely not." He seemed positive. But then, so did Manny, my one-time handler whose life ended with five of my bullets in his brain.

KC would have to be deaf not to hear the threat in my tone. "Last chance. Are you positive he's not one of yours?"

"Ariel, I understand what you're asking. We're not The Company, and I'm not your partner working against you." KC knew far more about my previous employment than he should.

"I'll give you a pass on this. Don't make me regret it."

"I repeat: it's not me, nor is it my immediate superiors. How long have you been followed?"

"A couple days. I'm in Rock Springs and picked up the tail on my way south."

"You couldn't shake him?" KC asked.

"That's why I'm calling. I ditched the man forty-eight hours ago but just watched him drive past."

I ate a slice of tomato while he took his time answering. "You're certain it's not coincidence?"

"Can't be. Same guy, same car on a back street looking at my truck in a big town."

His next words shocked even me. "Then kill him. If you consider this person a danger to you or our mission, put a bullet in his head." He said it so matter of factly that his statement took my breath away. "We're a nation of over three-hundred million, Ariel. One mistake isn't going to destroy her. Shoot the tail and call for cleanup."

No answer I could give would be constructive or positive. I ended the call and slipped the phone into my pocket. If KC sat across the table from me, I'd be tempted to do something bad and damn the consequences. I wasn't in the business of taking innocent life, deliberately or otherwise. Contemplating my boss's repugnant suggestion, I finished my entire breakfast.

Knowing it's easier to ask for forgiveness than for permission, I exited the restaurant through the kitchen over grumbles of the cooks after squaring my bill. I thought it best to find another way back to my rig and circled away from the building through employee parking to where my Suburban was visible. The green Kia was nowhere to be seen.

My phone rang while I walked. "Hi, honey," I answered. A block from where I started, some of the residences were unsavory. My plan for a wide circle was drastically reduced. "How're things at home?"

Dawson chuckled. "Good. How soon can I expect to see my beautiful wife?"

"We've been handed a setback. I've been warned to expect a possible influx of bad guys. I'm not sure if you've heard the news lately, but it seems they've been having success in Europe."

He changed from hopeful to enraged in an instant. "Goddamn it, Julia," Dawson shouted. "No more. Tell Carter you quit."

I gave him a few moments to calm. "I'd like to, but not now, my love. I've met this man and his lovely family and have broken bread with them. A part of me would die if they perished because I let them down."

"Will I even see you again?"

"Of course, you will. I've got to go now, Dawson. I'll call you later this evening."

Crossing at the end of the street, I cut back to where my ride waited. The Kia became visible as I closed in—parked at the end of the alley near the café. No wonder I couldn't see it. A man sat inside and watched.

I wasn't willing to continue working while being hunted. My suppressed Ruger lay covered on the front seat by the towel I kept handy. I retrieved it from the passenger side, closing the door and stepping away. Holding the gun under my jacket, I rounded the front of my Suburban and crossed the empty street at a sprint. Catching the tail by surprise, I tapped on the passenger window with the barrel of my gun before stepping back. He stared into the suppressed muzzle. "Open." I didn't raise my voice with the demand.

It went down perhaps six inches. "I don't have money if it's what you're looking for," he said.

"Unlock your doors and put both hands on the wheel at eleven and one." I heard the clicks of the front and rear locks and slid into the backseat. "Who do you work for?" I asked after making myself comfortable.

The man filled the seat with more left over. Muscles bulging his clothing made me remember the male outside Father Timothy's room. Wearing a long-sleeved shirt, expensive trousers, and polished shoes, my watcher appeared to be any businessman. "No one you'd know. If you're robbing me, take my wallet and phone and go."

He didn't seem as panicked as someone who feared he was being robbed would be. "Where are they?"

"On the console."

I wasn't going to reach forward and put my arm where he could grab it. "Use your right hand and pass them over your shoulder to me. Make it slow." A couple pedestrians crossed the sidewalk in front of us and didn't bother to glance in our direction. I took first the wallet and then the phone in my left. "A burner cell? Really?" It was no different than mine, likely with as little info, but I slipped it into my jacket pocket. I went through his wallet to find twenty-eight dollars and what I assumed was a fake driver's license. A single credit card bore the same name. Greg Atwell. "Okay...Greg...tell me why I should let you live?"

He shifted to where our eyes could meet in the rearview. "I've got a wife and kids. A good job and people who depend on me."

"Yet you've chosen to follow me for days. You've got to do better at convincing."

"I'll see you in jail. "You'l—"

"Strike one. You won't see anything in about thirty seconds," I warned. "Clock is ticking." I guessed KC was right. Kill the man and call for cleanup. Our eyes met as I made the decision. Apparently, he understood time was expiring.

"Marta Boyd," he said quickly. "I work for Mrs. Boyd."

"See? That wasn't so hard, was it? What does Mrs. Boyd want with little ol' me? I'm nobody."

His hands slipped to ten and two. "I don't know. My job is to watch and report."

"Report what?"

"Your whereabouts. Where you live, your daily life...who you socialize with."

His left hand slid to eight on the wheel, where his right lowered below three. "Strike two. I said eleven and one." I whispered. "I guarantee you won't like the ump's next call." His grip quickly rose to where I suggested. "Why is Mrs. Boyd interested in me? Take a few moments to consider your answer before you say the wrong thing. It's the bottom of the ninth with two out and the count full. Don't die at home plate."

"She didn't tell me, honest." He closed his eyes—I guess expecting the worst.

I didn't want to kill him. My problem was he knew too much. Nor did I want to watch over my shoulder while battling to keep Early Hollister alive. "Where you do you live, Greg Atwell?"

"New York."

"As in New York, New York?"

"Yes."

"Your car is a rental?"

"Yes."

"You've worked for Mrs. Boyd before?"

"No. This job was going to make a name for me. Make it easier to get higher paying clientele at home."

I dialed a number and put my phone on speaker. Rather than let KC answer, I broke in. "I'm having a heart-to-heart with the man I spoke to you about earlier, and I'm trying to come to a decision. His name is Greg Atwell of New York, New York. Would you offer us your suggestion again?"

"Kill him." The cold disembodied voice carried to us both. "Phone for cleanup after it's done."

"Thanks. Call you back in a few."

"Don't do it, lady. Give me the chance, and I'll leave on the first flight available."

I didn't feel good about it, but I let him walk after leaving a Walther PPK, his phone, and key fob with the promise of never returning to the west. He also seemed to take my warning to heart when I apprised him of his impending death if I saw him again. No matter the circumstances, I'd shoot first and ask questions later. I'd planned to put a bullet in his foot to get answers. Fortunately, my conversation with KC worked better.

Perhaps Marta Boyd would stop meddling after losing her employee.

Chapter XI

I drove north to the Come Horn Inn soon after leaving Greg Atwell afoot. Rather than stop and surveille on my way, I chose to regroup my thoughts in bed. First, Dawson and I carried on a constructive conversation during the trip. He needed to understand how badly I wanted to return to Salmon and never leave again. While I wasn't sure my arguments were convincing, I felt better after parking and locking up.

A fifteen-minute shower and clean sheets worked wonders. I got snuggled in with lights out by 7:30. Memories of droning tires and V8 engine dissipated.

Another four days passed while I both searched for my targets and worried about my class in Salmon. My first school year in my adopted hometown was grinding to an end while I missed most of it. The idea of tendering my resignation grew stronger each day. If I couldn't be counted on to do the job I loved, why should I expect the school to keep me on their payroll? KC's plan of leaning on the schoolboard to keep me employed seemed unreasonable. Perhaps substituting again was best for everyone. I could choose the days I was willing to work and have more time to spend with my husband. Besides, I wanted to raise my children—not leave them in daycare.

With days growing longer, my sleep got reduced. Concerned my targets might attack after dark while spring temperatures rose, I donned night vision and carried my carbine while I prowled darkened landscapes as an apex predator. I grew more irritable each day from a lack of rest. Doing my best not to take it out on Dawson when we spoke, I didn't hold back when KC called. "I think whoever is feeding you intel is full of shit. Either find help for me or do the job yourself."

"I know, I know." I was damned tired of his patronizing. Jackson was feeling more like my hometown than Salmon. "We've been busy formulating a plan but can't implement it until the latest incursion is neutralized."

At least they were thinking. I hoped he understood how close I was to giving my notice. I'd hate like hell to learn ISIS got to Hollister, but I was equally worried about my husband, our homelife, and the future. "I'm listening."

"Huh uh. Your phone isn't secured. We'll discuss it in person."

Several times driving the 77 miles on Route 189 from Jackson Hole, I stopped at Pinedale's Wrangler Café, only to come face-to-face with Hollister and his family. He and Shaye looked up at the bell over the door, and we made eye contact. Warm smiles directed my way along with a wave drew me over. "Hi," I said and scuffed the toe of a boot against the floor. "Nice to see you again...this time as sober as a Sunday school teacher."

Shaye was the first to speak. "Hello, Mrs. Woodman. Would you like to join us?" Their boy—Tryn—got his own seat, where Anna was in a highchair pulled close to her momma.

I hesitated. On one hand I wanted to learn anything I could. Yet I needed to avoid them on the other. "You should eat as a family."

"We're a family whether you sit with us or not," Early pushed the fourth chair out with a toe. "Take a load off."

They'd already ordered, and I was barely seated when their food came. Steaks and lobster tails for the adults, a hamburger for their boy, and a hotdog for the little girl. I was breaking my rule again of never getting to know those who might die.

"Would you like a moment to peruse our menu?" our server asked after she got my tablemates taken care of.

My belly growled. "What's your biggest steak?"

"We have bacon wrapped fillets as our special tonight. Six, eight, or twelve ounces."

Crap. I'd been thinking of something closer to twenty-four. "Got anything bigger?" Not only did our server's eyebrows raise, but Early and Shaye's attention pivoted from their kids.

"You're in cattle country. We've got rib eyes ranging from twelve up to forty ounces and prime rib as thick as you'd like."

"Could I get a twenty-four-ounce ribeye rare?"

Our server, a woman perhaps a few years older than me, tried to contain her smile. "Sure. A baker and steamed vegetables okay?"

"Would it be okay to trade the potato for more greens?"

"You've got it."

Early whistled quietly after she left. "Are you hungry, or do you plan to take enough home for three extra meals?"

I shrugged. "This'll be the first time I've eaten a square in forty-eight hours. Been too busy. My application for a teaching position is in, but I haven't heard back. I took a part-time job to fill the gap with a company who's employed me before."

Early looked up from his lobster. I couldn't help but grin to myself—I hoped. "A company I might know of?"

"Huh uh. From out of state."

He caught me watching when he was about to take a bite of lobster. "What?"

I shook my head as my smile grew. "It's nothing."

"Come on, spill it."

"My husband and I spent two weeks in Central America over the winter." I nodded at his crustacean. "We ate those constantly. He sometimes went through eight or ten each day, and..." I held my palms a foot apart. "...their tails were this long!"

Early looked from me to Shaye. "We're going on vacation. I don't think it's possible to get sick eating these..." He looked at the sad chunk of meat on his fork. "...but I want to try."

My steak still hissed and popped when our waitress delivered the impressive meal. Damn. I'd forgotten the size of a pound and a half slice of beef. I cut into it to check and found the chef was a master. Blood ran and I dredged a chunk of broccoli through it, the flavor combined with spices overwhelming my senses.

Halfway through my meal before looking up, I saw my appetite was sheer spectacle. Not only did another table observe me eat, but those at mine and even the server watched. I turned my attention to Shaye. "Hey, I said I was hungry."

I finished every bite and considered desert. When Early and Shaye passed, I followed suit as to not make a pig of myself. Our server returned with our bills, and Early snatched both. "Dinner's on us," he said.

"Thank you." I replied graciously and winked at Shaye. "I'd've ordered their apple pie if I'd known sooner."

Early cocked his head and looked at his wife. "I like this one."

Finished with our meal and ready to go, movement outside the door caught my attention. I recognized the man about to hold it open. "I need to use the restroom," I said quickly and stood. "Thank you for dinner." A sign for DOES rather than BUCKS pointed to a hallway. I turned the corner and got away from prying eyes in ten quick steps.

I needed to go, but the emergency exit sign at the hall end beckoned. Outside and almost free, I hurried around the front to where I could see inside. Near where I sat only moments before, a tall blonde woman with her back to me embraced Shaye before tousling the dark hair of Tryn. It wasn't until after she squatted to lift Anna before I was sure my quick identification was correct. She turned and looked toward where I watched.

I'd nearly bumped into Marta Boyd and her husband Jack.

* * *

I left Pinedale in haste for Jackson. I called Dawson the following morning, and he was no happier, so we ended our conversation on a sour note. I needed a place to practice to burn off growing frustration and hone slowly eroding skills. Contrary to the way Hollywood portrays marksmen, shooting capabilities diminish remarkably fast. I handled my handguns and carbine each day, but familiarity alone couldn't replace shots fired downrange. Nothing to do but make a call. "KC," he answered.

"Need some help," I said.

"I was about to call you. Is there trouble?"

"Not really, other than Marta Boyd came very close to finding me. What I need is a chance to practice somewhere."

"I think my information might change your mind."

"Oh?"

"We've been infiltrated. We got eight pings on our radar. We were too late in all but in one instance. We've got a guy in custody now."

"Eight? Were they together?"

"Negative. Each came over borders in different locations. Texas, Arizona, California, and Minnesota."

My mind raced. Eight enemy combatants. They traveled in groups of seven—I thought of them as animals after watching Shaye fight for Anna's life. Could it mean as many as fourteen? God, no single person could handle so many. Certainly not me on my best day. I wet suddenly dry lips. "How long ago?"

"This morning."

I could only think of Dawson. How alone he'd be. How could I have done this to the man I considered my soulmate? He would be lost without me. An epiphany struck. "Is this a first wave? One of many?"

"Not sure. We have trained professionals trying to get information. So far, he's not broken."

"Can I have a crack at it?"

Although I was serious, KC laughed. "No, we need him alive, Ariel. Don't worry, he'll eventually tell us everything he knows."

"Eventually."

He ignored my obvious jab. "You're on the clock. Do what you're best at. What can you tell me about Mrs. Boyd?"

I explained getting caught at the Pinedale eatery and dining with the Hollisters. "She and her husband were obviously interested in something. Not sure if it was me, but she looked at the window where I watched."

"She didn't see you?"

"Huh uh. It was dark outside and impossible to discern through the glare when I was eating."

"Could have been a simple coincidence. Pinedale is where her family lives. She was probably expected. Remember, the simplest explanation is usually correct."

"Yeah," I grumbled. "Except, no one mentioned she was coming. Wait until the next time she sticks her big nose where it isn't needed."

"Do not engage with her, Ariel. It's a direct order. She is not to be considered collateral damage under any circumstances. Understand?" His command was backed by a steely tone. Damn. The one woman I wouldn't mind removing from the fray, and she's hands off. "Do you understand?" he asked again. "Not a hair on her head is to be harmed."

"I understand. You'd better hope she doesn't foul what we're doing here. It'll be on you."

He sighed. "It always is. Now, get to work...you've got a job to do."

* * *

My chance to test KC's word came sooner than I imagined. Packing gear and preparing for my drive to the Green River and the Hollister home, a hard knock on my door and a shout startled me. "This is the Teton County Sheriff. Open the door!"

My heart pounded with two suppressed firearms lying on the bed and my Glock holstered beneath my arm. "Just a moment. I've got to finish dressing." My SIG carbine and Ruger handgun were quickly pushed under the bed, and I slipped into my jacket.

More bangs against my entry followed. "Now," another voice shouted. "Open this door...or we'll kick it in."

Three males and one female waited outside my room with their hands resting on gun butts when I unlocked and opened. "Yes?" I asked coolly. "How may I help you?"

The tallest wore four brass stars on each uniform collar and HORACE THIELMAN etched on a gleaming plaque over his breast pocket. "Your name?"

I had no doubt of the official nature of the demand and who wanted to know. "Ariel Woodman. What's this about, Sheriff?"

"I'm responding to a complaint." His eyes canvassed what he could see of my suite as he spoke. "Are you alone?"

"Yes. What did I allegedly do, and why is the highest law enforcement official in the county asking?"

He motioned with his fingers. "We'd like you to come to my office to answer our questions."

"Absolutely not."

"Are you refusing my request?"

"Yes, sir, I am."

"I can get an arrest warrant."

The female deputy retrieved a phone from her belt and punched in a number. "Judge Mahoney, please," she said.

"Whatever complaint brought you to my door can be easily explained." I reached for an inside pocket of my coat and unzipped it without exposing my handgun. I withdrew a badge. "This should help."

He studied it and read aloud: "US Department of Homeland Security—American Defense Shield." Thielman glared. "What the hell is the American Defense Shield? I've never heard of it." I handed him my official card showing my name, photo, and commission date. "Agent Ariel Woodman?"

I nodded. "My boss's name is on the bottom. Call Homeland Security and ask for Agent Kevin Clark."

He squinted at my ID again and handed it back to me. "Stay put until we straightened this out."

I stepped aside and gestured. "Why wait? You're welcome to come in." The female terminated her call as she entered behind the men.

My employers surprised me with their efficiency. Instead of bureaucratic red tape to wade through, Thielman was soon connected to KC.

"Agent Clark, my name is Horace Thielman, Teton County Sheriff. I received a complaint about a woman who is now passing herself off as one of yours. She carries a badge and commission card... Ariel Woodman...no, we wanted to contact you first." I offered the sheriff and deputies my brightest smile. None returned it. "Yes, I understand. Uh huh...an hour? Sure, I'll be there. Look forward to meeting you,

Agent Clark." He ended the call and handed my credentials back. "Who in the hell are you?" he asked.

"Another cog in the machine like you, Sheriff." I held my coat wide to replace my identification in the inside pocket, allowing him to see my handgun. "Nothing more...nothing less."

"We were advised to back off and to offer our assistance only if it's asked for...you're working a federal case. Shouldn't you or your boss have contacted my office first? Sharing information is beneficial to both of our agencies."

I shrugged. "Not my call. Instructions I received were to follow a tip. I'm sure Agent Clark will explain later."

"Homeland Security planned an exercise at Pinedale in the next county some weeks back," Thielman said. "Did you take part?"

I recalled what was detailed as a snap Homeland Security drill. A boy or small woman was reported to have been involved. "I'm not at liberty to discuss operational details of Homeland Security. Besides, you haven't answered my questions. What am I alleged to have done, and why is the high sheriff of the county himself asking?"

Thielman gave a wry smile. "I'm not at liberty to discuss operational details."

My expression was equally frosty. "Then, I guess I'll have my boss or higher up ask you."

* * *

Jackson was in my rearview within the hour. It was a sunny day without a cloud I could see. Still cool for early April, but only time would warm the soil after such a cold winter. I wore a pair of Oakley's most expensive wraparound sunglasses. I didn't pay so much because I had an expense account. They simply fit my face and eyes best. Not too dark as so many are but keeping the glare from reaching around the edges. More than once Dawson told me how professional I looked wearing them. The thought of my husband made me fish my phone from a pocket. He picked up on the first ring. "To what do I owe the pleasure of your call, beautiful lady?"

His heartfelt words and tender tone drove a knife into my chest. "I needed to hear your voice and tell you how much I love you, honey."

"Are you okay?"

"Yeah..." I trailed off not knowing what to say.

His normal rumble intensified. "Julia? What aren't you telling me?" He was obviously alarmed, although I didn't sense panic.

"There's not much to say, except I needed to tell you how much I love you. I will until the day I die."

"Goddamn it. Come home, Jules. Come back right now."

"Soon. Very soon."

I hated to hear him plead. My man was one who dictated terms, not groveled. "Please, Jules. Don't make me beg."

"You don't have to. It should be any day now when I'm finished here."

"You've got intel?"

"Yeah, KC promises this'll be it. They've come up with a plan to end the attacks, but we've got to neutralize this group first."

"Group? How many?" Dawson's alarm could be felt more than heard.

"Not sure." God, I hated to lie. "Probably one or two like the last time."

"Come home. Please."

"Soon as I can, Dawson. I love you. Talk to you later." I ended the call before he could hear me weep. I wiped my cheeks and continued my journey.

The day got spent watching the log house from high on the mountain near Union Pass. Glassing was difficult at such long distances. Even with a cool breeze, heat waves distorted the images. Finally, switching from my binoculars to spotting scope set on low magnification, I could make out mule deer feeding on the hill behind their home and not much more.

A nap before dusk left me rejuvenated. I idled down the mountain and drove past their house forty-five minutes later. Already dark, I parked over a knoll and prepared to continue my vigil. Armed with my

Sig Sauer carbine, I slid extra ammunition in each rear pocket. I could feel my butt moving them as I walked when the magazines rubbed my low back. No matter, I wasn't sure how many nor when I would face an impossible number. Better to be safe than sorry.

Light from a waxing moon lit the landscape when I switched on my night vision goggles. It was an awkward struggle to mate them to my binoculars. With little to do but watch, I wandered where my feet and curiosity took me. A ravine behind their home led west between two ridges. I guessed it drained water from both hillsides.

A bobcat hunted any game he could catch. He stalked and killed two small creatures I assumed were mice after he chewed and swallowed them whole. The cat avoided a small herd of mule deer does and fawns, choosing to circle and pursue other prey elsewhere. Burnt Mountain lay to the northwest where winter snow finally melted. Swinging my binoculars to the east, I could make out the cold ridges of the Wind River Range. They were rugged—I'd explored them online using Google Earth. They called me in the same fashion the winds from my own River of no Return Wilderness whispered my name.

My phone rang shortly before daybreak. In my truck and considering options for badly needed shuteye, I answered the moment I read the name. "Woodman."

"I think we're weeding them out," KC said. "HS identified and arrested another six overnight in Florida, New York, LA, and Seattle. They're probing every border or port of entry for weakness and hoping to exploit it. Be aware we're doing what we can...but stay alert."

"You haven't learned an approximate number?"

"Working on it. Thus far, we've received conflicting accounts. We hope to triangulate stories and zero in on a realistic figure. I know it's difficult but hang tough. Have you got anything to report?"

"I spent the afternoon and overnight near Hollister's home. All was quiet. I'm leaning toward catching a few hours of sleep in the back of my Suburban. Did you speak with Thielman?"

He chuckled. "Sure did. I learned Marta Boyd pointed him in your direction. It explains the sheriff busting out of his office to handle it himself. I imagine the guy tailing you to Rock Springs called with any information he learned."

"Bastard. I hope he didn't get on the plane. I told him the next time we met would be his last moments alive."

"He boarded it all right. HS got tipped to keep an eye on him. He's home working as we speak."

"Will Thielman back off?"

"He promised to. If not, call immediately. I've got superiors who make me look like a nice guy. They'll make him wish he never went into politics."

"I hinted as much and hope you're right. We don't need anyone getting between me and whatever storm is blowing in."

"Don't hesitate to contact me if you need backup, you hear? I've got both fixed wing and rotary aircraft at my disposal."

I remembered the way he initially reached out to contact me with a show of force, using what my husband explained was an armed AH-64 Apache helicopter. His ham-fisted way of impressing us and getting my attention nearly made me lose control. Facing twenty soldiers, the fear of Dawson losing his life stayed my hand. "I remember," I said in a flat tone.

He ignored my obvious jab. "Stay in contact." Dead air followed.

I chose to drive to the bottom of the hill and a few hundred yards toward the main highway. There, where I could spy on the cutoff leading to the Hollisters, I found a nice area to park near the road overlooking the river. Morning brightened as the sun rose, while I inflated my mattress in the back and lay my sleeping bag atop. Afraid I might miss something, I ate a huge apple and chewed store-bought jerky and struggled to stay awake. Finally, tired and useless to anyone, I lowered the two windows facing the gravel thoroughfare. Vehicles would alert me as they passed. Crawling into my makeshift bed, I was asleep before my head touched the pillow.

Only seven hours fitful shuteye left me weary. I was grumpy but alert. Although a half dozen vehicles roused me from sleep to look, only one of them turned up the hill. I'd fallen back into slumber after I recognized the pickup of the rancher and his sidekick.

I changed socks and undershirt before stepping outside. A cool breeze rushing down the river raised goosebumps, forcing me to shrug into my coat. I filled my coffeepot with fresh grounds and water from a jug and put my single burner camp stove atop a round of pine someone cast aside. Choosing another large apple and a hard-fleshed pear, I took my time eating and sipping water until my java perked.

My belly no longer complaining, and with a filled travel mug and thermos, I idled past the log house I shadowed before turning around. Perhaps a trip to Pinedale and then back to Jackson were in order. I opened a small bag of chips, but a queasy stomach made me stop near where I spent the night. Afraid I might throw up, I got out only moments before retching. Chunks of fruit and acidic coffee hurt as they came up. I couldn't blame my meal, although I didn't wash it before eating. Perhaps it was somehow contaminated.

I stopped at the grocery where Shaye and Anna nearly lost their lives. After tossing away what I bought earlier, I purchased more inside along with any other item that caught my eye. An eclectic combination of more fruit, bread, potato salad, jerky, a pound of sliced turkey, and artificial crab filled my basket. Last but not least was another bag of my favorite chips.

An hour of driving and surveilling the main drag netted me nothing. I drove another thirty minutes southward before I changed my mind and retraced my travels. Two hours later—munching fake crab meat—I swung through Hoback and south to the Endicotts' place but identified both fishing the banks of the Snake River below the highway. I got a good look at them as I leaned over the guardrail and vomited. Christ! If it wasn't a foodborne illness, I couldn't afford to catch a virus at such a critical phase in my hunt.

With little time left if I was to reach Hollister's place before dark, I forewent continuing to Jackson and fueled in Hoback instead. As luck would have it, an SUV bearing *Teton County Sheriff* on its doors parked next to me. The female who called for an arrest warrant against me lowered her window. "I thought I'd tell you if you haven't heard...the order came down to assist you in any way we can. Got a radio?"

I shook my head. "Huh uh. Just my cell."

"Let me give you my number and Sheriff Thielman's, too."

It took me a bit to get to contacts on my phone. "Okay, I'm ready."

"My name is Mary Ratched, and the number is..." She saw me staring slack-jawed and wide-eyed.

I couldn't stop my grin. "No way!"

She smiled back. "Should I be a nurse at a mental institution rather than a deputy?"

Dawson's nickname while he cared for me after getting wounded was Nurse Ratched. We had a lot of fun with it. "Either that or share the identical moniker I call my spouse." I hastened to explain. "Nurse Ratched is the nickname I gave my husband the first time he cared for me after I got wounded."

She laughed. "It's what I call my husband whenever I get sick. Although, in my case, he really is a Ratched."

I got their numbers before we parted. Mary was a smart woman and dedicated to her job. She'd been a sheriff's deputy almost fifteen years and loved every day at work. Not so long before, she would've gladly arrested me or worse.

Another two days of watching netted me nothing. HS intercepted another suspected ISIS fighter, but KC admitted those being interrogated hadn't broken. With ten enemy fighters in custody, he assured me one would soon break leading to a cascade of information. Vomiting sporadically, I finally returned to Jackson for a long night of sleep and to wash five days of stench from my body. A bag of soiled clothing was given to room service with their promise it would be available before I left in the morning.

It wounds my heart to admit home was the furthest thought from my mind. Not only Jake and work, even Dawson was rarely considered. He didn't call nor text while I focused on an attack, intent on stopping one before it began. Nor did I attempt to contact him. My center of attention was on one thing only.

A long shower helped relax me. I let the water pound my neck and upper back before I stepped out. Chairs propped under my suite and bathroom doorknobs helped to keep me safe, along with my work gun under a towel. After dressing for bed, a knock on the door was a welcome sound. A hamburger and bowl of soup ordered before my shower was delivered. I made myself comfortable at the dinette and watched the news as I ate. While the fight over building a border wall raged, nothing was mentioned of apprehended terrorists. It made wonder as I mulled what little news was actually reported—did Americans really want to be so sheltered from the real world? One where wolves actually hid and sometimes came through what we considered doors safe from outside forces? The little time I spent with Homeland Security and the American Defense Shield opened my eyes to lurking evil even I couldn't imagine.

Ten hours of unbroken sleep left me refreshed. Not sure when I would get another, I enjoyed a second shower and dressed in clean clothes. Loathe to leave my beautiful room, a last look was afforded it before closing the door. Would I live to return for my things?

I called KC on my drive southeast to the Green River. "Yeah?" Although alert, sleepiness in his tone made me realize he needed rest the same as all of us.

"Any news?"

"Oh...uh...no." He sounded disoriented.

"Is Hollister still alive?"

"Hope so. I've heard nothing on my end. Do you have something to report?"

"No. I spent the night in Jackson. First time I haven't been surveilling throughout the night. I've been afraid he might get hit while I'm getting some rest."

His voice rose. "You've gone without sleep since the last time we spoke?"

"I've been getting naps in the truck. A few unbroken hours here and there."

"You're going to kill yourself, Ariel. ISIS won't have to do it."

"It isn't like you've given me any help. If I'm asleep, there's no one to keep watch."

"Pretend you're human, Ms. Woodman. We're not infallible, nor can we be everywhere at once. I'm expecting you to do your best, not be perfect. Do you understand me?'"

My turnoff was coming up. "As long you're working on a solution, I'm going to do my best to save this guy's life."

He sighed loudly. "Go ahead and give it all you have, but don't kill yourself doing it. Do you understand? There'll be other missions as important or more so after this. We need you, Ariel. Your country needs you."

Yeah, fat chance, I thought to myself after ending our call. The moment this job was finished, I was done working for the government.

Chapter XII

I intended to set up surveillance on the road leading to Union Gap. From there, I could see downslope onto the home and property of Early and Shaye. I thought of them more as people rather than a job since dining with them a second time. They became as human as my own small family after getting to know them—no longer faceless targets for our nation's enemies. To be a part of Shaye's terror while she fought to save Anna was to observe the young mother in her most primal form. I could not, would not fail in my mission.

A glint caught my eye. Someone was parked above where I normally set up on the graveled road. Attaching the window mount of my spotting scope while stopped along the Green River, I was unable to identify the truck. If someone were seated inside, I couldn't see through the raised window and reflection. With my first plan stymied, my alternative was to idle past the Hollister driveway.

Lazy smoke rose from their chimney. Although the days warmed, there was a chill in the spring air. With no movement outside the home, and any vehicles either gone or parked inside the garage, I could find little to watch. Turning around, I retraced my way to where I camped along the river. There, I could watch anyone take or leave the spur they lived on.

I'd brought a box filled with complimentary snacks from the Come Horn Inn lobby. Settling in for the long haul, I opened a bag of chips. Before I could eat one, a whiff caused my stomach to churn. Throwing the Suburban door wide, I scrambled out quick enough to lose my breakfast on the ground. My retching stopped only after my stomach was emptied. *Jesus, don't let me get sick before the storm catches me.* No way could I do my job properly if taken down by a bug.

The rig sitting on the road leading to Union Gap was visible from where I parked. Though I nodded off from time to time, I woke and ran my field glasses over the truck and nearby terrain. Perhaps it broke down and was waiting to be towed. However, an extended cab pickup could be packed with six or more men. Best not to dismiss it. I felt the enemy closing on me as if the crushing fingers of a giant hand.

Holding a depleted roll of toilet paper, I stepped out to use natures bathroom. Before I could walk over the bank behind a copse of brush and pines, the sound of tires on the graveled thoroughfare stopped me. A Jeep came around the corner before I could blend in. It immediately slowed and stopped next to my rig when the driver saw me. "Hey, I know you, lady!" Early Hollister leaned forward and peered around his aging Brittany copilot. "What in the hell are you doing out here again? You spend another late night closing a Pinedale bar?"

I strolled to his passenger window with the roll held behind. "Hey, girl." I let his dog smell my hand before carefully scratching her ears. An infected bite wouldn't do. "Fancy meeting you again," I said to Early.

"What brings you out this way?"

"Sight-seeing. I don't get tired of exploring God's country."

"It's beautiful," he agreed. "Got plans for this afternoon?"

His question caught me by surprise while I was worried about keeping my lies straight. "Oh...I...I..."

"Good enough for me," he said. "We're burning steaks and chicken on the barbeque today. You might as well bring your appetite and help us eat. I've seen the way you can shovel food away."

"I don't want to put you out," I said, looking for a way to avoid more interaction with the couple. "Besides, I don't have anything to bring."

"Naw, it's all right. You and your hollow leg are enough. Believe me, there'll be more food than we could eat in a week."

"You're certain I won't be a burden?"

White teeth gleamed in the shadowed interior. "Yeah, I'm sure. Mount up and follow me home. Shaye'll be happy to see you."

I called KC the moment the door closed, and I started my rig. "You got anything to report?" he asked.

"Yeah, I'm driving to the Hollister place. They invited me to a barbeque, and I couldn't get out of it. Any news on your end?"

"Yes and no. Our interrogators have gotten nowhere. From what I understand, our prisoners only smile."

"Boss, bring me one. I'm serious. Get one to me today." I'd started down the road I found myself on after taking two men apart with bullets and they sang like birds. I could do it again.

"As much as I'd like to, it's impossible. Once they're remanded into custody, we have to follow specific rules. None of them make our jobs easier."

"Fine." I put the Suburban in gear and took the left branch where the road split at Tosi Creek. "Don't put the next one you intercept on the books. Fly him directly here."

"Look, I understand—"

"No..." I broke in. "...you *don't* understand. I need answers, and I need them now. I'll do what a bunch of limp wristed men seem unwilling to do."

"Doesn't work that way, Ariel. You're a team player now...not a lone wolf."

"Seems like my team is supposed to play blindfolded without suiting up or knowing what game is being played. The rest of you sit in your climate-controlled offices and wait to see if I won or got steamrolled by the other side."

"We need to meet. You'll understand if I can explain the bigger picture. If you dispose of this group and we implement our plan, it's over. You can return to Salmon and play little Suzy Homemaker, wiping the noses and butts of your students." His voice rose. "I know who and what you are. No one does what you do without loving their job. You'll get bored, and I'll watch you jump at the next one offered. I've seen your drive and excitement, Ariel. You can't turn it off."

I gave serious consideration to KC's comments before answering halfway up the hill to intersect with Early's driveway. "Forget meeting with me again. There's a good chance you won't leave it." I ended the call before I could offer more threats. One thing I was sure of—my time working for the government was coming to a rapid close.

Tryn and Anna played in the front yard when I came over the rise. When they saw me, their little legs carried them inside as fast as they could. Early and Shaye appeared on the porch moments later, while I parked in front of their garage nearest the house. I waffled over stuffing my work gun inside my jeans. In the end, I left it on the seat next to my carbine covered by the towel.

Shaye's first question caught me unaware. "When did you get the Suburban? Weren't you driving a black Tundra last time?"

I froze for a moment while searching for a plausible answer. "My husband needed it. I drove home and swapped him."

Like Dawson with his Colt, I wasn't sure I'd seen Early without an old thumb buster revolver on his belt. I wondered if they were kindred spirits and how they'd react to the other. The military record of the gunfighter facing me didn't matter. I'd put my man up against anyone on earth, no matter who Father Timothy considered the most dangerous. "I hope you've already eaten," Shaye said. "We only have a couple hundred pounds of meat."

I laughed. "Guess I shouldn't have made such a pig of myself."

She took my hands in hers, pulling me close to kiss each cheek. I'd seen their family welcome each other in the same manner, but it was all I could do not to pull away. While I've never considered myself aloof, such a greeting was outside my comfort zone. "Nonsense. You were hungry. Besides..." She squeezed my shoulder for effect. "...you could stand a little extra to cover your bones."

"I've always been skinny." We stopped where I could see bloodstains from the first ISIS member I killed on their porch. I smiled at the memory, remembering how one of the most feared terrorists met his fate.

Shaye led me inside, while Early fussed over the barbeque. Their house was larger and more open than I remembered. Her kitchen appeared to be filled with food—the table and counters covered. She pointed to a chair with a pair of tongs. "Make yourself comfortable."

"Good Lord. Are you cooking for an army? Even I'm not going to help you make much of an inroad!"

Her back was to me. "We invited a few friends over. I hope you don't mind."

Shit. It wouldn't do to be exposed to their family and friends again. I needed to look for a way out. "No problem. I won't be able to stay long anyway."

Shaye turned. "Oh, I'd like to spend time together. We don't often get company."

"Is there something I can help you with? My husband does most of our cooking, but I know my way around a kitchen."

"Sure! We've got vegetables to cut up. I hope roasted is okay."

We spent an hour working and talking before their first guests arrived. We heard boots on the porch before a door opened. Ionella Endicott entered in the kitchen with her arms loaded. "We brought pies!" she said. "Two apple and a couple mixed berry from the freezer."

The beautiful woman was well along in her pregnancy. I thought she was expecting the first time I saw her. She set the pies on the counter and wiped a forearm across her brow, where I saw a curious mark before her bangs fell back into place. It looked as if a blemish or scar had been removed.

Shaye came to my side after kissing her friend. "Nellie, this is Ariel Woodman. She's a new friend."

Ionella took my hand. "We've met. I can't say she's a regular, but Ariel often dines at the Upchuck. How are you?" Her grip was strong and her shake firm.

"Good. I never noticed how pregnant you are. How far along?"

She gave her stomach a familiar rub—one all pregnant women seem to do. "About twenty-two weeks."

"Do you know if it's a boy or girl?"

"We don't care. Russ told the doctor to surprise us."

Nellie and Shaye compared maternity stories while I worked and absorbed their chatter. There wasn't much I could add having never been pregnant, but I enjoyed being a part of normal conversation where the death of a bad guy wasn't being planned. We were three women discussing the joys of bringing life into the world rather than ending it. I finished my tasks before sitting with Ionella.

The door opened and closed, while boisterous laughter from the porch heralded another arrival. I knew her immediately. Christ, I needed to find an excuse to leave.

I'd never spoken to the tall willowy blonde, but knew her from reports and saw from afar. Shaye wiped wet hands on her apron before she stretched high on toes to greet the new arrival. "Anna, this is Ariel Woodman. We've gotten to know her through an odd series of events. Ariel, meet Anna Boyd."

I got the same treatment from her as from Shaye—a kiss to either cheek. "It's nice to meet you," she said. "Are you new to the area?"

"Yes. My husband and I are thinking of relocating."

A slam of the door and heavy bootsteps preceded Early and Russell. "Time to put the meat on the grill, my dear," Early said.

Shaye handed him a cookie sheet with two butterflied chickens already seasoned and another to Russell. "Holler when they're done and you're ready for steaks, hamburgers, and hotdogs." She turned to me when both men disappeared. "You're in for a treat. Early's chicken is amazing."

I found sitting and talking to three women about my age a refreshing change. At home, Robin was my closest friend, but our common past sometimes made for awkward moments. Some topics weren't to be broached. Not so with the trio with whom I found myself chatting. All were mothers or a mother-to-be—something I hoped was in my future. To listen to them discuss their lives, children, and common friends relaxed and drew me in. I answered when addressed and nodded my head at the proper times but simply took in the atmosphere. It was easy to see what I longed for my future to be. These women were the best of friends no matter their social standings. I knew from reports that Russell and Ionella worked hard for every penny they earned, where Early and Shaye were comfortable with their business. Only Emerson and Anna were wealthy with the money she brought into their marriage. Even then, Emerson toiled in their orchard.

More voices when the front door opened and alerted us. Anna looked at Shaye. "Are they here?"

A female's voice with a husky timbre set me on edge. Unable to escape my predicament, I scooted forward on my seat ready to bolt. Before I could make up my mind, Marta Boyd entered the kitchen carrying Shaye's daughter, Anna. I tried to make myself small, hoping the older woman wouldn't notice. After hitching the child to a hip, she kissed her daughter, Shaye, and even Ionella before spying me. Marta froze, unable and unwilling to believe I sat in her cousin's kitchen. "Jack," she called. "Jack!" Her voice lifted before the front door opened again.

I heard his footsteps as he hurried to the kitchen. "Whatcha need, woman? Early isn't ready...says he's got almost an hour before the hamburg..." He stopped when he saw where his wife stared.

Shaye couldn't help but notice Marta and Jack's reaction as did Ionella. Anna looked from her parents to me, realizing something was amiss. Shaye stepped forward to make introductions before the atmosphere could become openly hostile. "Marta, Jack, this is a good friend of Early's and mine," she said firmly.

Marta stepped in my direction away from her husband. "Ariel Woodman. We have met." Her tone wasn't combative, nor was it friendly. I recognized a hint of an accent in her precise manner of speech—obviously English was a second language.

I rose to my feet and shifted my shoulders. Best to have my holster where I could reach the gun under my coat easiest. While I wasn't an enemy to these people, only Marta and Jack felt my appearance constituted a threat, however vague. I hoped they hadn't learned what I represented and cringed inwardly when holding out my right hand. It was too far away from the easiest protection I carried. "Mrs. Boyd. I'm sorry we didn't get a chance to speak long at our last meeting," I said coolly. I'll be damned if I was going to show fear no matter who I faced.

Her grip was strong and sure. "I thought you had left town. In fact, I was certain you were gone."

"No, ma'am. Too much going on for me to leave. Why, even the sheriff of Teton County couldn't run me off." Ionella and Shaye laughed with me. I shifted to Marta's husband and offered my hand. "You must be Jack." His grip was tighter than I was comfortable with but not enough to injure.

"I am," he said. "Nice to have a formal meeting. I've heard quite a bit about you."

Alarm bells clanged wildly in my mind as he released me. Did his wife dig deep enough to know more than she should? Obscene wealth could open many doors. "All good, I hope."

His chuckle wasn't friendly. "Remains to be seen, I reckon."

I remembered something Dawson once told me. "You should know that things are never what they seem," I said.

We were at a stalemate when the door opened again and we heard claws scratching for purchase, followed by the screams of children. The Hollisters' Brittany ran into the kitchen with four children giving chase. One, Anna's son, a little boy of perhaps five or six ran into me and fell to his bottom. "Sowwy," he said.

I automatically squatted and lifted him to his feet. "It's all right. You're not hurt, are you?"

Suddenly shy, he drew back to stand next to his Grandpa Jack and shook his head, a finger going into a nostril. Anna pulled it away. "Keep your hands away from your nose, Little Jack."

His name made sense. I stayed crouched at his eye level. "Are you named after your grandpa?" The blond boy nodded. "It's a good name," I said. "Will you grow up to be as strong as him?"

Little Jack finally grinned and made a muscle with one arm. "Stwonga," he said.

I stood during the laughter following his proclamation. The dog wasn't as cornered as the children playing thought she was, and Little Jack followed his sister and friends screaming out the front after the poor girl. Something told me the pooch enjoyed the chase as much as

174

the kids loved the pursuit. Moments later, men from outside tromped in. "Ready for the meat and to roast the vegetables," Early said.

We sat at two picnic tables on the long porch. Before it was time to eat, I took a few moments to walk to the end where I shot the second man. As with the stain near the front door, it seemed impossible two murderers lost their lives while hoping to kill this beautiful family. A cool breeze meant I could keep my jacket zipped and gun hidden from prying eyes.

Shaye was right. Early's chicken tasted incredible. She, Anna, and I sat with the children, while Nellie and Marta ate with the men. I deliberately avoided eye contact with the older woman. No sense in a simple glance being misconstrued as a challenge. I wanted to eat and run. The less I was around the formidable tycoon, the better. Marta learning her efforts didn't result in my arrest or expulsion from the county was all the enjoyment I needed.

I learned Anna's daughter's name was Lola. "You have a very old and pretty name," I told her. "Were you named after someone?"

Blonde like her parents and younger brother, the young girl nodded. "Yes, ma'am," she said. "After my dad's grandmother. My middle name, too. Violet," she added.

"What grade are you in?"

"Fourth."

"You're ten years old?" She nodded, but it was hard to imagine. The girl was tall for her age, well spoken, and poised. Pretty like her mother and grandmother, she would someday be a stunning young woman

"Do you have children?" Anna asked.

I shook my head. "No, but we hope to start our family very soon."

"Have you been married long?" I could almost see the ears of Jack and Marta straining to hear our conversation.

"Two years in August."

"I understand your husband farms in Oregon?" I nodded and scraped a healthy pile of roasted vegetables onto my plate. "Where do you live?"

A gust of wind blew hair into my face and I pushed it aside, hoping any stray blonde tresses stayed hidden. "Astoria. It's at the mouth of the Colombia River. We can watch ships traveling on it from the windows of our house."

"What's his name?"

"Dawson..." I almost blurted Pelletier until I caught myself.

"What kind of farming is done near the ocean? Anna asked. "Surely not root crops. Oats? Corn? Soy?"

My lie was easy to tell, if not to stomach. "Cranberries. His family have owned bogs for generations."

Shaye's head cocked in confusion. "I don't understand. I thought you told me he was retired?"

Crap. Falsehoods were beginning to come back to bite me. "He's mostly stepped back. His younger sister runs the operation now while he slowly makes an exit."

Although not planning to, I ate until my middle felt distended. At least I didn't get sick again, something I worried about. Perhaps the virus ran its course. A girl could hope. When Shaye got ready to clear our table of dishes, I stood to help. Most were paper plates and cups, but platters, bowls, and silverware needed washing. She protested, saying I was company, but it gave me a chance to repay before leaving.

We returned to the porch to check for a last load only to find Anna bringing it. The men were already making themselves comfortable in deck chairs against the log walls. Marta stopped me before I could return inside or leave. "Walk with me," she said.

"I really have to be going."

"Can I come?" Lola asked.

"You can give me a few minutes from your busy schedule," Marta told me. She turned to Lola. "I'm sorry, but this is private between adults, honey. We'll be back soon."

I was sure all eyes followed us as we hiked up the ridge. Marta stood almost a foot taller than me, and I felt more the quaking student than teacher. Far off was Burnt Mountain, and neither of us spoke nor stopped until we topped a rise. For a woman nearing sixty, she was in amazing shape.

Marta stared into the high, craggy peaks of the Wind River Mountains before turning to me. "Do you love your family?" I returned her gaze without flinching or answering. "Do you?" she asked again.

"My family is dead," I said flatly, "with the exception of my husband."

Her brow knit. "Your parents and any siblings are deceased?"

"Yes."

"You loved them?"

"You ask a stupid question. Of course, I did."

"You love your husband and feel strongly about his family?"

"Obviously." My mouth twisted with distaste for her questions.

"I also love my family. Nothing on earth is more important than blood. Not money, possessions, nor the adoration of others. Nothing." I dipped my chin in response. "You killed the women behind the restaurant." Her statement wasn't a question. "The men and women with you were officials or law enforcement. Yet somehow you did not fit...were not like them...and disappeared soon after. I saw it in your eyes when you aimed your gun at me. Where others were doing their jobs, you were different. You were there to kill. Your finger was on the trigger, and you wanted to pull it. I watched as you aimed at a spot on my head to put a bullet. Only the man who demanded I be arrested stopped you."

Her rendition wasn't entirely accurate, but I would neither agree nor disagree. "My job was finished when you appeared."

"What exactly is your occupation?"

"Money you've spent trying to put your nose where it isn't needed and getting nowhere should tell you all you need to know."

"I don't understand."

"Nor should you. Stay out of my business."

"Mrs. Woodman, I suggest—"

"Mrs. Boyd, quit suggesting. Cease trying to understand. Stop telling me what I should or should not do. Stay out of my way. The less I see or hear of you, the better off we'll be. Your private eye was nearly sent home in a box, and you'd have been directly responsible."

"You have entered my family's life. I observed you watching us. Then, a woman dies by your hand a short time later wearing a dynamite vest. I don't believe in coincidences."

"I'm not at liberty to discuss operational details."

"Then you do work for law enforcement or the government. It would explain why Sheriff Thielman didn't take action against you."

I turned away from Marta, finished with our conversation and ready to leave before pausing to face her again, our eyes locking. "I'm willing to offer a suggestion and little else. If you want to save the lives of your family and friends, put them onboard one of your jets. Fly them to..." Where? Europe left them more vulnerable, even South America and Australia weren't safe from the scourge of ISIS. "...fly them to Alaska. Find an obscure location and disappear. I'll make sure word is sent when it's safe to return."

She blinked and frowned while assimilating my counsel, trying to make sense of the warning. "You expect me to believe we are all in danger from someone other than you?"

"I've said all I'm going to and far more than I should have. However, don't make the same mistake you did when hiring a PI to tail me."

I didn't care whether she followed or not. Our conversation had ended, and I left Marta behind on my way back to the house. At the corner of the log home, I glanced behind to see her where I left her. "Where's Yaya?" Lola halted a few steps away.

"She's enjoying the scenery," I said. "It's so beautiful from up there."

Jack passed me without a glance, hustling in the direction of his wife. Not wishing to run for my Suburban and drive away, I hurried inside to tell my new friends goodbye.

Shaye was the first to express her sorrow at my departure. "Can't you stay longer? We haven't cut into Nellie's pies."

"I hadn't planned to be out so late. It's past time to return home."

Getting hugged by the much taller Anna was reminiscent of Robin's embraces but without the overflowing bosom to contend with. Nellie was just as friendly. All three strolled outside with me, trying to make a lunch date. Movement in my peripheral vision caught my eye. Jack led Marta by at least a hundred yards. He pointed to me standing at the porch edge. "Stop her," he shouted.

Emerson came to his feet where he'd been sitting with Early and Russell. "What?" he hollered back.

"Woodman. Stop her."

I damned near turned and ran. The only reason I didn't was to learn the reason behind Jack's anger. "Ariel?" Shaye was pulled away by Early as Emerson's enormous mitt closed around my neck and upper back.

"Take your hand off me," I demanded quietly as Jack closed.

The elder Boyd stopped at the bottom of the stairs while I seethed at getting manhandled. "This woman isn't who she pretends to be. She's a danger to us all."

Anna came to stand next to me. "What's going on?"

"Marta admitted she saw this...this woman's handiwork," he sputtered.

"Jack?" Marta called as she jogged. "No, Jack."

Whether he was aware or not, Emerson's hand squeezed tighter. "I suggest you take your hand off me," I whispered. "You won't get another warning." I pressed the tip of the razor-sharp mini tanto I carried against his thigh, feeling the threads of his jeans part. A hard jab would sever his femoral artery.

"Do it, Em," Marta panted when she reached Jack's side. "She will kill you."

Pressure let off as he took his hand away. "This woman isn't who she seems," Jack said to the group before he looked at me. "I want you out of here and don't come back, you hear? Out of Jackson and Wyoming all together. I see you again, I'll kill you, understand?"

Whispers and scuffles alerted me to Nellie chasing the children inside. The door closed before I spoke. "You have no idea what you're doing," I said while deliberately holstering my knife.

"I don't need to hear more. Marta told me." Jack gestured toward the hill. "I know what happened behind the Upchuck." He shook her arm off while he spoke. "We're aware you stay at the Come Horn Inn in room fifty-six. Pack your shit and git."

I mulled a response before answering his challenge. "I imagine it's a bit more comfortable than the cave you live in." His eyebrows rose in surprise. "Helluva door you have on it."

He accepted my provocation by mounting the stairs only to be held back by Marta. "No, Jack. Not here...not now," she said. "Allow her to leave."

"Not anytime," I said. Jesus, these people were stupid. I turned to Early who stood with a protective arm around Shaye and pointed. "Ever noticed that before?" My finger jabbed at the bloodstained plank in front of their picture window. "Best figure it out before these two..." I jabbed a thumb over my shoulder. "...get you killed."

Marta pulled Jack away as I skipped down the stairs only to hear Emerson's exclamation. "Shit, she cut me. I'm bleeding!"

"Serves you right, Emerson Boyd." Shaye's voice was close, and I turned at her touch. Early divided his attention between his wife and the spot on his porch. He no longer trusted me—none of them did—and I couldn't blame him. Not after Marta and Jack's reaction. "Tell me they're wrong. Explain that it's all a big misunderstanding. Please?"

She and I had connected in the brief time we spend together. The young woman's pleading undertone was clear. "They're wrong, and it's all a misunderstanding." I sighed. "Unfortunately, I can't tell you why. Only that I have nothing but your best interests at heart."

I noted Early's hand close to the butt of his revolver. I'd learned it belonged to his grandfather who carried it before him. Shaye frowned. "You mean it's all been a lie? You aren't a teacher?"

Finally, I could tell a truth. "Yeah," I grinned. "I'm a third-grade schoolmarm. My students are wondering where I am."

"Please." Marta left Jack with a hand cautioning him to stay. "Make us understand. Show me where I'm wrong."

I shrugged. "I can't. I can only affirm you couldn't be more mistaken."

"Then..." Marta shook her head and shrugged. "...I guess we're done here."

Shaye plucked at my coat sleeve. "Can't you do something?"

Marta's gaze softened a little when I met it. "There's only one thing I can try." My phone was inside a coat pocket, and I drew it out, punched speed dial, and put it on speaker.

KC answered immediately. "Didn't expect to hear from you so soon, Mrs. Woodman. Besides, I thought you planned to kill me the next time we met?"

Chapter XIII

I grimaced at his declaration and wished I hadn't switched my cell to speaker. "Big problems, KC. Need assistance ASAP."

His joking tone changed immediately. "Assets are on standby awaiting your orders."

"We're on speakerphone with Marta Boyd standing next to me. I need your explanation as to who we are and then perhaps speak to her? Otherwise—" I trailed off.

"Who am I conversing with?" Marta asked. "I recognize your voice."

"Agent Kevin Clark with the Department of Homeland Security. How may I help you?"

"I'm going to let you explain to Mrs. Boyd, Agent Clark." I handed my government issued phone to her after switching it to single user.

Marta strolled away while I unlocked my truck. Shaye looked first at Early before glancing at Marta easing up the incline toward the road. "I don't understand," she said.

"Nor should you. I blew it. This's a royal screwup I never should have allowed to happen."

"Let what happen?" she asked.

I leaned against my rig when I saw Early closing the distance. His look told me everything I needed to know. "It's me, isn't it?" he asked.

My shrug didn't put him at ease. Instead of the easygoing man I'd shadowed far too long, his eyes didn't stop roving. With him suddenly on edge, I could see the warrior he'd once been. "Not my call," I said.

"Reckon I always knew this day would come. When did HS learn?"

"Mrs. Woodman?" Marta hustled toward us. "Agent Clark would like a word." She returned my cell and fumbled for her own.

I took it to press against my ear. "Ariel."

"Intel came in while I spoke with Mrs. Boyd. They're suggesting as few as four are headed your way or as many as eighteen. I'm sorry I can't be more helpful. We have ten in custody, Ariel. You could face a small army."

Marta's voice elevated. "This is Marta Boyd requesting immediate evacuation for thirteen…"

"Twelve," Early said and pointed at me. "You go…I'm staying."

"Yeah, twelve," I repeated. "You're going, Hollister. Not me."

"This's my home," he said.

"Nothing is more important than your family. Stay and die. You lose and so do your wife and kids."

"Early?" Marta called. "Is there not an airstrip nearby belonging to a rancher?"

"It's dirt and far too short for fixed wing capable of takeoff with a dozen people."

She spoke into her phone again. "We need a helicopter. A big one. There is a small landing field a few miles away…" Marta turned back to Jack.

"Ariel?" I heard KC's tinny voice from where I held the phone against my chest.

"Yeah?"

"We're ready to move at a moment's notice."

"I need Hollister and his family out of here now. There're twelve, men, women, children, and a dog. Preferably by helicopter."

"Her call was forwarded to us. We're talking to her now."

Shaye followed Early into the house with Emerson and Anna. All their children were inside. "There's something I don't understand. How did ISIS learn where Hollister lives?"

"We've been working on multiple leads since learning of their planned incursions."

My patience was wearing thin. "So? Are you getting anywhere?" I asked before struck by an epiphany. "Did it come from inside?" I got dead air in response. "Well?"

He sighed. "Possibly. There's a ten-million-dollar price tag on our man's head."

"Ah." It made sense. Marta was no longer on the phone as she and Jack neared me. "Do me a favor when this is over and I survive, will you?"

"If I can it's yours," KC said.

"I want to be your first call when you locate the leak. Give me the name or names of all involved. There'll be no charge. Consider it a freebee." The thought of one of our own giving up a patriot to our enemy both sickened and incensed me.

"You've got it if it's at all possible." I heard him speak to someone nearby before he gave me his attention again. "We're commandeering a fancy helicopter parked in Jackson. Some sheik or head of state uses it while in the US. They're in Wyoming on vacation."

"Commandeering? You can do that?"

"I can do anything I want. I've got agents armed with badges and rifles putting two of our pilots on board with coordinates to your airfield. Advise Mrs. Boyd ETA is twenty-two minutes."

"Is it big enough?"

He chuckled. "Yeah, it's a BELL 525 Relentless. Seats for sixteen plus two crew members. It's not particularly fast, but it is plush. The bird is popular among royals and the rich around the world. Take care of it, or we'll be out fifteen or twenty million."

Early held the front door of his home for his family and friends before closing it behind. Amy—their Brittany—was on a leash held by Lola. Emerson was armed with a semi-automatic pistol, while Hollister added another revolver to his belt and carried a bolt action rifle with a daunting scope. "I've gotta go," I told KC, "unless you've got more."

"Not at this time." His voice softened. "Take care, G-Dub." Huh. The bastard even listened to conversations between me and Allen Fryxell. I couldn't wait to tell Al. He'd be pissed as hell.

I ended the call with our group waiting for any news I could offer. "Your ride is twenty minutes out. They'll meet you at the airstrip."

"What about you?" Marta asked.

"I'm going to make sure no one follows. My job is to provide enough time for you to get off the ground if the bad guys are nearby." I stripped my coat off and reached inside the cab to retrieve the SIG carbine, tossing my wig inside. No need to hide any longer. Detaching the one-point sling, I slid it over my head and shoulder before shrugging into my outer garment again. I held the long gun lazily in one hand by the pistol grip. "Good chance they're days away."

Shaye and her girlfriends startled in surprise at my natural look. She hugged me first, followed by Ionella and Anna. About the same height as me, Shaye whispered in my ear, "Marta was wrong, and I was right about you. Take care."

Early hung back while the others squeezed into two rigs. "You know what you're doing?" he asked.

I gave in to building excitement and fear and shuddered before meeting his gaze. "Yeah. I know."

Even exposed to the gray woman, his lips pulled back, and for a fleeting moment I saw the same eagerness before he chuckled and nodded. "I think you do."

"Get your family out of here. Don't come back until you're given the all-clear. Understand?"

He ignored my order. "How long before the cavalry arrives?"

I couldn't help my ferocious grin. "I am the cavalry." Lord forgive me, but I was ready for the fight even if it killed me.

"You can't handle—"

I didn't let him finish. "You did."

Early jolted. Only a handful knew he and a partner held off hundreds of ISIS fighters after Early killed their leader. Airstrikes were called in, but as a ground campaign always did, it came down to men with rifles. Now, the terrorist group planned to return the favor on American soil. "Early!" Shaye shouted. "Let's go."

"Get out of here," I said. "Follow me to the end of your driveway, and I'll block the road leading out."

He nodded. "Don't get killed, okay?"

My guts twisted at his remark, but I grinned. "That's pretty much the condensed version of my plan."

I led and parked the Suburban blocking the graveled thoroughfare leading past their home. Not bothering to make eye contact or wave goodbye, I turned my back and swept the surrounding hills and road leading to Pinedale with field glasses. I couldn't be everywhere at once and prayed the coast was clear for them. If not, the family would be lost. Nearby sage tops swaying in the ever-present breeze made my heart leap while expecting a horde of swarming fighters.

Distant thumps announced the helicopter's arrival. I wondered if the unannounced landing would anger the strip's owner. I hoped not. It was probably the same guy who stopped and spoke to me. The sleek bird coming in fast became visible from the west before disappearing behind a knoll. The roar of its blades continued. Although knowing nothing of battlefield tactics, I'd have to be an idiot not to understand any aircraft was most vulnerable between descent and accent. Its pilots would keep the engine at full power ready to claw back into the sky at a moment's notice. Too slow to suit me but quicker than I feared, the 'copter appeared over the rise and banked west. I breathed a sigh of relief when it disappeared and could no longer be heard. I was alone again as I'd spent much of my life.

* * *

Tossing my cell onto the seat, I used the extra pocket in my jacket for a carbine magazine. More were loaded and strewn across the seat and console for both the SIG and my work gun. If I wasn't ready, I couldn't imagine what was.

I stopped at the edge of the hill to face down along the banks of Tosi Creek to where it crossed under the road and ran into the Green River. Although I could see miles in three directions, no vehicles were visible except one toward Union Gap where it continually parked. Fed up, I decided to confront the driver and learn the reason for its regularity. Perhaps it was innocent—an employee of the US Forest Service, someone repairing winter washouts, or even a rancher working. No matter the reason, I needed to understand who it was.

Disappointingly, it vanished before I could intercept to calm my concerns. Certain where it parked, I got out to examine the tracks and noted their aggressive tread. I assumed the road leading through the mountains to Dubois was made treacherous by snowdrifts, a sensible cause for good tires. They disappeared north, so I reasoned the driver found a way to return to the tiny town north of the Wind River Mountain Range. Not ruling out terrorists, I returned to my camping area between the road and river below the Hollister home.

My ringing phone while crouched over my coffee pot boiling on a camp stove startled me. KC's name made my heart leap—afraid of his news. "Ariel," I said.

"Nothing new?"

"Huh uh. I'm at the junction below Hollister's house where I can monitor traffic. Nothing yet."

"I thought you deserved an update. Our chopper is on its way north to a rendezvous with a jet out of Missoula."

"Do you know where she plans to take her group?"

"They're being allowed to liftoff without a flight plan. However, we'll monitor their progress through our air defenses with a couple F15s as shadows."

"I'm glad. Why don't you and your team take over from here? Neither Hollister nor their friends can ID you."

"I've dispatched teams of three in civilian clothing. We're monitoring in and outflow through Pinedale, Hoback, and Jackson. The only way to beat us is backroads through the mountains. "We're not concerned about high passes. Most continue to be snowed in."

I was exhausted from the day's activities and adrenaline rushes. "Then, I'm done here? I can return home?"

"Negative. You're our last line of defense. Should they infiltrate, we need you in place to slow them long enough for us to enter the fight and kill or capture those we can.

"Can I return to my room in Jackson? I could stand some shuteye."

"Sure," he agreed. "I'll make contact if we learn anything."

My bed almost stopped me on my way to the bathroom, but I needed a shower in the worst way. After propping a chair under the front door, I took my work gun in with me. I texted Dawson while sitting on the toilet. *I need to tell you how much I love you.*

Without waiting for an answer, I started my shower and let hot water cascade over my neck and upper back. I leaned forward to brace my forearms against the wall. Tired...I was so tired. Barely able to keep my eyes open, I let it almost scald me before scrubbing my body and sliding into a nightgown. No reply from my husband, and however much I needed to be in contact with him, I couldn't wait and slid between the sheets. I would slumber until my weariness was gone rather than use my phone alarm.

Sleepy eyes startled me awake when I opened them enough to see the clock. Nine-thirty a.m. I sat up to rub them and remembered my exhaustion. Flopping to my back again, I prayed Early and his family and friends made their escape unscathed. KC would have certainly called me if something went awry. However, I contacted him on my way to the Suburban. My growling stomach needed attention. The day was warm and sunny without a breeze when I stepped outside the Inn.

He was speaking the moment he answered. "Our mutual interests are safely away along with parents, sisters, and their families."

"Have your teams discovered anything of interest?"

"Negative. Are you en route south?"

"Just woke up. I plan on a big breakfast and enough coffee to float a battleship."

"Don't let your guard down, Ariel. No telling where the enemy is. Now isn't the time to underestimate them."

"I don't underestimate anyone no matter what side they're on," I answered coolly. I wasn't over my snit with him.

After parking, I waffled on how well armed I should be. Dad's Glock was always under my arm, but was it enough during a time of heightened alert? Not able to decide, I installed the suppressor on my work gun and chambered a round before I stuffed it inside my waistband at an angle. My carbine would stay on the seat covered by the hotel towel.

Father Timothy was the first person I saw after entering the Upchuck. He sat in the window booth I sometimes took and beamed at my entrance. "Ariel! How nice it is to see you." If he could have stood easily, I'm sure he would have.

I leaned over to hug my ancient friend. "How are you this morning, Father?" He wasn't quite halfway through a patty melt, and an unopened bag of chips lay next to his plate.

He gestured at his meal. "I think I bit off a little more than my stomach could handle. Could I interest you in the other half?"

"No," I laughed. "I plan on eating the rest of the cow before I leave." Angie held a coffee carafe high, and I waved my cup in response. She brought it and a glass of water. "Do you have a special today?" I asked.

"You just missed the breakfast we offered," she said. "Prime rib from last night, hash browns, eggs, and toast or a biscuit."

"Got any left?"

She shrugged. "Not sure. Want me to check?"

"Please."

I tried the coffee and found it as robust and flavorful as always. Very late in the morning, I didn't have to strain to observe each person who passed our window. Traffic was sparse as shoppers. Timothy offered his chips. "Go ahead. They give me heartburn if I eat too many."

The aroma wafted, and I caught the smell. Immediately, my stomach lurched as anything remaining fought to come up. I burped and leaped to my feet, anxious to make the women's room before vomiting. Not quite making it, I left a mess from the door to the sink. There, I dry-heaved until bile came up.

Angie appeared with a bucket and mop as I cleaned my face and mouth. "Are you okay?"

I swallowed hard before I could answer. "I don't know. Guess I've caught a bug I can't shake." I ran water into my palm to better wash my mouth out. "Can I help you with the mess?"

"I've got this," she said. "Go keep Father Timothy company. I'll be out in a couple minutes."

I took my time and peed first. Angie cleaning my vomit embarrassed me. If she'd allowed me to take over, I would have and felt better for it. Checking to make sure the handgun in my waistband rode correctly, I left the stall to wash my hands again.

Angie came out of the bathroom with me. "We've got prime rib left if you're still interested."

"Give me a few minutes to see if my stomach'll settle. Could I get a glass of milk to help?"

I wobbled to our booth where my concerned friend waited. "Are you okay?" Timothy asked.

I noted the bag of chips were no longer in sight. "Yeah, I think so. I've been struggling for a few weeks with some stomach bug I picked up." I gave Angie my most grateful smile when she appeared with milk. "It comes and goes when I least expect it."

"I could help you make an appointment for a checkup if you're interested," he said. "Lord knows they see me enough in my old age."

One of the biggest trucks UPS runs parked across the street. Four men exited and came in our direction. "Thanks, but I don't think so." They entered the Upchuck and sat at a nearby table. Other than the priest and me, a table of six businessmen and the quartet were the only patrons.

Angie stopped and dropped off menus where the four waited before coming to us. "Have you decided?"

Food no longer sounded good. "Yeah, half a tuna sandwich and a cup of corn chowder, please."

My tablemate waited until our server left. "Are you still working?"

I finished the milk to coat my stomach before taking a sip of my coffee again. It still tasted good and went down easier than I feared. "I'm glad we got a chance to talk again, Father. This is likely our last meeting."

"Oh? Have you finished and plan to return home?"

I shook my head. It hurt to speak the words aloud, but the man across the booth was the only person I could say them to. "No, I'm not done. Do you have a piece of paper and a pen or pencil?" He dug inside a pocket and came up with the stub of a pencil and an envelope. I thought about what to write and glanced outside. It dawned on me the UPS truck moved, and a Mercedes sat in its place. Finally, I scribbled Dawson's full name, our address, and both his cell number and Melissa's home phone. "This's my husband's number and his mom's, too."

Timothy read them and glanced up. "What do I do with these?"

"I'll need someone to contact him and offer what comfort is possible. You're the one for the job, Father. You know more about me than any other person alive, but for the man who's going to wait in vain for my return." Angie brought my meal, and I held off until she was gone before I tried a bite. It was good, and I ate two more before tasting a spoonful of the soup.

"Are you saying what I think you are?"

I glanced into his calm watery eyes and nodded. "You need to tell him how much I loved him and what he meant to me. He'll be angry, but don't take no for an answer. Dawson's a violent man, but you'll have nothing to fear from him. Pester him until he lets you in. Promise me you will." Timothy regarded me carefully before he nodded, and I bolted the rest of my sandwich and washed it down with water, then a sip of coffee. Time to earn my money.

One of the four men shifted earlier where I could see something hanging from a vest or a similar garment under his coat. It dawned on me the UPS doesn't allow civilians to ride in their trucks. The vehicle left behind those who I naturally assumed were employees in casual wear and not brown uniforms. Nothing added up until he moved and I recognized a grenade.

With two of the men facing in my direction and the other two with their backs to me, I stood and drew my work gun, sliding the safety off as the muzzle raised. The first bullet took the nearest one armed with explosives in the eye. As he slumped, the second was dying, too. The last pair hadn't yet turned, and I didn't give them the opportunity. Two more silent shots before a crash to my right diverted my attention. Angie stood petrified after dropping an armload of dishes.

The initial terrorist spasmed violently while I tried to put a finisher in him. He finally stilled enough for me to stick the muzzle near his ear and put a bullet inside. Another attempted to lift his head only to receive the same treatment. My gun was empty when I finished. Stuffing it inside my waistband, I drew my Glock. "Call Sheriff Thielman," I demanded of Angie who hadn't moved. "He'll understand when you tell him my name. Father? Clear the building and don't allow anyone to touch the bodies for any reason." I strode past him with a glare. "Don't you dare forget what you promised me."

A sprint across the street almost got me hit by a speeding pickup. Its tires screeched and smoked as the driver cut the wheel hard to avoid a collision. I didn't slow and unlocked the door and leaped to the seat of my rig. The truck was moving before I buckled my seatbelt. My targets got a significant head start in our race to Early Hollister's house. It was up to me to stop them.

* * *

Accelerating to eighty upon leaving the city limits south, I passed two slower cars after turning east toward Pinedale. Longer stretches allowed my speed to blast past ninety and sometimes approach a hundred. What I loosely planned was to shoot a front tire or somehow cause the truck to lose control and crash. Then, it would be easier to dispatch any survivors. Meeting them in a head-to-head gun battle would leave me woefully under gunned. Instead, I got hung up behind a combine and oncoming traffic, slowing me to a crawl before it dawned on me— a call to KC could direct a gunship or perhaps a 'copter filled with soldiers to the Hollister residence. An opening to pass the tractor and three cars in front came when we topped the short hill. I reached for my phone while I swung in from the opposite lane only to find my pocket empty. Searching the others and then the passenger seat, I last recalled it on the table between me and Father Timothy. Damn. Not only was I on my own but likely hurtling to my death—nor could a last conversation with my husband take place. *Lord, forgive me,* I prayed. *Take care of Dawson and give him a good life. Let him find another woman who loves him as much as me.*

Sorely disappointed I didn't catch them before leaving the main highway, I turned north toward the Hollister home and slowed after the asphalt turned to gravel. Unless I was woefully wrong, I would find them searching the house and premises for their target.

The backend of the brown truck was visible for only a moment when it topped the rise past Tosi Creek where the Hollister driveway began. I stopped to make a new plan rather than rush headlong into the fight. Chambering a round in the SIG carbine, I flipped the scope covers up and switched the electronic sight on. Two extra magazines went into my knapsack and another in my coat pocket. I couldn't imagine needing or having an opportunity to fire over a hundred rounds but running dry wasn't an option.

I parked short of the slope apex and driveway before I exited my Suburban. After giving it thought, I left the key in the ignition. My heart was racing when I attached the carbine to the sling over my neck and shoulder and left it to hang at my side. Mulling my suppressed .22/45, I put it on the seat covered by the hotel towel as a last-ditch weapon.

My heart fell as I closed enough to see though tall sage. From where I crouched, seven men armed with rifles waited with the truck between them and the house. Another two holding handguns were mounting the porch steps. Still more disappeared behind the garage. Far too many to take on alone. Yet what choice did I have?

My suppressed 9mm was anything but silent. Quieter with a muzzle device but not noiseless like my .22/45. Nor was a nine a long-range round. However, I practice out to two-hundred yards and sometimes beyond. The pair on the porch were banging on the door and peering through windows. Taking a deep breath, I concentrated on those closest with their backs to me. Feeling virtually no recoil, I could quickly move from target to target. Rising high enough to clear the sage between us, I settled the green dot on the ISIS member farthest right. He could conceivably reach cover if I started at the other end.

My first shot went between his shoulders, and he dropped as if I cut his spinal cord. Shifting the barrel minutely, I moved from terrorist to terrorist as quickly as my finger could squeeze the trigger. Not all were killing shots, but when I hesitated to assess, five weren't moving, and two were crawling beneath the huge van. A last shot went into the rear-end of one, while the other squirmed out of sight. Each of the five lying motionless caught another bullet to help keep them down and hopefully dead.

I figured to take the fight to them until a fully automatic Kalashnikov sprayed bullets in my direction. They came from the corner of the garage. A couple whizzed close enough I heard them pass. Falling to my belly, my only chance at survival was to retreat. The hammering of rifles kept me pinned until I realized my mistake. More were possibly closing on me under the cover of gunfire. Crawling backward, I reached the graveled road and ran bent at the waist in the direction of my truck with the recoil pad against my shoulder.

A fast one burst from the brush over the hill. His appearance shocked me but not into inaction. As I'd practice so many times before, my sprint didn't slow as I lifted the muzzle and opened fire. I hit center mass with most of five rounds and three more as I passed his corpse. Stopping at the door of my truck, I switched magazines before leaping inside. The engine started as another three assassins appeared. Throwing the transmission into reverse, I sped backward on the steep hill. Bullets struck my vehicle and broke the windshield. The inside filled with shattered glass as I focused on staying on the road. It's not as easy as it sounds while dividing my attention between mirrors and those trying to end my life.

Smoke boiled from beneath the hood, and I lost control enough to allow the rear axle to drop into the deep ditch. A sitting duck positioned sideways, another burst of gunfire struck my truck. I switched into four-wheel-drive and gunned the engine. Rather than pull forward, the steep bank slid the Suburban farther down the slope. Finally, as bullets tore through my door and blew out the window, howling tires caught and bit at the firm surface. My rig lurched forward out of control as I whipped the wheel away from danger.

I stopped when bullets no longer struck around me. Unfortunately, I sat at the three-way and was pointed toward the mountains instead of my escape route into Pinedale and possible help. A thick cloud poured from beneath the hood, and the power steering no longer functioned. I was surprised when the truck I'd watched so many times was again parked on the mountain above. Two choices awaited me. Hope my engine continued to run and try to reach the mystery vehicle, or stay low along Green River and the shorter drive to timber and rocky hillsides in hopes of escape on foot.

The van appeared behind me while I stalled. Slamming the gas pedal to the floor, my choice was made when I couldn't make the turn without power steering. I barely missed hurtling into the river by half standing and pulling on the steering wheel. The laboring beast came around until I faced open road and timbered slopes far ahead.

Steam and smoke shrouded my front end while I struggled to see through it. The engine faltered and caught again, allowing me to reach almost forty miles per hour. I used one hand to fill my knapsack with spare magazines as the motor labored. A glance into the mirror allowed me to see the huge van closing.

A stand of timber beckoned less than a mile away when the Suburban died. It rolled to a stop while I attached the carbine to its sling and leaped out with my knapsack only to collapse in the gravel. My left leg wasn't responding as it should, and I was horrified to see the UPS truck hurdling closer as I struggled to stand. Hobbling along the road and searching for a suitable place to climb the slope, I found a good spot and started upward.

Boulders from a previous ice age lay strewn across the hillside and offered brief concealment. Reaching the first less than two hundred yards from my truck, I paused to assess. The lumbering van slowed to a stop behind my rig. Keeping the huge rock between me and my pursuers, I continued upward while laboring to breathe. Shouts below got my attention. I peeked to see what appeared to be a dozen or more armed men being given orders. With the nearest timber a thousand yards away, I didn't stand a chance of reaching it.

Chapter XIV

Waving arms left no doubt they watched the direction I fled. Rather than stay hunkered behind the rock, I was about to be forced to flee for my life. Curiously, although my jeans were saturated with blood, I felt little pain. To give myself extra time and room, I opened fire with the SIG at a single target. He went down with a shout after my sixth round, only to drag himself to concealment. My next ten shots were aimed at the engine compartment. I wasn't sure what damage an underpowered 9mm hollow point could do at long range, but if I disabled their van, perhaps they could be tracked easier in the event of my death.

None were visible when I turned to scale the steep slope. My goal was another boulder a hundred yards away, but a yell sounded before I could reach it. Gunfire hammered from below as bullets struck around me. Throwing myself the last few feet, I crawled behind the rock panting with fear and debility.

A quick peek clinched my assumption the men advanced toward me. I fired twice to keep their heads down but not waste valuable ammunition. Making myself as small as possible while I considered options, a loud smack and scream below made me peer again. One rolled from concealment and lay unmoving in the open as the distant reverberation of a gunshot floated to me.

A second shout alerted me before the far-off thunder of a rifle sounded. With yet another man down, I took the opportunity to put more distance between us. I used my carbine as a walking stick to shuffle uphill, fearful of bullets tearing through my body.

A third and then fourth shot were on target. Whomever my guardian angel was, he or she could shoot. Two more men fell, but one regained his footing and vanished. Another appeared as he edged away from the distant marksman and into my sights. Though more than four-hundred yards downhill, I emptied my carbine in hopes of wounding him. I smiled when he jerked and sagged before crawling away. I dug into my pack for another magazine, only to find one filled and the other partially. Inserting the former, I chambered a round, turned, and increased my separation from my enemies.

Distant booms continued intermittently. While I didn't hear more shouts of pain or fear, it offered me the chance to reach the timberline and any protection it offered. Resting against a tree where I could still see below, I took a moment to assess my wound. I guessed it passed through the door and struck above my knee, missing the bone and exiting. How it hit my left leg but missed the right I couldn't imagine. While my pantleg was soaked, bleeding seemed to have slowed or even stopped. I found the field first-aid kit in my pack and pushed my jeans down. I'd been shot before and knew what to expect, but it still made my guts lurch to see the damage and discoloration. After packing the entrance and exit holes with a coagulant, I wrapped it tightly with gauze.

Mind-numbing exhaustion struck before darkness fell. My leg throbbed with each heartbeat. It no longer bent easily as I climbed. Walking awkwardly added to my weariness. I searched for a spot that offered both concealment and a windbreak. A cold breeze from snow banks lying not far above chilled skin beneath my sweat-soaked clothing. It surprised me how far desperation pushed me even when wounded.

I stopped in a bramble of jack pines. Higher lay a couple of windfalls and good-sized boulders. They wouldn't stop a freezing wind, but beggars couldn't be choosers. I only hoped my pursuers turned back. Whoever manned the rifle saved my life. Now, it was up to me to honor my unknown savior by keeping hypothermia at bay.

Building a fire would be impossibly stupid. I kept two survival blankets in my knapsack for emergencies and removed one from its wrapper. The moment I coiled it around my shoulders I felt the warmth of my reflected body heat. As long as shock didn't kill me overnight, I was fairly confident hypothermia wouldn't win. The second blanket went between me and the cold ground.

Racking my brain to decipher the sharpshooter's identity didn't bring me closer to a name. I knew KC put together a diverse team, but they couldn't have located me so quickly after I engaged the enemy. Could it be the driver of the truck that parked on the mountain above the Hollister home? Nothing made sense as I finished the first of five water bottles kept in my pack. A handful of energy bars were also stored, and I nibbled at one while my stomach rebelled. I needed to take care. Vomiting much-needed liquids might kill me if a bullet didn't get me first.

Wrapped in my coat with the hood pulled low over my eyes and the emergency blanket around me, I dozed intermittently. I would begin to drift only to hear a sound and have my eyes fly open. My carbine lay scant inches away. Although uncomfortable, I wore my dad's Glock and spare magazines. It wouldn't do to be caught unprepared and leave it behind in my haste. Any of fifty-one rounds from the handgun might well save my life.

Dawn came sooner outside the forest than within. My lids were heavy with exhaustion when it was time to move. I'd decided overnight to cut east and attempt to escape in a wide circle. Perhaps I could intersect with the Green River again and find a ride to safety.

Panic set in when I tried to stand. My injured leg had swelled to the point of almost bursting my jeans. It would no longer bend at the knee, making travel difficult, and each step was excruciating as I picked my way through the timber, using deer and elk trails. Remembering what Dawson taught me while hunting big game, I took great care with each step, making sure I didn't break any sticks. The slope below was heavily timbered and steep. I feared stepping wrong and losing my balance. Not only for the noise I'd create, but I worried about being able to stand again.

A shrill scream sounded long before I heard the distant shot. I stopped to rest and smiled. Someone continued to have my back. I made a pact with myself should I live through this to kiss the sharpshooter soundly when I learned the mystery identity.

The forest ended at a rock-covered slope. It was even steeper than where I'd followed animal trails. I feared a single misstep would send me careening over a cliff as I inched my way across its expanse. My breathing labored enough that I stopped to rest and drink a third bottle of water.

Realizing my eyes closed under the dim cloudy overcast, I forced them open. It wouldn't do to be caught on the slope. Although the earlier scream came from the west, any surviving members willing to press their attack could come upon me at any moment. What seemed like a dozen or more might be whittled in half judging by the response to the sharpshooter's prowess.

I'm coming for you, Dawson, I whispered. *Wait for me, honey. You and Jake. If I make it home,* I promised myself, *I'll never leave your arms again. Lord,* I prayed, *help me return to my boys and our family, and I'll never ask anything of you again.*

Bone crushing fatigue slowed me to a stumbling shuffle. Setting a goal of reaching a certain rock or spot, I continued my painful trek east only by counting steps. Gone were thoughts of stopping the team of terrorists as I battled for survival. Somehow, I found myself lying on my side without recalling how I came to be there. Struggling to a seated position, I rested and drank my fourth bottle. One remaining would have to see me to safety. Standing was no easy feat after setting the plastic jug aside. I hated to litter. Unfortunately, getting my knapsack off again would take too much energy.

A series of gunshots below didn't make sense. They weren't far away, so it couldn't be my guardian angel. One struck my upper chest and pack, causing me to stumble before a volley tore into my back.

I crumpled facedown. My carbine was still attached to the sling inches from my hand. Numb from pain, sucking sounds from my chest when I breathed told me all I needed to know. *I love you, Dawson.* I'm pretty sure I said it aloud, but can't say with absolute certainty. *You, too, Jake. A better boy never existed. Take care of your master. He's going to need you now more than ever.*

I struggled to roll to my side. A wheezing cough brought up the coppery taste of blood. *Huh, just like the old westerns I used to watch with Dad,* I mused. Wiping the back of a hand along my cheek, I stared in surprise at the smear of blood. I wasn't sure what to expect, but dying from gunshots didn't hurt as bad as I envisioned. My body felt less sensation than I anticipated. I guessed my demise was apropos after so many met their ends by my hand, although far more mercifully than waiting to pass from shock and blood loss. I wondered if I would make it long enough to be given a finisher through my skull.

Rocks slides below alerted me to company. *Bastards,* I thought. *I'm taking a couple more of you with me.* Anger drove me to a seated position against a boulder where I could see movement farther down. None were within my rifle's range, but they soon would be. I tried to uncap the last water bottle while I waited. Hands weakened by a lack of blood weren't strong enough, and I dropped it. *Doesn't matter,* I supposed. *It isn't as if I'm going to need it in a few minutes.*

My once-light rifle weighed a ton when I lifted it. Creeping movement got closer as I waited, rocks tumbling to bounce down the steep slope. *Come on, you bastards,* I raged to myself. *Get up here before I die.*

Only four appeared. Either I miscounted, or my guardian angel was far more efficient than I realized. My vision was blurry, making it difficult to see through my scope. Finally, they were within fifty yards, unaware of where I lay when I opened up. My rate of fire was slowed by a weak trigger finger, but two were down before the other pair ducked and retreated. *Ha! Got you sons of bitches!*

Too exhausted to lift my head, I reclined. I hadn't noticed the sky looked like rain until I stared up. My long gun was too heavy to lift as I waited for the end. I remembered Dad's Glock as the seconds ticked by. Ability to unsnap the safety strap and draw it left me faintly surprised. Fully automatic gunfire sailed above me—my unseen assailants not able to reach me over the lip between them and where I lay.

My eyes closed for what I expected was the last time. *Forgive me, Lord,* I prayed. *Forgive my terrible choices and the sins I've committed. Help Dawson through the next few years. He's going to need you. Mom? Dad? I hope you're waiting with Meghan because I'm on my way.*

Gravel crunched nearby. My lids fluttered, but I willed them to open. Two of the most frightening men I could imagine stood near my feet and peered down. Both wore huge thick beards. I didn't have to comprehend their language to understand their surprise. A damned woman killed them.

I don't think they saw the pistol in my hand where it rested against my thigh. It was louder than I remembered without the earplugs I normally wore during practice. My bullet tore into the guts of the ISIS radical standing on the right. Unlike soldiers who fire full metal jacket projectiles in battle, I used hollow points for better results. I shot a second and third round—each lower than the other before I could no longer raise my handgun. It fell to the side, leaving me fully exposed for what was still to come.

Where I expected a quick death by a final bullet, the last man standing had other plans and drew a fearsome knife. Damn. The bastard was going to saw my head off. While I didn't understand a word he said, an interpretation wasn't needed to feel his rage. When he squatted and gripped a handful of my hair, I could only wait and hope it was quick and relatively painless.

"No!" A deep voice sounded like the roar of a lion from the direction I'd hiked. A bullet slammed through my assailant's ribs, followed by a long volley. He released my locks and fell near my feet on his butt before rolling to his side. "No!" the shout came again. Someone ran toward me and continued to fire into what I assumed was already a corpse. My eyes closed as I smiled. *We got 'em all, Early. You're free and clear.*

A shadow blocked out the sky. My lids tried to open, but it was no use. "Oh, God…God…Jules…" Fingers opened my jacket and plucked at my blouse while I wheezed for oxygen.

Jules? The deep tone and nickname could mean only one thing. Somehow, against all odds, Dawson located me. Hundreds of miles from home and running for my life along the edges of a vast wilderness, my man discovered my whereabouts. While somewhat surprised, I wasn't shocked. Nothing about him astonished me any longer.

He tore my shirts open to expose my chest. I felt them tremble as he ran fingers over my wounds. "Oh, no-no-no...God, no, Jules," he whispered. I tried to take a breath to speak only to hear sucking sounds in my torso. I gurgled and choked, spraying a mist of blood from my lips. A mike keyed. "Al? Goddamn it, Al, answer me," Dawson shouted.

Allen's voice boomed. "I got you loud and clear, sir. Have you put eyes on G-Dub?"

"Julia's shot to shit. I'm afraid she's dying. We're above the Green along the southeasterly portion of the Wind River Range. Can you give me an ETA?"

The radio crackled. "Less than four minutes. Keep her alive, Cap'n."

"I'll fire a flair when I hear your rotors."

"Roger that."

"Stay with me, Jules. Don't you dare die on me, woman." Hands fluttered over my torso again, searching for more wounds. I felt him close to my face. "Can you hear me? Julia, can you hear me?" he hollered.

I wanted to answer. Truly I did. Yet I couldn't muster the energy to respond—only gasp helplessly like a fish out of water.

The flair fired before I recognized the sound for which Dawson waited. Seconds later, I heard thumps as Allen Fryxell piloted his helicopter closer. The two-way squawked. "Too steep, sir. There's a wide flat on a rise two-hundred meters to your south."

Dawson scooped me from the ground. I felt the sensation of flying between the jarring impacts of his feet. We met a worsening roar drowning out even my thoughts. I floated high until another set of arms took me. "Get in, sir," Al shouted.

I couldn't catch my breath after Allen's violent takeoff. No matter how hard I tried, the sweet taste of oxygen was denied. "She's not breathing," came Dawson's yell. "She's not breathing!"

"Check for obstructions and start CPR," Al hollered back.

No longer did my body hurt, nor did I feel the need to inhale. Elevating to see better, I observed Dawson performing desperate chest compressions as he fought to stimulate my heart. Once, he stopped and pinched my nose, blowing two long breathes into my mouth. Oxygen escaped from the holes in my chest without inflating my lungs. No longer did my husband stop to blow, he continued with hard, steady compressions with a steely look of concentration.

Suddenly visible in the distance, I didn't need to get closer to recognize my mother, father, and Meghan. Waving a hand overhead to catch their attention, I ran to them with overwhelming delight at our reunion until realizing I wasn't shortening the distance. I stopped, hopeful they would meet me halfway. For a moment, I thought Dad gestured me closer until I could see he waved me back. At least I got to hear his voice again so strong and clear after silenced for far too long. I nodded my agreement when he finished, and his radiant smile filled me with joy.

"Clear."

A jolt flung me back into my body. Something covered my mouth and pushed oxygen in. The pain of being sent away rivaled that of my damaged and dying vessel. I heard the tormented moans of a wounded soul and knew instinctively Dawson watched from nearby. His pain was more than I could bear. Scratching and clawing, I sought to break free again of my earthly mooring.

"Clear."

My escape was halted by another painful shock.

"We've got a pulse. Let's get her into surgery!"

* * *

I floated under a vague surface, aware of sounds of scuffling and anger. "Get the hell out of here and don't come back." I didn't have to see Dawson to feel his unbridled rage. The heavy thud of a blow and a falling body followed. "You son of a bitch. I'll kill you next time." I could only guess who he hit, but I was willing to put money on KC. A closing door made me hope it was over.

Father Timothy's tone was no different than if we conversed at the Upchuck or in his quarters. "Julia warned me you were a violent man, Mr. Pelletier," he said. "Was it necessary to strike him?"

Dawson's fury didn't lessen. "Keep your bible handy, Father. You'll be performing last rites again if I see him one more time." Again? I wondered who died and hoped the dominee believed him, because I didn't doubt my husband.

A door opened, and I heard the strong quiet voice of Melissa. "In the hall, boy. Now." Unable to hear more, I concentrated on Father Timothy and his quiet prayers. I needed every bit of help I could get.

* * *

Waking was a luxury denied me. I got close—often able to hear conversation. Timothy and Dawson grew closer with the priest sometimes being called to calm the hoarse bawling of my husband. Since I rarely saw him shed a tear, his cries tore at my heart. *Help me through this, God, and Dawson will never feel pain caused by me again,* I swore.

Time held no meaning. A machine breathed for me as I lay unmoving. I sometimes heard familiar snores and knew Dawson waited for me to recover. A door closed once, and I listened to hushed voices. I recognized Scotty's. "How is she?"

"Better," my husband said.

"How long before they bring her out of her coma?" Robin asked.

"Not sure. Doctor Richards suggested a couple more days before they reassess." A coma? No wonder I couldn't wake. "They're concerned about her cognitive abilities after going without a pulse for so long."

I heard Scotty very close. "Christ. Julia's the only person I can imagine absorbing this much abuse and surviving."

"She's not out of the woods yet," Dawson said. "We've got a long way to go. Even if she heals physically, it's too early to say if she can function normally...if at all."

"What about..." I'm not sure if Robin stopped talking or if I no longer listened. I drifted away to get much needed rest.

* * *

I struggled to wake. "Jules? Can you hear me? Open your eyes for me," Dawson crooned and stroked my cheek.

"Give her time," a voice said. "The medication needs a chance to flush from her system, and she has to want to come back."

"Come on, honey. I know you can do it."

"Keep talking, Mr. Pelletier. Use the call button if she shows signs of response before I return."

The door closed, and I felt Dawson take my left hand in his. "Jake's at Aunt Bess's waiting for you. They say he stares at the front door and stands anytime he hears a car. You'll be happy to know six of your hens each hatched a clutch of eggs. Scotty said we've got about forty of the little bastards running around the yard chasing bugs. Old Bill Spencer was selling rabbits...all of them Flemish giants. I gotta pay Scotty back because he bought three does and a buck for us. Spencer swore two of the females were already bred. If he's right, we should have plenty of rabbit meat pretty soon."

It was nice to know my hens were setting. I figured to keep more than usual over the winter. Perhaps as many as two dozen. Dawson and I hadn't talked about bunnies, although I planned to purchase more. His news pleased me, but the thought of Jake pining for his mistress was almost more than I could bear. I was directly responsible for his worry I might not return.

"I've met your Father Timothy. Nice man. Can't believe you were able to keep him from me. I'm not sure how he learned, but he was the first person after Al and me to appear. You were in bad shape, and he performed last rites when we weren't sure you'd survive. Never would have dreamed you converted to Catholicism. Reckon you and me need to have a heart-to-heart over how you spilled your guts to him."

I'd never thought of last rites. Otherwise, I would have asked Timothy to say them if the worst-case scenario came about.

"Mom's been here since the first day. Al left to get her the moment you were stabilized enough to leave the ER. She's at the hotel getting much-needed sleep. Scotty and Robin drove. They must have been on the road within a couple minutes of my call. Jose and Ox were ready to jet in, but I asked them for another favor instead. They weren't happy to miss cheering you on in person."

For a girl who often felt alone, it certainly sounded as if more friends than I realized were in my corner.

"You've also gotten visitors I've never heard of...except for one. Does the name Marta Boyd mean anything? Father Timothy explained who she is, but I still have a hard time understanding how you came to know such a wealthy woman. Can't wait to get your version of the story, you hear? A bunch of others visited I don't remember the names of. Someone they called Early and another one as big as a damn mountain. You've been keeping strange company, Jules." I felt his lips touch the back of my hand. "Mark and Mandy called. They heard from Jose before I could make contact. They wanted me to give you their best, but they've got a baby to worry about with another on the way. Speaking of babies, when were you planning to tell me you're pregnant?"

Pregnant? The news startled me into awareness. Light blinded as I struggled to open my eyes. "Pregnant?" I croaked.

"Jules? Jules?" Dawson's voice rose. "Hang on. I'm buzzing the nurse's station."

"Yes? How may I help you?" a voice sounded over an intercom.

"Call the doc. Julia's awake!" Dawson shouted.

"Pregnant?" I asked a second time against a dry and raspy throat sore from being intubated.

"Yeah. You didn't know?"

My vision cleared enough to see him looking down. I tried to shake my head. "No." I whispered. My odd vomiting made sense. I suffered from morning sickness while working in Wyoming. "How far...am I?"

"Around thirteen weeks. They warned me you'd probably miscarry while your body fought to survive, but you surprised us all."

Pregnant. The satisfaction of hearing the term in relation to me was both overwhelming and soothing. I needed to live so I could be a mother.

Bodies entered my room and crowed around. "Hi, I'm Doctor Richards," a man said. "Can you tell me your name?"

"Julia Marie Pelletier."

"Excellent. Can you tell me who the man holding your hand is?"

"Dawson. My husband."

"Good...good..." No matter how many questions I got, I couldn't tear my gaze from my love. I made promises to both God and myself I planned to keep. Nothing could sway me from a future I could finally see. Dawson, me, and our first baby. Who knows how many after?

***

My wounds made for an extensive list of notes. Eight .30 FMJs tore through my back and chest. Any other style of bullet would have killed me instantly. Another went through my left thigh, and a slug injured my right arm. I spent nine days in an induced coma while my body knitted. After I woke, a long line of guests stopped to visit and pay their respects. Marta Boyd and her husband Jack came immediately after friends and family like Allen, Melissa, Scotty, and Robin.

Marta didn't wait to apologize. "I am so sorry for jumping to the wrong conclusion. You did not fit with those I found you working with. You saved my family, and I shall be eternally grateful. Should you require anything, do not hesitate to make contact."

"I didn't know what else to do. My job was to be invisible and shadow Early and his family. Tough to introduce myself and continue working under the radar."

She nodded. "You performed remarkably, Julia. Even with an old woman sticking her nose where it did not belong."

Shaye and Early were next. "I figured it out. It was you behind the grocery in Pinedale and then on Pine Street, wasn't it?" Shaye asked. "I'm indebted to you for Anna's life...and mine, too."

"You don't owe me anything," I said.

"It was you," she insisted. "I know it was."

"I can't thank you enough," Early said. "For everything. All you gotta do is say the word, and I'm there for you."

I grinned. "I wasn't drunk, you know."

"Drunk?" Dawson said. "You rarely drink. I can only remember you going overboard once or twice."

Early's eyes narrowed. "You should think of a second career in acting. You sure as hell sold me."

"He caught me by surprise one morning after I'd kept watch throughout the night," I explained to my husband. "KC advised me the threat was imminent. I thank God my nap in their basement refreshed me, because it was later the same day in Pinedale—" I stopped after realizing I divulged too much.

"I knew it!" Shaye boasted. She leaned close to kiss both of my cheeks. "Thank you. Early, Tryn, and my baby thank you, too."

"Cripes. I make a crappy secret agent," I said.

"We heard you're pregnant. Is it true?" she asked.

"Uh huh. About thirteen weeks."

My admission earned me another kiss to each cheek. "We have to stay in touch, okay? Oregon is a long way from here, but-"

"About that," I broke in. "It was part of my cover story. We live a lot closer in eastern Idaho. I'll text you our address."

My eyes felt gritty, and Dawson noticed. "She's wearin' down, folks," he said. "Stop again tomorrow if you're still in town. Right now, Jules needs her rest."

***

Nothing comes easy for me outside of bad guys using my body for target practice. Getting discharged from the hospital was no different. Once Dawson felt confident I would survive, he left me to sleep alone for long stretches. KC must have bided his time until my husband was away.

Agent Clark woke me from a nap with his boy Friday in tow. "I understand you're doing much better, Mrs. Pelletier," KC said.

I stared back. "My doctor tells me I should live."

"Apologies are due. My men should have never missed the UPS truck. Nor should we have been so late in locating your Suburban. For some reason, your tracker went dead. It wasn't until your friend Mr. Fryxell was airborne with you and your husband before we learned where you were."

"It's just as much my fault. I stupidly forgot my phone at the Upchuck after the excitement there. I was too far out of Jackson to go back. My plan was to catch the van and cause it to crash."

He debriefed me as much as he could in the non-privacy of a hospital. Dawson eventually calmed and met with him to explain what he knew and where to find most of the bodies. "We located your suppressed .22 in the Suburban. Later, we found your SIG carbine and a Glock where you were wounded last. I hope you don't mind we left all three with Mr. Pelletier."

I didn't care if I saw any of them again. Even Dad's gun. They represented my past. "That's fine," I said.

He stood from where he sat at my bedside. "We'd better let you rest. Your husband made it clear I wasn't to be in contact. However, we needed closure." His boy Friday handed KC a newspaper, and he passed it to me. "Tell me what you see on the front page."

The writing was in Arabic, but I didn't need to be fluent in the language to understand the huge photo. It was an exploded log house with Early Hollister's body clearly propped against the burned remains. A woman and two children could be identified, too. "I...I don't understand." Early and Shaye stopped to see me only yesterday.

"This's what we've worked on. Building a reasonable facsimile of his home. Digital recreation makes it appear as if his body is in the foreground. We've paid to have this published in over two hundred newspapers in the Middle East, North Africa, and Asia, proclaiming the Sziria Hill shooter was murdered. Intelligence suggests our enemies have been rejoicing."

"It's over, then?"

KC nodded. "We think so."

"Have you learned more about someone on the inside? I stand by what I offered."

He shook his head. "Not yet, although we're working on it." He took his paper back and stopped at my door. "I'll be in contact after you've healed."

I shook my head. "I prefer not to see or hear from you again unless it's to point out the guilty mole."

His return smile irritated me as he left, but with his scar it was tough to tell if it was a smirk. Angering me further was his boy Friday stopping at the door to turn with a grin. He pointed at me and dropped his thumb as if a gun went off while winking.

I didn't mention my meeting to Dawson when he returned. Let him think Kevin Carter and Homeland Security were out of our lives for good. As far as I was concerned, they were. I suspected they'd take care of anyone found aiding the enemy internally as much as I'd prefer to handle it.

Chapter XV

Dawson was in my line of fire when I got strong enough to confront him after he and Al returned from supper laughing. I was in no mood after brooding two days without an opportunity to challenge events, and my tone wasn't friendly. "You drove the truck I watched on the hill above the Hollisters, didn't you?"

My husband dragged a chair over from against the wall and sat. He didn't attempt to avoid my accusation. "Yep."

"I'd better get out of here, sir," Al said. "Give you two some private time."

"Sit, flyboy. You're up to your neck in this," I told Al, then swung my imaginary front sight back on Dawson. "How'd you know where I was?"

He didn't flinch and stared back steadily with a hard edge. "I was aware of your location from the first time you drove away to work again. I installed a GPS tracker under your rig. Each time you changed vehicles, I attached another. Downloaded one onto your phones. A couple other apps, too."

"What apps?"

He shrugged. Of one thing I was certain: Dawson had no clue when it came to electronics. "You didn't work alone." My gaze shifted again to Al who looked everywhere except at me. "Someone helped you. Without assistance, you don't even know how to turn your cell on and off."

"You're right. Al directed the operation and relayed info."

"Did you intercept my calls?" I asked Dawson's partner.

He didn't hesitate. "Yes, ma'am."

"Anything else?"

Allen didn't look at me after finding a fingernail he considered more interesting. "Yes, ma'am."

"Well?"

He spoke to the fingernail. "I sometimes listened to your exchanges. One of the apps allowed me to switch your speaker on when it notified me of a conversation."

"You listened to my private discussions?"

Dawson broke in. "Al refused til I ordered him, Jules."

"You are *not* his commanding officer any longer. He could have refused."

"I leaned pretty heavy."

Dawson could be fearsome if needed; however, I'd never witnessed it toward Al. Most of the time, the two were thick as thieves. One would lie and the other swear to it, although not to me as far as I knew. "Is that true, Al?"

"Did he threaten me? No. Nor did I consider it an order." Al rose like a thundercloud and stormed to my bed. For the first time since we met, he glared in anger directed at me. "It was worse. He was panicked and perilously close to tears, Julia. I won't listen to a friend and partner beg me to help save the life of his spouse."

Dawson sniffed and no longer looked at me. *Oh, Jesus, what have I done?* I gripped his sleeve. "It was you, wasn't it...behind the Upchuck?"

His eyes were moist with memories when he nodded. "Yeah. You damn near got everyone killed includin' yourself."

I raised an eyebrow. "Me?"

"It was pretty obvious she carried explosives of some sort. Otherwise, they would've opened fire inside as a team. One at the front door...the other from the back. Even Al figured it out from listening to your calls. You should've killed the male first, then capped the female when her vest didn't explode. I was left with no option after you focused on the woman."

"Given an extra ninety seconds, he could've helped you face the squad in Pinedale," Al said. "After I relayed what I learned, Dawson got in place and took a rest across the hood of his truck too late. Carter and his cavalry rolled into town to help you finish." His eyes narrowed.

"I listened to a few of his calls until he got wise and blocked me. Only worked a few minutes until I got around their firewall. Figured there was something off about the guy or his office, but my suspicions were never verified. It's why we didn't contact him after Cap stretched his rifle out along the Green to give you a fighting chance. All I could do was fill my tank with JP-five and wait overnight in a sleeping bag at the Jackson airport."

I shook my head. "It never dawned on me it could be you. I assumed it was a sharpshooter from KC's group."

Dawson snorted. "You put your trust in the wrong people, Jules. You noticed they never had your back until after the fact, didn't you?"

He was right. A convenient excuse always explained why I was on my own. Even if I remembered my cell and called, KC would have remained in position until I summoned for cleanup or died. "Dawson asked for my assistance on an open channel, Julia," Al said. "At the very least, they should have answered it with a gunship to mop up. Someone has it in for you. KC's corporal contacted us after you were in surgery to learn where to find the bodies. I believe your health and wellbeing were an afterthought."

No wonder I heard my husband strike my boss. It was real—not a dream. Nevertheless, to ask for confirmation might well anger him further. "How many did you tag," I asked.

Dawson wasn't happy with himself. "Not as many as I should've. You were hobbling up the hill and then pinned down when I was still at fourteen hundred meters...almost a mile. I was forced to leave the truck I borrowed from Al and double-time it cross-country. It would have taken too long to drive around. I battled a downdraft and a crosswind, but I got three and missed a pair while givin' you cover. I kept 'em hunkered down until you hit the timber. I got time to close inside of seven hundred while they regrouped. Killed or wounded eight before it got too dark."

I understood why so much of his ammunition supply was missing at home. He knew well the ranges he may be called on to deal with. Only practice could help, and Dawson lived by an ingrained belief in it. One shot in practice for every yard a marksman may be called on to shoot. If he thought the ranges might approach a mile, I could guarantee he fired a minimum of seventeen hundred rounds.

Our conversation stilled when the door opened. I think we all sighed in relief when Father Timothy appeared. "Am I interrupting?" he asked.

"No," I said as Dawson and Al both answered yes.

"I'll come back later," the old man muttered and turned.

"Please stay. Dawson, he knows."

My husband wasn't happy with me. "Knows what?" His tone dripped disgust.

"Everything."

"I understand you and Timothy have spoken in-depth. Define 'everything.'"

"From the time I was born to all that's happened between then and now. He's heard my confession four or five times."

The priest remained silent on matters concerning confession.

Dawson retrieved his work Stetson from where he left it on my bed. He squinted and dog-eyed the little dominee before digging at an imagined spot on the stained brim with a thumbnail. "Reckon I'll have to give the idea a bit of thought," he said. "Ready for a cup of jo, Al?"

Our private lives were nobody else's business according to my husband. Judging by the way he scowled at my friend suggested Dawson hadn't changed his mind. "C'mere," I said. "I need a goodbye kiss."

While his lips touched mine, I slid my left hand beneath his coat. Dawson felt where I touched and tugged. "Are you sure?" he whispered.

I left my fingers where they were. "Yeah, slide your belt from the loops." He did as I asked before coiling it to slip into a jacket pocket. He drew back, and I placed my hand under the blanket to warm.

"Got your phone?" He'd brought mine so I could talk, text, or peruse the internet. I figured KC kept my government issued version. Perhaps Timothy had it. I planned to ask. Pictures of home to keep me grounded should be deleted.

I brought it out from where I kept my cell on my stomach beneath the sheet and blanket and smiled. "Right here."

"Need somethin' day or night, call or text me or Al, okay?" He left the room after I gave him a serious nod. There were only two in the area Dawson trusted my life to—himself and Allen Fryxell.

* * *

Lying in a hospital bed offered plenty of time to catch up with Father Timothy. According to Dawson and my nurse, the ancient priest spent much of his time visiting patients in the hospital. Even so, he set aside a significant amount to converse with me. "I'd like to apologize for scaring you at the Upchuck," I said. "It seems as if you're always nearby when bad stuff happens. You shouldn't have to see things like that."

"You were certainly quick and efficient," he said.

"I needed to work fast. I was afraid they were there to set off a grenade after I spotted one."

"What if they weren't? What if you were wrong, and they stopped for lunch?"

I closed my eyes. Even killing an enemy wasn't to be taken lightly. I usually second-guessed myself until it came time to squeeze the trigger. The four in the restaurant were an exception to the rule. The moment I identified the explosive, I hungered to end their time on earth. A big lesson was learned with the woman laden with explosives. These people existed outside the parameters of humanity and needed to be put down. "Should I have sent you over to bargain with them?"

He chuckled. "No, not after what we saw when police arrived. Between them, the four carried six fragmentation explosives, and two were armed with handguns." Timothy clucked his tongue. "Poor Angie. She's tough, but I'm not sure she'll ever recover. The world suddenly became smaller to her when evil knocked at our door."

I liked the woman. She worked hard as a single mother with boys in high school and college. By all evidence, she played just as intensely, and the years weren't kind to her. She was pretty and shapely from afar, but etched lines aged her beyond the woman's years. "I'm sure you'll see her first. Would you apologize for me? Let her know how sorry I am?"

"Certainly," he said. "However, it might be better coming from Early."

His news made me frown. "Why him?"

The priest chuckled. "Did you notice Russell waiting their table the day you stopped the suicide bomber?"

I thought back to the barely averted catastrophe. Angie waited on me and Timothy but never approached the group. "Yeah."

"She and Early were an item throughout high school, and they still talk. When he returned to Jackson after a stint in the military followed by a failed marriage, most figured they'd get back together. Instead, he met a girl while camping, and they married. Rumor has it Shaye's green with jealousy when it comes to his old flame, and she doesn't care who knows it."

His story made me grimace when I applied it to me, Dawson, and his old girlfriend, Nancy. I felt the pangs of jealousy but not in the same way as Shaye. Instead, I tempered my resentfulness with pity for his previous girlfriend and considered it best to change the subject before too much time on my hands let me overthink it. "Have you been in contact with the Hollisters or Marta? Do you know if they returned home?"

I felt better after learning their lives returned to normal, although Marta planned to stay in contact with Homeland Security whether they liked it or not. The news made me almost glad after what I learned about KC from my husband and Allen. Promises made to God aside, I could no longer work with the man.

Unexpected visitors proved delightful. Shaye and Anna made their journeys from Dubois and Pinedale to see me. I suspected my predicament made for a convenient girls day out. However, knowing the ladies viewed me as a friend tickled me. They missed my nurse by moments after I was given a sponge bath. My wounds were healing but not yet enough to chance a shower. Short walks in the halls got easier, although I was plagued with a significant limp from my leg wound. My ribcage and lungs hurt with every breath I took.

Dawson sat beside my bed when the cousins entered my room. He texted with Melissa, who insisted she be kept up to date on my condition. A quiet knock dispelled any notion of a nap after I recognized my guests. They stopped at my bedside dividing their attention between me and my husband, whose dark complexion handsomely mixed equal parts of Mediterranean and North American native. "Ladies," I greeted. "What brings you so far from home?"

"You," Shaye said. She touched my uninjured knobby knee hidden safely beneath the blanket. "We hoped to see how you fared."

I found it hard to believe my visitors were related. Shaye was barely as tall as me with auburn hair and a muscular figure. By contrast, Anna stood nearly a foot taller with honey-blonde tresses and a willowy build. Together, they reminded me of a female version of Mutt and Jeff. "I'm on the mend," I said. "Doctor Richards thinks I can go home in a couple days. I'm performing better on cognitive tests as well as walking each day." Only Dawson's refusal to give up on chest compressions kept my brain alive. Even so, I struggled with finding words when I least expected it. Few obvious holes were left in my memories, although I'm warned to be prepared for them. My doctor and nurses explained memory loss would crop up when I was least ready.

"Mom sends her regards," Anna said. "She feels responsible for your wounds."

I shook my head. "She had nothing to do with it. Tell her to forget it. This is little more than a job injury."

Shaye took my hand. "I...we...Early and I can't thank you enough for what you did. We've met with Agent Clark twice and learned how long you've been protecting us."

Dawson stood and put his phone away. "Reckon I'll leave you ladies to yourselves." He kissed my forehead. "Call or text if you need anything."

I grinned at the way both women watched him leave, and my heart swelled with pride. To me, he was a catch by any measure. "Wow!"

Shaye said. "Someday you're going to have to share how you snagged that one!" Anna smiled at her cousin's reaction, although she didn't remark.

"Next door neighbor," I said and waggled my eyebrows to their giggles.

Shaye took the seat Dawson vacated. "You must be ready to get out of here."

"You can't imagine. Where's Ionella?"

"Waiting tables. She would have liked to be here and asked us to give you her best."

"She's a hard worker. I like her."

"She feels the same about you, too," Shaye said. "Hey, Early and I looked on the map and found Salmon. I thought we'd been through your town at least once. I was right."

"Is there a chance both of you could visit after I get out of here? Ionella, too?"

Their heads bobbed. "Absolutely," Shaye said. "Anna and I talked about it and thought it would make a nice road trip with the kids. Show them new country. Salmon has motels, doesn't it?"

"Yeah, but we have plenty of room. Nothing like your home," I hastened to explain. "Two spare beds and space for your children if they don't mind couches and the floor."

"Mom told us you don't have any family but your husband's," Anna said. "Is she correct?"

"She's right, though I have Dawson's mom and her sister's family. His brother lives in Texas."

"I think we met his mother," Anna said. "Melissa, isn't it?"

"Uh huh. I couldn't ask for a better mother-in-law."

Shaye couldn't wait to unveil their surprise. "We did the math, and your due-date should be sometime in early December. We'd love to help when the baby is born."

Their excitement was contagious. I'd have Melissa and Robin and now Shaye and Anna to help me. They left in the afternoon with the promise of returning in early evening. Dawson stopped to see me but departed to find his own supper when he saw I'd eaten and was tired. My eyes closed before the door.

Scraping sounds woke me. The overhead light was off and the curtain around my bed closed, cutting me off from the room. I sighed, not ready for my evening checkup. Instead of Judy, my nurse for the day, KC's boy Friday shouldered his way in. I never learned his name, only that he was a corporal again. He didn't deserve my interest after how shabby he treated Dawson and me at our initial meeting. I fumbled for the call button, but he leaped forward and jerked it away, throwing it to where I couldn't reach. Rather than complain or show fear, I groped for my cell instead. Behind him, a chairback had been pushed under the door handle, explaining the noise of metal on linoleum.

His smile was satisfied and triumphant. "Dirty little bitch. Ain't so tough without a gun, are you?"

No word enraged me more than bitch. I loathed the expression no matter how it was used. "Come a little closer, asshole. I'll knock your teeth down your throat."

He accepted the challenge and stepped next to my bed. "I wish there was more time so I could enjoy this longer." While the man was short, the hand he struck me with felt as big as a ham. My head buzzed and swam while my cheek ached from the cruel blow.

Although my eyes watered, I stared back in defiance. No way was I going to show fear to a man who would strike an injured woman recovering in bed. "It was you, wasn't it?"

He grinned and nodded. "Figured it out, did you? When?"

"Just now."

Boy Friday snorted but stayed out of reach. "Clark thinks he runs a tight ship. Who do you think talked him into letting you do the heavy lifting? He's got too many irons in the fire, and I run things in the office. Thought for sure you'd catch a bullet or get waxed in the restaurant blast. Turns out you've got more lives than a cat." He offered his creepy grin again. "I'm confident you've used the last of them."

"You sold out your country and a fellow soldier and his family for what? A little money?"

"Ten million. And my own island. Tough to say no to that."

"Only to a gutter sucking scumbag like you," I said, preparing myself for what was to come. If only Dawson returned from his meal or a nurse noticed my door was barred. It might be enough to frighten my executioner away. None of my strength returned, leaving me too weak to go toe-to-toe with a strong man determined to murder me.

He jerked the pillow from beneath my head. "Don't make the mistake of thinking you bother me. In a few minutes you'll be dead, and I'm going to be a rich scumbag. A call to the right number after you're in the ground to let my contact know the photo of Hollister was faked will take care of him." He clucked his tongue. "This's too easy. One minute you were about to be released, the next you couldn't breathe and suffocated. So sad."

He was right. His plan was too simple to go wrong. His grin twisted into a snarl as he pushed the pillow over my face with both hands, smothering any cry for help. Although I couldn't see, I felt him lean in to use his weight to stop my struggles and seal me away from oxygen.

I loved how my husband didn't hesitate to do anything he could to make me feel safe, and I gripped the hilt of the knife he left me. It stayed under my thin mattress until now. Sliding it free of the scabbard while boy Friday gloated, I struck with the razor-sharp six-inch blade. It sunk to the hilt in what I hoped was the area of his liver before I sliced across his belly, sawing as I fought to open him.

Our life and death struggle lasted only seconds before the pressure on my face disappeared. I threw the pillow off and gasped for air. Dark spots dissipated as he reeled away, his face drained of blood while he used both hands to hold his guts in.

Throwing my thin cover aside, I slipped my legs over the edge of the hospital bed and stood to face him. Blood gushed from between his fingers as he sought to stem the flow. I guessed my aim was true when I hoped to cut into his blood-cleansing organ. We both heard bangs on the door and shouts from outside while I pointed to his gaping wound.

"Who's the bitch now?" I said. My hand wet with blood, I wiped my palm and regripped the handle tightly. Boy Friday dropped to a knee, then slipped to his side on the floor. I rolled him to his back with my good leg and knelt. "This's for Early and the harm done our country." I positioned the blade above his heart and slowly pressed it through his shirt and between his ribs. I pushed using both hands and my weight until it stopped at the hilt. Shouts outside grew louder as bodies hurled against my door. I waited until I was sure it was over before sitting back. Getting up was difficult even with the foot of my bed as a lever to help me stand.

The door flew open the moment I pulled the chair aside. "Jules!" First into my room, Dawson uttered my name, then stared along with staff, Shaye, and Anna. Blood dripped from the fingers of my left hand. Someone switched the light on.

Doctor Richards stepped around my husband. "Get her on the bed."

Someone—Shaye, I think—pulled the curtain aside. "Holy hell," a nurse blurted. Boy Friday and much of what should have been inside of him lay exposed. The hilt of Dawson's knife protruded from where I left it in the man's chest.

Police were summoned while my husband helped me into bed, and a resident pronounced my attacker dead. I offered a brief explanation of the attack while we awaited authorities. My doctor examined me to set my husband's mind at ease.

KC beat Sheriff Thielman by five minutes. Dawson bristled when my old boss appeared, except Agent Clark was too shocked to notice after he recognized who lay on the floor. I gave him the short version while we waited for police.

Thielman and his deputies took over the investigation. I took my personal items when they wheeled me to another room for an interrogation. KC and Dawson sat in while the sheriff prepared to question me. "Did anyone witness the attack?" Thielman asked.

I smiled at him while my former boss and Dawson shook their heads. "In a way."

"I don't understand."

Dawson waited impatiently with the other two while I unlocked the screen of my cell. Once I realized my memories were filled with holes, I moved the icon for my voice recorder to the upper left corner of the screen. My husband could help me with questions I left on it if he wasn't nearby. I'd activated it the moment the corporal woke me and snatched the nurses call button away. I lay my phone on the table. "All you have to do is listen."

* * *

The hospital released me forty-eight hours after my attack. Information gleaned leading up to the corporal's death were keeping KC and those above him busy. Our government needed to know how much damage the man wreaked. Sheriff Thielman wished me goodbye, and I could tell he hoped I'd never come back. Unfortunately for him, I planned to return frequently. Me, my new besties, and our kids would see a lot of each other. Shaye offered us a ride to the airport where Allen waited with his helicopter fueled.

I didn't notice Dawson's boots until we were airborne and I pointed. "Are they new?" We spoke on headsets over the 'copter's roar.

"Picked 'em up about a month ago. I used your gift card."

Crap. I'd planned a road trip where we'd have him fitted and then return for them later. Oh, well. At least he got a pair. "I'm glad. Are they comfortable?"

He winked. "Fit like a glove. I can't thank you enough, Jules."

I enjoyed my ride home over the Bitterroot Mountains. Snow lay deep in shaded areas in early June, and not a cloud was in sight. Bright sunlight allowed me to see bleached stains on the helicopter floor. They made me remember looking over Dawson's shoulder as he struggled to save my life. Nor could I forget the peace and serenity I experienced when I perceived my family and heard Dad speak. I wasn't ready to share with Dawson until I fully processed my experience.

Rather than touchdown behind the house, Al landed along the driveway in the field. I guessed Dawson worried about my animals—especially our new bunnies. With two does pregnant, we didn't need them spooked. Thinking about their condition made me consider my own, and I found myself touching my stomach. Al throttled down and started the process to stop the engine.

Dawson removed his headset before he unbuckled and opened our door. Offering a hand after he stepped outside to help me down, he said, "Wait here while I get your Jeep. My truck's at Al's place in Missoula."

I judged the walk ahead of me. At least four hundred yards—a quarter-mile. "No need. I can do it if you'll carry my things."

"You sure?"

"Yeah, just give me your arm."

Al insisted he tote our gear rather than Dawson. It allowed my husband to help me if needed. I was proud of myself—if not out of breath and exhausted—when we reached the porch steps. Instead of climbing them, my tears could no longer be held in check. Remembering the promises I made to God, I thanked Him again for guiding me back. Al's cheeks were wet, too, while Dawson's chin quivered, and his eyes shone. "Our place, Jules," he said. "You're home."

"I didn't think...I mean...I didn't know if—"

"You're here," he butted in. "You made it."

He helped me one tread at a time. I touched the back of my rocker while he unlocked the door. I planned to spend a lot of time in the old chair, one I found at the local antique store where Dawson purchased my rolltop desk. Our baby would grow in my womb while I rocked and sang. Both men were smiling through brimming eyes when I turned my attention back. They stood aside and allowed me to enter first. "Oh..." I slid a chair out and collapsed on it at the kitchen table. Returning to Salmon and our place took my breath away.

My counters were clean with everything in their own places. The interior smelled as if it spent time empty. Dawson noticed the same odor, because he opened the front and back doors for airflow. The sweet odor of early season sage warmed by the sun wafted through. He returned and opened the fridge door. "Got soda or beer, unless you'd rather drink coffee, Al."

"Beer me, Cap."

"Jules?"

"Water." Thinking of the sweet liquid from our well sounded best.

"Comin' right up."

"You want to fly to Missoula with me and drive your truck back?" Al asked.

"Jules? Mind if I leave you alone for a few hours. I could be home by six or seven."

"No. I mean, no, don't go," I said. "Stay with me."

He nodded. "We'll figure something out later, Al."

I couldn't wait to see my bed after I finished the glass. Before rising under my own power, I patted the back of Al's hand. "Thank you. Thank you for everything."

He nodded and took mine. "It was pure pleasure, Julia. Let me know if you need anything."

I slow-walked to the bathroom after kissing Dawson's bearded cheek. Finished washing my hands, I stopped in front of the mirror. Although my eyes were sunken and my cheeks drawn, I felt content. Limping my way to the bedroom, I waved to Al as I passed the kitchen.

Dawson left the bed made as he always did—tight enough to bounce a quarter. I struggled one-handed to pulled the covers out rather than feel trapped. Awkwardly changing into my favorite nightgown, I slipped beneath the covers and drank in the quiet and peacefulness of our place. The door opened and closed quickly only a moment before slumber. Dawson checking made me smile. At last, I was home.

Chapter XVI

Light streamed through the curtains when I woke later to the roar of Allen's departing helicopter. It didn't distress or irritate me—the sound represented a machine expertly piloted by a man who saved my life. I rolled carefully to my side and fluffed my pillow to raise my head. Dawson's familiar step echoed on the porch a moment before I heard the kitchen door. I was almost asleep again when he slipped into our bedroom and into bed. Scooching close, he gently wrapped an arm around me, avoiding my wounded arm, back, and chest. Instead, he rested his forearm and hand on my hip and growing baby bump. I sighed rather than speak and pressed against him to show I was aware. His added warmth lulled while his breathing slowed. My husband was as tired as me.

I woke a second time in confusion not knowing where I was until my eyes flew open. The nightlight I kept by the door helped me to remember. Home. I was home. My nightstand clock read 2:38 a.m. and I realized how badly I needed to pee. Dawson snored quietly when I crept from our bed.

My bladder barely released when a tap sounded on the door. "Jules? You okay?"

"Yeah. I had to go," I said.

"Need any help?"

His question made me giggle. "No, I've done this most of my life, thank you."

I drank in his deep chuckle. "Okay, I'll use the upstairs toilet and meet you in bed."

Dawson finished quickly and already waited outside after I washed my hands. He loomed tall and naked when I opened the door. "You were fast," I said. "I thought you planned to meet in bed?"

His teeth gleamed in the low light. "I'm here to offer an arm...or two."

My knee ached from overuse. I wondered if I would ever heal and regain strength lost. "I'll take you up on it, but let me hold onto you." He wanted to carry me...I know he did. However, his only attempt in the hospital made me cry out in pain. My knee, chest, and back weren't ready.

Dawson's side was empty when I opened my eyes. The angle of sunlight coming through a window alerted me to midmorning. The bedroom door stood ajar—I guessed so Dawson could hear me. I'd slept eighteen hours according to my calculations. Sore from yesterday, I stifled any groans and stuffed my feet into the pink kitten slippers I preferred. I smiled and wiggled my toes to make their ears move. Although better suited to a young girl, even Dawson thought they looked cute when I shuffled around the house.

He wasn't downstairs anywhere I could see on my way to the bathroom. I called for him the moment I was done. "Dawson? Are you in here?" My voice wasn't loud—taking a deep breath hurt my lungs and chest. Nevertheless, he would've heard me in the dead silence.

I started my day with a big glass of water before changing to coffee. My favorite cup was left next to the full pot. I filled it before beginning a plodding search for my husband. Unable to locate him in front through the kitchen window, I shambled to the backdoor and opened it wide to better see him tossing handfuls of scratch to my chickens. Although he fed them far too much cracked corn, I didn't mind a bit when his clucking and soft tone struck at my heart. I'd been convinced I wouldn't be a part of all this again. Tears welled until they spilled over and eventually dripped from my chin. He disappeared inside the coop with my wicker basket to gather any eggs.

Dawson realized I was up when he came through the back door I left open. "Jules?" Boots clomped as he searched, and his voice was louder and deeper the second time. "Jules?"

He found me in my rocker on the front porch. I couldn't see through tears until I blotted with a tissue. An attempted smile twisted with emotion. "Good morning, my love." My voice broke.

Two long steps put him next to me. Sinking to one knee, he asked, "Are you okay? I can run you into town if you need a doctor...or call for an ambulance."

A sip of coffee helped clear my throat. I patted the seat next to me. "I'm fine. Will you sit and just hold my hand?"

"For you, anything," he said.

Morning at our place is perfection on such a beautiful day. It took good ears to hear a truck passing on the highway. Clad in only a thin nightgown, I welcomed hot coffee to negate the effects of a chilly breeze. A hummingbird with a blue neckband zipped in to see if the hanging feeder contained his breakfast. Neither Dawson nor I moved while the tiny bird sipped sugar water from the plastic flower. He flew in the direction of the garage and garden area. My plot looked sad and full of weeds. With no one home to tend it, my strawberries and raspberries were grown over.

I remembered the wild rabbits Dawson and I killed when they pilfered my vegetables. He showed off his prowess with his .44, and I used my suppressed work gun. I broke the silence. "I bought something for you."

"Oh?"

"A revolver."

He lifted my hand and kissed the back. "Thank you."

"Don't you want to know what it is?"

"Doesn't matter. It's from you."

He'd talked many times about buying one, but never—forgive the pun—pulled the trigger. "I stopped by the Freedom Arms factory."

Dawson twisted toward me, his eyes wide. "You didn't?"

"A premier grade forty-four mag with adjustable sights. I wasn't sure about barrel length." I dipped my chin toward the familiar Anaconda on his belt. "Your Colt is a four inch, so I went with four and three quarters. Is that okay? It won't be ready until August, so it's not too late to call and modify the order."

"Is it okay?" he echoed. "I prefer a short-barreled belt gun, so it's better than okay, Jules. Your gift is perfect."

"I wanted to get something you'd use."

He sighed and looked across the field toward the road before putting a hand on the butt of his Colt. "Been plannin' to retire this one. A bit...well...too many memories go with it now."

I sniffed and dabbed at my nose with a tear-soaked tissue. "I-I'm sorry."

"Ain't your fault. Besides, I wouldn't have it any other way." We were silent with our own thoughts for a few moments before he glanced at me again. "August, huh?"

"They were backordered."

"I'll be damned. Reckon if I ordered today, I could have a holster delivered about the same time." He preferred a company out of El Paso for his leather. The Texas saddlery shop had been around long enough to build sheaths for gunfighters of the nineteenth century such as Tom Threepersons and Wes Hardin—a lawman and an outlaw.

"I hope you like the model I chose," I said anxiously. If Dawson hung up his Colt, I wanted its replacement to be perfect.

"I have no doubt I will," he assured. "Your cup's almost empty. Want a refill?"

"Please." I handed it to him as he went past.

My God, girl, what were you thinking? Leaving my beautiful home and perfect husband for others? Yes, I'd performed my job well and kept those who I was hired to shadow alive. I'd also nearly lost everything. Dawson was subjected to another round of bitter tears when he returned. He elected to say nothing before setting my cup on the little table and offering his kerchief.

I rocked and sipped my coffee. Pushing down with my left foot hurt my knee. A half-hour passed while I absorbed our life. Robins landed and listened for worms before hopping to a new location. A doe and two spotted fawns fed along the drive. I hoped one would someday grow into a magnificent buck to draw Dawson's attention.

"Done."

I glanced to see what my husband was talking about. He was busy fiddling with his phone. "Done what?"

"Ordered a holster. I should get it in eight weeks or less."

"You've learned to go online with your phone and buy things?" I asked incredulously.

"Yep, Al taught me."

"I could have."

"Never felt the need."

I changed the subject. "I want Jake."

"Figured as much. I can be to Mom's place and back in a few minutes. Are you okay to stay here alone?"

No, I wasn't, but I needed my best boy. We'd been through thick and thin together. "How long?"

"Twenty minutes, tops."

My eyes closed while I considered. "Okay, but can you bring me a blanket first? It's chilly in the shade, and I can't seem to get warm."

Rather than chide me over leaving my bathrobe behind, he draped a comforter far too thick over me and tucked it in before hustling to the garage. Dawson rarely drove my Wagoneer, and he looked funny in the driver's seat when he backed out. He shot me one last look and waved before shifting into drive. Dust raised from the tires as he drove, blowing across the field in the light breeze. While I enjoyed the scenery of northwestern Wyoming, I never got used to the constant wind.

My watch showed fourteen minutes from the time Dawson drove away until he appeared again. Seventeen before he parked next to the garage. I loved the rumble of my Jeep's V8 until he stopped it. Jake didn't wait for his master to open the door—leaping through the open window instead. He must have smelled me on Dawson, or else my name got mentioned. My boy is a smart dog who recognizes a number of words. We were sometimes forced to spell certain terms. "Easy, Jake," Dawson bellowed.

I held a hand out and called softly, "Hi, Jakie." One moment I thought he would leap into my lap, the next he smelled my bandaged arm and knee. My boy knew I was injured and calmed.

Dawson came up the stairs with a glower. "He didn't hurt you, did he? Damn dog didn't give me a chance."

"No, I'm fine." Jake's chin was in my lap with his big brown eyes trained on mine.

"Ready for breakfast? Don't forget...you're eating for two," he said with a grin.

We'd not spend much time talking about my pregnancy. I mostly slept and healed in the hospital unless I got visitors. "French toast?"

"Coming right up."

I couldn't help but cry while stroking Jake's head and muzzle. He never ceased to amaze—always excited to meet me when I came home from a job or each evening from school.

I'd fallen asleep and Dawson woke me when breakfast was ready. Our pointer lay next to my rocker. "Would you rather eat inside or out here?"

"Oh...I..." I'd been running for my life through a forest and my mind was still clouded with fear and pain. "...uh...at...at the table if you don't mind."

He didn't miss my frantic search for an enemy. "You okay? You were moanin' in your sleep, Jules."

I let a shaky breath out. "No, it was a bad one." I covered my face and wept again.

"Here, now." He tossed my blanket aside and helped me stand where I clutched at him, desperate to never let go. "I've got you. I've always had your six, girl." His strong arms were careful to avoid my bandages. "I'll never let you down."

He was right. Even when I didn't realize it, Dawson kept vigil over me as much I provided the Hollisters. I could attribute my every breath to his resourcefulness. My life continued because he refused to listen.

I returned to bed after finishing one slice of toast covered in syrup and a few bites of scrambled eggs. Nothing sounded or tasted good.

Dawson covered me after I got comfortable, and Jake curled against my side. We were a sleeping team again, my dog and me. He'd put in all the hours he needed to nurse me back to health. "Will you stay in the house?" I asked.

Dawson frowned. "Of course, I will. Sleep easy...I've got you," he repeated. "Want the door left open or closed?"

"Just a crack, okay?"

It hurt a bit, but I rolled to my side where an arm could be thrown over Jake. He moaned and groaned and snuggled closer. I squeezed my lids tight to keep from soaking my pillow with more tears.

* * *

Voices woke me, but I think it was Dawson hushing them that caught my attention. His distinct bass was hard to miss. Jake didn't leave me, but his head was up, and he was listening. "I'll just peek," a female whispered. The kitchen door opened and closed, and I heard boots retreating.

Red hair was visible first. "Hi, Robin," I said.

She stepped inside. "Oh, good. You're awake."

"It was time. I'm about to sleep the day away."

My friend sat on the edge of the bed. "How are you? Dawson said you were up and ate this morning."

I yawned. "Tired. What brings you and Scotty out here today?"

"Delivering groceries. Dawson called and asked if I could fill an order. Not a lot...mostly stuff for you."

"Fruit?" I asked.

"Uh huh, and vegetables, juice...things like that."

"I'm not sure I'll be able to be your matron of honor," I confessed.

"Why not? All you have to do is stand there and not look so pretty." Robin grinned and winked.

Pretty? Those days were long gone if they ever existed. I was the girl never asked to dances nor out on dates. In the meantime, passing years and brutal trauma took their toll. If Robin saw me naked, she'd be horrified at my scars. I'd never wear a lowcut top again. I struggled to slide to where I could sit against the headboard. With my right arm of little help, the effort left me exhausted. "Don't misunderstand," I panted. "I want to be there, and I'm grateful to be alive, but I'm sick and tired of always being sick and tired. Weak, too. I feel as if I'll never have enough energy to do chores again, let alone attend you at your wedding."

Robin patted my arm carefully. "You'll be up and around before you realize it, Julia. I know you. Nothing can hold you back. Not even pregnancy will slow you."

I rubbed my growing belly. "I'm not entirely sure how this happened."

Her brows lifted in humor. "Do you need me to explain the birds and the bees?"

"It's not that," I protested. "I haven't been home often."

"I bet if you count back, you'll know exactly when."

We got a chance to discuss her and Scotty's upcoming nuptials. They were watering their backyard heavily beneath a pair of huge walnut trees and adding fertilizer. She wanted a thick carpet of grass to walk on for where they wanted to marry. I hoped plenty of seed got added. The last time I saw it, there was more dirt than green. Neither planned to invite many guests. It'd be only close friends and family. I was happy to hear Robin contacted The Jumping Salmon to cater their reception. I thought it might be a good time to intervene and pay the bill anonymously.

Although he and Robin went out of their way to shop for us, I didn't get a chance to thank Scotty for everything. Sometime while Robin talked, I faded and missed her leaving.

The squeak of our bedroom door woke me. "Jules?" Dawson rubbed my shoulder. "Better get up. Supper's ready, and Doctor Richards said you need to walk."

Jake stretched and yawned. Like me, he could sleep until tomorrow morning except for a pesky bladder. His yawn was catching. "Help me, please?" I relied on my husband more than ever.

Dawson assisted me to the table after waiting outside the bathroom. I continued to limp hunched over as if I were ninety. "I fixed chicken soup. Lots of veggies in it." He pushed a plate closer to me. "A batch of biscuits, too."

As much as I enjoy and appreciate his culinary skills, nothing sounded, smelled, or tasted good. I tried a few spoonsful before nibbling at the bread. Dawson said nothing as I forced myself to eat, although he cast a critical gaze. I finished most of the broth and a biscuit before I pushed my bowl away. "I'm sorry, but I can't eat anymore."

"No problem…it's a start. Are you ready for a walk?"

I made it to the garage door before stopping to rest. Jake followed and watched in concern when I quit. The evening breeze felt no warmer than when I was out earlier. Dawson helped me return to the porch and my rocker. Birds were getting ready for bed as I glided and listened. The blanket from before lay folded nearby and I wrapped myself in it. Our place couldn't be more peaceful, and I wondered if I ultimately returned only to die at home.

A week got wasted while I napped on the couch by day and slept long hours in bed at night. Dawson didn't complain when I kept him from chores and daily life. I needed him nearby to savor what I almost lost. Through it all, I was unable to stop dwelling on my conversation with Dad.

"Rise and shine, Julia Marie." Dawson's voice was no longer hushed when he strolled into the bedroom.

"Another hour," I complained and struggled to roll away.

"Now. You need to hurry. We don't have much time."

His steely tone caused my eyes to open. "Why?"

"I made an appointment for you in Salmon with Doctor Wells for your prenatal care, and he ordered your records from St. John's Med center. He's in for a shock, but I'll ask for him to personally check under your bandages. No nurse."

Dawson's schoolmate was my attending physician. "Dawson…Julia," he greeted when he swept into the room. "I understand someone has a bun in the oven?" I nodded. Dr. Wells gave a professional smile. "Cutting to the chase, I've studied your records, been briefed on national security, and threatened by government thugs. It appears they don't want you treated by some country hick friend of the family, but here we are. What are your wishes, Mrs. Pelletier?"

I looked at my husband. "Dawson thinks . . ."

Wells interrupted, taking my words in another direction. ". . . doesn't matter. Do you want him out of the room?"

"I-I . . . no. He's the father."

"Again, it doesn't matter. He'll eventually get my bill. What counts at the moment is what you want."

I didn't have to think. "I want our baby delivered here by people we know."

"Then let's get to it," Wells said, his real smile back.

It turned out Dawson didn't need to ask that no staff be present. KC already made the "request." My husband's friend assessed my injuries and prescribed a refill of antibiotics. Before we left, I was given a list of prenatal vitamins and a date for my next checkup. It felt good to have my bandages removed, and he felt confident my stitches could be taken out. The doctor frowned while he listened to my breathing, something that worried us both. It continued to hurt with each lungful I drew.

We got a load of chicken and rabbit feed in town. I stayed in the Jeep while Dawson purchased it and the boys tossed it in back. A wince from one that shook the rig got hidden from my husband. We needed his truck back from Missoula, but I wasn't up to the trip nor letting him out of my sight.

I guess The Jumping Salmon beckoned, because we turned into the parking lot instead of going home. "You heard what Gary ordered," Dawson said. "You've got to eat more if the baby's goin' to get enough. This ain't like when you don't feel good and can't. The little tyke's gonna cannibalize your body if you don't shove some vittles in."

I lifted an eyebrow when he parked in the handicapped zone. We could afford a fine for no permit, but one look at me would give us a pass, so I didn't refuse his arm on the way inside. His infinite patience as I shuffled almost made me weep again. A couple leaving held the door, their pity clear as they waited without comment for us to enter. Although the time was between lunch and supper, enough patrons were seated inside to make me uncomfortable as every eye followed us. The local gossip mill ground away at full speed.

Allison Edwards saw us come in and waited at a table with the chair pulled out. She held it while Dawson seated me. "We heard you were injured again, Julia," she said. My husband drew his chair closer so our knees touched. "Are you doing better?"

I glanced at Dawson who answered for me. "Still hurtin' a bit, but she's healing. You know how clumsy she is." He quickly changed the subject. "Say...what's the daily special?"

"Our bison burger and all the fries you can eat...or substitute onion rings. Your choice."

He handed the menus back unopened. "We'll take two. Fries for me and substitute a baker for Jules with everything on it." I nodded. His choice was as good as anything else.

"Something to drink?"

I wasn't one to order a sugary beverage, but the thought of one made my mouth water. "A Sprite, please."

Dawson looked surprised. "Make it two."

I finished the first and was almost done with the second when our meal came. For some reason, I could smell the goop the restaurant used on the buns. I got half the burger down and almost all the potato. Pushing my plate to Dawson, I offered what was left. "You might as well finish it. I can't eat another bite."

Our server came to clear our plates away. "Unlimited fries, Dawson," she reminded. "Might as well let me bring another order."

"No, but thanks. Got things to do, and I'd better get Julia home." We both adored Allison, and I didn't complain when he left a fifty percent gratuity behind.

I got in a long nap and was sitting on the porch with Dawson when Jake's head came up. A low woof told us we were about to have company. I recognized the silver SUV as Dawson's aunt and my boss. She parked next to the garage and got out looking around. Finally, Bess came up the steps and leaned against the bannister. "I'm embarrassed to admit this's the first time I've been here, Julia." She nodded to my husband. "How's one of my favorite nephews?"

He snorted at her attempted humor. "I'm one of two, Auntie. Either I'm your favorite or I'm not."

She winked and said, "You're right," before turning her attention to me. "Melissa kept me up to date on your progress after the...the...well, your accident. She cried every night over how badly you were...wounded." As a pacifist, Bess was uncomfortable with the idea of violence and those involved. "How're you feeling?"

News of my mother-in-law's tears didn't surprise me. The sisters were almost as tall as Dawson, and they could weep at a moment's notice. "A little better each day," I said. "Thank you for asking."

She hemmed and hawed around the reason for stopping until I yawned. "The reason I'm here..."

I held my palm out. "You can stop right there. I plan to resign my position at school. Not only was I absent much of the year, but I'm pregnant now and plan to be a stay-at-home mom." There was another reason, but I wanted to talk it over with Dawson first.

Bess was visibly relieved. "I'm so happy for you and Dawson. We've all hoped you'd have children soon. Melissa didn't mention anything...are you keeping it a secret?"

I nodded. "For now."

Dawson waited until his aunt waved and disappeared. "She was here to fire you."

"It's her job. I would've done the same in her situation."

He sighed. "Maybe. You worked hard for your position."

"You're right. However, our life has taken an abrupt turn." I instinctively rubbed my baby bump.

"Have you thought of names?" he asked.

"I've always known what I'd name a girl. Bethany, after my mom."

"It's beautiful. Beth for short?"

"Huh uh. My mom was Beth. Our daughter'll be Bethany."

"Got a middle one picked out?"

"Anne."

"I like it. It's Mom's, too. She'll be pleased."

Although I wanted to, I refrained from rolling my eyes. Men could be so thickheaded. Of course, I knew. It's why I chose it. "I hope you don't mind what I'd like to name him if it's a boy." The thought came to me while I lay in the hospital.

"Let me have it. I've got a few ideas, too."

"Timothy after Father Timothy. He saved my soul."

I think Dawson was surprised. He frowned and thought about it before turning his attention to me again. "I like it. Mind if I help with the middle name?"

"Sure!"

"Allen."

"After...you mean after Al?"

"Yeah. He was a good soldier to serve with, and the best business partner a man could hope to have. We're also having this conversation because of his flying skills, along with his love and admiration for you. He saved your life, Jules. We can't forget it."

"Timothy Allen Pelletier," I articulated slowly, letting the name roll off my tongue. "I love it."

He grinned. "Bethany Anne Pelletier. It's got a nice ring to it, too."

Jake insisted on walking with me while Dawson started supper. After a late lunch, we weren't having a big meal. His suggestion of toasted ham and cheese sandwiches and tomato soup even sounded good. I used a walking stick he insisted on making for me, derived from a rare straight section of vine maple. It was a little taller than me and as thick as my wrist. I stopped a little farther than where Al landed his helicopter before I rested for my return.

The kitchen actually smelled good when I got back. I didn't miss Dawson peering anxiously through the window during my trek back. His attention increased when I stopped at the bottom of the stairs to catch my breath. "Need a helping arm?" he called through the screen door.

I didn't answer until I got on the porch and went inside. "Nope. I got it."

He pulled my chair out. "Have a seat. Got a sandwich and bowl ready for you."

"I saw a series of stakes to the west of where Al landed last time. Are you planning something?"

After serving himself, Dawson sat across from me. "We need to hit the sack early tonight. Tomorrow's gonna be a long day." he said, ignoring my question.

I yawned. His plan sounded good to me. My walk was exhausting. "What's going on?"

"We're meeting Ox and Jose in Belize City. We'll fly into Missoula on our way home and pick up my truck."

"Oh, honey...I'm not sure I can..."

He didn't let me finish. "Don't worry. I've got this. Mom agreed to keep Jake, and we're meeting the Leer belonging to Al's buddy in Salmon at zero six hundred. Finish your sandwich and soup, and I'll help you into bed."

Not only did I eat it all—I fell asleep fast enough I didn't hear Dawson clean the kitchen and start a load of clothes in the washer. Our flight south would take every bit of energy I could muster.

Chapter XVII

I was relieved to find Dawson and Al planned ahead so our flight south wasn't as taxing as I dreaded. Seats on one side of the fuselage were replaced with a comfortable bed. I slept until we stopped to refuel and used the restroom while we waited. Dawson sat within an arm's length—I could reach out and touch him—where he enjoyed movies during our flight. My greatest joy during the trip was occasionally waking and able to see him inches away.

Jose and Ox waited outside their van when we taxied in. Both hurried up the steps the moment they were lowered. Ox knelt next to where I sat at the edge of the bed, and for a moment I thought he would cry. "How are you, little one?"

I couldn't smile. "A little better each day, my friend."

Jose leaned around Donny where I could see him. "Welcome to Belize, señora." His dark and expressive eyes were full of mischief when he winked.

"Thank you, Jose. I needed this."

The trip to our villa was far less frightening than my first. Jose drove with his attention on keeping me comfortable rather than making good time. With an hour added to our journey, I was exhausted when the gate to our southern home opened.

I held tightly to Dawson's arm while we went inside. Something looked odd when my gaze traveled down the slope to the water's edge where we swam. My husband beat me to the punch. "I see you got it finished in time."

Ox stood next to us where we stared out the window. A long dock extended into the bay from an open building. Donny and Jose's boat was moored beneath it. "We would've preferred flying into the states rather than oversee the job, Cap'n," he said. "The crew worked hard and stayed under budget."

Rather than slope to the lapping waves, the hill stopped short of the new building where a rather large flat area was paved with cement. Chairs, a table, and an open barbeque made an alluring picture. "We went a little farther out than you suggested," Jose said. "The dock stretches fifty feet. Got enough room to cover two boats and moor another pair if you want. Ox and I broke in the barbeque, and it works better than we hoped. Ran electricity to the building, so we've got lights and power outlets. We could put in a refrigerator under cover to make it even more handy. There's lots of room inside."

"Do it," Dawson said. "Choose a large model and have it delivered and installed ASAP."

Wide concrete steps led from the backdoor and merged with others going from our bedroom patio to the dock below. Dawson took one side and Ox the other when I insisted going down to see it. The steel-covered building was even bigger close up. Our gathering area was cut in an oval shape, with a cement retaining wall not visible from above holding the hillside back. I asked Dawson, "Do you mind if I walk to the end of the dock?"

The boys stayed behind as my husband helped me. I noted a built-in ladder on the end for swimmers. The clear water was deep, and I could see fish swimming below. "Careful," Dawson said as I leaned out.

"Help me sit." Although my feet couldn't break the surface, I swung my legs above it after Dawson got me into position and made himself comfortable next to me. "How long are we staying? Don't forget we have a wedding to attend."

"Long as you want or need. Scotty and Robin will understand. Our time schedule is wide open. Other than Jake and my family, there ain't no reason to go back until the baby is ready to be born. We'll return to Idaho whenever you decide and not a moment before."

***

Jose grilled fresh fish caught before they left to get us at the airport. Pineapple and vegetables rounded out our supper. Conversation was subdued while we enjoyed our meal. I found myself surprised when the food tasted better with every bite. What started as a six-pound grouper was reduced to a skeleton when we finished.

Jose kept an eye on me until afterward. "We understand you're preggers, señora."

I nodded. "Almost four months now."

"You must eat more," he said.

"My appetite is returning." The bison burger and now the fish and vegetables seemed to have kickstarted my salivary glands.

"How're your wounds?"

I rubbed my gritty eyes. "I got the stitches out yesterday."

"Take a day...perhaps two...then exercise in the saltwaters. It'll help you recover and increase your desire to eat more."

"You're tired, Jules," Dawson said. "Let me help you to our room."

I didn't argue. Although I'd slept most of the way south, exhaustion had set in. Our villa seemed miles away as I took the cement stairs to our bedroom patio one at a time. Finally, Dawson could stand by no longer and swept me into his arms. I gritted teeth and waited for lancing pain that didn't materialize. Perhaps I was on the mend.

Other than once to use our private bathroom, I slept through the night until noon the following day. I woke on my side and rolled to my back before stretching. My wounds pulled but didn't cause undo discomfort. The door was open a few inches, and I was sure Dawson listened for my call. Instead, I rubbed my growing belly. Although I felt the bump, I found it hard to believe a baby grew inside.

Rather than get my husband's attention, I rose and looked inside empty bags before realizing Dawson put our clothes away. Choosing a light blouse and a pair of cargo shorts, I went into the bathroom to change. Huge mirrors and bright lights didn't allow me to avoid the sight of my scars. They weren't enormous but were red and obvious for what they represented. I ran my index finger across them and marveled at how they missed vital organs. My chest ached with each deep breath, but it didn't bother me while I was inactive.

My shower was only long enough to rinse sweat and travel fatigue away. I ignored a subtle breeze before shutting off the water. As I suspected, Dawson waited in our room when I stepped out fully clothed. "Afternoon, sweet thang," he drawled. "Sleep well?"

My stride already felt surer when I crossed to where he sat on the bed. "Like two babies," I said while rubbing my tummy.

"The boys and I ate early this morning, but there's plenty remaining to fix." Though I didn't need it, I took his arm when he led me to the kitchen, and helped me onto a high stool at the bar before perusing the fridge. "There's some sort of fish I don't recognize, shrimp, mushrooms, cheese, bacon, eggs..." He trailed off while he searched through the icebox.

"Can you cook an omelette?"

He stood and turned to face me. "Can I cook an omelette?" he echoed. "Dear woman, I can knock your socks off with my breakfasts."

"I want three eggs, shrimp, bacon, mushrooms...and some of that chopped up." I pointed to a ripe pineapple on the counter.

Dawson impressed me when he also used heavy cream found in the refrigerator door. My mouth watered while he fried bacon. I talked him into dropping four extra strips in the pan for me to enjoy while he prepared my breakfast. He slid my plated meal across the counter to me as the boys returned from whatever errand they ran. Ox was first to me. "Smells good! I'm your man if you can't eat it all."

"Stick around," I said dryly. "You'll get plenty." I didn't mention Jake usually finished my breakfasts.

"Did you locate a refrigerator?" Dawson asked Jose.

He held his arms wide. "Got a big one. They deliver and install tomorrow. I warned 'em where it went, but they said no problem."

I liked the big shrimp and chunks of pineapple. My burgeoning appetite surprised me as I worked through the meal. A lull in the conversation caught my attention, and I looked up to see our friends staring and Dawson smiling. I wiped my mouth with a napkin. "What?"

"It's nice to see you hungry again," he said. "You worried me."

I gauged what was left and figured I could finish rather than feed the last of it to Ox. Ignoring the peanut gallery, I bent to the task of eating six big bites washed down with milk. "I'd like to go to the dock if you don't mind."

Dawson looked up from where he read the bill presented to him by Jose. "Hang on, and I'll go with you."

"I'll take her if you don't care, Cap," Ox said.

"Do you mind, Jules?" Dawson asked. I glanced around the kitchen while I considered. It took too long to decide, and he made the decision for me. "I've got her, Ox. Thanks."

My first full day went fast. Dawson sat with me on the dock, while I lay and absorbed radiant heat from the fire in the sky. Thankfully, he brought a cooler filled with cold bottled water. We shared them, and he helped me stand after the last one was drunk. The sun was hot and my fair skin would burn long before his. I was tired but climbed the steps without help. Perhaps there was light at the end of a dark, frightening tunnel.

I slept until noon and sometimes longer during our first four days. My appetite increased until I felt hungry most of the time. Although I went to bed very early, I woke at 8:30 on the fifth. Dawson caught me when I left the bathroom wearing a bathing suit covered by a loose caftan. "Plans?" he asked.

"To catch a few rays before we eat. Interested in tagging along?"

Going down the steps hurt my knee, but each day was better than the one before. Dawson was ready to catch me if I fell, yet I made it to our picnic area without stopping. The new fridge was filled with bottled water and soda. I led us out to my favorite spot at the end of our pier. There, I spread a large towel and left room for him when I sat without help. The lapping of waves and distance roar of the ocean as it crashed against rocks guarding our lagoon soothed my soul. I soon found myself lying on my side with my head in Dawson's lap. He rested his hand on my hip taking care not to irritate my wounds. "I need a journal," I said. "We need to record these days while our baby is growing inside of me."

"Good idea. I'll see if one of the boys knows where we can buy one."

"We need to keep track of everything. Where we are and what we're doing on a particular date. Perhaps even the weather. She can read it when she gets older."

"She?"

"It's a girl. I'm sure it is."

He chuckled. "I'll take your word for it."

The water lapping below us beckoned. Grains of sand were visible deep in the turquoise ocean. I stood and threw off my caftan. Grinning at Dawson, I stepped off and fell feet first with my toes pointed and barely caused a ripple. The lagoon was even warmer than I remembered, and I surfaced to see his concerned face. I relaxed to float on my back and drifted away using a slow backstroke that pulled at my arm wound. "C'mon in," I called. "The water's fine!"

Dawson pulled his shirt over his head and tossed it aside. Sandals kicked off left him wearing only his swim trunks. Using two long strides to the edge of the dock, he launched himself in my direction and powered below the surface like a torpedo. I twisted belly down and watched him knife beneath me. It made me laugh when he popped up fifty feet beyond where I floated. Checking to see I was still okay, he turned with sure strokes toward open ocean a half mile away. He paused after a couple hundred yards before returning in the same easy glide.

Dawson stopped within touching distance to tread water. "Are you okay? Need help getting out?"

"Not yet."

Rather than swim away, he literally freestyled laps around me. We didn't talk while I enjoyed the salty brine. Once he came close enough to kiss me before twisting and diving. Without his long hair in a braid, it fanned out as he explored the seafloor. I feared for his safety after a minute passed, but he barely breathed hard when he appeared again. I caught his eye, and he swam to me. "Ready?"

I hated to get out. Dawson helped brace me on the ladder so I could climb. My chest hurt from deep breathing, and he saw it when he followed. I answered his unasked question. "I'm okay. It's going to take time."

Ox and Jose waited at our picnic area, the barbeque hot with eight lobsters on the grill and a table covered with fresh fruit. Mangos, bananas, soursop, and pineapple were my favorites among many. I dripped my way to a chair after helping myself to a banana and the plate of pineapple. Ox grinned, while Jose gazed critically. "Already you look better, señora. Belize looks good on you."

Although three angry bullet wounds showed above my swimsuit, I couldn't agree more. "I feel better," I admitted. Dawson brought a mango and chunked watermelon and sat beside me. I took his hand in mine. "I owe everything to this guy." My sight misted as I remembered, and my chin quavered before I could stop it. Would controlling my emotions over my brush with death ever become possible?

Jose's dark eyes gave nothing away while he considered me before glancing at Dawson and then Ox. "Don't we all, señora? Don't we all?"

*＊＊

Days turned into weeks while I recovered. Each morning I rose earlier until I finally woke at my normal time of 5:30. With Jose driving and Ox riding shotgun, they showed us what they'd learned of the tiny country. They took us to beaches, Mayan ruins, museums, and caves I refused to enter. We also frequented bustling outdoor markets where Ox and Jose delighted in bargaining. Nothing was off-limits, and I saw how the locals loved to barter. Rarely did we walk anywhere when I wasn't holding Dawson's hand. Simply the memory of what I nearly threw away was enough to make me burst into tears.

Leave it to Ox to make sense of my emotional responses while the hour was late and we were sitting around the firepit. A cheery blaze was fed with dried brush the boys cut back our property's perimeter. "It's normal, Julia. My wife was the same way during her pregnancy. Your hormones are moaning." His eyes twinkled at his play on words.

"I'm tired of it. It started when I arrived in Wyoming the last time."

"You were pregnant and didn't know it yet," Dawson said.

"What were you doing there?" Ox asked.

We all heard the distaste in my husband's tone. "She was working. How in the hell do you think she got shot full of holes?"

Jose's eyes narrowed in the flicking light. "I thought The Company was disbanded and defunct, señora."

I nodded. "It is."

"Who bought your services?"

A glance to Dawson earned me a shrug. "The government."

My admission earned a whistle from Jose. "They came to you?"

Dawson's voice was low with a dangerous rumble. "Yeah. Damn near got themselves killed."

"What part?" Ox asked.

"I worked for a subsidiary of Homeland Security. They swore me in, and gave me a badge and everything."

Jose sounded surprised. "What were you tasked with?"

My husband snorted. "What do you think?"

"Ah," he said. "Our current administration is carrying out assassinations at home?"

"Not of US citizens. These were bad guys. Really bad guys," I said.

Jose wasn't sold. "Uh huh."

Dawson's bass was hushed. "They were ISIS."

After their initial shock, I was forced to give the pair some highlights. My explanation went into how smoothly first contact went but also the difficulty of performing my assignment. I explained about the female suicide bomber when I stopped her outside the restaurant but learned later it was Dawson who saved the day. Nor did I leave out details of how little Anna Hollister was nearly murdered behind the Pine Street grocery.

"Hah!" Ox suddenly roared with a shudder of muscular release. I felt the energy dump the huge man generated with his guttural bellow. The poor guy lost his own daughter—about the same age as Shaye's girl—to a drunk driver. His reaction and tears put the rawness of his loss on display. "You could've called us, Julia. You should've."

"I'm sorry, Donny. You know I work best alone."

They were riveted by my tale of engaging the final group in Jackson. Jose's smile was dark and unpleasant when I told of encountering the four inside the Upchuck. I shared it only to explain why I left my cellphone behind.

"You didn't mention this particular encounter," Dawson said. "Father Timothy surprised me with the highlights."

I shrugged. "Not much to it. I watched them exit the UPS truck and identified a grenade a few minutes after they sat. Following my encounter with the female suicide bomber, I wasn't going to take a chance and made quick work of them."

"Timothy said the same thing," Dawson said dryly. "The way he put it...one minute you were talking, the next you were shooting."

"Yeah, that's about right." I didn't let myself think about the subject, lest I burst into tears again. At least the priest followed up on his promise and helped my husband through the worst of my recovery.

"Jesus," Ox breathed.

The final engagement was nothing I was ready to discuss—my emotions were far too raw. It was well past my bedtime, and I stood and looked up the hill. "If you boys don't mind, I think I'll hit the sack."

Dawson jumped up. "Let me help you."

"I'll be fine. Stay as long as you want."

He shook his head. "G'night, men. See you in the morning."

* * *

Dawson stepped from the bathroom drying his hair with a towel and another around his waist. He stopped abruptly. "What?" he asked. I twisted away, unable to halt my weeping. His weight rolled me toward him as he knelt on the bed. A hand squeezed my shoulder as he continued turning me to him. "You can tell me anything, Jules. Are you in pain?"

Except for crying, I opened my arms to him without speaking. To his credit, Dawson took me into his, holding and rocking me. If anything, my response to his quiet gentleness bordered on hysterical. His embrace tightened as if it were possible to protect me from memories. Shushing me and rubbing my back, Dawson did what he could to be a calming influence. My sobs eventually abated, leaving me to occasionally hiccup while I caught my breath.

How to explain something I didn't understand? Yet no one had more faith in me than my husband. "Y-you are-aren't going to believe me."

He didn't stop rubbing my back as I struggled with coherency. "Try me," he said in a bass so low I felt it more than heard.

I sighed, my breath catching again. "I-I don't know h-how to t-tell you."

"Relax and take your time. It'll come out, Jules."

"I talked to Dad." To say the words out loud sent me into another frenzy of tears.

Dawson waited until I calmed. "Tell me," he whispered.

His reaction didn't surprise me. My husband was far more open minded than me. "When...when Al was flying us to the hospital after you found me."

"You spoke to your dad?" I nodded my head against his neck. "How?"

"I couldn't catch my breath after we were onboard. You hollered at Allen I wasn't breathing, and he told you to start CPR. I didn't stay in my body and watched from above as you tried to breathe in my mouth. When they didn't work, you continued with chest compressions. Al flew low and fast over the Hollister place. A couple times I worried you'd crash when he barely cleared treetops."

"You got it right," he murmured.

"That's when I saw my family. Mom, Dad, and Meghan."

"Where were you?"

He posed a good question. "I-I don't know. We just *were*. They remained in the distance, and I couldn't get closer no matter how hard I ran."

"You're sure it was them?"

"Oh, yes! As certain as I'm here with you. When he spoke to me, his voice was as clear as yours is now."

"What did he say?"

"We talked about everything. Especially how all of my family were anxious to see me again, but it wasn't my time. He looked and sounded so good...Mom and Meghan, too. They were happy...no...they were overjoyed to see me. I wanted to stay, but Dad said you and our children needed me."

"Children?"

"Yeah. I felt he was very proud of me, even with the things I've done. We talked about so much in such a brief time...I can't remember it all. One thing I do...he warned me of danger to you and me and our family."

"Did he say what it was?"

"No, only that you and I are a team, and we should always cleave together. Never allow anything to come between us. Oh...Dawson? They love you and are so pleased with who you are. All three were certain you're my perfect mate."

"Do you recall anything else?"

"Not really. I get flashes when I least expect them. Dad faded, and I woke in my body." Memories of my husband's pain stabbed me. "You-you were crying s-so hard I couldn't stand it, and I-I t-tried to leave again. But the doctor s-shocked me and made me stay."

"I'm glad he did," Dawson whispered. "Life without you isn't worth living, Jules."

"You believe me?"

He pulled back to arm's length in surprise. "Of course. Why would you think differently?"

"Because my family died a long time ago, and I'm telling you I saw and spoke to them."

His eyes narrowed as he cocked his head. "I've never doubted you, Julia. If you came in the house telling me the sky turned green and the grass blue, I'd expect to see it exactly as you described. I don't have to make excuses for what you're certain of. You're sure you talked to your family, and so am I."

My family was right. Dawson was my perfect mate.

***

My strength built quickly as my appetite returned. Our afternoon swims grew longer each day until finally reaching the breakers holding the sea at bay. Early mornings saw us fishing from Ox and Jose's boat far into the Caribbean. We caught and ate enough food from the ocean that I welcomed the occasional hamburger or hotdog. However, I enjoyed hooking odd-looking fish sometimes tipping the scales at half my bodyweight. It felt as if my stomach grew daily as my clothes got tighter.

Dawson left the boys and walked to where I worked on my tan. "Have you paid attention to the calendar?" he asked.

I blocked the sun with my hand and peered at him through my dark glasses. "Not really. It's probably August now, isn't it?" Realization hit me with the significance. "Oh, Lord. How long until Scotty and Robin's wedding?"

"Today's Sunday. They get married in six days."

"But I don't want to leave."

He lifted a shoulder. "Then, we won't. I'll call and offer them an excuse…as if we need one. The boys are right. Belize looks good on you, Jules."

I sighed. "No, I promised. We both promised. They've never let us down, no matter how frightened they were. We can do the same."

"Shall I call for a plane?"

"Yeah, I guess." I still needed to find a dress to wear. None of what I owned would fit my growing belly.

"Are you sure?"

"Of course, I am." I rolled over and stood. "We're coming back this winter, though."

Dawson cupped my chin and leaned down. "Whenever you want and for as long as you wish," he vowed before kissing me.

I pulled away when our lips parted and hobbled as fast as I could to the end of the dock "Race you!"

I dove and traveled barely twenty yards in the water before I heard a splash. Then, Dawson's head appeared ten feet ahead of me while churning the lagoon with hard kicks and long arms. He didn't let up until reaching dangerous water along the reef. There, he waited and treaded water until I reached him, his arms going around me as he pulled me close. "Me and you and little Bethany against the world, Jules, for the rest of our lives."

Not only Bethany. My father promised us children.

* * *

Telling Ox and Jose goodbye was far more difficult than at the conclusion of our first stay. As Dawson did, I considered them a part of our family. We made it clear not only did we want them to stay as long as they wished, but they would soon have company again. I'd purchased airline tickets far in advance for Scotty and Robin to fly south the day after their wedding. We hoped their stay would be as memorable as ours. After apologizing at being unable to meet us, Al left Dawson's truck parked at the Missoula airport. I wished I would have listened more carefully—I swear my husband sighed his content after he started the diesel engine and settled into his seat.

Our flight arrived at 4:00 in the afternoon, and I delighted at the higher temperature than Belize with far lower humidity. Highway 95 was a welcome relief as we traveled through Lolo, Hamilton, Darby, and Conner on our way up Lost Trail Pass. It was a few minutes after 7:00 when we passed Melissa's driveway. "Aren't we stopping to get Jake?" I asked.

Dawson wore an impish grin when he turned his head to me. "Later."

I frowned. "Okay, but not too late. I'd like to be in bed early."

His smile grew when we turned onto our drive. Something didn't look right when we left the timber where we could see our house set against the mountain rising behind it. We drove past fencing that wasn't there when we left, when two horses and four mules lifted their heads. I gasped. "A barn. Dawson! Horses and mules, too," I added excitedly.

"You can thank Scotty. He's been ramrodding two crews. One putting in fencing and the other raising the barn."

We idled past the stock. "Isn't that Tonto? I recognize the mules...it's Erlene and Aztec! Where's..." I craned my neck to see a second horse. "...Betsy?" The appaloosa I rode into the Middle Fork with Scotty and Robin was nowhere to be seen. Instead, a young mare I thought was a Morgan watched us pass with her head high and ears forward. I didn't recognize the extra pair of mules.

"Scotty didn't want to let her get away. She's his go-to when a rider needs a gentle mount. He found the new mare for sale in Challis. Says she's trail-broke and steady."

Our barn was raised as a monitor style. The center section stood taller than both sides. Rather than built of steel, it was sided with wood and far larger than I first imagined until Dawson parked next to it. He laughed when I mentioned we could stable a dozen horses and mules in my initial excitement. "Need space for a tack room, not to mention tons of hay and sacks of grain."

I couldn't believe it. We finally owned horses, mules, and a place to stable them. Our children would be raised with an appreciation of working animals and the mountains surrounding us. What more could a woman want? I had a beautiful homestead, wonderful husband, and now the start of our family to make my life complete.

***

Dawson and I sat under a walnut tree enjoying the excitement of both Scotty and Robin. We stood with them in front of God and twenty-two witnesses as they said their vows and now mingled with guests, receiving well-wishes from them all. My husband looked nice in new jeans and the gray long-sleeve shirt I admired most on him. I couldn't help but rub my growing belly stretching the new dress I purchased for our friends' special day.

"Never thought I'd see it," Dawson said. "Even when Robin and he hit it off, I expected him to do or say something dumb enough to scare her away."

Melissa heard him as she came up from behind where we sat and put her hands on his shoulders. "All we have to do is see the way he looks at her, son. Scotty and Robin are no less in love than you and Julia." Dawson's mom squeezed my shoulder for effect. "Is it true they're going to honeymoon at your place in Belize?"

"Our gift to them, Mom. Jules got 'em first class tickets, too. They're flyin' in style."

"Bless your heart, Julia," Melissa said. "It'll be an experience they'll never forget. I certainly haven't."

"Donny and Jose are getting ready. They'll pick up our newlyweds tomorrow afternoon."

"I like those boys," she said. "If you don't mind, I'd love to vacation there again when we have a chance."

"Anytime," Dawson said. "You've got from the time Scotty and Robin get back until Julia goes into labor. We're countin' on your help."

She chuckled. "There's no keeping it a secret any longer is there?" We all looked at where my stomach stretched my dress.

No, there was no more subterfuge about my condition. Nor would friends believe I'd been badly wounded only a few months ago. Deep breaths still hurt, and so did walking down a steep hill. My knee sometimes rebelled and warned me I expected too much from it. No worries, according to my doctor. Like I found in most circumstances during my life, good things come to those who wait.

Chapter XVIII

Bethany rode on the seat rise between me and the pommel with a tight grip on the saddle horn. Every so often, she would kick with her heels and try to cluck with her tongue in a vain effort to mimic. My right arm circled her little body to keep her safe while I held the reins in my left. Ahead, Dawson occasionally turned in his saddle to keep a close eye on us and our mule train. When he did, our daughter caught his eye and wave wildly as if he didn't know we trailed. "Daddy see, Momma!" she said excitedly.

I leaned forward to kiss her crown. "Yes, Daddy sees Bethany, honey. Daddy loves his girl." Jake led our group in a trot ahead of us all.

"Daddy see." Her repeating murmur was filled with satisfaction.

Our journey into the Middle Fork of the Salmon River was Bethany's third—the first as an eight-month old in a baby carrier on my chest. Her first steps were taken in camp at Thomas Creek. At thirty-two months now, I expected her to be a handful in and around our wall tents. My growing stomach made our seating arrangement tight, but she'd gotten tired of riding with Dawson.

Summer rafters caught her attention. With her trying to stand to better be seen, I held Bethany in her seat. "Careful...we don't want to scare Bliss, do we? She might buck us off!"

Her arm wigwagged in return to friendly waves from occupants in a pair of huge boats. "Dey saw! Momma, dey saw!"

Dawson drew our string to a halt before dismounting and strolling toward us with Jake at his side. I love everything about my man—from his dusty Stetson down to leather chaps and scuffed boots. He ran a hand along Bliss's neck to her withers while wrinkling his nose at Bethany. "My girls doin' okay?" he asked.

Our daughter leaned forward—her arms held wide. "Take me, Daddy."

He gathered her against his chest with both hands where they could kiss. I noticed he kept her high enough she couldn't kick the Freedom Arms revolver I purchased for him in another lifetime. He immediately fell in love with the .44 magnum after filling out the proper paperwork and bringing it home. In the three years he'd carried it, Dawson's taken two mature mule deer bucks and a nice bull elk. We've realized my dream of living a largely self-sufficient life, growing a garden, raising livestock, and filling our freezer with seasonal fish, birds, and big game.

"It ain't far. Should reach camp in less than an hour," he said. "I'll take Bethany to give you a break if she doesn't mind." Judging by the way her head bobbed, our girl was prepared for a switch.

I rubbed my second baby bump while they mounted and Dawson got her firmly seated. My due-date was in fourteen weeks—a boy to continue the family name.

Letting the string get started while I stayed behind to minimize dust in my eyes and mouth, I couldn't help but marvel at the place we found ourselves. Miles from the trailhead in some of the wildest country the lower 48 has to offer, a wolf, bear, moose, or elk could make its presence known at any time. Although it was the last day of July, the weather wasn't unbearably hot. I clucked my tongue and tickled Bliss's ribs with my heels. It would be a relief to reach our destination and erect our tent—my pregnant body grew more tired with each clink of an iron shoe.

Dawson kept turning in his saddle on every corner, fearful of me lagging too far behind. I recognized where we were long before I saw pitched tents ahead. Somewhere near where they stood a hot spring beckoned. The excited screams of children and shouts from men meant our arrival hadn't gone unnoticed.

Scotty held Tonto's reins after Dawson handed Bethany to Robin and dismounted. He hurried back to where I rode into camp. "Looks like the whole gang's here," he said. "Let me give you a hand." Jake watched carefully as his master crowded close to his mistress. My left knee never fully regained its strength and occasionally lets me down when I least expect it, but always when I mounted or dismounted. It was lucky he was there to catch me when it buckled and gave way.

Shaye was first to reach me after Dawson helped me stand. A kiss was administered to each of my cheeks before welcoming me into her arms. I hugged her back and viewed at our crowd over her shoulder. Scotty, Early, Emerson, and Jack Boyd, along with Russell Endicott helped Dawson unload our pack train and lead the animals to where Scotty's horses and mules were picketed. Little Jack and Tryn were along the river skipping rocks, while Lola and Shaye's daughter Anna—named after Emerson's wife—were gathered around Bethany. Anna Boyd, Marta, and Ionella stayed in their chairs next to the firepit and out of the way, but I returned their enthusiastic wave. What a group! Although all my friends were pretty or striking, I counted Ionella as the most beautiful woman I've ever met. Other than Melissa and Allen Fryxell, everyone I loved was gathered in one place. "We're glad you're here!" Shaye said. "Our plane landed about ten this morning, and the boys got our tents up and camp ready by noon. We've spent the afternoon hauling more firewood from along the river." She squatted to stroke my pointer's muzzle and scratch behind his ears. "Who's a good boy, Jake?"

Robin was next to embrace me. "Scotty and I rode in the day before yesterday," she said. "He worried about getting our camping spot since all of us enjoy the hot spring and it's rafting season. How'd you hold up to the ride in?"

"Good. We spent the night at Loon Creek and got a late start this morning." I watched with concern as Lola and Anna led Bethany away to play. "Be careful with her, Lola," I called. Ionella held her and Russell's sleeping toddler in her arms. Lois Mae was only a few months older than my daughter.

"Can we offer you something to drink, Julia?" Anna asked. She leaned forward to open a cooler left within an arm's length. "We've got Coke, Sprite, Orange Crush, or water."

I plopped into an open chair next to the seated women. "Orange soda sounds good." I accepted it, popped the top, and took a long pull. "How can I be so tired after sitting all the way here?" Jake made himself comfortable on the ground beside me, his muzzle still dripping with water from the river below.

Our camping and pack trip got planned for the end of July and beginning of August every year. This was our third without anyone missing. Seemed we'd have a new member joining us next summer if my delivery went as normal. Two weeks of nothing but rest and relaxation with great people who loved the same backcountry lifestyle. Al begged off my heartfelt entreaties—turned out he wasn't lying when he once declared bugs and any creepy crawlies were the bane of his existence.

We invited another wonderful friend to join us, but Father Timothy died last winter. He wasn't doing well when we got the call. I'm thankful I got to be at his bedside before he passed. He needed to know our son would carry his given name when we had one. Also, I wanted him to understand I continued to follow through with my penance to teach Sunday school and at our local Catholic school. Each month my wages were donated back to the general fund. I swear Timothy heard my words whispered in his ear and crossed the great divide with a smile.

The priest was another who accepted without blinking my account of speaking to Dad. He suggested I ponder any warning either heard or felt and act accordingly. To him, my previous employment was part of God's grand design, and He may not be finished with services I could provide. Dad was merely His mouthpiece to warn me to keep my skills up to par and my head on a swivel. I didn't know how to live any other way.

Dawson and Early hit it off. Marta's husband, Jack, wanted to dislike the man I loved simply because he struggled to forget seeing me as an enemy. Instead, the three men shared a past the rest of us couldn't comprehend. All were army men who served in the same region of the world and were privy to similar horrors. They would sit up late, drink, laugh, and tell stories long after the rest of us retired.

Eight wall tents formed our camp. The men arranged them in a rough circle with the fire and gathering area inside. Scotty provided a large one as our refuge from hordes of bugs proving worst at sunrise and sunset. Our children were kept within the boundary unless accompanied by an adult or one of the older girls. Lola was freshly fourteen—a burgeoning beauty—yet still responsible. Any time now, Emerson would be hard-pressed to keep the boys away.

I napped on the cot Dawson erected for me after finishing my soda. A soft voice woke me after what seemed only moments. "Mrs. Pelletier? Mom said to tell you it's almost time to eat." Only Lola's face was visible inside.

"Ohh..." I kicked my feet off the edge and twisted to sit upright. I slept hard in the afternoon heat and was aware of having drooled. "Could you help me?" Cots were difficult to rise from during the best of times, but a protruding middle made it doubly so.

"Sure!" Eager with a hero complex her mother warned me of, the gangly teen hurried inside and took my hands. "One...two...three." Already taller than me, she set her feet and pulled when I heaved myself forward. My knee threatened to buckle, but I've grown used to it and caught my balance.

"Tell them I'll be out in a minute, okay?" Lola nodded after waiting a moment to assure herself I wasn't going to fall.

My blouse was drenched in sweat. I removed it and used a hanger to allow the fabric a way to dry. After erecting our tent, Dawson slid my duffle beneath my bed to give us added space. Wrestling it out wasn't easy, nor lifting the bag. Unzipping it, I went through shirts until finding one I wanted. Movement in my peripheral vision startled me as Shaye entered with Robin following. "Bethany's getting tired, but—" Shaye stopped and Robin behind her. I stood in only my maternity pants and bra and held the long-sleeved garment in one hand. Shaye covered her mouth with a palm—eyes already brimming—while Robin stared. I knew what they saw. Ugly scars from bullets tearing their way through and exiting my chest. I lifted the top in embarrassment to cover my front.

Shaye's arms opened as she came to me already weeping. "Oh, Julia, I'm so sorry."

I returned her embrace and could barely answer. "Not your fault." Robin moved behind me where she traced entry wounds with a fingertip. Until my friends accidentally walked in on me, only my doctors, a few nurses, and Dawson viewed my blemishes. After they healed and were no longer a threat to my life, I'm not sure my husband noticed them again. He loved me unconditionally.

"I feel responsible, though."

"Sweet Jesus, Julia," Robin whispered. "I knew you were badly hurt, but I never dreamed it...it..." She stopped and bit her lip.

"It's okay," I said stiffly and pulled the top over my head, making sure it wasn't too tight around my midsection. "I don't know about you two, but I'm ready for supper." Not prepared to revisit a subject I wanted left behind, I strode past them to eat.

Our camp bustled with activity. It seemed as if the kids and I were the only ones who didn't help prepare our meal. Dawson caught my eye and jerked his chin toward a chair. Bethany already sat between her older friends, jabbering and waving a hotdog like a sword over her head. I barely made myself comfortable before my man came to sit next to me with mounded plates for each of us. Hamburgers, hotdogs, baked beans, even potato salad and a Greek version.

"Doin' okay?" Dawson asked before stuffing his face. I swore I wouldn't cry, even with my hormones off kilter again, but my chin quivered after I pressed my lips together. "Jules?"

I waved a hand to fend away more questions while doing my best to compose myself. One-by-one, our friends gathered in a circle around the fire. Someone touched my shoulder as another lawn chair went on the other side of me. I looked up to see Shaye. "May I?" she asked. I nodded without saying anything while she got herself situated. Staring at my plate, I willed myself not to weep. Shaye was beautiful with her blemish-free skin and auburn hair swept back lazily—something I could never pull off.

Dawson pushed a bottle of water into my hand. "Something to drink?"

"Thanks," I said quietly.

Conversation rarely slowed, even while we ate. I finished everything, plus a piece of apple pie Marta flew in, before I tossed my plate into hot coal. Bethany grew bored after feeding most of her hotdog to Jake and crawled into my lap to snuggle. "Tired, Mommy."

I hugged and kissed her. "Mommy's tired, too." A hard kick from within reminded me I ate for a second tummy.

"Did you and Robin see anything interesting during your pack in?" Jack asked Scotty.

Dawson's oldest friend's brow furrowed while he thought. "A few does and fawns, a couple cow moose and their calves...anything else, honey?" Scotty looked at Robin.

She used a valley girl accent. "Well, yeah. Duh! Don't you remember the mountain lion with a rabbit in its mouth? Or the cinnamon-phased bear standing in the pathway a mile from the trailhead?" Robin's response made me grin. Barely five years in Idaho with six months of each spent in the backcountry, and she was already an old hand.

"Julia..." The crowd quieted anytime Marta spoke. Rarely did she have to raise her voice. "Are you enjoying your teaching position? I understand private schools do not pay as well as public." Her eyes danced when she finished. She obviously learned I taught for the love of it and as penance. Anna once told me her mother needed only to make a brief phone call or text to learn the answer to any question, no matter how tightly the subject matter was protected.

I didn't have to fib. "Absolutely! I love it. I'm stepping away the upcoming year for maternity leave, but once Timothy Allen is walking and getting under foot, he's all Dawson and Melissa's." Dawson was the greatest stay-at-home father I could imagine, although Grandma Melissa often kept Bethany.

When our first child arrived, Melissa, Shaye, and Anna stayed with me in split shifts that included Robin. Although Dawson never complained, our house felt full during the first three weeks of our daughter's existence. Never in my life did I feel as pampered as I did when my friends took care of my newborn and me. However, I was careful to keep my scars covered with a blanket while feeding Bethany until we were left alone.

Almost six months pregnant, I spent much of my time on the banks of the Middle Fork and fished and napped while my body got ready to give birth a second time. Getting enough fresh fruit and vegetables to satisfy my palate wasn't a problem. A plane arrived with supplies—including ice—every three days. Marta enjoyed camping with us, although she preferred not to do without.

Bethany was asleep on her cot one evening as I prepared to join her. Dawson planned to sit up with Early and Jack after I kissed him goodnight. A call surprised me after I turned away. "If Dawson doesn't care, would you mind sitting with us for a few minutes, Ariel?"

I sighed to myself. Early was never at ease with the feeling he left me behind. Taking the seat across from him, I made myself comfortable—not an easy feat in my condition. "It's Julia, Early. You know that."

His gaze was sharp and direct when he stared in the firelight. "It might be your name, but you'll always be Ariel Woodman to me."

"Most days I answer best to Mrs. Pelletier."

"My family is alive because of you," he said abruptly.

"Thank KC. He's the one who hired me to keep the bad guys away."

Early nodded. "I have. He's okay taking the occasional call to set my mind at ease. Chances are he'd never tell me if danger lurked again. He'd hire you or someone similar."

"Huh uh." I shook my head. "I'm done being a patsy for others. My focus is on me and my family." Only Dawson was privy to my continuing target practice at home. No sense in allowing an intrinsic skillset to become rusty. Dad warned me to be vigilant. With one child and another on the way and married to a husband I loved more than my life, woe to any who might come against us.

"You're aware Marta keeps eyes and ears everywhere, aren't you?" he asked. Jack listened to our conversation with a stone face.

"I guessed as much."

"Not just in the US but around the globe. The Middle East, Europe, Africa, Asia...anywhere a threat to her family could emanate."

"Good. Bad guys are everywhere." I kept my voice as quiet as Early's and hoped the kids were asleep and couldn't hear our conversation over the crackling of burning wood.

"Julia..." Jack's chiseled features reanimated as he cleared his throat noisily and spat in the fire. "...family is a loose term. It goes well past blood ties to those who we consider kin." He stared hard before changing his gaze to Dawson and then coming back to me. "Doesn't matter you were a hired gun. You took lives and nearly gave yours on our behalf. Dawson, too. Marta's net of protection extends not only to your immediate family but Dawson's as well. Hell..." He tipped his head toward his son's tent. "...she even keeps tabs on Emerson's best friend in Washington state because she knows me and my boy love him."

Marta Boyd was a frightening woman. Remembering I once planned to eliminate her until KC stopped it made me feel sick. While she wielded power I couldn't comprehend, I considered her one of the sweetest ladies I've met. "We thank you. I appreciate her and everything she does," I said. "There's a chance...albeit slight...we may face challenges ahead. I've been warned..." I bit a lip and glanced to Dawson who dipped his chin. "...by someone very close to me to not get complacent. At some point in the future my family will face a threat to our survival."

Both Jack's and Early's eyes narrowed in the firelight before glancing at one another. The former gave a curt nod. "You're sure of your source?"

I couldn't help but smile—not with malice, but absolute joy. "As certain as if it came from God's mouth to my ears."

"Good enough for me," Jack said. "I'll let Marta know to keep her feelers vigilant."

"I'll take it as a personal affront if your family faces difficulties and I'm not the first one you call," Early said, his eyes reflecting crimson in the firelight. "I owe a debt to you not easily repaid."

Later in the evening, my husband hardly made a sound when he pulled back the canvas to enter our tent. Waking immediately, I didn't make a sound in case he was extra tired. Bethany slumbered so quietly I could barely hear her breathe. "You brought some frightening people into our lives, Jules," Dawson whispered as he unlaced his boots. I'm not sure how he knew I was awake.

"They're your friends, too." It was true. He and Early developed a bond I couldn't fathom.

"Yeah...they're a good crew. Early let me know we're welcome to give them a hand next summer. Seems Russell, Ionella, and Lois Mae live in a camp trailer. They've saved enough cash and plan to erect a stick frame home next summer. If we all pitched in, we'd save 'em a basketful of money."

"It's about time," I said quietly. "They have a beautiful lot to build on. I suppose it'd go where their trailer is parked now." I envied the way it sat on the hill above the Snake River. It was only a few minutes' walk to wet their lines.

I heard the surprise in Dawson's voice. "You've been there?"

"Part of my job was to keep a watchful eye on the Endicotts. They don't know it, but I drove to their home a handful of times. Both of the Boyds' places, too. I think it would be fun to take the kids and help raise a home," I whispered.

His cot squeaked as he made himself comfortable in his sleeping bag. "Don't say anything. It's supposed to be a surprise. I'll tell Early first thing in the morning we'd like to help."

There was no sense in answering. Dawson barely finished talking before I heard his first snores.

***

A long walk was impossible in my condition, so I insisted Dawson and I ride to the lookout we'd previously hiked to, where we'd once met a group of silly girls who insisted we disarm. Since then, we'd made the trek an annual pilgrimage. Shaye put together a picnic basket we shared after reaching our destination. Below stretched the Middle Fork of the Salmon River in all its glory, surrounded by peaks jutting over ten thousand feet. Early and Shaye loved to tell stories of their rugged Wind River Mountains—and although I saw them from afar, I couldn't imagine anything rivaling what I considered my glorious backcountry. We ate our meal while observing a herd of mule deer on the slope below. Tomorrow we'd break camp for the long trek out. I was loath to leave our high lookout, but our group was already packing their things.

We stopped where our base wasn't far below. Children were playing tag, and I identified Bethany's wobbly run while she chased Lola. Anna's oldest child tripped and fell dramatically, only to be caught by our toddler shrieking and laughing as she landed on her target. It wasn't the way I remembered playing the game, but our daughter seemed to make her own rules. I swallowed hard and sniffed—my eyes misting. Dawson tore his gaze away from our family and friends and grinned. "It doesn't get any better than this, does it?"

I shook my head and knuckled tears away. "If I were to write the story of a perfect life, I would only need to record what we have here."

He cocked his head and looked from me to our camp and then back again. "There've been a few bumps and bruises along the way, but I gotta agree with you, Jules. It's been good since you came into my world."

His world. Yes, I certainly crashed into his orbit. Yet somehow, we were able to form a bond that grew stronger each day until we could no longer live without the other. My farmer—once a leader of men in combat—and me, a schoolteacher turned assassin turned teacher again—coming together to form a growing family. No matter what, as long as I kept my husband and children safe, I'd never be alone again. A kick inside my belly reminded me our three would soon become four. *Thank you, Dad,* I prayed silently. *Thank you for telling me to go back. You were right. It wasn't my time. The pain I endured was worth it.*

Dawson clucked his tongue after shooting me his boyish grin, one that made my heart flutter, while thumping his boot heels against

Tonto's ribs. Bliss needed no incentive to follow, her sure steps always giving me confidence.

Bethany noticed our return and flew on unsteady little legs to meet us, except Lola caught and scooped her up, keeping our baby safe. More than one of our friends raised a hand high at our return.

Dawson dismounted first and let me fall into his arms. I clutched at him longer than needed to catch my balance, my man's strong embrace holding me tight. When a hand grabbed at my maternity pants, it was Dawson who bent to lift our daughter. To feel them both in my arms, I would suffer all the angst and aches again.

Dad was right. My family needed me, and I would never fail them.

CPSIA information can be obtained
at www.ICGtesting.com
Printed in the USA
BVHW030821110821
614085BV00010B/682